Jacqueline Winspear is the author of two previous Maisie Dobbs novels, *Maisie Dobbs* and *Birds of a Feather*, which won the Agatha Award for Best Novel. A *New York Times* Notable Book, *Maisie Dobbs* was nominated for a record eight awards, including the Edgar Allan Poe Award for Best Novel, and won both the Agatha and Macavity Awards for Best First Novel, as well as the Alex Award for an adult novel suitable for young adults. Born in England, Winspear now lives in California.

Also by Jacqueline Winspear

Maisie Dobbs

Birds of a Feather

Messenger of Truth

Additional Praise for Jacqueline Winspear's *Pardonable Lies*

Winner of a Macavity Award

"Will thoroughly delight existing fans and should garner her new ones . . . Winspear carefully crafts each sentence, building toward a thrilling and emotional conclusion." *—Library Journal*

"If you haven't read the Maisie Dobbs stories, you are missing a treat." *—The Ledger Independent* (Kentucky)

"Fans of Miss Marple and Precious Ramotswe are sure to embrace Maisie, a pitch-perfect blend of compassion and panache." *—Booklist*

"To give an idea of how much I liked *Pardonable Lies,* I immediately went to my local bookstore and ordered the first two in the series. Long live Maisie Dobbs!" *—Mystery News*

"Maisie is immediately captivating. . . . Dobbs ponders the mysteries of life as well as the mysteries she is hired to solve. . . . Surprisingly eloquent, even moving." *—Saint Paul Pioneer Press*

"Jacqueline Winspear's historical mysteries prove exactly what this subgenre can achieve, offering a prism of the past and a mirror of the future. . . . Fascinating." *—Sun-Sentinel*

"A fine examination of a young woman making her way amid the economic and social dislocations of 1930s Britain . . . *Pardonable Lies* is a reflection, a meditation even, on how those of us who have experienced war carry with us the scars that can reopen in an instant." *—The Sunday Patriot-News*

"Winspear again treats us to a story broad in scope and rich in detail and suspense. . . . An excellent series." *—The Orange County Register*

PARDONABLE LIES

A Maisie Dobbs Novel

JACQUELINE WINSPEAR

Picador

Henry Holt and Company
New York

For Anne-Marie
With much love and gratitude
for our lifetime friendship.

PARDONABLE LIES. Copyright © 2005 by Jacqueline Winspear.
All rights reserved. Printed in the United States of America.
For information, address Picador, 175 Fifth Avenue, New York, N.Y. 10010

www.picadorusa.com

Picador® is a U.S. registered trademark and is used by Henry Holt and Company
under License from Pan Books Limited.

For information on Picador Reading Group Guides, as well as ordering, please contact
Picador.
Phone: 646-307-5629
Fax: 212-253-9627
E-mail: readinggroupguides@picadorusa.com

Designed by Victoria Hartman

Library of Congress Cataloging-in-Publication Data
Winspear, Jacqueline, [date]
Pardonable lies : a Maisie Dobbs novel / Jacqueline Winspear.
    p.   cm.
ISBN-13: 978-0-312-42621-7
ISBN-10: 0-312-42621-6
    1. Dobbs, Maisie (Fictitious character)—Fiction. 2. Women private
investigators—England—London—Fiction. 3. Air pilots, Military—Family
relationships—Fiction. 4. World War, 1914–1918—Missing-in-action—
Fiction. 5. London (England)—Fiction. I. Title.
PR6123.I575P37 2005
823'.92—dc22   2005046388

First published in the United States by Henry Holt and Company

10   9   8   7   6   5

Truly, to tell lies is not honorable;

but when the truth entails tremendous ruin,

to speak dishonorably is pardonable.

—Sophocles (c. 496–406 B.C.), *Creusa*

Pile the bodies high at Austerlitz and Waterloo.

Shovel them under and let me work—

I am the grass; I cover all.

And pile them high at Gettysburg

And pile them high at Ypres and Verdun.

Shovel them under and let me work.

Two years, ten years, and passengers ask the conductor:

What place is this?

Where are we now?

I am the grass.

Let me work.

—Carl Sandburg (1878–1967), *Grass*

PART ONE

London, September 1930

ONE

The young policewoman stood in the corner of the room. Plain whitewashed walls, a heavy door, a wooden table with two chairs, and one small window with frosted glass rendered the room soulless. It was a cold afternoon and she'd been in the corner since coming on duty two hours ago, her only company the rumpled and bent girl sitting in the chair that faced the wall. Others had come into the room to sit in the second chair: first, Detective Inspector Richard Stratton, with Detective Sergeant Caldwell standing behind him; then Stratton standing while a doctor from the Maudsley Hospital sat before the girl, trying to get her to speak. The girl—no one knew her age or where she had come from because she hadn't spoken a word since she was brought in this morning, her bloodstained dress, hands and face showing a month's worth of dirt—was now waiting for another person who had been summoned to question her: a Miss Maisie Dobbs. The policewoman had heard of Maisie Dobbs, but with what she had seen today, she wasn't sure that anyone could get this young scrubber to talk.

The policewoman heard voices outside the door: Stratton and Caldwell and then another voice. A smooth voice. A voice that was neither loud nor soft, that did not need to be raised to be heard or, thought the policewoman, to get someone to listen.

The door opened and Stratton came in, followed by a woman she presumed to be Maisie Dobbs. The policewoman was surprised, for the woman was nothing like she had expected, but then she realized that the voice had revealed little about the owner, except that it had depth without being deep.

Wearing a plain burgundy suit with black shoes and carrying a worn black leather document case, the visitor smiled at both the policewoman and Stratton in a way that almost startled the uniformed woman, as her eyes met the midnight-blue eyes of Maisie Dobbs, psychologist and investigator.

"Pleased to meet you, Miss Chalmers," said Maisie, though they had not been introduced. The warm familiarity of the greeting took Chalmers aback. "Brrr. It's cold in here," added the investigator, turning to Stratton. "Inspector, can we bring in an oil stove? Just to take the edge off?"

Stratton raised an eyebrow and inclined his head at the unusual nature of the request. Amused at seeing her superior caught off guard, Chalmers tried to hide a grin, and the seated girl looked up, just for a second, because the woman's voice compelled her to do so.

"Good. Thank you, Inspector. Oh—and perhaps a chair for Miss Chalmers." Maisie Dobbs removed her gloves, placing them on top of the black bag, which she set on the floor, before pulling a chair around so that she was seated not opposite the girl, on the other side of the table, but close to her.

Strange, thought Chalmers, as the door opened and a constable brought in another chair, left the room, and returned with a small paraffin stove, which he placed by the wall. They exchanged quick glances and shrugged shoulders.

"Thank you," said Maisie, smiling.

And they knew she had seen their furtive communication.

Now, sitting alongside the girl, Maisie said nothing. She said nothing for some time, so that after a while Chalmers wondered what in heaven's name she was there for. Then she realized that the

Dobbs woman had closed her eyes and had changed her position slowly, and though she couldn't put her finger on it, it was as if she were talking to the girl without opening her mouth, so that the girl—as if she couldn't help herself—leaned toward Maisie Dobbs. *Blimey, she's going to talk.*

"I'm getting warmer now." It was a rounded voice, a west-country voice. The girl spoke deliberately, with rolled *r*'s and a nod when her sentence was finished. A farm girl. Yes, Chalmers would have pegged her for a farm girl.

But Maisie Dobbs said nothing, just opened her eyes and smiled, but not with her mouth. No, it was her eyes that smiled. Then she touched the girl's hand, taking it in her own. The girl began to cry and, very strange again, thought Chalmers, the Dobbs woman didn't reach out to put an arm around her shoulder, or try to stop her or use the moment as Stratton and Caldwell might have. No, she just sat and nodded, as if she had all the time in the world. Then she surprised the policewoman again.

"Miss Chalmers. Would you be so kind as to poke your head around the door and ask for a bowl of hot water, some soap, two flannels, and a towel, please."

Chalmers gave a single nod and moved toward the door. *Oh, this would surely give the girls something to chew over later. They'd all have a giggle about this little pantomime.*

A bowl of hot water was brought to the room by the police constable, along with the flannels, soap, and towel. Maisie removed her jacket, placed it over the back of the chair, and rolled up the sleeves of her cream silk blouse. Reaching into the bowl, she rubbed some soap on a wet flannel and squeezed out the excess water. Then she lifted the girl's chin, smiled into her reddened and bloodshot eyes, and began to wash her face, rinsing the flannel and going back again, dabbing the hot cloth on the girl's temples and across her forehead. She washed her arms, holding first her left hand in the hot flannel and working the cloth up to her elbow, then reaching for the girl's right hand. The girl flinched, but Maisie showed no sign of noticing the movement, instead massaging her right hand with the cloth, gently working it along her arm to the elbow, and then rinsing again.

It was as she knelt on the floor, taking one filthy bare foot after the other and washing the dirt and grime away with the second flannel, that the policewoman realized she had become mesmerized by the scene unfolding before her. *It's like being in church.*

The girl spoke again. "You've got right soft 'ands, miss."

Maisie Dobbs smiled. "Thank you. I used to be a nurse, years ago, in the war. That's what the soldiers used to say: that my hands were soft."

The girl nodded.

"What's your name?"

Chalmers stared as the girl—who had been sitting in that room without so much as a cup of tea since she was brought in twelve hours ago—replied immediately.

"Avril Jarvis, miss."

"Where are you from?"

"Taunton, miss." She began to sob.

Maisie Dobbs reached into the black bag and brought out a clean linen handkerchief, which she placed on the table in front of the girl. Chalmers waited for Maisie to take out a sheet of paper to write notes, but she didn't; instead she simply continued with her questions as she finished drying the girl's feet.

"How old are you, Avril?"

"Fourteen next April, I reckon."

Maisie smiled. "Tell me, why are you in London and not Taunton?"

Avril Jarvis sobbed continuously as Maisie folded the towel and sat next to her again. But she did answer the question, along with every other question put to her over the next hour, at which point Maisie said that was enough for now; she would be taken care of and they would speak again tomorrow—only Detective Inspector

Stratton would have to hear her story too. Then, adding fuel to the tale that Chalmers would tell the other policewomen lodging in rooms upstairs at Vine Street, the Jarvis girl nodded and said, "All right, then. Just so long as you'll be with me, miss."

"Yes. I'll be here. Don't worry. You can rest now, Avril."

TWO

Following a debriefing with Stratton and Caldwell, Maisie was taken back to her office in Fitzroy Square by Stratton's driver, who would collect her again tomorrow morning for another interview with Avril Jarvis. Maisie knew that much rested on the outcome of this second interview. Depending upon what was revealed and what could be corroborated, Avril Jarvis might spend the rest of her life behind bars.

"You've been gone a long time, Miss," said Billy Beale, her assistant, running his fingers back through his sun-burnished hair. He came to Maisie's side, took her coat and placed it on the hook behind the door.

"Yes, it was a long one, Billy. Poor little mite didn't stand a chance. Mind you, I'm not sure how deeply the police are looking into her background at this point, and I would like to have some closer-to-the-bone impressions and information. If I'm required to give evidence under oath, I want to be better prepared." Maisie took off her hat, placed it on the corner of her desk, and slipped her gloves into the top drawer. "I'm wondering, Billy. Would you and Doreen fancy a trip down to Taunton for the weekend, with everything paid for?"

"You mean like an 'oliday, Miss?"

Maisie inclined her head. "Well, it won't be quite like being on holiday. I want you to find out more about Avril Jarvis, the girl I interviewed this morning. She said she's from Taunton and I have no reason to disbelieve her. Find out where she lived, who her family are, whether she went to school there, if she worked, and when she left to come to London. I want to know why she came to London—I doubt if she knew it was for a life on the streets—and what she was like as a child." She shook her head. "Heavens, she's only thirteen now—all but a child. It's wretched."

"She in trouble, Miss?"

"Oh, yes. Very big trouble. She is about to be charged with the crime of murder."

"Gawd—and she's only thirteen?"

"Yes. Now then, can you go to Taunton?"

Billy pressed his lips together. "Well, it's not as if me and Doreen have had much of an 'oliday together, ever, really. She don't like to leave the nippers, but you know, I suppose me mum can look after 'em while we're away."

Maisie nodded and took out a new manila folder, which she inscribed AVRIL JARVIS and passed to Billy, along with a collection of index cards upon which she had scribbled notes while waiting for her debriefing with Stratton and Caldwell. "Good. Let me know as soon as possible if and when you can go. I'll advance you the money for the train, a guesthouse, and incidentals. Now then, let's get on as I've to leave early this evening."

Billy took the folder and sat down at his desk. "Oh, yeah, you're seein' that old friend of yours, Mrs. Partridge."

Maisie turned her attention to a ledger before her. She did not look up. "Yes, Priscilla Partridge—Evernden, as she was when we were at Girton together. After two terms she joined the First Aid Nursing Yeomanry in 1915 and drove an ambulance in France." Maisie sighed and looked up. "She couldn't stand to stay in England after the Armistice. She'd lost all three brothers to war, and her parents to the flu, so she went to live on the Atlantic coast of France. That's where she met Douglas Partridge."

"I reckon I've 'eard that name before." Billy tapped the side of his head with a pencil.

"Douglas is a famous author and poet. He was badly wounded in the war, lost an arm. His poetry about the war was very controversial when it was first published here, but he's managed to continue with his work—though it's very dark, if you know what I mean."

"Not really, Miss. I'd 'eard of 'im, but, y'know, poetry's not up my alley, to tell you the truth."

Maisie smiled and continued. "Priscilla has three boys. She calls them 'the toads' and says they are just like her brothers, always up to something. She's back in London to look at schools for them for next year. She and Douglas have decided that the boys are growing up and need to have a British education."

Billy shook his head. "Don't think I could part with my nippers—oh, sorry, Miss." He pressed his hand to his mouth, remembering that Frankie Dobbs had sent Maisie to work as a maid in the home of Lord Julian Compton and his wife, Lady Rowan, when her mother died. At the time, Maisie was barely thirteen years old.

Maisie shrugged. "That's all right, Billy. It's well past now. My father was doing what he thought best for me, and no doubt that's what Priscilla is doing. Each to their own—we've all got to part one day, haven't we?" Maisie shrugged. "Let's just get these bills finished and go home."

For the past year, Maisie had lived at Lord and Lady Compton's Belgravia home. The accommodation had been offered to Maisie in the context of a favor to Lady Rowan, who wanted someone she trusted living "upstairs" during her absence—Maisie was now an independent woman with her own business, since her mentor and former employer, Maurice Blanche, retired. So instead of a lowly bed in the servants' quarters at the top of the mansion—her first experience of life in the household—Maisie occupied elegant rooms on the second floor. The Comptons were spending more time at Chelstone, their country home in Kent, where Maisie's father was the groom. It was generally thought that the Belgravia property was now retained only to pass on to James, the Comptons' son who managed the family's business affairs in Canada.

For most of the time, Maisie was alone in the house but for a small complement of servants; then at the end of summer, Lady Rowan would sweep into town to take up her position as one of London's premier hostesses. However, extravagance had been curtailed since last year when Lady Rowan, with a compassion uncommon among the aristocracy, declared, "I simply cannot indulge in such goings-on when half the country hasn't enough food in its belly! No, we will draw in our horns and instead see what we can do to get the country out of this wretched mess!"

Upon arriving at Ebury Place that evening, Maisie brought her MG to the mews behind the mansion and noticed immediately that Lord Compton's Rolls-Royce was parked alongside the old Lanchester and that George, his chauffeur, was in conversation with Eric, a footman who took charge of the motor cars when George was in Kent.

George touched his forehead and opened Maisie's door for her. "Evening, m'um. Very nice to see you."

"George! What are you doing here? Is Lady Rowan in London?"

"No, m'um, only His Lordship. But he's not staying. Just a business meeting and then to his club."

"Oh. A meeting at the house?"

"Yes, m'um. And if you don't mind, he's said that as soon as you returned he'd like you to join him in the library."

"Me?" Maisie was surprised. She sometimes thought that Lord Compton had merely indulged his wife in her support of her in the early years of her education, though he had always been nothing less than cordial in his communications.

"Yes, m'um. He knows you're going out later, but he said to say it wouldn't take long."

Maisie nodded to George and thanked Eric, who stepped forward with a cloth to attend to the already shining MG. Instead of entering through the kitchen door, an informality that had become her custom, she walked quickly to the front entrance, whereupon the door was immediately opened by Sandra, the most senior "below stairs" employee in the absence of the butler, Carter, who was at Chelstone.

"Evening, m'um." Sandra gave only a short curtsy, knowing that Maisie hated such formalities. "His Lordship—"

"Yes, George just told me." She passed her hat and coat to Sandra but kept hold of her document case. She checked the silver nurse's watch that was pinned to her lapel, a gift from Lady Rowan when she was sent to France in 1916. The watch had been her talisman ever since. "Thank you, Sandra. Look, could you run me a bath, please? I have to meet Mrs. Partridge at the Strand Palace by seven, and I really don't want to be late."

"Right you are, m'um. Pity she couldn't have stayed here. It's not as if we don't have the room."

Maisie patted her thick black hair and replied as she sped toward the sweeping staircase. "Oh, she said she wanted to be waited on hand and foot in a lavish hotel now that she has a few days' respite from her boys."

Outside the library door, Maisie composed herself before knocking. The men's voices carried; Lord Compton's was sharp and decisive. The second voice seemed deep and resolute, and as Maisie listened she closed her eyes and began to mouth the overheard words, automatically moving her body to assume a posture suggested by the voice. Yes, this was a man of decision, a man of bearing, with weight upon his shoulders. She thought he might be a solicitor, though one thing sparked her interest in the seconds before she knocked on the door and walked into the library: The man's voice, as Maisie interpreted it, held more than a hint of fear.

· · ·

"MAISIE, GOOD OF you to spare us a few moments of your precious time." Julian Compton held out his hand to Maisie to draw her into the room. He was a tall, thin man, with gray hair swept back and a debonair ease of movement that suggested wealth, confidence and success.

"It's a pleasure to see you, Lord Julian. How is Lady Rowan?"

"Apart from that wretched hip, there's no stopping her! Of course, there's another foal on the way now—perhaps another Derby promise in a couple of years!" Lord Compton turned to the man standing with his back to the fireplace. "Allow me to introduce a very good friend of mine, Sir Cecil Lawton, KC."

Maisie approached the man and shook hands. "Good evening, Sir Cecil." She noticed the man's discomfort, the way his eyes did not quite meet her own, focusing instead on a place over her shoulder before looking down at his feet, then back to Lord Julian. *I can almost smell the fear*, thought Maisie.

Cecil Lawton was only one or two inches taller than Maisie. He had dark-gray wavy hair that parted in the center and was swept to the sides. He wore half-moon spectacles, and his bulbous nose seemed to sit uncomfortably above a waxed mustache. His clothes were expensive, though not new. Maisie had met many such men in the course of her work, barristers and judges who had once invested heavily in making an impression but, having reached the pinnacle of success in the legal profession, did not regard Savile Row with the reverence of their younger days.

"I'm delighted to see you, Miss Dobbs; you may remember that we have met before. It was when you gave evidence for the defense in the Tadworth case. The man might have been on his way to Wormwood Scrubs, had it not been for your acute observations."

"Thank you, Sir Cecil." Maisie was now anxious to know the reason for her being introduced to Lawton, not least to allow her time to get ready for supper with Priscilla. She turned to Lord Julian. "I understand that you wanted to see me, Lord Julian. Is there a matter I might assist you with?"

Lord Julian looked at Lawton briefly. "Let's sit down. Maisie, Sir Cecil requires confirmation of information received some years ago, during the war. He came to me, and I immediately suggested that you might be able to help." Lord Julian glanced at Lawton, then brought his attention back to Maisie. "I think it best if Sir Cecil explains the situation to you in private, without any commentary from me. I know you would prefer to hear the details in his words, and any questions you put to him can be answered in absolute confidence. I should add, Maisie"—Lord Julian smiled at his friend—"I have informed my good friend here that your fees are not insignificant and you are worth every penny!"

Maisie smiled and inclined her head. "Thank you, Lord Julian."

"Very well. Good. I'm off to my lair for ten minutes or so. I'll be back shortly."

SIR CECIL LAWTON fidgeted in his seat, then stood again with his back to the fire. Maisie leaned back slightly in her chair, a move that caused Lawton to clear his throat and begin speaking.

"This is most unusual, Miss Dobbs. I had not imagined that I might one day be seeking assistance in this matter. . . ." Lawton shook his head, his eyes closed, then looked up and continued. "My only son, Ralph, was killed in the war."

"I'm sorry, Sir Cecil." Maisie issued her regret softly. Sensing that Lawton had a burden to shed, she leaned forward to indicate that she was listening closely. He had pronounced his son's name *Rafe* in the old-fashioned manner.

"I was in a position to ask questions, so there was—is—no doubt in my mind that Ralph was lost. He was in the Flying Corps. Those chaps were lucky if they were still alive three weeks after arriving in France."

Maisie nodded but said nothing.

Lawton cleared his throat, held his fist against his mouth for a second, folded his arms, and continued. "My wife, however, always maintained that Ralph was alive. She became very—very *unstable*, I think you would say, after we received the news. She believed that one day he would come back again. She said a mother knew such things. Agnes suffered a nervous collapse a year after the war. She had become involved with spiritualists, mediums, and all sorts of quackery, all in an attempt to prove that Ralph was still alive."

"There were many who consulted such people, Sir Cecil. Your wife was not alone in that respect."

Lawton nodded and pressed on with his story. "One of them even said that a spirit guide—" He shook his head and once again took a seat opposite Maisie. "I'm sorry, Miss Dobbs. The mere thought of it all makes my blood boil. The fact that one person can wield such power over another is abhorrent. Is it not enough for a family to endure loss, without having a witch—" Lawton appeared to falter, then regained composure. "Anyway, my wife was told that a spirit guide had passed on a message from the other side that Ralph was not dead, but very much alive."

"How difficult for you." Maisie was careful to maintain a middle ground as she listened to the story. There was something in Lawton's manner as he spoke of his son that made her feel uneasy. Her skin prickled slightly at the nape of her neck, where the scar left by an exploding shell was etched into her scalp. *His regard for his son was compromised.*

"My wife spent the final two years of her life in an asylum, Miss Dobbs, a private institution in the country. I could not afford rumors that might jeopardize my position. She was cared for in very comfortable circumstances."

Maisie looked at the grandfather clock in the corner of the room. She needed to move on. "Tell me, Sir Cecil, how may I be of service to you?"

Lawton cleared his throat and began to speak. "Agnes, my wife, passed away three months ago. There was only a small funeral and the usual notice of her passing in *The Times*. However, on her deathbed, she begged me to promise that I would find Ralph."

"Oh." Maisie placed her hands together and brought them to her lips, as if in prayer.

"Yes. I promised to find someone who is dead." He turned to face Maisie directly for the first time. "I am duty bound to search for him. That's why I have come to you—at Julian's suggestion."

"Lord Julian was at the War Office during the war. I am sure he has access to records."

"Of course, and the search only revealed what we already know: Captain Ralph Lawton, RFC, died in France in August 1917."

"What do you want me to do, Sir Cecil?"

"I want you to prove my son dead, once and for all."

"I'm sorry, but I must ask: What about his grave?"

"Ah, yes, the grave. My son died in an inferno when his aeroplane came down. There was little left of the craft, let alone my son. His remains are buried in France."

"I see."

"I am taking this step to keep a promise to my wife."

Maisie frowned. "But such a search could go on indefinitely, and difficult to bear, if I may say so, Sir Cecil."

"Yes, yes, quite, I understand. However, I have decided that there must be a time limit set for such a task."

Maisie sighed deeply. "Sir Cecil, as you no doubt understand, in my work I am familiar with unusual requests and have taken on assignments that others have refused or abused. In a case such as this, my responsibility must extend to your well-being—if I may speak frankly."

"I'm perfectly all right, you know. I—"

Standing, Maisie walked to the window, glanced at her watch, and turned to face Lawton. "Brutal honesty is often a requirement of my work, and I must—as I said—be frank. You are recently bereaved, and your wife has burdened you with a terrible promise: to find a son who, to all intents and purposes, is dead. It would seem that, since you received word of his death, you have not been able to seal his passing with the rituals that we must all go through to release those who are lost to the past."

Maisie paused for a moment, looked back at Lawton, and continued. "It is only through such a pilgrimage of mourning that we are free to remember the dead with a fullness of heart. In taking on this case, your passage through grief and remembrance will be of paramount consideration. You see, Sir Cecil, I am not yet sure how I might proceed with such work, but I know only too well how difficult it will be for you to relive your loss as I go about my inquiry. And of course I would be investigating those your wife consulted in her search for confirmation of her sense that he was alive."

"I see. At least I think I see. I thought you could just search records, go over to France, and . . ." Lawton's words stalled. It was clear he had no idea what Maisie might do in France.

"Allow me to make a suggestion, if I may, Sir Cecil. Consider all I have said, and the implications of my investigation. Then please telephone me at my office, and we will proceed from that day if you still wish me to search for the truth regarding Ralph's death." Maisie reached into her document case and pulled out a calling card that she passed to Lawton. It was inscribed with her name, followed by *Psychologist and Investigator* and her telephone number.

Lawton studied the card for a moment before pushing it into the pocket of his waistcoat. "Yes, quite. I'll consider the breadth of my request."

"Good. Now, if you will excuse me, Sir Cecil, I really must hurry. I have a supper engagement this evening."

A single knock at the door heralded the perfectly timed entrance of Lord Julian Compton.

"I thought you'd be just about finished by now."

"Yes, Julian. Miss Dobbs has been most helpful." Sir Cecil held out his hand to Maisie.

"I look forward to hearing from you in due course, Sir Cecil."

Maisie shook the proffered hand and turned to leave. "One more thing regarding your wife's assertion, Sir Cecil: Should you choose to commence with the investigation, I will be curious to know if your wife ever attributed a reason for Ralph's not returning home— if she thought him alive."

THREE

Returning to her rooms, Maisie bathed, then styled her hair quickly before putting on her black day dress. She had no gowns or evening wear, choosing instead something from her wardrobe that would "do" for supper at the Strand Palace Hotel. She applied rouge sparingly, along with a swish of lipstick, and patted her hair one last time. Her long tresses had finally met the hairdresser's scissors in early summer and, though the new haircut was stylish, she found she missed the weight at the back of her head and along her spine when she unpinned her chignon. Now the chin-length bob was growing out, which Maisie liked: For once in her life she was following fashion.

Collecting the freshly polished MG, Maisie sped off toward the Strand Palace, where she was to meet Priscilla. Though they had kept in touch, the women had met only once or twice after Priscilla left England to live in Biarritz. At first, Maisie had questioned her friend's decision to reside abroad, but she knew Priscilla needed to reignite an effervescent personality numbed by loss and grief. In Biarritz she had immersed herself in a round of parties but was saved from a life of postwar decadence by the quiet strength and resolve of her husband, the poet Douglas Partridge, who welcomed

Priscilla into his home on the coast and into the calming influence of his life of artistic endeavor and introspection. Maisie was happy for her friend and considered the union sound. Priscilla had discovered true joy again and in so doing encouraged Douglas's confidence in company. Now, with three sons, Priscilla's enviable energy was often sapped by the end of the day, though Maisie wondered how her friend would ever fare if she lost the boys' nanny.

It wasn't just Priscilla and her family that occupied Maisie's thoughts as she maneuvered through the London traffic. She was troubled by the meeting with Sir Cecil Lawton, by a case that might be lucrative but seemed fraught with ambiguity. She liked to bring her cases to a complete close, to know her notes could be filed away with all loose ends tied. She could not fail to notice that Agnes Lawton had clearly asked her husband to find their son, whereas Lawton had briefed Maisie to prove him dead, a distinction that hinted at a client who might be more troublesome than most. She hoped Lawton would decide against the investigation.

Maisie parked the motor car. As she rushed into the grand entrance of the Strand Palace, she caught a glimpse of herself in the newly refurbished modern and very avant-garde mirrored glass foyer and sighed. In truth, there was one aspect of the reunion that she was dreading: Priscilla was a self-confessed fashion hound. Her long limbs, aquiline features, and shining chestnut hair seemed to lend themselves to any style, any ensemble—always brand-new and very expensive. As she had written to Maisie, "I spend much of my day on my hands and knees or otherwise steeped in the life of three impish toads, so I never begrudge myself the odd shopping trip to Paris." Maisie knew she would feel hopelessly drab in her company.

MAISIE NOTICED PRISCILLA immediately, sitting on an armchair at the agreed-upon meeting place. She stopped for a moment to regard her old friend. Priscilla wore wide trousers of heavy black silk, with a pale gray chemise tucked into the wide waistband. A black silk jacket, shorter than the thigh length Maisie favored, was set upon her shoulders. Pale gray piping edged the jacket, and a gray silk handkerchief was tucked into a breast pocket. Maisie brushed a few specks of lint from her dress, which she suddenly felt to be pitifully behind the times. Priscilla turned to face her; then, with a beaming smile, quickly but elegantly unfolded her long legs and rose from the chair.

"Maisie, darling, you look absolutely smashing. It must be love!"

"Oh, come on, Pris." Maisie kissed Priscilla on both cheeks before the women stood back to appraise each other.

"Well, I'll say this for you, you don't have wrinkles." Priscilla reached into her bag and pulled out a fresh cigarette, which she pressed into an ebony holder. Maisie remembered the flourish with which Priscilla would smoke her illicit cigarettes when they were at Girton, waving the holder to emphasize a point, sometimes blowing a perfect smoke ring before saying, "Well, if you want my opinion . . ." which she would give without waiting for a response.

Priscilla put her arm through Maisie's and led her conspiratorially toward the Grill Room. "Now then, I want to know everything and I mean *everything*, especially about whoever it is that has given you a twinkle in your eye. I know you've had a couple of suitors, and I know that twinkle. I remember seeing it when we went to Simon's leaving party. Do you remember—" Priscilla stopped suddenly. "Oh, God. Sorry, Maisie, I didn't mean—"

"Oh, not to worry, Pris. It was a long time ago. And it *was* a wonderful party, the best of my life." Maisie smiled to let Priscilla know that a reference to Simon was not ill-timed. Captain Simon Lynch was the young army doctor whom she had loved, but whose terrible injuries in the Great War had rendered him incapacitated in body and mind.

Priscilla stopped and looked into Maisie's eyes, her own glistening with tears that revealed the depth of her remembered grief. Maisie rubbed her friend's hand as it rested on her arm. "Come on, let's have that drink, Pris. I know I'd like one."

"My, you have changed! Now all I have to do is take you shopping."

Maisie turned to Priscilla as they were shown to a table. "I knew it would be only a minute or two before you tried to take me in hand."

"All right, I'll leave that topic until later. You may be seeing a country doctor—it *is* him, isn't it?—but there's no need to go all frumpy and pearly yet."

"But I'm not—"

Priscilla held up a hand playfully as she ordered a gin and tonic. Maisie asked for a cream sherry.

"So. Come on, out with it; tell me all about him. Is it that Andrew Dene? *Dr.* Andrew Dene? The one you wrote about in your last letter?"

"Look, it's not serious courting, we're—oh, thank you." Maisie smiled at the waiter, glad for the interruption of their drinks being set upon the table.

"Not serious? I'll wager, Maisie, that it's serious for Dr. Dene! Has he asked you to marry him?"

"Well, no. . . ."

"Oh, come on. Here you are, a successful woman of professional standing, and seeing you blush I feel as if I'm talking to my lovesick nanny." Priscilla stubbed out her cigarette and took a hefty sip of her gin and tonic. "Who, I might add, has almost given me gray hair by conducting an affair with a man I consider to be a very nasty piece of work."

"Thank heavens the comparison ends there. Andrew's actually very nice."

"So why aren't you marrying him?"

Maisie sipped her sherry and set her glass down. "If you must know, he hasn't asked me. For goodness' sake, we've hardly seen each other since we first went to the theater. I enjoy his company— he is such fun, you'd like him—but apart from spending the odd day together at the weekend, or an evening during the week if he's in town, we are both busy."

Priscilla pressed another cigarette into the holder, raised an eyebrow, and leaned toward Maisie. "Are you sure you've only spent the odd *day* at the weekend? Not the whole weekend?"

"That's it; no more, Priscilla Evernden. You are a devil!" Maisie laughed, joined by Priscilla. "Oh, it *is* good to see you, Pris. Come on, tell me about the boys. Have you found a suitable school for them?"

The waiter returned to take their order for supper, and as he left, Priscilla went on to bring Maisie up-to-date with family life and the search for a school that would accommodate three boys, used to a certain freedom in their fashionable French coastal resort but who must now begin to prepare for a more restrained life ahead. The conversation continued over the meal.

"So, we're sort of between the devil and the deep blue sea, trying to get them educated without having the life whipped out of them if they so much as put a foot wrong." Priscilla placed her knife and fork on her plate and reached for her wineglass. "Anyway, I'm to see three more schools this week, plus I have to meet with my solicitors to discuss upkeep of the estate. Part of me wants to sell, but on the other hand I'd love to keep it for the boys." Priscilla shook her head. "Anyway, far too boring for supper talk. Now then, what about you? What's your latest case?"

"You know I can't tell you about my cases."

"Not even a snippet for a hard-pressed mother?"

"That will be the day!" Maisie smiled. "All right, let's just say that my next case, if I am awarded the assignment, involves proving that someone who died in the war really is dead." Maisie was careful not to say *aviator* and was aware that the information shared with Priscilla was more than she had ever before disclosed to someone not directly involved in an investigation.

Priscilla pulled a face. "Gosh, I wish I hadn't asked now—mind you, it's not unusual when you think about it. After all, so many were listed as *missing*, which caused terrible heartache."

"And I may well have to go over to France to complete my inquiries," continued Maisie. "Though I can't say I'm looking forward to it."

"Then you must come to Biarritz—consider it a break following all that hard work. Heavens, I've been trying to get you to come for years!"

"It's probably a bit out of my way. If you were at your flat in Paris, I might be able to visit you there."

Priscilla shook her head. "I'm hardly ever in Paris except for the odd shopping expedition. Douglas goes to the flat to write sometimes. There's a sort of League of Nations bookish set in Paris that he finds stimulating. The Americans are rather fun, but it appears to me that a fair bit of backstabbing goes on, you know."

"I wouldn't know, Pris. There's a similar set in Fitzroy Square, but I hardly see them. We're not even on nodding 'good-morning' terms."

Priscilla was quiet for a moment, and as she ran a finger around the rim of her wineglass, Maisie regarded her closely. Her demeanor had changed; a tension had moved into her shoulders that Maisie knew came from Priscilla's heart.

"What is it, Priscilla?"

"Oh, nothing. Nothing, really. . . ."

Maisie leaned back as Priscilla in turn leaned forward, resting her elbows on the table. She began to unburden her troublesome thoughts with a nervous half laugh and a joke.

"You know, *my* father would have sent me from the table for this. 'Only cooked meat on the table' was a favorite quip as he pricked you on the arm with a fork."

"Those who are gone are never far away," said Maisie.

"Yes, I know. I'm seeing it more and more in the boys as they get older. Though they never knew their uncles, I see reminders every day, even when one of them is just about to box another around the ears! God, I miss them; I still miss my family, Maisie." Priscilla took up the ebony holder and, despite disparaging looks from two matrons dining nearby, lit another cigarette.

"But there's more, isn't there?" Maisie rested her hands on the table, not with palms down but relaxed and slightly upturned.

Priscilla blew a smoke ring and smiled broadly at the neighboring diners. *She doesn't change*, thought Maisie.

"It's that case you mentioned, Maisie." Priscilla seemed to falter but then continued. "It made me think of my eldest brother, Peter. As you know, I was the youngest; the boys were all older. Phil and Pat were both killed in 1916, within two weeks of each other, but Peter—I don't know about Peter."

"Don't know?" Maisie resisted the urge to lean toward Priscilla, instead leaving room for her to continue her story.

"No. I have no idea." Priscilla looked at Maisie directly. "It's my boys growing up so quickly, I think. I pushed it all back after the war, after Mummy and Daddy died. Off I went to France like a shot, drank myself silly for a year, and, thank God, along came Douglas to drag me from the abyss. I adore him, Maisie, and I adore my boys. Douglas and I have helped each other, really, and I don't want to look back, but . . ."

"But?"

"We never knew where Peter died. His body was never found, though that wasn't unusual, was it? I never even saw the telegram. My parents had already lost Patrick and Philip, so they burned it, and I've been troubled about it ever since. I'll put it to the back of my mind for a while, and then something—and sometimes it's something really simple, not a big thing like this case of yours—brings it all back again."

Maisie did not respond for some moments. Then she reached across to her friend and took her hands in her own. "Look, Pris, I want you to consider something—and please don't dismiss my suggestion immediately. I can direct you to someone who, in conversation, can help you to put Peter to rest in your heart. I'm your friend, too close for such work, but Maurice—"

Priscilla pulled her right hand from Maisie's grasp, holding it up to stop her speaking. "I know what you're suggesting, Maisie. I've heard all about these newfangled talk therapies, and they're not my bag. I'd rather listen to an old gramophone record and have a drink and a cigarette until misery finds someone else to pick on." She paused briefly and changed the subject. "Have you received a letter from Girton asking for contributions to the new fund-raising campaign? I thought I'd send something."

MAISIE AND PRISCILLA remained together for another hour or so, reminiscing over dinner about their time at Girton College and their lives since the war. They agreed to meet again for lunch before Priscilla flew from Croydon Aerodrome back to France. But as she left her friend, driving back to Ebury Place with the top down on the MG, for it was a warm Indian-summer night, Maisie considered the possibility of a return to France, a prospect she anticipated with dread in her heart.

FOUR

Maisie went to the office for just one hour the next morning, before being collected by a Scotland Yard driver in a black Invicta motor car. However, there was time to spend with Billy before embarking upon her day.

"Mornin', Miss." Billy had arrived early at the office. "Nice evenin' with Mrs. Partridge?"

Maisie removed her coat and hat, hung them on a hook behind the door, and went to her desk, where she placed her handbag in a drawer and her black document case—a gift from the Comptons' staff when she first went up to Girton in 1914—on the floor next to her chair. She sighed. "Yes, it was a lovely evening. Thank you for asking."

Billy looked up, not used to hearing fatigue in his employer's voice. "A late one, was it, Miss? I know you said Mrs. Partridge used to be a bit of a girl for the long nights and parties."

Maisie nodded and leaned back in her chair. "Well, it was a bit later than usual, but no, that's not the reason for my malaise this morning, Billy. I can't say I slept very well."

"Not comin' down with somethin', I 'ope."

"No—just a few concerns."

Billy frowned. "What, about that girl from Taunton?"

"Actually, no. There may be another case coming in that I'm not—"

Billy reached across and picked up a buff-colored folder. "Was it"—he turned the folder sideways; a piece of paper flapped on top—"Sir Cecil Lawton?" Billy didn't wait for an answer but continued, leaving his desk to bring the folder to Maisie. "The dog-and-bone was ringing its 'ead off when I got in this mornin', and this bloke said to tell you that 'e'd thought about what you'd said and wanted to assign the task—that's what 'e called it, a *task*—to you, and could you place a telephone call to 'im in 'is chambers today, so—"

"Oh, damn it!" Maisie leaned forward and rested her forehead on her hands.

Billy's eyes opened wide as he placed the folder on the desk in front of her. "I beg your pardon, Miss. Did I do somethin' wrong? I mean, I took the message, got the file ready for the particulars, and—"

Maisie looked up. "No, it's all right, Billy. I'm sorry, that was rude of me. The truth is, I'm just not sure about this case."

Billy thought for a moment. "Well, you always said we've got the final decision as to whether we accept a job, didn't you?"

"I know, I know." Maisie sighed, scraped back her chair, and walked to the window. "And I never thought I would be compromised, but I have a . . . a very uncomfortable feeling about this."

"So, why don't you put a tin lid on it? Tell the man to go to someone else." Billy joined her at the window. They looked not at each other but across the square before them, where the sun was streaking across leaves beginning to take on hues of copper, deep red, and gold. Leaves that would soon litter the flagstones, rendering them slippery and brown.

Maisie did not answer but instead closed her eyes. Billy stepped away quietly, gathered a tray set for tea, and left the room, understanding that this was one of those times when she required some moments alone. Hearing the door click behind him, Maisie reached for a cushion on an old armchair set in the corner and placed it on the floor. She knew Billy would give her ten minutes before gently knocking at the door and entering with a freshly brewed pot of tea to refresh them both. Pulling up her skirt slightly to allow ease of movement, she sat on the cushion, legs crossed, arms loose in her lap, her eyes now half closed. Soon she would leave the office for Vine Street. For the sake of Avril Jarvis, she must be clear and ready, not fatigued by other concerns.

She allowed her mind to become still, as she had been taught so many years ago by Khan, the Ceylonese wise man to whom she had been taken by Maurice Blanche. Then she asked questions silently, questions she did not struggle to answer, knowing that insights and responses would come to her in the hours and days ahead, as long as she went forward with an openness of heart. What was at the source of her doubts regarding the assignment from Lawton? Was it a question of trust? Certainly she had intuited a certain . . . a certain . . . what was that sense she'd had? Reticence? Yes, there was fear, but why? Whatever could a man have to fear from a dead son, a son who was a decorated aviator? Without doubt, Agnes Lawton had exacted a terrible deathbed promise, so it was likely that Sir Cecil was reeling not only from her passing and state of mind in her final years but from the task he had assumed. A task he now wanted to pass on to Maisie.

Was she concerned because she felt Sir Cecil was interested only in making good on his word, giving the case an element of triviality? There would doubtless have to be a return to France, and to Flanders—*Oh, God, why? Why?* Maisie sat in silence, allowing her mind to clear again, so that mere seconds assumed an expanse that stretched into hours, in the way that, in slumber, one can have a dream of years passing, yet upon waking look at the clock and see that only the briefest of naps has been taken.

Billy knocked gently on the door, waited a moment, and entered. Maisie was standing now and walked toward the desk, her customary strong stride and ready smile greeting him.

"That's better, Miss. Now, get this down you before the old door-bell goes and you've to be off to Vine Street." Billy poured tea into a well-used tin army mug for Maisie, a vessel she had preferred since her days of service in France, when the hot, strong, almost-too-sweet tea had sustained her in the worst of times. "Do you think she'll talk—y'know, with Stratton in the room?"

"Oh, yes, I should think so, though perhaps with a little difficulty. Much of it will be repeating the story she told me yesterday."

"Poor little scrap." Billy sipped his tea, then continued. "Well, talking of the girl, Avril Jarvis, I've sorted it all out with Doreen and we're off this weekend to Taunton."

"Oh, good work, Billy."

"And you know what I'm like about leaving the Smoke! Anyway, me old mum is taking on the nippers, so we'll be on our own. Doreen says she don't mind that I 'ave to work, and all, it will be a nice little break."

"Good. Now then, Billy, please devise a plan for your inquiry, and let's look at it together before you go—we'll do that tomorrow. In fact, why don't you leave on Thursday, to allow a little more time."

"Right you are, Miss." A bell rang in the office, activated by a caller at the front door below. "Ay-oop, there's the Scotland Yard chappie now. You'd better be off, Miss."

"I'll see you this afternoon, Billy, all right?" Maisie quickly put on her coat and hat, and opened the door.

"Yes, Miss. Oh—Miss? Did you decide about Sir Cecil Lawton?"

Maisie turned to answer Billy before leaving. "Yes, I've made my decision. I'll telephone his chambers while I'm waiting at Vine Street."

Upon arrival at Vine Street, Maisie was ushered into an office to meet with Detective Inspector Stratton and his assistant, Cald-well.

"We've received the postmortem report from the pathologist." Stratton removed several sheets of paper from a folder but did not pass them to Maisie. "How a slip of a girl managed to kill a man of that size beggars belief, but the evidence is there for all to see: fingerprints all over the murder weapon."

"She maintains that she didn't murder the man; he was her uncle—"

"But with respect, Miss Dobbs," Caldwell interrupted, "she also has no recollection of the actual events, per her confession to you yesterday."

"I would hardly call her story a confession, Sergeant Caldwell." Maisie turned to Stratton's assistant, disguising her distaste for a man she considered an opportunist who rushed to premature conclusions. "Miss Jarvis recounted the events she could remember before her collapse."

"Yes, with a knife in her hand, right next to the body. She should have thought about her fear of blood before she thrust the knife into her beloved uncle's neck and chest."

"I think *beloved* hardly describes a relationship hallmarked by such brutal behavior, do you?"

"But, with respect, Miss Dobbs—"

Stratton sighed. "All right, that's enough, Caldwell." He turned to Maisie. "Let's see what we get out of this interview, shall we? In the meantime, we are trying to establish whether Harold Upton, the victim, was indeed related to Jarvis. I've been in touch with the constabulary in Taunton this morning, and we expect to hear shortly. Her people will be informed in due course."

"And *due course* is how long, Inspector Stratton?"

Stratton was about to answer when there was a knock at the door.

"Yes!"

Maisie noted Stratton's edgy response, an indication that her question would not be answered and that it was likely that Avril Jarvis's family would not yet be informed that she was in custody.

She was curious to know who would be offering legal counsel to the girl.

"Sir, she's in the interview room now."

"Very good, Chalmers."

The policewoman nodded and closed the door.

"Now then—"

"We were talking about her people being notified, Inspector."

"Ah, yes." Stratton looked at his watch. "We'd better get cracking, I've an appointment at eleven." He rose and opened the door for Maisie.

As they walked along the corridor toward the interview room, Maisie turned to Stratton. "Has Jarvis had the benefit of legal counsel yet, Inspector?"

Stratton opened a door into an anteroom and indicated for Maisie to enter before himself and Caldwell. "She refuses to speak to anyone but yourself, Miss Dobbs. A duty solicitor has been assigned"—he glanced at his watch—"who should have been here by now."

As if on cue, a young man rushed into the room in a flustered manner, clutching a new briefcase. Maisie shook her head, though it was no surprise to her that Avril Jarvis would be assigned a raw recruit to the legal profession. The combination of no money, as far as anyone knew, and a novice solicitor with no reputation or established contacts in chambers could only mean that, during her trial, Avril Jarvis would be represented by a junior barrister rather than counsel of some standing.

"I hope I haven't held anyone up here. I've been sorting out some very testy relatives fighting over a will. Sorry!" The solicitor was flushed and hurried, giving no reason for confidence. "Charles Little, duty dog assigned to Jarvis." He held out his hand to Stratton and beamed a boyish smile. Maisie watched Caldwell sneer. *Duty dog* might have been an attempt at humor, but even Maisie could not avoid thinking that he was more like the *duty pup*.

"Right then. Let's get on with it." Stratton turned to enter the interview room, but Maisie placed a hand on his arm.

"Inspector, look, I know this has to be done, but may I see Miss Jarvis alone for a moment, with only Miss Chalmers in attendance? I fear that if we all enter at once, nothing will be gained except another wall of silence."

"I must say, this is most—" Little stepped forward, grasping a possible opportunity to exert some influence.

"Oh, for God's sake!" Caldwell's complaint was almost drowned as the young solicitor pressed his position.

Maisie held up her hand. "This will take only a minute and may make the difference between accomplishment and failure."

Stratton turned to the two men. "I believe Miss Dobbs should have this opportunity, and I agree with her conclusion." Addressing Maisie he added, "Two minutes, Miss Dobbs, double the time requested."

Maisie inclined her head and stepped into the room where Avril Jarvis stood alongside a table and chair. She was not wearing handcuffs, but bracelets of raw skin on her wrists suggested that a pair had been removed after she had been brought into the secure room. Chalmers stood beside the door. Jarvis was dressed in a plain gray dress of prison issue and plain black lace-up shoes. Her hair had been drawn back sharply in a bun and her face and hands appeared to have been scrubbed roughly. She smiled as Maisie entered, but then her eyes filled with tears. She took a step toward Maisie, but Chalmers moved quickly. The girl was, after all, detained on suspicion of murder.

"It's all right, Chalmers." Maisie held up a hand and turned to Avril, who collapsed into her arms. She said nothing but allowed the girl to weep.

"I'm scared, miss. I'm right scared."

"Of course you are, of course you are. Now then." Maisie held Avril Jarvis away from her but kept her hands on the girl's upper arms, so she could feel the benefit of Maisie's strength. "The Detective Inspector is waiting outside, and so is your solicitor. Avril? Avril, look at me." Maisie lifted the girl's chin, for she had tried to rest her head on Maisie's shoulder. *She's exhausted.* "Come on now, Avril, look at me. All you have to do is tell the same story that you told me yesterday."

Avril Jarvis wiped her eyes with the back of her hand and sniffed. "Yes, miss, all right."

Maisie looked into her eyes deeply and smiled knowingly. *But you didn't tell me everything, did you, dear girl.* "Take a deep breath . . . yes, that's it. And another. . . . And again. . . . Shake your hands like this. . . . Good. Now then, stand with your hands at your sides, keep them loose, and"—Maisie walked behind the girl and pressed her fingertips into the middle of Jarvis's slender back—"let this go."

Avril Jarvis gasped and almost fell forward, feeling the tension in her spine escape as Maisie touched her. "That felt like burning, it did, miss. As if your hands was on fire. Like a hot poker going through me, it was."

Maisie nodded. "Keep your feet firmly on the floor, Avril, and stand tall, but not like a lamppost!"

Stratton entered without knocking, accompanied by Caldwell and Charles Little.

"Right, Miss Jarvis, let's get down to business. This need not be long and miserable if you cooperate and answer my questions. Then Mr. Little here will be able to speak to you alone—with only the policewoman in the room, that is."

"What about this lady?" Avril pointed to Maisie. "Can she stay?"

Maisie stepped forward. "No, Avril, I have to leave you with your solicitor. It's for the best, and it's also the law."

"But—"

Maisie turned to Stratton. "I think Miss Jarvis is ready." She smiled at Jarvis and nodded.

The questioning of Avril Jarvis continued for a good two hours.

Following the interrogation, Maisie waited to speak to Charles Little, who left the room anxious to return to his office.

"Mr. Little, may I have a word?"

"Oh, Miss Dobbs." He looked at his watch. "I have barely a moment. I'm sorry, but I really am very busy."

"I have only one question: Do you know whom you will brief to act as counsel for Miss Jarvis?"

Little sighed. "Well, clearly she's on a sticky wicket. She needs a legal miracle worker to get her out of this mess, and even with the assistance available to those with no funds, she'll not have access to the caliber of counsel I would like to brief on her behalf."

"I see."

"Well, then. I must be off. Cheerio, Miss Dobbs."

Maisie watched the young solicitor leave and shook her head. *A legal miracle worker.* She walked slowly toward the police constable who would summon Stratton's driver to take her back to Fitzroy Square. *So be it.*

FIVE

Maisie looked over the three pages of notes written in Billy's large curved handwriting and smiled. His deliberate forming of letters, large, like those of a child in primary school, reflected an innocence she found endearing.

"My only addition to this list, Billy, would be the newspaper offices. There's probably a local rag, so see if there are any references to the family. I know it's a tall order—after all, she's thirteen years old—but some newspapers have a librarian to assist with deeper research. And in a place like this, I would say there are people who have been at the newspaper since the year dot; find out who they are. Mind you, be careful. This story is about to become big news. Don't give anything away that might end up on the front page of the *Express*."

Billy made a notation in his book. "Right you are, Miss."

Maisie handed back the pages and smiled. "Good work, Billy. Now all you have to do is follow your plan, but you must allow room to add new possibilities for inquiry. And remember, leave no stone unturned. Keep an open mind and don't jump to conclusions. Be vigilant for coincidences. Every detail, even one that is seemingly unimportant, could be vital."

"Yes, Miss."

"Now." Maisie walked to her desk, took a key from her black case, and unlocked a drawer on the right-hand side. "Here you are." She handed Billy a brown envelope. "You should have plenty there for train, guesthouse accommodation, dining requirements, and a bit left over for yourselves."

Billy looked at the envelope and pressed his lips together. "S'very kind of you, Miss. You know, not just this"—he flapped the envelope back and forth—"but for trustin' me to go off on me own on a case. I won't let you down, Miss."

Maisie allowed silence to linger before she spoke again. "It's not for me, Billy. It's for a young girl who is scared to death. Just one small detail in her favor may mean success or failure in defense of her case."

Billy nodded. "And D.I. Stratton doesn't know what I'm up to?"

"No. There's no need to inform him at the moment. This is a private investigation, expenses paid for by the business."

"Well, like I said, I won't let you down—or Miss Jarvis. Mind you, I read in the *Daily Sketch* that they don't fancy the killer's chances, not when it comes to trial, what with the victim bein' a family man and all."

Maisie locked her desk and replaced the key in her case. "No jumping to conclusions. Leave the path open for the truth to make itself known; do *not* hamper the way with speculation. *Questions*, Billy, are at the heart of our success—the more questions you ask, the better equipped we will be to help the girl."

Billy nodded.

"Right." Maisie looked at the silver watch pinned to the breast pocket of her navy jacket. "I have to leave for the Inns of Court now for my appointment with Sir Cecil Lawton at his chambers. You'll have left for the day by the time I'm back. Best of luck to you tomorrow." Maisie held out a hand to her assistant.

"Thank you, Miss."

She smiled, collected her hat, gloves, and bag, and quickly left the office.

· · ·

MAISIE TRAVELED BY underground to Holborn and from there walked to Lincoln's Inn Fields and the chambers of Sir Cecil Lawton, which were in a building first constructed in the fifteenth century. Maisie was deliberately a few minutes early for the appointment and used the time to walk around Lincoln's Inn, one of the first residential London squares. Maurice Blanche had instructed her time and time again that the solution to a problem or question was rarely to be found in sitting alone and that movement of the body also moved the mind. It was a crucial part of the pilgrimage, the journey toward truth.

Though there remained reticence in her heart regarding the assignment, she was bound by her loyalty to Lady Rowan Compton and her husband, Lord Julian. And though Lord Julian would never have exacted an obligation to assist his friend, she felt compelled to take on the inquiry, given her association with the family and all that they had done for her. However, she now had another reason for accepting the case.

Maisie was ushered in by the clerk of chambers, and waited only a moment before being shown into Lawton's private office. Cecil Lawton stood up and came from behind an ornate carved mahogany desk, the sheer heft of which seemed to underline the standing of one of the great legal orators of the day.

"Miss Dobbs, please, do sit down." Lawton indicated two leather Queen Anne chairs, with a small carved table between them. There was a knock at the door, and an assistant entered with a tray and two cups, together with a coffee pot and cream jug. "One of my clients, some years ago, owned a coffee plantation in British East Africa. It seems that, in addition to my fee, he has felt it necessary to keep my office well stocked with coffee. Hence all juniors have to learn the art of brewing a fine cup at midmorning."

Maisie smiled and reached for the cup that was held out to her as she settled herself in the chair. "My former employer was brought up in France and continues to enjoy a French breakfast with very strong coffee each morning, though he now lives in Kent. I have acquired the taste."

"Ah, yes, Maurice Blanche. Always a man to have on one's side in court." Lawton took a sip of coffee, set his cup on the table, and turned to Maisie. "I am most grateful to you for taking on this inquiry."

Maisie had noticed a more relaxed manner in comparison with their first meeting. *The weight on his shoulders has passed to me.* She set her cup next to Lawton's on the table. "Before we begin, I would like to discuss my terms."

"Of course. As I said on the telephone, your fee is perfectly acceptable and I also appreciate your advice regarding closure of the inquiry. All expenses will be met with immediate refund when presented to my accountant. In fact"—Lawton took an envelope from the inside pocket of his black jacket—"I felt an advance was in order."

Maisie took the envelope and placed it on the table, next to her cup. "Thank you. However, I have another request, Sir Cecil." She reached into her document case and took out a copy of *The Times.* "You have no doubt read about this case." She handed the newspaper to Lawton, indicating a column on the front page with her right index finger.

Lawton reached into the folds of his gown, to the jacket pocket again. He took out his spectacles and read the news that Maisie had pointed to. "Oh, yes. Of course. But I can't see—"

"I would like you to act as counsel for Miss Avril Jarvis, Sir Cecil."

Lawton took off his spectacles. "Miss Dobbs, I don't know. This is most unexpected."

"I realize that, sir. I have never before made such a request a condition of my taking on an inquiry, but I have been involved in the case—I consult with Scotland Yard on occasion—and know that the girl will not otherwise have access to counsel of any stature. I must add that, in my estimation, her case merits such representation."

"You believe her innocent?"

Maisie took care to retain eye contact with Lawton. "I believe in her *innocence*, Sir Cecil. My assistant leaves tomorrow for Taunton, to conduct further inquiries as to her background and the question of her appearance in London."

Lawton sighed, tapping the newspaper. "But this seems all too familiar: a poor girl leaves home to seek her fortune in London; she falls on hard times, is taken up by a pimp and, in this case, exacts a payment for her sins." He rose and walked toward the window that looked out across the square. "If I agree to act for the girl—and I do not need to remind you that I have to be briefed by her attending solicitor—does that mean your fee is waived?"

Maisie took a deep breath. Lawton was a wealthy man. He did not need to strike such a bargain, though she suspected the move was born of habit by a man used to the verbal jousting of the courtroom. She had been cautious with her money for years, but her pockets were not *that* deep; however, she had made her decision. Avril Jarvis needed a legal miracle. "The fee will be halved, though obviously not my expenses."

Lawton leaned across his desk, took up a fountain pen and made a note. "I agree to your terms, Miss Dobbs. Now, let us continue."

"Thank you, Sir Cecil." Maisie smiled, pleased that an agreement had been reached. She proceeded to remove a wedge of index cards from her case as Lawton took his place again in the chair opposite.

"I would like to know what happened when you received word of Ralph's death."

Lawton sighed. "It was on August seventeenth, 1917. I was about to leave our home in Regent's Park when the telegram arrived. It stated that Ralph was missing, presumed dead. A letter received later confirmed that his aeroplane had been shot down over enemy territory and he had perished."

"How long had he been in the Flying Corps?"

"A long time, all things considered, but only a few months as a pilot."

"Oh?"

"He enlisted fairly soon after leaving school, then transferred from the Royal Engineers to the Flying Corps, where he was a mechanic before becoming an observer."

"A mechanic?" Maisie realized that she had taken the step she'd warned Billy about only a couple of hours earlier. She had made an assumption, in her case that Ralph Lawton had joined the Royal Flying Corps as an officer.

"Yes, Ralph went into the army straight from school." Lawton rubbed his chin. "He was a singular sort of chap at St. Edmunds, didn't really have close friends." He paused again. "Anyway, my son enjoyed solitary pursuits and had something of a mathematical mind, passable at physics and so on, and liked tinkering with engines. Essentially, Miss Dobbs, it would be fair to say that Ralph preferred his own company, liked to be left alone."

"Did he enjoy his schooldays?"

Lawton frowned. "I do not believe such a time in one's life is there to be *enjoyed* as such. Sadly, my son was not a scholar, nor did he excel on the sports field. In fact, I understand he was rather shunned when it came to such pursuits. He wasn't one who was at home on the cricket field, and he was far too sensitive for rugby."

"Sensitive?"

Lawton seemed uncomfortable. "Well, you know, didn't care for the camaraderie or, indeed, the demands of such a sport. Look, is this really necessary, Miss Dobbs?"

"Yes—yes, it is." Maisie was thoughtful. "Tell me, Sir Cecil, what would you say was at the heart of Ralph's *singular* character?"

"If you must know, I think it was my wife's fault. Ralph was very much his mother's son, Miss Dobbs."

"And you think that was detrimental to his future?" ·

"Miss Dobbs, I had hoped that my son would demonstrate more

acceptable ambitions to a father in my position. His performance at school was average at best, except in mathematical subjects, as I have indicated. His reluctance to take a full part in the recreational aspects of scholarship at such a prestigious boys' school, together with his insistence on joining up with the enlisted men rather than taking up a commission, all served to convince me that my son wished only to cross me."

"I see. So there was a rift between you?"

Lawton was silent for a moment before replying. "He may have been my son, Miss Dobbs, but I did not care for his character, I'm afraid."

"And your wife?"

"Adored him. She lost two sons in childbirth before Ralph was born, and our daughter's death from rubella meant he was to be our only child. My wife elevated Ralph's importance to a ridiculous level. She didn't care what he did or who he became, as long as he was *there*, hence this stupidity in continuing to believe he was alive. And now I am charged with continuing the charade!"

Maisie leaned back into the chair and breathed deeply. She was taken aback by the strength of feeling revealed in Lawton's voice, which had become quite loud. Instead of encountering a father crushed by the loss of his only son, Maisie found herself keen to temper his frustration and bitterness. As Lawton began to regain composure, Maisie stood up. "Sir Cecil, it is such a pleasant day today. I know this is somewhat unusual, but may we continue our discussion during a stroll around the square?"

Lawton frowned. "Julian suggested I should expect you to have a somewhat irregular approach to such an inquiry." He sighed and consulted his watch. "I can spare another half an hour."

Maisie stood up. "Then let us walk. Before I leave I would like the names of those your wife consulted in her quest to prove your son alive. I will need whatever information you have on Ralph's service record and also, if you have further recollections of his friends,

I will require the details. Please make a note of these things. Perhaps one of your assistants can begin to—"

"Oh, no, Miss Dobbs. I will compile this collection of information myself."

Maisie nodded. "I will need to make arrangements to visit Ralph's room in your house; even if it has been changed since his death, I'd like to see it. I will require any belongings that you have retained, for just a short time." She paused and looked directly at Lawton. "And Sir Cecil, this is only the first of several discussions. There is much for me to learn, much for me to understand about Ralph. Now then, shall we?"

Maisie stepped toward the door, but not before she had noticed the line of perspiration across Lawton's forehead, and the shaking of his hands as he took out a handkerchief and held it against his brow. She would not press him too much during the walk. No, it was important to lure him back into her field of influence with lighter questions. But she would visit him again, and soon. For Maisie had understood something very quickly. Ralph Lawton had failed his father in some way, and Cecil Lawton, the famous Cecil Lawton, the great legal miracle worker, could not forgive him for it—*even in death*.

SIX

Sir Cecil Lawton had furnished Maisie with several names, per her request, along with an invitation to visit both his Regent's Park home and his country estate in Cambridgeshire, where Ralph had enjoyed school holidays. Billy and Doreen Beale had left Paddington Station for Taunton on the early morning train and, after lunch with Priscilla the following day, Friday, Maisie planned to drive to Chelstone, where she would visit her father, before continuing on to Hastings on Saturday morning. As Maisie considered the next two days, her inquiry plan taking shape on a large sheet of paper referred to as a *case map*, the telephone rang.

"Fitzroy, five, six, double-oh," said Maisie, leafing through a box of papers that had just arrived by messenger from Lawton's chambers.

"Maisie, darling, I thought I'd give you a quick ring."

"Hello, Andrew." Maisie bit the inside of her lip. Though they had planned a day together, she felt torn, wanting to have time alone to consider the two cases now uppermost on her mind.

"Oh, dear, I know that voice. You're knee deep in a case and you want to be still and think about it for hours without any interruption, planned weekends with the unflappable Dr. Andrew Dene notwithstanding." He paused briefly. "But, dear Maisie, I will hold you to your promise. In fact, I have a surprise for you, so I expect you at my door by eleven on Saturday morning."

Maisie smiled as she looked up from her papers, seeing Dene in her mind's eye. His unruly hazelnut-brown hair would doubtless be flopping into his eyes. His tie loosened as he came into his office, he would have thrown his woolen jacket across the back of his chair and would be trying to pull on his white coat while talking to her.

"All right, all right, I confess, I was going to try to weasel out—"

"I knew it!"

Maisie heard a pile of papers and files fall from his overladen desk, then a scuffle as he tried to retrieve them and listen to her at the same time.

"—but I will come to Hastings on Saturday morning."

"Excellent. I'll take you out for fish and chips on the beach, if you play your cards right!"

"Oh, how could I turn down an offer like that?"

"You couldn't. Righty-o, I must dash. I've got a new patient this morning, a youngster crippled with polio, I'm afraid. See you Saturday."

"Until then, Andrew." Maisie replaced the receiver and stared out of the window for a moment. In truth, she suspected that Dene had fallen in love with her but would not ask her to marry him until he felt confident that her answer would be yes. And they both knew that time had not yet come. For her part, the relationship had been an easy one, given Dene's happy-go-lucky character. Yet one aspect of her response to their relationship bothered Maisie: the fact that, when apart, she seldom thought about Dene; then, when she saw him again, she was quick to remember how charming she found him to be. He, too, had risen above difficult circumstances—the death of both parents at an early age—and he had worked hard to put himself through medical school. After serving in the war, he was now an orthopedic specialist with a bright future at a rehabilitation and convalescence hospital high on the cliffs above Hastings Old Town, in Sussex. Maisie sometimes envied the way in which Dene refused to allow the weight of his past to be a burden, though she suspected he used his lightness and good humor as an antidote to his own sufferings and those of his patients.

She turned to the papers once more and made a notation on an index card. She glanced at her watch. Lawton had given her the names of three women claiming to be psychics whom his wife had consulted, and she planned to visit each woman today. She remembered only too well the many psychics and others like them who feigned a special relationship with the dead and claimed to have heard from a son, father, brother, or husband who had been killed. She also remembered the grieving, those whom her mentor, Maurice Blanche, had counseled following such disappointments—and the practitioners he had challenged and effectively put out of business.

During her apprenticeship they had worked together to break a ring of fraudulent psychics who took money from the bereaved in return for bogus messages from the dead. It was a landmark case that tested Maisie to the core, not least because it was the first time she was personally required to give evidence in court. According to the newspapers, it was the youthful innocence of one of the witnesses, Miss Maisie Dobbs, that swayed the jury to find Frances Sinden, Irene Nelson and Margaret Awkright guilty, a result that would pack them off to Holloway Prison for a very long time indeed. Now, having checked to see whether there had been any previous convictions or complaints against the women on Lawton's list, or whether she and Maurice had investigated one or all of them years ago, she set off.

BARROW ROAD, ISLINGTON, was on the cusp of change. The large Victorian houses had been divided into flats, some of them run-down, some clinging to a haughty grandeur despite paint that was beginning to peel. The downstairs flat at number 21 might have seemed gray and damp if someone who cared less than Lillian

Browning was in residence. The soot-blackened exterior was made bright by window boxes with pink and red geraniums, and on each step down to the flat a medium-sized terra-cotta flowerpot overflowed with brightly colored blooms. Mrs. Browning had planted an ivy in a larger pot, and it was now furiously making its way along the recently replaced iron railings, the original railings having been torn up for use in the armaments factories at the outset of war in 1914.

Maisie knocked at the door.

Lillian Browning was about forty years of age, with light hazel eyes and mousy brown hair recently treated to a permanent wave that had resulted in frizz rather than a smooth curling of her locks. Her plain pale-green dress seemed a little tight across the middle, indicating, perhaps, that Mrs. Browning had enjoyed a slender figure in girlhood but had reached an age when some restraint in food consumption might be advised.

"Yes?" Browning squinted as she smiled at Maisie, then took out a pair of wire spectacles from the pocket of a black cardigan, placed them on her nose, and scrutinized her visitor.

"Mrs. Browning?"

"Yes. How can I help you?"

"My name's Maisie Dobbs. I wonder if you might be able to spare me a moment or two?" Maisie smiled and inclined her head, a seemingly insignificant move that she used to great effect.

"Here for a reading, are you?"

"Well, I *am* intrigued by your line of work, Mrs. Browning. May I come in?"

The woman nodded and stepped aside, directing Maisie along the narrow passage and into the parlor to the right. "Recommended by a friend, were you?"

"Yes, sort of." Waiting for an invitation to be seated, she looked around the small room. A Victorian anaglypta decorating paper adorned the walls, overpainted in a deep creamy gloss that had become stained across the ridges of the pattern. The faded velvet curtains were edged with a fraying silk fringe, but though the room revealed additional evidence of rather worn gentility, it was comfortable and clean, if musty.

"Please do sit down, Miss Dobbs." Browning nodded toward an armchair with threadbare cushions. "May I offer you a cup of tea?"

"No, thank you." Maisie smiled again. She was actually somewhat relieved, for she knew she had nothing to fear or shield herself against in this house. No otherworldly spirit had ever entered the room. Browning was nothing more than a fake trying to make ends meet. But she might yet be useful.

"What can I do for you, Miss Dobbs?" Browning reached toward a wooden box on the top of the sideboard and took out a pack of tarot cards. "I charge one-and-sixpence for the cards. More if I have to summon the spirits."

"No, there will be no need, Mrs. Browning. I should have told you immediately that I am here to ask you about one of your former clients, Lady Agnes Lawton."

Browning stood up quickly, replaced the cards, and folded her arms. "Well, like you said, you should have mentioned it at first, I could've told you on the step that I have nothing to say. You from the authorities?"

Maisie leaned back in her chair. "No, I'm not from the authorities, but I am trying to . . ." Maisie paused. "I'm trying to assist Agnes Lawton's husband in putting the memory of his son and wife to rest. I understand that she came to you for help."

The woman sat down again and pursed her lips before speaking. "I knew she'd passed on. I go down to the library once a week to read the obituaries, and I saw that she'd shaken off this mortal coil."

Maisie looked down at her hands. There was something sadly amusing about this woman, who spoke again after giving the matter a little thought.

"Well, as long as you're not here to close me down, I s'pose it's all right. I can hardly get by as it is, being a war widow. Of course, that's why she came to me, having been through losing someone. I have a very highly respected clientele, I'll have you know, and they trust me."

Maisie nodded.

"Of course, I couldn't forget that one, even though it was years ago that I saw her. Very posh, she was. Very well heeled, though she never called herself *Lady* at the time, said she was *Mrs.* Lawton. Poor woman thought her son was alive."

"And what did you tell her?" Maisie leaned forward.

Browning avoided meeting Maisie's eyes as she answered. "Well, I told her that he hadn't come to me, you know, in spirit."

"And you led her to believe he wasn't dead?"

"I never said any such thing, not exactly. Now then. I think, Miss Dobbs—"

"Did she ever say why she thought her son was alive?"

Browning stood up and walked toward the window. Maisie knew the woman's desire to protect her reputation would prevent her from sending her from the house; after all, she might be well connected. "Mrs. Lawton said a mother knows, and he would have come to her. You heard about it a lot, sons coming home to their mothers for just a second; then the next thing you know, the telegram's arrived. Happened to me, it did, so I knew what she meant. I thought I saw my Bernard walking down them steps there; then all of a sudden he was gone. Vanished. A week later the telegram arrived, telling me he'd been killed. That's how I knew I had the sight."

"I'm sorry—"

"So I knew what she meant. If he hadn't come to her, just for a glimpse, then he must be alive."

Maisie stood up, ready to leave. There was nothing for her here, except perhaps an impression of Agnes Lawton's desperation. She imagined the woman making her way to Browning's dark parlor— despite her attempts to cheer the exterior with flowers—and sitting while the fake spiritualist feigned communion with the dead, allowing her to believe her son was still alive. Even though she loathed such deceit, Maisie was filled with compassion. There was an immense sadness in Browning's work, though the woman could not see the harm inherent in her claims.

"Do you have many visits from the bereaved nowadays?"

"Oh, I still get the odd one here and there, but not like it was during the war. I get a lot of young girls now wanting to know who they are going to marry, whether they'll marry well, that sort of thing. I put it down to the talkies, you know. They all want to know if they'll meet the likes of Douglas Fairbanks or Ronald Colman, or if they'll be rich and live in a big house." She looked up at Maisie. "Now, I notice you aren't engaged, Miss Dobbs. I do think I see a tall man in your future, wears a hat—"

Maisie raised a hand. "Not me! I'll be on my way, Mrs. Browning. Thank you for your time."

And before Lillian Browning had even a chance to say goodbye, Maisie was gone.

THE NEXT STOP was Camberwell and a Miss Darby. The small terraced house backed onto the railway line, with air acrid from the constant to-ing and fro-ing of steam trains belching in and out of the main London stations, the residue of raw boiler fuel from the Welsh coal mines lingering in the gardens. Maisie knocked at the door of number 5 Denton Street, and a small thin woman of about sixty opened the door. She held a handkerchief to her mouth and nose and only removed it to say quickly, "Yes?"

Maisie coughed. "Maisie Dobbs to see Miss Darby. If you have a moment."

The woman nodded and stood aside, saying nothing until they were inside and walking toward the sitting room. "I tell you, there's days I can't even sit in my own garden. I put my washing out, and it's all splattered with black spots. Mind you, always the same, it is.

Always been like it ever since I first came to live here, but lately, since I went down with the flu in—oh, sorry, Miss Dobbs. Do take a seat." The woman pointed to a wooden Windsor chair and pulled an identical chair alongside. She took Maisie's hand in hers. "Now, then, has a dear one passed on?"

SEVEN

The visit to Miss Darby proceeded much as Maisie had anticipated. Though the woman's compassion for her clients was obvious, Maisie detected no authentic ability to communicate with anything other than flesh and blood, which she did very well and to her advantage. Darby had taken care not to make promises that could not be kept and—from her account of their meetings—it would seem that Agnes Lawton gained nothing more than an hour or two's comfort. Maisie left the house with a sense of frustration and pity: frustration that Agnes Lawton had not seen the fakery behind the claims, and pity for a woman who had clearly been in deep crisis, her grief so deep that common sense could not prevail. The thought of a third such visit was almost too much to bear, but Maisie tried to shake off all preconceptions as she drove to Balham, where she would visit Madeleine Hartnell.

After parking alongside Dufrayne Court, a modern block of flats surrounded by landscaped courtyards, Maisie stood for a moment, leaning with her back against the MG to observe the white building. Designed to resemble an ocean liner, each of the building's three floors seemed enlarged by a wraparound balcony in the same white finish, though portholes in the balcony allowed glimpses of the floor-to-ceiling French windows of each flat beyond. Maisie imagined the occupants as rather well-to-do people who entertained, who enjoyed being at the forefront of life on the outskirts of London. They were people who might have been thought to be going places, though the speed with which they made progress may well have been curtailed by the depression that now gripped the country. It seemed an unlikely choice of accommodation for a woman who, according to the claims she made to Agnes Lawton, kept company with the past.

Maisie located the bell for Hartnell's apartment, alongside her surname on a glass-fronted directory of residents. She pressed the button, and an intercom crackled.

"Who is it?" The voice was difficult to discern, given the sputtering line.

"Maisie Dobbs to see Miss Hartnell." The line crackled again.

"I'll ask Miss Hartnell."

There was more noise on the line as Maisie waited; then she heard the receiver being picked up once more.

"Miss Hartnell will see you now, Miss Dobbs. You'll hear a buzz, then a click, and all you do is push the door and walk in. All right?"

"Yes." The buzzer sounded and Maisie entered a light, airy entrance hall with a carpeted staircase in front of her. The main door to each flat was only accessible from an inner courtyard.

Maisie climbed the stairs to the second floor, where the door to number 7 Dufrayne Court was open and the housekeeper stood waiting.

"Good afternoon, Miss Dobbs. Lucky for you Miss Hartnell had a cancellation this afternoon. Do come in." She closed the door behind Maisie, then walked ahead.

For her part, Maisie hoped for a moment or two of solitude before meeting Hartnell. Though it began as only the whisper of sensation while she regarded the building from outside, she now felt a stronger prickle across her neck, her most vulnerable place. A chill air seemed to embrace her, just for the briefest moment, as they walked along the hallway. Maisie knew only too well the source of such chills, though she was not afraid. Hartnell may have misled Agnes Lawton, may have encouraged her to believe that her son was not dead, but even when the housekeeper had left for the day, Hartnell was never completely alone in her home.

A large drawing room was visible through glass double doors ahead, and Maisie could see a red brick fireplace against a white background. The polished wooden floors were covered with rugs and a shaft of light seemed to sweep from the left, where Maisie imagined the French windows and balcony to be. Before reaching the drawing room, the housekeeper stopped and indicated a smaller room, also on the left.

"Miss Hartnell will be with you directly. I'll bring tea in a moment."

"Oh, that's not necess—" Maisie began, but was interrupted.

"Miss Hartnell always has a cup of tea at three." The housekeeper pressed her hands together, nodded, and left the room, closing the door behind her.

Maisie quickly appraised the room. There was no circular table, no heavily fringed lamp that she had seen in the rooms of others plying their trade as mediums and psychics. Instead, two armchairs were set in front of a window, and a low table with just enough room for a tray was positioned at an angle to the chairs. There were no curtains, only blinds partially drawn against a fierce afternoon sun. A vase of lilies had been placed in the corner, and in the air a sweet fragrance lingered for which Maisie could detect no immediate source, for as she leaned toward the blooms, no scent was apparent. Maisie stood in front of the window and closed her eyes. She brought her hands together and imagined a circle. She saw the circle moving toward her before slipping over her head and down the length of her body, enveloping her in a protective shell. As the circle dropped to her feet, she breathed deeply again. She would be safe now.

The door opened.

"Miss Dobbs. Please do take a seat."

Though she had expected someone younger than the two women visited earlier, Maisie was not prepared for Madeleine Hartnell to be quite so youthful. She appeared to be only about twenty-four years old and was fashionably dressed in a pale blue crepe costume. She was a very attractive woman. Hartnell held Maisie's initial look with her piercing blue-green eyes, her platinum-blond hair catching a narrow shaft of light that had forced its way through the blinds. *She understands exactly why I am here*, thought Maisie, as she felt the skin at the nape of her neck prickle again. She would have to take great care with Madeleine Hartnell.

"Mrs. Kemp will bring tea in a moment." Hartnell held out a hand to indicate the chair just as the housekeeper entered with a tea tray. "Ah, there she is now." Hartnell smiled. "Thank you, Mrs. Kemp."

Without first asking, Hartnell poured tea for two, placed a cup in front of Maisie, and leaned back into the chair with her own cup of tea. She sipped once, then turned to her visitor.

"So. You have some questions for me, Miss Dobbs?"

"Yes, I do. And thank you for seeing me."

Hartnell nodded. Maisie noted the woman's relaxed manner. *Too calm, much too calm.*

"I understand that Lady Agnes Lawton was a client." She framed her words as neither question nor statement, allowing Hartnell to respond as she wished.

Hartnell looked at her for a few seconds, sipped again, and leaned forward to place her cup on the tray.

"Please, Miss Dobbs, put all your cards on the table. It would make our conversation so much easier."

Maisie felt as if she were engaged in a game of chess, a player looking for the next strategic move. "Of course. On her deathbed, Agnes Lawton exacted a promise from her husband, Sir Cecil Lawton. As you know . . ." Maisie paused and held Hartnell's piercing eyes with her own. Hartnell did not flinch. "As you know, Lady Agnes never accepted the death of her son, despite the fact that his remains were buried at the Faubourg-d'Amiens Cemetery, along with other members of the Royal Flying Corps who gave their lives." Maisie paused. "I have been retained by Sir Cecil Lawton to prove that his son is dead."

"Is that so?"

Maisie did not respond immediately but allowed a pause before replying. "Yes, that is so." She moved in her chair, mirroring the woman's position. Hartnell was confident and calm, though as soon as she noticed Maisie change position, she uncrossed her legs, and leaned forward, smiling. *She's anticipating my every move*, thought Maisie.

"I had hoped you might be able to help me, Miss Hartnell, to throw light on the issue of Ralph Lawton's death," said Maisie.

Leaning back again, Hartnell shook her head. "I'm afraid there's little I can say, Miss Dobbs. Lady Agnes believed her son to be alive, and I saw no reason to doubt her. I should add that my clients expect and receive a promise of complete confidentiality. I know she's dead now, but"—again she held Maisie's eyes with her own—"that doesn't have a bearing on my work. Death is not the end of the line as far as my responsibility to my clients goes."

"I see."

"I know you do, Miss Dobbs."

Maisie inclined her head, a move emulated by Hartnell.

"You see farther than you let on to most people, though I am not most people." Hartnell reached forward, poured a small measure of still-hot tea from the pot into her teacup, and added milk. "You get it from your mother's side, don't you?"

"Miss Hartnell, I'm afraid—"

"No, you're not afraid. You have no reason to be, because she walks with you. She's always with you, your mother, watching over you."

Maisie felt a lump grow in her throat. She felt protected against any darkness in the spirit world, but not in the most vulnerable places of her heart. She sat straighter, but Hartnell was ready.

"Yes, it's one thing protecting oneself from the dead, but only too easy to forget the damage that the living can do, eh?" Hartnell smiled at Maisie, then at a place beyond Maisie's shoulder, as if sharing a secret with another.

"You make a good point, Miss Hartnell." Maisie was anxious to gain control of the conversation, though she wanted dearly to reach behind her chair, to touch, just once, the soft yet strong hand that had once grasped her own small one. *Come on, Maisie, love, skip along, we've to be back from the park and have your dad's tea on the table by five. Come along, my girl, come along, skip along with Mummy.* Maisie spoke quickly before any more memories flooded into her mind's eye. "Have you any information that might help me? I seek only to assist my client and to bring a measure of peace into his life."

"And knowing will bring him peace?"

"I have, of course, suggested that peace may not come with such knowledge, but in the meantime I have a commitment to search for truth."

Hartnell moved to the window and opened the blinds, using a pulley secured to the wall. She closed her eyes and turned to Maisie, her blond hair now haloed by a bright ring of sunlight. "I can tell you nothing more, Miss Dobbs, though I will say this: You would be advised to withdraw from the agreement immediately."

"I have given my word."

"Yes, I know. And you can't abandon the girl either, can you?" Hartnell closed the blind and moved to the door. The meeting had ended.

Taken aback by the comment and her abrupt dismissal, Maisie stood, gathered her document case, and opened it to take out a calling card. She knew very well what Hartnell meant but would not acknowledge the accuracy of her words.

"Miss Hartnell, thank you for your time, it is most appreciated." She held out her card. "Perhaps you would be so kind as to telephone me, should you think of anything that might assist me in my search for proof of Ralph Lawton's death."

Hartnell held the card in one hand, the doorhandle in the other. She glanced at the card. "Psychologist and investigator? Well, well, well. . . ."

Maisie again said nothing and moved toward the now-open door. "I have been asked to tell you two things, Miss Dobbs."

"Yes?" Startled, Maisie turned quickly, her senses alert.

"First, that you look beyond the town, the town in the west country."

Maisie nodded.

"The other is that you have two from the other side who protect you, though one has not passed over." Hartnell closed her eyes. Maisie could hear the housekeeper's footsteps as they *click-clicked* closer along the parquet hallway. "It is strange; he is between this world and the next: caught in life, yet his spirit wanders. It is so very sad." Madeleine Hartnell did not say goodbye but left the room with tears in her eyes.

Maisie thanked Mrs. Kemp and left the flat at Dufrayne Court quickly. Slipping into the driver's seat of the MG, she leaned back and exhaled deeply. Madeleine Hartnell was formidable, without doubt. Maisie placed her hand on the buckle at the front of her belted dress and took another, deeper, breath. *Calm, become calm.* A moment or two passed before Maisie leaned forward to start the engine. As she pulled away, she considered all she had learned about Madeleine Hartnell. She did not doubt that Hartnell had command of the abilities she claimed—indeed, she had proven as much. Or had she? Were her comments a shot in the dark? No, she was too close to the target—so much so that Maisie made a mental note to contact Billy with instructions to make inquiries in the villages close to Taunton. She thought of Hartnell's parting words. Suddenly, Maisie felt her eyes prickle. *Oh, Mum, I have missed you so much, so much.* But it was as she drove toward the West End that Maisie felt her heart ache and a vision of her former love, Simon, came to her. She imagined him in his wheelchair with a blanket across his knees, a gentle breeze catching the leaves of exotic plants in the nursing home conservatory as he sat alone. *Caught in life, yet his spirit wanders. . . .*

What was it about Madeleine Hartnell that Maisie mistrusted, more so than either Browning or Darby? The latter were both certainly fakes trying to make a living in difficult times. *Be careful.* The words echoed into Maisie's mind. *Be careful.* It was her mother's voice she heard.

Something else intrigued Maisie. For all her sophistication, command, and supersensitivity, there was a vulnerability about Madeleine Hartnell that reminded her of Avril Jarvis. As she pressed her foot harder on the accelerator, it occurred to her that she saw a girlishness in Hartnell, though she could not put her finger on the reason for such a thought.

EIGHT

Maisie was at her desk early on Friday. In preparation for lunch with Priscilla, she had gone through her entire wardrobe and found it wanting. She held up a cream silk blouse, one of three she owned, to see if it might look too dowdy with the burgundy suit she had considered so very stylish several months ago. Instead, the black day dress was chosen again, along with black shoes and the hat with a broad ribbon of claret satin. She would wear the suit jacket over the black dress. *There, that will add a bit of something. . . .*

As she sat at the case map and tapped a red pencil on the broad sheet of white paper, the thought occurred to Maisie that the source of much of her discombobulation was Madeleine Hartnell. Maurice had been of little help—or was it that his answers had not immediately given her rest? It was obvious that he had no intention of providing comfort, though she knew his counsel to be true as she reflected upon the telephone call she had made to him immediately upon returning to her rooms at Ebury Place.

"Remember, Maisie, that such people come to us on two levels, so to speak." He had paused during their conversation to draw deeply on his pipe. "On the one hand, yes, you must take great care with the likes of Hartnell. We have seen her sort before, and with due care we have come to no harm. And it is clear that she might be of further use. My advice would be to seek the wisdom of our friend Khan."

"I haven't seen him in a long time, Maurice. I'm amazed he's still alive, to tell you the truth."

"Khan seems to be above such notions as age." Maurice paused. "He is the one to whom *I* have turned, Maisie, in times of spiritual darkness."

"Oh, I wouldn't say that I'm—"

"The second level, Maisie, is the task that we are all sent to accomplish in each other's lives. It is a task of which we have no conscious awareness, but it is there all the same. Hartnell's appearance at this time will indubitably require you to address . . . a conflict, perhaps? It is a rhetorical question. Consider your discomfort and welcome it as the ache necessary for you to become more deeply attuned."

Maisie sighed, the sound of her own exhaled breath bringing her back to the present. She looked at the scribbled notes and diagrams on the case map in front of her and began working again. In a circle centered on the paper, she had written RALPH LAWTON; in another, AGNES LAWTON. Drawing connecting lines between the circled names of each person already identified as someone known to Ralph, she wondered who might be able to shed light on his character and how she would approach them. There was specific groundwork to do, so she made a note to investigate the aviator's military record herself as soon as possible. The word HOUSE was circled, and as Maisie looked at the chain of thoughts, guesses, questions, and known facts linked by the series of lines, she knew her next visit must be to the Lawton country home.

She worked for several hours, checking her watch and waiting for Billy to report in. She had written the words FRANCE and FLANDERS on the case map; then, in a corner, she had faintly penciled in the word BIARRITZ, as a frivolity if time allowed. The telephone rang.

"Fitzroy—"

"S'me, Miss."

"Billy, hello! How are you?" Maisie leaned back in her chair and looked out at the square as she spoke.

"Awright, thank you very much. Doreen's gone out for a stroll, and I'm in this telephone kiosk talking to you."

"So, any news for me?"

"Not a lot yet, Miss, not a lot. Mainly because the papers 'aven't got 'old of the girl's actual name, though when they do it'll be all over the place, I can tell you."

"Not a lot happens in country towns, Billy."

"Well, I wouldn't say that, Miss—ay-oop, got to put a bit more money in." Noises on the line indicated that Billy was pressing coins into the telephone box and then the button to continue the call. "I've been to the library already and looked up *Jarvis*. They've got a very good librarian who was over in France you know—very inter-estin' woman, said what she did was something she couldn't talk about—but anyway, I told 'er I was looking for an old mate of mine from the sappers, who lived down this way and that we'd lost touch in 1917 when I was wounded. So she drags out all sorts of books and papers and ledgers and what 'ave you—"

"And?" Maisie wanted to chivvy Billy along. Given the chance, Billy Beale could talk the hind leg off a donkey.

"Anyway, interestingly enough, turns out there was a family of Jarvises lived outside the town, in a village not far from 'ere, and—you are never goin' to believe this, not that it has anything to do with my investigation—but—"

Oh, get on with it, Billy, thought Maisie, tapping her pencil against the table again.

"But apparently this 'ere Jarvis family was involved in some strange doin's."

"What sort of strange doin's—things?"

"Well, some years ago, one of the womenfolk got 'erself put away for a bit for meddlin' in medicinal work—you know, giving people tinctures and mixtures."

"I don't think there's an actual law against that, Billy."

"There is when it kills people."

"Oh, I see."

"They weren't exactly fitters-in, if you know what I mean. Now then, I don't know if our Avril Jarvis is of the same family, but it does seem a bit of a coincidence, don't it, Miss."

"Look into it, Billy. What's the name of the village?"

"Downsmarsh-on-Lye."

"Sounds very postcardy."

"Not from what I've 'eard, Miss. More like, the only people are farmworkers and tinkers who ain't got enough money to put clothes on the backs of their children. Mind you, at least they can grow a bit of food down 'ere."

"Will you go to the village today?"

"There's a branch line with a train every three hours. I'll get the half-past-eleven."

"Good."

"Talk to you tomorrow mornin', Miss. Shall I telephone Chelstone?"

"Yes. Better make it early, as I'm leaving for Hastings. Telephone at seven—and Billy, take care."

" 'Course I will, Miss. What they goin' to do, whop me one over the 'ead with some 'erbs?"

"You know what I mean." Maisie shook her head and placed the receiver in its cradle.

So, it appeared Madeleine Hartnell was right: The girl came from a village outside Taunton. The accuracy of the prediction unsettled Maisie even more. She felt vulnerable, as if she were crossing a lake covered in ice. Just one false step and. . . . She tapped the table again. She was to meet Priscilla at the Strand Palace at one o'clock. There was just enough time to go to Khan. *He is the one to whom I have turned, Maisie, in times of spiritual darkness.* She would go now, before the cloud she felt looming ahead came any closer.

· · ·

THE LARGE HOUSE in Hampstead had not changed since she first entered it as a young girl, brought by Maurice Blanche to meet Dr. Basil Khan on what he described as an *educational visit*. It was from Khan that Maisie learned that seeing was not necessarily something one did with the eyes; there was a depth of vision to be gained from stillness, a vision that had stood her in good stead ever since. And it was to Khan that Maurice brought Maisie again, in the early days of her return from France in 1917, so that his insight, calm, and healing presence might bring peace to a young woman wounded in body and spirit. He had not failed her but simply asked her to tell her story again and again and again, and in the telling she had begun the journey of ridding herself of death's ugly stench, a clinging vapor she thought had laid claim to her senses forever.

A young man in a white cotton robe answered the door and bowed to Maisie, bidding her to enter the spacious yet plain hexagonal hallway.

"I have come to see him—if I may?"

"I shall ask. It is Miss Dobbs, is it not?"

"Yes. Thank you."

The young man bowed, his hands pressed together in front of his chest, and left the room.

Maisie walked to the bay window that looked out across the garden at the front of the house. A dense privet hedge obscured a view of the road, offering privacy from the curiosity of passersby. There were two statues in the garden, which was fragrant with flowers and shrubs not immediately familiar to Maisie. One statue had been brought from Ceylon. It was of the Buddha, sitting with legs crossed. Rose petals had been left at the base of the statue and around the neck. The other, perhaps surprisingly, was of St. Francis. At the foot of this statue, a small feeding platform for birds had been placed. Maisie smiled as a thrush settled on one of St. Francis's arms before hopping down for a repast of bread crumbs.

Khan's students came from all over the world, accommodated in the many rooms of the large house. In addition to the young men and women who stayed for months at a time, Khan held daily audiences with others who sought his counsel. Those who came represented a broad spectrum of influence, be they men of politics, commerce, or the cloth; it was from such sources that bills for upkeep of the house and property were paid—though the material needs of its occupants were few.

The young man entered again, and Maisie was led to Khan's rooms. The reception room was much as she remembered it as a girl, though today the floor-to-ceiling windows were closed and the white curtains did not billow majestically as they had on that first visit. She removed her shoes before entering the spartan room. Khan sat cross-legged on cushions, positioned so he faced outward, to the natural light. Maisie moved toward him, and as she came closer he turned. She took the wizened clawlike hand extended to her and leaned forward to brush her lips against his forehead.

"I am glad you are in my house again, Maisie Dobbs."

"And I too, Khan."

"You have only a short time, no doubt."

"Yes."

Khan nodded as Maisie silently knelt on a cushion close to him and then sat with her legs to the side. She rested one hand on the floor and smiled at Khan, and though he could not see her, he turned to her once more and smiled. As he faced the window again, Maisie saw a single fly land on his forehead and crawl to his ear and then his nose before flying away into the room. Khan did not even flinch. She knew she would have to speak first, and that her words must be from the heart.

"I am afraid, Khan."

He nodded.

"I have been asked to take on a case that I feel—no, I *fear*—will compromise my spirit. I do not feel on safe ground with this work, even though I have my practice, my stillness. And I have no evidence of such a threat, though I am required to be in communication with those who claim to open channels to the other side."

There was silence in the room. Then Khan spoke.

"Then what moves you to take this work?"

"I . . . well, at first I had thought to decline; however, a young girl needs legal representation, and it appeared that I could secure counsel for her as part of my payment."

Khan lifted his head as the sun warmed the windowpanes. "And which young girl are you helping?" It might have been Maurice talking.

Maisie's eyes became moist as she blurted out her confession. "I have missed her so much, Khan, so very much. I've always known she was with me, really, and I didn't want my father to feel he couldn't be everything to me, I didn't want him to know I grieved so deeply for my mother. Then, when he almost died, I—"

Khan turned to her, and she began to sob.

"I want to help this girl. I can't bear it that she could end up incarcerated for the rest of her life. That she be sent away. . . ." Maisie fought to compose herself. "And I have been afraid that if I go to France, the memories—"

Khan allowed her to weep, her shoulders shaking as he laid a hand upon her head. Then he spoke.

"My child, when a mountain appears on the journey, we try to go to the left, then to the right; we try to find the easy way to navigate our way back to the easier path." He paused. "But the mountain is there to be crossed. It is on that pilgrimage, as we climb higher, that we are forced to shed the layers upon layers we have carried for so long. Then we find that our load is lighter and we have come to know something of ourselves in the perilous climb."

Maisie looked up as he spoke, his melodious voice compelling her to listen carefully.

"Do not seek to avoid the mountain, my child, for it has been placed there at a perfect time. It will only become larger if you seek to delay or draw back from the ascent."

Maisie said nothing, but she moved away and pulled a handkerchief from her pocket to wipe her eyes and nose.

"Know that you are protected, child. That in your practice and belief lies your strength." Khan closed his eyes and appeared to be sleeping. He was a very old man, and he was tired, but he had one final message. "And you are blessed, both in those who protect you, and in those you seek to protect."

Maisie came silently to her feet, kissed Khan once more on the forehead, and walked away, slipping on her shoes at the door before leaving the room. A student escorted her to the front door, and she pressed a half-crown into his hand. He bowed, turned, and was gone. The door closed behind her. The mountain loomed ahead. She squared her shoulders to face it. *Yes, but what do I believe in?*

MAISIE ARRIVED AT the Strand Palace Hotel ten minutes late for her appointment with Priscilla. Though the country was in an economic slump, the modern hotel, with its silver revolving doors and ultramodern design, welcomed guests into a land of optimism, if only for a night, for dinner, or for a cocktail. Priscilla was standing in the lobby waiting. Wearing a slate-gray costume, clearly from an expensive Paris atelier, with matching shoes and bag, she seemed to be observing those who came and went, confident in their admiring glances yet somewhat amused by her surroundings. She saw Maisie and smiled. Maisie noticed immediately that Priscilla carried a large brown envelope.

"Darling!" Priscilla pressed her cheek to Maisie's, then drew back. "Whatever is the matter with you, Maisie? First, I have never known you to be late in your life and, second, you look like hell."

"Don't spare me, Pris." Maisie straightened. Why did she always feel so small next to Priscilla, even though she loved her friend?

"Are you ill?"

"No. Look, let's have some lunch. I'm just a bit busy, that's all."

"Hmmph! I hope that doctor hasn't turned out to be a cad."

Maisie looked around for the dining room. "No, of course not. I've just taken on a lot of work recently."

"Over here." Priscilla linked her arm through Maisie's and led the way. "You know what I think? I really do think you need a holiday. Come to Biarritz, Maisie. I'm sure your Billy and your doctor will be able to do without you for a couple of weeks."

Maisie shook her head as they were seated. "Not a chance, I'm afraid."

Priscilla raised an eyebrow as she reached into her bag and took out her cigarette holder and a packet of cigarettes. She pressed a cigarette into the holder and lit it with a silver monogrammed lighter that she placed on the table, drawing deeply through the holder. She looked closely at Maisie. Then she reached forward and extinguished the cigarette, leaving the holder in an ashtray.

"You know what I think, Maisie?"

Maisie sighed. "I'm *all right*, Priscilla."

"Well, I'm going to tell you anyway, like it or not. Number one, you need a holiday. No two ways about it. If your idea of fun is a weekend with a country doctor while thinking about your work non-stop, it's about time you had a few more options to choose from."

Maisie opened her mouth to speak, but Priscilla raised her hand.

"I haven't finished yet. The other thing I think you should do is get a place of your own—a flat or something."

"But it's not as if I haven't done *that* before."

"No, you haven't, not really. Think about it. You came back from France, recuperated from your injuries—and remember, I know all about wounds—returned to Girton to complete your studies, and of course you spent some time in Scotland, didn't you? At that grue-some place, what was it, where you worked with some of Maurice Blanche's cronies? The Department of Legal Medicine. Ugh! Then you came back to London to work for Blanche. And where did you live then? You went straight to Lambeth, where you lived in a rented room for years. *Lambeth.* Back to the womb, so to speak. There was that little sojourn in a room next to your office in Warren Street; how you could ever have lived in such a place is beyond me. Then you went to live at Ebury Place at Lady Rowan's insistence, to the home of 'she who couldn't come out and say that she really wanted to give you something' but, instead, couched the invitation as if you were a sort of unpaid overseer while they were away in Kent. All very nice, I must say, but you've kept to the safe places, haven't you? If you don't watch it, you'll end up living in a dusty old beamed cottage in Sussex."

Maisie looked at Priscilla, who shrugged her shoulders, placed a fresh cigarette in the holder, and proceeded to smoke for a moment, saying nothing. Eventually, Maisie broke the silence.

"Not everyone gets the opportunity to have a flat in town on their own, you know. Most women go straight from their father's home to their husband's, and a good many live under their in-laws' roof for a few years before being able to afford the rent on their own flat, if they're lucky."

"There you go again, sackcloth and ashes! But you are *different*, Maisie. A *professional* woman. You've worked pretty damn hard, so for goodness' sake, enjoy a bit more freedom before Sir Lancelot comes racing up on his charger and drags you off. And, not to digress, but I must say I'd like to know why he's still a bachelor. After all, it's not as if there aren't enough available spinsters. But back to my point—frankly, I'm glad I had a few years on my own, even though it wasn't exactly my best time."

Maisie wanted desperately to change the subject. "What's in the envelope?"

"I'll get to that in a moment. I haven't finished yet." Priscilla waved the waiter away for the second time, then called him back to ask for two gin and tonics. Maisie opened her mouth to protest, but the waiter left the table. "Look," Priscilla continued. "I've decided to invest in some property. It appears I have to, according to my advisers. My inheritance was pulled out of stocks in the nick of time, I really must do something constructive with it, and there's nothing more constructive than bricks and mortar, is there? I want to buy a couple of flats, perhaps a mews cottage in Chelsea—now *there's* an ideal location for a professional woman."

"But if I rent from you, it'll be like living at Ebury Place, Priscilla!"

"Not at all. It's . . . it's younger, for a start. None of this crusty old nonsense. Victoria, God bless her cotton socks, is dead. Move on, Maisie."

"Let's talk about the envelope. I know it's for me."

"All right." Priscilla rested the cigarette holder on the ashtray, her hands shaking, and leaned toward Maisie. "I'll come back to my point later." She picked up the envelope. "It's to do with Peter."

Maisie noticed Priscilla's knuckles become white as she clutched the envelope, and as she began to speak it was not with her usual strong authoritative voice but with a stutter, as if she did not know quite where to begin.

"I—well, I have . . . no, let me start again." Priscilla opened the envelope and closed it again. "I have been pondering, you know, since our supper together. I've been thinking about asking a favor of you."

"Me?"

"Yes. You see, I think—no, I *hope* you might be able to help me." Priscilla reached for her drink. "Look, Maisie, I know you are terribly busy, and I wouldn't ask if it were not fiercely important to me— to my family—and it's really only if you are coming to France after all, as you suggested. . . ."

Maisie frowned, observing the tears in her friend's eyes. "What on earth is it, Pris?"

"It was when you first mentioned this case you are working on and having to go to France. A light went on, and—"

"But how can *I* help you, Pris?"

"I think . . . no, I *know* I must find out where Peter was lost. I've wanted to know for ages, wanted to put his memory to rest, lay a few flowers by the nearest village memorial, that sort of thing. I've paid my visit to Pat and Phil's graves, ages ago, but Peter still lingers. For a long time I've felt I must do this, if not for me then for my boys, so they know it's important that I don't let these things go."

Maisie nodded. "Yes, I understand."

Priscilla waved to the waiter and ordered another drink; then she turned back to Maisie. "I know this isn't really up your street—I mean, there's no criminal here to track down—but when you mentioned this case of yours it struck me—I mean, I thought that if you were taking on this sort of thing, you might be able to find where Peter was lost."

Maisie breathed in deeply. In truth, she did not want to accept such an assignment, even an informal one for a dear friend, any more than she really wanted to prove Lawton's son dead. She thought that if her mentor, Dr. Maurice Blanche, were to counsel her, he would draw attention to the fact that both calls for help pointed in the direction of France and that there might be something there for her, something for her to learn about herself. She was about to decline, but looked at Priscilla and saw the appeal so clearly etched in her eyes and mirrored in her tension. It was an appeal that touched her heart.

Maisie bit the inside of her lip and thought for a moment longer, picked up her drink and swirled the liquid around without raising the glass to her lips, and looked at Priscilla again.

"Look, Pris, I'll do what I can for you, but don't expect any results by a certain time. This must be an informal assignment. It's the best I can do, the most I can promise."

Priscilla beamed and reached across the table, taking Maisie's hands in her own. "Oh, Maisie, that's good enough for me. I cannot thank you enough. I know it's a terrible imposition, and I wouldn't do it if it weren't—"

Maisie released her hand from Priscilla's grasp and pointed to the envelope. "So, what have you got for me to look at?"

Priscilla reached into the envelope and began to pass various documents to Maisie one by one. "These are letters after Peter enlisted. He was in Surrey somewhere. They are mainly to my parents, but there's a couple to me, before I joined the First Aid Nursing Yeomanry." Priscilla reached into the envelope for more letters. "And these are from France. You can always tell the ones from France; the ink gets noticeably thinner. I think the shops must have had such a run on it they watered it down to make it go farther." She shrugged, then continued. "Now, these are from England again. From a barracks in Southampton, from which it would seem he made trips to London for courses."

"Promotion?" asked Maisie.

"I really don't know. I do know that his communiqués were extremely brief, and he commented that he really didn't have much time to write."

"Not surprising, really."

"Then here are a few more from France." Priscilla passed the letters to Maisie, becoming quiet as she clutched a final piece of paper. "Oh, blast! It does this to me every time, every single time, no matter how many times I look at the bloody thing!" She took a handkerchief from her handbag and dabbed at the corners of her eyes. "This was the last letter my parents received from him. Just a half page of nothing much at all."

Maisie took the letter and looked back and forth through the envelopes. "Priscilla, it seems he was in France for some time before the final telegram was received, yet there are only three or four letters postmarked quite close together after he went over again. Of course, we're assuming this is his last letter."

Priscilla shrugged. "Yes, I'd noticed the same thing. I expect Mother and Father burned them. I understand they burned all subsequent letters from the Army."

"But why only the ones for that second posting? Why not all of them?"

Priscilla looked at Maisie directly. "Frankly, I haven't a clue. Why do people do what they do, especially in a time like that? Perhaps he didn't actually write any more, though I have to say that would surprise me, knowing Peter; he was always talking, always had a story to tell. But then I thought I'd be writing to my brothers all the time, 'The Dastardly Wartime Exploits of Priscilla the Younger,' but apart from a letter here and there I frankly fell exhausted into my bed, such as it was, every single night."

"Well, I certainly assumed Peter was the sort to write often. From everything you've told me, I would have thought he'd have a lot to say." Maisie inclined her head and frowned, her curiosity piqued.

"Well, yes. But . . . oh, I don't know, Maisie. I just want to know where he might have died, and seeing as I don't have a 'regret-to-inform' letter, I am completely in the dark."

Maisie collected the papers and placed them in the envelope once again. "Well, this may surprise you, but considering the terror and chaos, fairly good records were kept. It's interesting that you haven't been able to locate the information." She smiled at Priscilla, knowingly yet kindly, for she knew her friend had probably not tried particularly hard to procure details pertaining to Peter Evernden's death.

Priscilla was thoughtful. "The only thing I can say that might help is that I heard from my parents—this was just before I went over to France—that Peter was being transferred to another job and he was very excited about it. Then the next thing you know, he'd clammed up and they were dying to know what he was doing. My father had a map pinned to one wall of his study so he could follow, as best he could, all four of us. After Southampton he had nowhere to put Peter, because he didn't know where he was sent next, and I was certainly never told anything about where he went missing. Then, of course, the pins came off one by one until I was the only one left." Priscilla had relighted her cigarette while speaking; now she drew deeply, blowing a smoke ring as she exhaled. "I came home, Father rolled up the map, and that was that."

Maisie allowed a silence to seep into the space between Priscilla and herself. She could not help but be drawn by parallels in the two requests, one from a stranger and one from her dearest friend. One inspired by the other. Two men dead in France, two grieving relatives unable to rest, one of whom she loved dearly. She reached over and placed her hand on Priscilla's arm. "I'll do everything I can to find out where he was lost, Pris. Now then, come on, let's get something to eat. I'm starving." Maisie stared at Priscilla until she turned to her. "And I want to talk to you a bit more about finding a flat. But I don't want to live in someone else's property. I've been saving my money and I've paid off my motor car. I think I want a home of my own."

Priscilla beamed a mischievous smile, as Maisie knew she would. "Excellent!"

NINE

Maisie did not return to Ebury Place directly after seeing Priscilla but, instead, decided to consider where she might live, if she moved. There were other things to think about too.

Dusk was descending as she made her way to the Embankment. She loved to walk by the water, though when the tide was out the Thames mud was less than fragrant. Pondering the luncheon with her friend, Maisie wondered why she always found herself giving in to Priscilla whenever they met: One minute she was full of resolve, the next she could hear herself agreeing that a flat of her own was the best thing in the world for her, while at the same time *knowing* that she would have given the idea short shrift if she were alone or if anyone else had made the suggestion—Maurice notwithstanding. Not only that, but she had found herself agreeing to visit Priscilla in Biarritz when she went to France. But Maisie loved Priscilla and, after all was said and done, she valued her honest opinion, which she was never slow to offer. Without doubt, they were chalk and cheese, but there was a bond that no one could deny. And she had missed her.

Priscilla had said Maisie should draw up a list of attributes her new home should have. Maisie pulled her jacket collar up as a chill breeze nipped at her neck. It was the sort of thing she would have suggested herself, yet apart from being near the water, she really didn't know what she liked in terms of a place to live. Her accommodations had always been something of a fait accompli, established already rather than chosen to reflect her own tastes. *What do I want?* Priscilla had decreed that her flat must be close to places where she could go to meet people, a social set.

Turning back, Maisie was now walking in the murky darkness with only the streetlamps for guidance. It would not take long to provide answers to Priscilla's questions, once she consulted Peter's records at the War Office Repository, a task she would get out of the way as soon as possible. Maisie considered what sort of training Peter might have been undergoing, especially as he was brought back from France to complete his promotion, if that's what it was.

Billy would be back on Monday with news of his investigation into the Jarvis girl's background, and she would also be driving up to Cambridgeshire, to the childhood home of Ralph Lawton. This weekend she would see Maurice on her return from visiting Andrew Dene. She would tell him of her plans to go to France, probably within the next few weeks. Of course she would tell Andrew first, after he had shared the surprise he had mentioned. She wondered about that surprise and hoped very much that it would not be one to force her hand in a way that upset them both.

"OH, M'UM, THERE'S been a telephone call for you, from Dr. Dene." Sandra reached for Maisie's coat as she entered through the front door of the Compton mansion at Ebury Place.

"Really? What did he say?"

"Very sorry he was, m'um. Said to tell you he'd been called out in an emergency. Apparently there was an accident on a building site this afternoon, lots of back and leg work, so he said, and he's been summoned to Hastings General to assist in the circumstances. He'll be busy all weekend."

"Oh, dear." Maisie hoped the relief was not as visible on her face as she felt inside.

"I bet you were looking forward to the weekend away, m'um. You've been working hard lately." Sandra curtsied and began to walk away as Maisie moved toward the stairs.

Thinking quickly, Maisie turned and stepped back into the entrance hall. "You know, Sandra, I think I might not stay in London in any case, so no need to count on my being here this weekend. My bag is ready, so I'll leave first thing tomorrow morning for Cambridgeshire; it's just the opportunity I need to see a client at home."

"Right you are, m'um."

HAVING TELEPHONED HER father to explain why she would have to postpone the fortnightly visit that had become her routine since his accident in the summer, Maisie made sure that she packed the collection of letters from Ralph Lawton to his parents, most of which were sent specifically to his mother, though there were one or two addressed to his father. She also flicked through Peter Evernden's correspondence again, replaced the items in the brown envelope, and packed them alongside the other notes and files in her bag. The Lawton country home was in the village of Farthing, about five miles outside Cambridge. She hadn't been back to the area since her Girton years.

Lord Compton had left Ebury Place for Kent, and once again Maisie was alone. It was unusual for her to have a Friday evening with nothing to do. Not that she was ever idle; no, finding something to do was never an issue to contend with. Yet as she undressed, ran a bath, and lounged in her dressing gown for a while, Maisie sat in the armchair close by the window and sighed. *A holiday in Biarritz.* She had never had a proper holiday, not a real going-away holiday for which special clothes were packed and salt sea air or long walks in the country anticipated. Before her mother was taken ill, a holiday was two weeks spent picking hops in Kent in September or a few days with her grandparents on her mother's side. Later in life, her grandfather had taken a job on the waterways as a lockmaster, so the Dobbs family would travel by train to Marlow and then by bus to the hamlet where her grandparents lived in a small cottage alongside the canal.

Now Maisie smiled at the memory, for her grandparents and her mother were long gone. It seemed that with them had gone any inclination to go away on holiday.

She knew she had been driven, at first to forget the war, then to complete her education. She had been determined to excel in her work with Maurice Blanche, and now her energy was directed into making her business a success. Maisie strove to bring each case to a close in a way that ensured that those whose lives she had touched were at peace with the outcome of her endeavors, as far as such a thing might be possible. But there had been no break in that work, except for a day or two here and there and, for several months now, alternate weekends when she spent a day either in Kent with her father or with Andrew Dene in Sussex. They were weekends when she always took work along in her bag, and her thoughts were never far from her office.

She thought of the posters adorning the railway platforms, the temptation to travel overseas that greeted her as she reached the turnstile at Warren Street station. Hadn't it been the same since the war, with those who could afford such forays traveling via ship, train, motor car and aeroplane—to the Riviera, to Africa, to the Mediterranean, or even to Devon and Cornwall? Not that travel was expensive, for the ships of war had been converted for civilian use and prices had tumbled. But one had to have some independent wealth to have the time to travel, so Maisie had ignored those compelling illustrations of a grand ship's prow or a deep azure sea seen through the branches of an orange tree: the lure of travel to take away memories of trenches, of cold, mud, and blood. *For those who are free to leave.*

And here she was on a Friday evening with nothing to do unless she worked. Or read, which was of course her other distraction; the quest to learn, to expand her knowledge of the world without taking another step overseas. Perhaps that was why her meditation practice had suffered, for Maisie did not always like the message she heard when she was alone at the end of the day. It was a voice that spoke of her isolation and of her choosing not to move beyond the boundaries of those worlds in which she felt a modicum of safety. What was it that Maurice said, one of his favorite challenges? *Seek the opportunity to swim beyond your own little pond.* She knew every reed, mudbank, and fish in her pond. Perhaps it was time to look for that flat after all, sooner rather than later.

After bathing, Maisie telephoned the Lawton residence, expecting Sir Cecil to be there. He was known to enjoy various country pursuits and also the company of a circle of academics with whom he dined at weekends. Lawton agreed to her proposed visit to the house in order to look through Ralph's belongings, personal items that had been saved by his wife, who had believed that her son would return one day. Maisie was extended an invitation to be a guest at the house, but knowing that the offer was one of protocol, and in the spirit of her musings on travel, she declined in favor of staying at a good hotel—after all, she had been given a generous expense allowance in advance. Yes, she would splash out, she would spoil herself.

ON SATURDAY MORNING, Billy telephoned, just as Maisie was pulling on her coat, ready to leave Ebury Place.

"Billy, how are you?" Maisie took the call in the library.

"Awright, doin' well, Miss. Yourself?"

"I'm well. Now then, what news?"

"Turns out Avril Jarvis is from that family. This is what I've found out so far: There's four kids, Avril's the oldest, but the others ain't fully related."

"What do you mean?"

"Her real dad was killed in the war. She never knew 'im, because she weren't born when 'e went back over there after bein' 'ome on leave. Mrs. Jarvis was married again after the war to a fella who was in the town lookin' for work. Little Avril was about four at the time."

"Go on."

"The family have gone through difficult times—mind you, so 'ave a lot of people, 'aven't they?"

"Billy. . . ."

"Well, I've found out that the father—the second one, that is—was in some trouble with the law. Done time: theft, burglary. Seems to me as if Avril's mum married a lot of trouble there, because 'e drinks as well. There are the kids wantin' for a good meal, and the man's knockin' back pints in the local."

"How did Avril get to London, did you find out?"

"From what I can make out—and I got quite a lot of this from a neighbor—"

"You didn't say anything?"

"No, said I was from the school board because they ain't been at school—which was a pretty good guess, because they ain't. The littl'uns 'ave been put out to work in the fields, doin' their bit for the family."

"Poor kids."

"Poor kids is right. And you should see the mum, all drained and lookin' double 'er years, she is."

"Anyway?"

"Well, anyway, apparently the stepdad said that Avril could earn good money in service in London, so—this is what was told to the mum, accordin' to the neighbor—'e puts 'er on a train to London where a bloke 'e knew arranged for 'er to work at a job in service, with 'er wages bein' sent to the family, leavin' the girl with a bit of pocket money to get by. The mum told the neighbor that the 'usband's mate'd said that accommodations and keep were all found."

"I'm sure." Maisie shook her head. "And what about this business with the medicines?"

"That's on 'er dead father's side. Turns out they didn't much like Avril's new stepdad but couldn't do anything about it. The family were in a tricky position, what with the business about the woman who'd killed a man with the 'erbs and what 'ave you. From what I know, it was the father's sister, the girl's aunt—apparently they was tight, the two of 'em."

"Can you find out more about that, Billy, and the aunt's activities?"

"Workin' on it already."

"Good. And if you can, find out the name of whom she was sent to in London. By the way, any sign of the newspapers, or even of Stratton's men?"

"Not a dickey bird. Bit strange, that, ain't it, Miss?"

"Yes, it is. Anyway, you'll be traveling back tomorrow afternoon. We'll talk first thing Monday morning."

"Very good, Miss. I'm glad I caught you, only telephoned on the off chance. I was a bit surprised when they said you was still up there in the Smoke."

"Change of plan. I'd best be off now, Billy. See you Monday. Take Doreen out for a nice dinner tonight."

"Right you are, Miss. Ta-ta."

Maisie replaced the telephone receiver. *So Avril Jarvis was sent to London by a violent stepfather. To whom did he send her?* It was common for a family friend to be called *uncle*—so was this a relative of the stepfather or did *uncle* have another connotation? Billy would find the answer.

THE MOOR'S HEAD Hotel had been built in the early 1800s. Following a period that could only be described as "genteel decline," it had been refurbished by new owners in 1925 and was now a rather sumptuous place that regularly drew visiting academics, families of students, and an influx of American travelers keen to enjoy a much-admired city. Maisie arrived just after noon on Saturday and, following lunch in the hotel dining room, claimed her MG from the garage that had once been stabling for carriage horses and made her way to the Lawton country home.

As she drove across the Cambridgeshire fens to the village of Farthing, she remembered how captivated she had been by the flat farmlands, so very different from the soft hills of Kent and Sussex. Farthing was a small yet busy village, with a number of people out and about their business, whether visiting the grocery shop, the post office, or the butcher. It was still too early to see a steady stream making their way to the King's Arms, though at evening opening time she was sure the local hostelry drew quite a few customers. Saplings, the Lawton home on the edge of the village, had originally been built as a vicarage but was subsequently deemed too grand for a country parson. The Lawtons had bought the house before Ralph was born, when it was customary for a man in Cecil Lawton's position to own not only a house in London but a country home to which he would travel when his work in the City was done at the end of the week. For some years now, Lawton's work was frequently "done" on a Thursday and did not continue again until Monday afternoon.

A manservant answered the door and showed Maisie into the drawing room, where Lawton was waiting for her. Instead of the more formal clothes worn in chambers, Lawton was wearing plain gray gabardine trousers, a brushed cotton shirt with small checks, a cravat at his neck, and a tweed jacket with leather patches at the elbows. He immediately stretched out a hand to greet Maisie.

"Good of you to come so soon, Miss Dobbs. I'm glad you're cracking on with the work. Any conclusions yet?"

Maisie smiled. "Oh, goodness, no, it's far too early. As you know, I may have to travel to France after I have conducted inquiries in London at the records office. I hope to have the confirmation you require within the agreed time limit to my investigations, though as you know, there are no guarantees."

Lawton moved toward the door. "Right you are. Now then, I'm off for the afternoon. Shooting, followed by a spot of tea with Professor Goodhaven, a great legal mind. I'll have Brayley show you to the room that was Ralph's and have various boxes of his belongings brought to you."

"I see." Maisie frowned. *The room that was Ralph's,* not *Ralph's room.* "But Sir Cecil, I'd very much like to spend some time speaking with you about Ralph, in a more informal manner."

Lawton seemed agitated as he reached for the door handle. He stuttered and shook his head. "I—I'm sorry, Miss Dobbs, not today, previous engagements, you see. But to put your mind at rest, I've been in contact with that solicitor chappie, the one acting for the girl. I'll let you have further details next week. Good luck, Miss Dobbs. I hope you find something that might assist you, though frankly I can't see how Ralph's personal effects will prove anything. Now then, must be off."

He's running away from me. Maisie knew that Lawton, though prepared to support the promise to his wife with action, wanted little to do with the actual depth of inquiry that came with retaining the services of an investigator. *What intimidates a man like Lawton? What truth undermines a man in his position?* Maisie pondered such questions for a few moments, and then Brayley, Lawton's manservant, returned to the room and announced that Ralph's effects had been brought up to the room that he had occupied on the second floor.

The large room had been freshly decorated, the lead paint fumes causing her to hold her hand to her nose.

"Gosh, this is strong."

"It was only finished recently, m'um."

"I see."

"The work was booked just after Lady Agnes passed away."

"What was it like before?"

Brayley moved toward the windows, which he opened wide.

"Well, it hadn't been changed since Master Ralph lived at home. Of course, he was only here on school holidays and exeats, and he hardly came back after joining the Flying Corps, but his mother wanted it left untouched in any case."

"Because she thought he'd be coming home."

The manservant moved to the door and paused. Maisie was aware that, whenever she was about to ask a deeper question about Ralph, someone ended up at a door and was about to leave the room.

"Wait . . . please, just a moment, Mr. Brayley."

"M'um?" The man's eyes seemed to blaze for a second, and Maisie knew that his loyalty was to only one person: his employer.

Maisie adjusted her posture, so that she was not in any way reaching or leaning toward Brayley, and she took a step back, knowing that the movement would diminish any sense the man might have of being cornered. He would be more likely to speak freely if there was space around him, though there would clearly be a limit to his revelations.

"Mr. Brayley, I wonder if you could tell me if there was any reason for discord between your employer and his son."

Brayley became flushed, though only for a second, before composing himself. "I—I wouldn't say so, m'um. Of course, being father and son, they had their ups and downs, and the boy was very close to his mother, who had different ideas about how to educate him and so on."

"Yes?"

"A man likes to see himself reflected in his son."

"And Ralph didn't reflect Sir Cecil?"

"Well, not in the way of enjoying the same things. Master Ralph did not care for the hunting field or for shooting. He was more like his mother."

"And how would you describe Lady Agnes?"

"A softhearted soul and a very gentle person is how I would describe her."

"I see." Maisie walked to the window and looked out across the extensive grounds. "So it was a surprise when Ralph enlisted?"

"Oh, very much, m'um. We all wondered about that. It was before the war, you know." Brayley had become warmer. "To tell you the truth, we—I mean the household—thought it might be because he wanted to be off on his own, to prove himself to his father."

Maisie nodded, deciding to play her ace with the next question. "Mr. Brayley, as far as you know, was Ralph courting? Had he any young women friends that he admired? Did he bring anyone home to meet his parents?"

Brayley blushed again. "Not as far as I know, m'um. Mind you, a young man wouldn't confide in the likes of me, now, would he?"

Maisie nodded. "Quite right, yes, quite right. Thank you, Mr. Brayley, you've been very helpful."

The manservant executed a short bow and left the room.

MAISIE TOOK AN index card from her black leather case and made several notations. She included not only details of the conversation but a description of Brayley, the lighting in the room, the spare decor, and even the markings on the exterior of the three large boxes.

She placed the card and her pencil on a side table and, taking her Victorinox knife from her bag, proceeded to score the seal on the first box. Closing the knife, she opened the flaps to find a photograph album at the top of a closely packed selection of belongings. Taking up the album, she opened it to the first page, upon which a wedding photograph of the Lawtons had been affixed rather clumsily, as if Ralph had begun compiling the collection in boyhood. The images were mostly set against a formal background, with few taken in the gardens or the house. Indeed, it seemed that Ralph Lawton had been starched along with his shirts, so upright was his posture. Maisie turned over more pages, until she came to the first informal photograph, which seemed to have been taken when the subjects least expected it, but faced with the camera they were only too willing to smile. Two boys, approximately sixteen years of age, were dressed in tennis whites and laughing together, arms around each other's shoulders. The boy on the left, the one who was not Ralph, was looking straight into the camera and smiling. On the right, Ralph was looking not at the camera but at his friend. Maisie pulled the album closer. It was the look in Ralph's eyes that drew her, for it reminded her of the way she had once seen Dene looking at her. She had been putting on her hat in front of the mirror and saw his gaze reflected, though he was unaware of the feelings his countenance revealed.

TEN

Back in her room at the Moor's Head Hotel, Maisie sat on the bed, an array of papers and photographs spread around her. She had begun to sort the items, first in chronological order. Later she would create a different pattern, to reflect her observations and Ralph's inner life: perhaps letters gathered from one particular friend, a place mentioned in several different documents, a frame of mind revealed in a diary, or a new skill recounted in his flight logs, which she had not expected to find among his belongings.

Ralph Lawton had been shot down behind enemy lines in the murky light of dawn. His demise had been reported to the British by the German authorities, as was the custom, and his aeroplane was noted, along with metal identification tags found, miraculously, in the remains of the inferno that had consumed his De Havilland DH-4. According to a report sent via his commanding officer, a local gardener and several farmworkers venturing early to a field tried in vain to extinguish the blaze. Maisie was always amazed by the detail that could be recorded at such a time, for this was not the first report of a battlefield death she had read nor, she thought, would it be the last.

The letters Maisie had fanned out on the eiderdown were chiefly from his mother, with only a couple from his father and just a few from school friends. Of the school friends, most came from a young man named Jeremy Hazleton. Maisie closed her eyes and tapped her hand with one of his letters. Wasn't he now a Member of Parliament? Yes, he was the young, outspoken, wheelchair-bound politician whom many predicted would be prime minister in years to come, a man equally well regarded by the unions and a broad spectrum of the voting population. He had been a most vocal supporter of women's rights in earlier years; in fact, she remembered seeing a newspaper photograph of him being pushed along in his wheelchair by his mother, his young wife marching alongside, as he held a banner demanding VOTES FOR WOMEN. His rage against the equally long lines at labor offices and soup kitchens blazed in angry words across the daily tabloids: MARCH TO WESTMINSTER! HAZLETON TELLS WORKERS. There had been stories covering his visits to Lambeth slums and soot-blackened mining towns, and he had been photographed shaking the hands of workers and landed gentry alike. The trajectory of his political career was underlined by his legendary valor at Passchendaele: a hero for the masses. But, as many knew, Jeremy Hazleton was a rich hero, a man with a legacy from a landowning father. Maisie looked back at the photograph that had intrigued her earlier and compared it to the image she remembered from a newsreel she'd seen at a picture house. The youthful grin toward the camera had given way to a more serious pose in later years, but the likeness was unmistakable. Ralph's gaze had been directed at a boyish Jeremy Hazleton.

> 1500 hours. Went up with observer, Cunningham. Crossed over the line at 1540 hours. No movements to report. Followed line north for two miles, observed Fokker formation, and ascended to height of 10,000 ft. Set course for base, crossing back over line at 1600 hrs. Ground: 1700.

One report seemed much like the others; however, the accompanying journal gave details that would never be entered in a flight log.

The cloud formations were stunning this afternoon. One could almost imagine flying through candy floss at the seaside. Of course, the Hun on the ground tracing me with their guns was a bit of a blow to an otherwise very pleasant exercise. Then on another page: *Went up for training today. Well, went up, came down, went up, came down, up, down, up, down—and all without stopping! It seems I have been tested and, for once in my life, not found wanting. Wish the old man knew about that! Have received top marks for stop-start landings and expect an interesting job or two soon, before I become Fokker fodder.*

Clutching the journal, Maisie gazed out of the window. What did he believe in, this young man who was, it seemed, so isolated? What God might he have prayed to, knowing that as an aviator he had taken on war's most dangerous work? As his craft took flight, what did he cling to when even the slightest malfunction, the tiniest fracture in the wing or fuselage, might send him to a fiery death? And what angels lifted him when that day came, when he crashed to earth behind enemy lines? To whom did he profess love, as surely he must have, when he felt the descent into his grave?

She turned back to the journal and frowned. Would the journal have been returned with personal effects without being read by someone in authority? Possibly. Maisie rooted through the pile of papers and other belongings she had brought back to her room, then pulled out an envelope addressed to Ralph that had been flattened against books and albums. It was postmarked from Folkestone just one day before Ralph died. She placed the journal on top of the envelope, then inside. If the journal had been posted back to Saplings, it would appear that Ralph had sent it home to protect it. Had it not passed the censor? How would such a thing happen? Maisie remembered giving a letter to another nurse who was going on leave, asking her to post the letter when she arrived in England, so that her father might receive it sooner. Yes, it was possible. Instead of leafing through it, Maisie read the journal from the beginning, with the flight logbook on her lap to cross-reference dates.

One hour later, she knew two things: Ralph Lawton was still in touch with Jeremy Hazleton at the time of his death, though she could find no letters from the latter; and Ralph Lawton was, in fact, an accomplished aviator entrusted with work that was of the utmost importance. His unique experience as an engineer and then as an observer before being given command of an aircraft rendered him a very valuable individual indeed. Maisie leaned back again and frowned, frustrated with her lack of knowledge about the Flying Corps. Why would an aviator need to land and then take off again immediately?

USING THE HOTEL telephone that evening, Maisie made two calls. One was to the home of the Hon. Jeremy Hazleton, MP, in which she introduced herself as a constituent and asked if she might visit the following day. The second was to Chelstone, where she asked for the address in Canada of Lord and Lady Compton's son, James. He had been an aviator in the war and might be able to furnish her with some of the information she needed without her having to approach the Royal Air Force directly. She wanted answers to questions but did not want to answer any herself.

ON SUNDAY MORNING, Maisie was anxious to be on her way just after breakfast. A light drizzle was falling by the time she settled her account and left the hotel with her bag in one hand and document case in the other, so she was surprised to see Cecil Lawton's manservant waiting by the MG as she approached. Maisie had hurriedly thrown her mackintosh around her shoulders and pulled a waterproof hat low over her head. The man was drawn and gray, and he too was wearing a mackintosh, though Maisie suspected it might have been a castoff from his employer. Rain bounced off his black bowler hat, and he did not take his hands from his pockets as Maisie approached.

"Mr. Brayley, good morning to you, though it could be better, couldn't it?"

"Good morning, Miss Dobbs."

Maisie looked around. Rain was splashing down and around them, the shower now promising to turn into a lengthy downpour.

"Well, I know you didn't come here just to stand in the rain and bid me good morning. If you could help me with my bags—"

"Of course, I beg your pardon, m'um."

After Brayley helped Maisie stow her bags in the MG, she indicated that they should move into a shop doorway, out of the rain.

"Now then, Mr. Brayley, what can I do for you?"

Brayley took off his hat and turned down the collar of his mackintosh. Maisie could see the starched white shirt underneath, along with a black jacket that seemed a little shiny, as if it had been pressed many times during years of service. Brown liver spots crested his nose and cheekbones. Though balding, what hair remained on his pate had been combed back and oiled. It seemed to Maisie that Brayley bore a striking resemblance to a tired and aging faithful hound.

"I hope you don't mind, Miss Dobbs, but I wanted to say my piece about the situation with Ralph Lawton." Brayley had squared his shoulders, a move that, as Maisie knew only too well, is an indication of a person seeking strength they do not really feel.

"Please, feel free to speak in confidence." Maisie smiled and, as she spoke, placed a hand on Brayley's arm, just for a second.

Clearing his throat, Brayley continued. "I've worked for Sir Cecil since before his marriage—a long time by any standards. Some have said I was wed to my job, though my wife is in service at the house as well."

Maisie nodded. It was common for a husband and wife to work together, often being given a cottage accommodation on the estate.

"So, you see, I've seen a lot in that household."

"Go on."

"And what I want to say is that it's a terrible thing that Sir Cecil has been put through. First they lost two new babies, then a daughter, and they were left with a boy who was not the son his father wanted.".

"Yes, I understand there was some discord."

"Like I said, he was his mother's son, but he never did try to be a son to his father. Never tried."

"Are you sure, Mr. Brayley? Isn't it true that we never know quite what goes on in the houses where we work?"

Brayley's eyes blazed, and Maisie saw a loyalty so fierce it might color a true perspective of the situation.

Pausing just a moment, Brayley continued. "All I want to say is this: that she caused him so much grief, she did, with her believing the boy was still alive. My wife said, when she lost the babies, that it was enough to send anyone off their head. Look at her, look at what she put Sir Cecil through. She was a lunatic, right enough."

Maisie frowned. "And what do you want me to do, Mr. Brayley, for I am sure you have not come out in the pouring rain to tell me something I can deduce for myself?" She looked past Brayley and noticed a black bicycle propped against a neighboring shopfront. Brayley had cycled some five rainy miles into Cambridge. There was definitely more to say.

"She put him through some trouble, visiting those women who are no better than snake charmers. Could have ruined a man in his position. Then, to make him promise on her deathbed to find a son who's dead? It makes the blood curdle." Brayley paused to look up and down the street, which was still empty, though the rain had diminished somewhat. "I'm here to ask you, for his sake—because he is only going through the motions, you know—I'm here to ask you to not even bother raking up the past. Just make up a report, whatever it is that you people do, and have done with it."

Maisie was silent but continued to hold Brayley with her gaze. He looked up and down the street again, and when he turned back to her, she spoke.

"Mr. Brayley, no matter how I might assess the merits of this assignment, I have to bring an integrity to my work. If I did not intend to engage in a full and comprehensive investigation, I would not have agreed to assist Sir Cecil. I can, however, assure you that my work will be utterly confidential and I seek to protect all concerned. I will not fail Sir Cecil."

"I see." Brayley pressed his hat on his head again. "I'd better be off, then." He began to move out from the doorway but turned to Maisie once more. "And you know, don't you, Miss Dobbs, that I won't fail him either." Tipping his hat, he gave a short bow and walked away, collecting his bicycle by the handlebars and walking it along the road. Maisie suspected that he would not sit astride the bicycle to ride home until he was well out of her view, for the man's body had been rendered so unstable by fear and anger that he might well fall off.

As Maisie started the car and pulled away from the curb, she knew she would have to take great care with Brayley. The loyal servant had the tenacity of a guard dog, and certainly he had attempted to nip at her heels. Indeed, she was abundantly aware that she had just received a veiled threat.

FOLLOWING DIRECTIONS TO the letter, Maisie parked the car outside an Edwardian villa in the village of Dramsford, on the outskirts of Watford. The house had been built on an incline, so the front garden was a series of small terraces leading down to the pavement. It was a blustery day, and quiet because it was Sunday. Jeremy Hazleton had been cordial on the telephone, suggesting that Maisie arrive at midmorning so they would have time to talk before lunch, to which he did not extend an invitation. She watched an older couple leave the house before she alighted from her motor car, concluding that the Hazleton residence was probably open to visits from constituents whenever Jeremy Hazleton was at home rather than at Westminster.

Charmaine Hazleton answered the door herself, smiling broadly at Maisie as she welcomed her. She was a few inches shorter than Maisie and wore her dark blond hair in a chignon at the base of her neck, a style that framed her cheekbones before being drawn back. Her royal-blue dress was fashionably tailored, speaking of elegant good taste rather than indiscriminate expenditure. Her blue leather shoes were both sensible and stylish, a T-strap secured at the side with a delicate leather button.

"Good morning, Miss Dobbs. I trust your journey was not too difficult. The rain really can sweep across Cambridgeshire, can't it?" She stepped back for Maisie to enter and then led the way along a hallway decorated with floral wallpaper. She continued speaking, giving Maisie precious little time to greet her formally. "Jeremy has been busy since seven, with his first caller at eight. The work of an MP is never done."

Maisie studied Charmaine Hazleton's carriage as she walked briskly along the hallway. By the set of her shoulders, the short deliberate steps, the hands clasped in front of her, Jeremy Hazleton's wife revealed that, despite her welcoming smile, she would rather Maisie had never called and wished her husband's schedule were lighter that day. Though the meeting was to be with Hazleton alone, Maisie suspected that at some point there would be an interruption, and then it would be time for her to leave. Mind you, such skillful closure to the caller's time with her spouse was the prerogative of a junior MP's wife.

"Jeremy darling, Miss Dobbs to see you." Charmaine stepped toward the desk where her husband sat with a box of papers, many tied together with narrow red ribbon. Even in a wheelchair, Hazleton gave the impression of stature. Though it was cool, he had rolled up his shirtsleeves and wore a cardigan pulled carelessly across his shoulders. His brown hair was tightly curled and worn very short. Maisie suspected that if it were any longer it would be unmanageable, especially for a man with physical limitations. Boyish freckles were scattered across his nose, though his skin was fair. Before removing a tea tray that was set on the polished walnut desk, his wife squeezed his shoulder and he in turn patted her hand.

Hazleton turned his wheelchair so that he was facing Maisie and held out his hand. "Delighted. Please take a seat." He indicated an armchair set alongside the desk and turned to his wife. "Thank you, darling." There was no offer of tea for Maisie as Charmaine Hazleton left the room.

"Now then, what can I do for you, Miss Dobbs? You said that you wanted to speak to me in connection with Ralph Lawton. I must say, I thought it rather odd; after all, the poor chap's been gone for thirteen years."

Maisie looked toward the door for just a second, having noticed that she had not heard a click. The door was ajar by a good four inches.

"I trust our conversation will be in confidence, Mr. Hazleton."

"Absolutely. You have my word."

"Good. First of all, here's my card." Maisie took a card from her coat pocket—there had been no offer to take her mackintosh—and passed it to Hazleton. "I have been retained by Sir Cecil Lawton to prove that his son is, in fact, dead. It seems that Lady Agnes Lawton had a strong belief that her son was still alive, and—"

"What utter tosh!"

Maisie smiled. "That's as may be, Mr. Hazleton. However, Mrs. Lawton's belief was so strong that on her deathbed she asked her husband to continue her quest. Though Sir Cecil has no doubt that his son is dead, he feels duty bound to conduct a limited inquiry; hence he retained my services."

Hazleton looked at the card again. "Oh, I've heard of you." He drew out the *I* as if to suggest, perhaps, some previous knowledge regarding Maisie's reputation.

Maisie did not comment but continued with a question. "First of all, Mr. Hazleton, I understand that you and Ralph Lawton were at school together and were good friends—is that so?"

Jeremy Hazleton blew out his cheeks and shook his head. "I don't know about *good* friends, Miss Dobbs. Certainly we spent time together as boys, but we weren't each other's *best* friend, if you know what I mean. To tell you the truth, Ralph didn't have a wide circle; in fact, he took a beating from the other boys on more than one occasion, so I rather stuck up for him."

"And why might he have taken a beating?"

Hazleton shifted her gaze, turning his wheelchair away from her just slightly, and began to sketch a circle on his blotting pad, a sphere that he then spiraled inward. "Oh, you know how it is with children who are on the outside—and there's always one, isn't there? He wasn't very good at sports—positively hated anything involving the mud. That sort of aversion to the rough-and-tumble gives rise to a fair bit of ribbing."

"But a beating?"

"You know how boys can be."

Maisie moved on. "And how did you help him?"

Hazleton laughed. "Not to put too fine a point on it, Miss Dobbs, I enjoyed a measure of popularity as a boy. It was a position I used to influence the behavior of others."

"I see. Now then, I understand that you were still in touch with Ralph Lawton when he was killed in France."

Hazleton frowned. "To tell you the truth, I can't remember, Miss Dobbs. I believe we may have corresponded a few times."

"But didn't you visit him when he first enlisted?" Maisie took a clutch of index cards from her document case. "Yes. I noticed in Ralph's personal papers that he mentions several occasions on which you met after leaving school, one being when he first joined the Flying Corps; he had some leave and met you in"—Maisie turned over the card—"yes, in Ipswich, for a day or so. You stayed at a guesthouse there."

"Oh, yes, of course." Hazleton lightly hit his forehead with the heel of his right hand, a move Maisie thought rather staged. "It's so long ago, I can hardly remember. I think it was a coincidence, really. If I remember correctly, we exchanged a couple of letters, realized we both had a couple of days off at the same time, and thought we would go to the coast to have a bit of fun, meet some girls, what have you." Hazleton looked at Maisie and smiled. "Youthful high jinks, you know."

"And did you—meet some girls?"

"I daresay we did, though one stag weekend seems like the rest at that age."

Maisie heard the door handle rattle as Charmaine Hazleton came into the room. She looked at her watch and was about to speak, but Maisie spoke first.

"Mr. Hazleton, can you think of any reason, any reason at all, or any circumstance in which Ralph Lawton might still be alive?"

Shaking his head, Hazleton began to move his wheelchair back to the desk. "Miss Dobbs, I consider myself fortunate to have survived a bloodbath, a hell on earth. Ralph was flying behind enemy lines, as far as I know, and was shot down, his aeroplane on fire. There is no question in my mind that he is dead. I therefore cannot imagine any scenario whereby he is alive. Now, if you would excuse me."

Maisie stood up. "Thank you so much for your time, and on a Sunday. You have been most accommodating." She smiled. "I wonder, may I telephone you if I have further questions?"

Hazleton smiled in return, remembering that Maisie Dobbs was also a member of the voting public. "Of course."

CHARMAINE HAZLETON ACCOMPANIED Maisie to the front door, whereupon she took an umbrella from a stand in the hallway and proceeded to walk to the MG rather than bid her farewell on the threshold. As they negotiated the steps down to the pavement, Maisie turned to her hostess.

"Mrs. Hazleton, how did you meet your husband, if I may ask?"

"I was his nurse. I took care of him from the day he was brought back from Flanders."

"I see. I was a—"

Maisie was interrupted sharply by Charmaine Hazleton as they reached the street.

"Miss Dobbs, I wonder if I might ask you a favor?"

"Why, of course, Mrs. Hazleton."

The woman held her chin a little higher, as if it might bring her to Maisie's height. "I do not want my husband contacted with regard to Ralph Lawton again."

Maisie inclined her head. "Why not?"

The woman clasped her hands together firmly in front of her. "As you can see, my husband suffered in the war. Since that time he has gone forward with purpose and resolve; he has a successful political career in front of him. Such memories of the war, of friends lost, are troubling to him."

"But I would have thought that those living with wounds from the war form an important constituency for whom your husband represents a voice. Surely he is used to—"

The woman swallowed deeply. "That's different."

"Is it?"

"Yes, Miss Dobbs. Now then, please go and do not try to speak to my husband again. I tell you, I will do everything in my power to prevent his being troubled by memories. I will *not* let it happen!" She turned and walked away, her spine erect, her chin still held upward.

Maisie knew that Hazleton had lied. Lawton's papers revealed that he had continued a regular correspondence from the day they left school until the day the aviator was killed, and they had seen each other more than once. She understood, too, that Charmaine Hazleton's *favor* was out of proportion, given the seeming innocence of the MP's responses to her questions and to what he claimed was sporadic friendship at best.

As she drove steadily back toward London, the rain glancing off the MG's windscreen, Maisie tried to recall if there had ever been another time in her work when she received two threats in one day and for the same reason: Ralph Lawton had loved another man.

ELEVEN

 "You can tell your batman there to keep his nose out of proper police work, if you don't mind."

"Well, good morning, Sergeant Caldwell. I'm very well, thank you, and you?" Maisie had deliberately leaned back into her chair when she answered the telephone to an aggressive tone from Stratton's assistant. She would not allow someone for whom she had so little regard to have a negative effect on her mood at the start of a new week.

"Never mind about me, you just make sure that jack-the-lad there minds his own business."

"Sergeant Caldwell, I wonder if I might speak to Detective Inspector Stratton, if *you* don't mind." As she spoke, Billy came into the office, mouthed a good morning when he saw that she was on the telephone, and took off his coat and hat, hanging them on a hook behind the door.

"Inspector Stratton won't be in for a few days, so I'm holding the fort here on this case, and I'll be——"

"Sergeant Caldwell"—Maisie looked at Billy, who rolled his eyes when he realized the identity of Maisie's caller—"I fully appreciate your concern for the integrity of your investigation. However, I assure you that Mr. Beale has done nothing that might have an

untoward effect on the case of Avril Jarvis. Mr. Beale was acting on
my behalf and was undertaking very specific research in connection
with my responsibility to the case, which, as you will appreciate,
may well involve an appearance in court."

"I'll need to speak to you and Mr. Beale here at Vine Street, you
know."

"Yes, I had expected as much. Now then, shall we come along at
ten?"

Caldwell coughed, clearly caught off guard by Maisie's taking a
lead in the conversation. "Yes, that would suit very well. Ten o'clock
it is, then."

"Until then." Maisie replaced the receiver.

"Didn't take long for 'im to start breathing fire, did it?" Billy
stood in front of Maisie's desk.

"No, he was very quick off the mark, I must say." Maisie gathered a manila folder with several papers inside. "Come on, let's sit
over there and work on the case map until we're ready to leave for
Vine Street. Bring your notes, Billy."

They sat at the table together, rain slanting across the windows so
that the view to the square was obscured by rivulets of water running down the glass on the outside and condensation inside.

"Let's look at what we've gathered. Tell me about your inquiries."

Billy Beale shuffled his notes and fidgeted on his chair. There
were times that Maisie wondered whether she had done the right
thing in giving Billy a job as her assistant, yet time and time again,
often when she was at her wits' end, he had proven his worth to her.

"Well, I don't want to repeat myself, Miss, so I'll just take up
where I left off, if it's awright by you."

"Yes, go on, Billy."

"So, I told you what I'd found out about the stepfather. Now, according to one of the neighbors"—Billy looked at his notebook—
"on the day she was meant to go to London, young Avril was crying
and crying, 'oldin' on to 'er mum for dear life. Apparently the noise

of it brought out the neighbors, so everyone saw the stepdad when 'e pulled 'er fingers away from the mother's clothes one by one, slapped the poor kid around the 'ead, and told the neighbors to bugger off inside—sorry, Miss, but that's what 'e said."

"That's all right, go on." Maisie had pushed back the chair as Billy spoke and now had her back to him as she looked out of the window. She did not want him to see her tears.

"Well, 'e frog-marches 'er to the railway station and, as far as they know, went wiv 'er to Taunton on the branch-line stopping service, then put 'er on the train for London, where the uncle was to pick 'er up."

"Oh, God."

"Well, I don't know about God, Miss, because she certainly didn't get no 'elp when she needed it, and you can bet your bottom dollar she was praying."

Maisie turned to him. "All right, so we know she was sent to the uncle, who we now believe was probably the stepfather's friend rather than a blood relative. And we know she was not in service but was put to work on the streets, the uncle being a common pimp. Now, what about this aunt?"

"This bit is what you would call woolly, Miss."

"Yes." Maisie took her seat once again. This time, Billy noticed her expression as she pulled a handkerchief from her pocket.

"You awright, Miss?"

"Bit of a cold, Billy. This weather."

Billy nodded, knowing full well that Maisie had not suffered a real cold since they had begun working together and that England was enjoying a rather warm Indian summer, even with today's rainy humidity. "The stepfather is dead."

"Dead? How?"

"He died from so-called natural causes. A heart attack or something."

"But?"

"Turns out the aunt—now this is an aunt on the dead father's

side; you know, Avril's real father, who died in the war—anyway, locally they call 'er a witch. Not that she *is* a witch, of course, but she's
always out and about collecting plants and weeds in the woods and
beside the river, you know. And people go to 'er when they come
down with something. Trust 'er more than they trust the local
quack, and she's cheaper."

"How did the stepfather die?"

"Found dead outside the pub one afternoon. They'd called last
orders, and after everyone'd turned out, the landlord locked up and
that was that, as far as 'e thought. Then just before it's openin' time
again in the evenin', there's a commotion outside with a couple of
the locals bangin' on the door and shoutin' for 'elp. So the landlord
opens up, and there they are, standin' over the stepdad—dead on
the ground."

"Did you find out what the pathologist said?"

"There was an inquest, and it was put down to natural causes."

"And the local story is?"

"That the aunt did it, put something in the man's drink. She was
known to go into the pub for a swift one of a lunchtime, and there's
some what think she might've been in on that day, though no one
will say they definitely *saw* her. But the word on the street—and remember, it's only a tiny little place—is that she did it with some of
the tinctures she brews."

"I see."

"What do you think, Miss?"

Maisie made some notes on the case map pinned out in front of
them for several seconds, then turned to Billy.

"To tell you the truth, I might have done the same thing myself."

Billy's eyes reflected his surprise at her comment. He was about
to speak when Maisie continued.

"Good work, Billy. Let's get all the notes down now; then we have
to go to Vine Street to see Caldwell. I will need to make a detour on
the way back, so you should return to the office without me."

"Where are you go——" Billy corrected himself. After all, it was not right to question one's employer.

"That's all right, I can tell you. I am going to check the war service records for Peter Evernden. After that I'm off to Thomas Cook's to book tickets for passage to France at the end of the week."

"You goin' over there all by yourself?"

Maisie checked the time on her watch, today pinned to the lapel of her burgundy jacket. "Actually, no. I spoke to Dr. Blanche upon returning from Cambridge yesterday afternoon, and he has decided to come with me."

"Be like old times, won't it? You know, you and 'im together again, on a case." Billy clearly did not want to admit that he felt just a little left out.

"Well, we'll see. He insisted upon coming, to tell you the truth. Frankly, I can't see why, though I know he likes the opportunity to go to France, and travel alone is daunting when you reach his age."

"Gaw, I dunno, Miss. I reckon it's pretty dauntin' goin' to Taunton, if you ask me."

Maisie smiled. "Come on, let's get going. I'll tell you about Cambridge on the way, and we'll talk about our next move on the Jarvis case."

As they gathered their coats, Maisie knew Billy had hit the nail on the head. She *was* surprised when Maurice said that he would like to accompany her to France, and she had felt unable to decline. Without Maurice she might well have been a children's governess by now, at best. In fact, had she not been so fortunate, she might have ended up in Avril Jarvis's shoes. How then could she refuse Maurice, even though his request unsettled her?

THE MEETING AT Vine Street was predictable: an overlong complaint from Caldwell that Maisie later referred to as a "tedious longwinded slap across the knuckles," together with a request that Billy share the information he had gathered, which he did, to a point. For her part, Maisie was curious regarding the absence of Detective Inspector Stratton, only to be told that his son's illness had caused him to take a short leave. Caldwell added—rather sarcastically, she thought—that it was nothing serious and that his own nippers would have been over it all by now.

"That man makes me seethe!" said Maisie, as she and Billy left Vine Street police station.

"I must admit, Miss, I was a bit surprised that he wouldn't let you see young Avril, not after what you'd done for them," said Billy. "Mind you, I reckon they think that it's all done, seeing as they've received the bill and you'll get paid."

"That's exactly what it is, Billy." Maisie looked at her watch again. Frowning, she tapped the face and unpinned the timepiece, which she held to her ear. She wound the mechanism and listened again. "Oh, dear . . ."

The watch had kept perfect time ever since 1916, even in the most terrible conditions, including the shelling of the casualty clearing station in which Maisie was wounded. Maisie shook her head and continued.

"Well, it's not all done, not by a long chalk." She turned to Billy. "Right, I'll see you back at the office, Billy. There's one person whose response is missing in this Avril Jarvis case, and that's the mother. I know you couldn't see her, but the woman must be feeling *something*."

"Well, you'd 'ave thought so, wouldn't you?"

"Billy, look, get on with it. If you have to go back down to Taunton, so be it."

Surprise at his employer's manner registered on Billy's face, the lines between his brows furrowed even more. "Miss, I know I'm findin' out all sorts of background points, but I don't reckon I've discovered anything that proves she didn't do it—you know, the murder."

Maisie knew her exasperation was not with Billy but was a symptom of· the frustration she felt. There was so much that seemed close, yet untouchable, not only in the case of Avril Jarvis but of Ralph Lawton. She was not looking forward to going to France—was dreading it, in fact—and she felt pressured by the promise made to Priscilla. Then there was Andrew. Andrew with his surprise that she was avoiding, yet also knowing he would understand and tolerate her changed plans. She took a deep breath, closed her eyes briefly, and replied in a soft, modulated tone.

"Billy, I am not seeking to find an alibi but to give Cecil Lawton as much meat as I can for his defense of Avril Jarvis. It will mean the difference between murder and manslaughter, between a life behind bars or a shorter sentence, perhaps even an acquittal."

Billy was nonplussed. "But . . . but I thought you reckoned she 'adn't done it—the murder."

Maisie was still holding the watch, which she shook again, her attention to the stalled hands allowing her to think. "No, I didn't say I thought her innocent, though I do think she is keeping something under her hat." Placing the watch in her pocket, Maisie continued. "What's the time?"

"About twelve, I reckon, Miss."

"You're not wearing a watch." Maisie looked at her assistant, surprised.

"Nah, my old watch broke while I was down in Kent in the summer. One of the 'orses rubbed its snout against me ribs, and the next thing you know my pocket watch'd dropped to the ground for the big old lug to step on. 'Course, I was lucky to 'ave a watch in the first place, not a usual thing for the likes of me, if you know what I mean. But I can usually reckon the time, or there's the clock in the office, or in a shop if I'm out."

"But haven't we checked the time lately, ensured that both our watches were set to the very minute?"

Billy smiled and shrugged. "You've checked *your* watch, Miss. I've used me noddle." He tapped the side of his head.

Maisie frowned and shook her head. "Oh. Well, I'll see you at the office later."

Billy watched Maisie as she turned and walked away. He was sure he had never seen her so distracted.

MAISIE CONTINUED ON her way to the War Office Repository on Arnside Street, to make inquiries regarding Peter Evernden's service record. Having registered and stated her business, Maisie was escorted to a room where she was asked to wait at a table for the relevant records to be brought to her. The spacious main records hall had tall ceilings and a series of deep oak tables polished to a shine that mirrored that of the floor. Maisie walked on tiptoe as much to avoid slipping as to prevent the clatter of her heels along the floorboards. She took a seat at the table indicated by the clerk. Only two other people were in the room, an elderly man and woman poring over a series of papers taken from a folder. A shaft of light from the late-afternoon sun that had finally broken through illuminated their heads, close together as they read, passing pages to each other and whispering. Were they the mother and father of a boy who was lost, finally able to come to London to seek more information on a son well loved? Or perhaps their search was on behalf of another; they might be an aunt and uncle or from overseas.

"Miss Dobbs?"

"I—I—excuse me, I was miles away." Maisie shook her head and stood up to speak to the clerk, who had returned.

The young man smiled. "It gets very close in here, even on a chilly day. Now then. Captain Peter Evernden."

"You've found his records?"

"Well, that's the thing, there's nothing here."

"I understood that this is where I could see his military service records."

"Normally, madam, that's right. But they're not here. I double-checked and couldn't find a thing, although it seems as though they were here once."

"So what happened to them?"

"Might've been moved, you know. Perhaps mislaid, pushed in with another chap's records, that sort of thing."

"Do you think you can find them?"

The man shook his head, his light brown hair reflecting the sunlight that had moved across the room. Maisie looked around. The man and woman had left.

"Like a needle in a haystack. Thousands of records here, you know. I've looked at the files on either side, up and down, but no— nothing."

"Do you keep a ledger with names of those who have requested files?"

"Yes, of course, madam, but again, I would have to go back through the ledgers and unless I had an idea of who and when— well, it would take forever."

Maisie nodded. "I see. But they *were* held here, weren't they?"

"According to the indexes, yes, they were."

"But. . . ." Maisie sighed. "I suppose that unless we look into each one of the *thousands* of records, we won't find them; that's about the measure of it, isn't it?"

"Yes, it is, I'm afraid. Although I will note the loss; then we can keep a lookout for Captain Evernden's records. Shall I write to you, if and when we find them?"

"That might take years!" Maisie shook her head again but reached into her document case for her calling card. "You might as well have this, just in case. You never know, I may be lucky."

"Right you are. Good day, madam."

MAISIE'S MIND WAS still buzzing with conjecture throughout her entire conversation with the clerk at Thomas Cook's who issued her tickets for the ferry from Dover to Calais. Though a Mr. Stuart Townsend had been running his Channel ferry service for motor cars and passengers for several years now, using a decommissioned minesweeper now pressed into commercial service, she wasn't sure she would be able to look while her beloved MG was hoisted on board. Perhaps she should have looked into acquiring a motor to drive while in France, for surely the MG would not be comfortable for Maurice. But it was too late. She knew the elevated energy that caused her to fuss and fret now were a result of her earlier frustrations as well as another emotion: fear.

Maisie could see only one France, only one Flanders. She could see only a desolate landscape filled with darkness, with mud, lice, rats, and rivers of fetid water and blood. Though she had worked on days that were warm, days when even in the worst of times she could hear a skylark high above the land in the lull of shelling that was all too close, her abiding memories were of rain, mud-soaked skirts, and hands that were chapped and raw. And death. The abiding vision of death.

Maisie wasn't quite sure how she arrived at the Embankment. In the late afternoon she had felt her body shaking, the sweat trickling in rivulets down her spine from her neck to her waist, and known instinctively that she should make her way from the Strand to the water, the river that now soothed her. She breathed in the air, which was not fresh like Kentish air but calmed her all the same. How must she have looked, to those she had passed? A woman wide-eyed, seeing not the streets along which she walked but a path she had traveled at another time. A time when hell was closer and, she thought, the gods even farther away.

Maisie bit her lip and the tears—locked all day behind a round of determination and decisions—flooded forth. How would she hide this descent from Maurice, who had helped restore her spirit when she returned wounded from France? How would she conceal the fact that the nightmares had come again, spurred on, perhaps, by seeing Priscilla, by the dead young men—Ralph Lawton and Peter Evernden—and by the love of a man who cared so deeply for her? How could she admit that, like a young girl, she yearned to be ministered to by one who would surely have soothed the wounds of her child if she could? As Maisie felt the wave of grief break through the dam of her acquired resilience, she felt, too, a pressure on her shoulder, as if someone had reached out to her. She turned slowly, with hope in her heart, but there was no one there.

TWELVE

"Good evening, m'um." Sandra opened the door for Maisie, who had not, after all, returned to her office but had instead walked for some time along the Embankment before making her way to the underground and, ultimately, to Ebury Place. "You can tell the nights are beginning to draw in. Look at that mist out there. There'll be some nasty fogs soon, what with all this funny weather we're having."

Maisie nodded, taking off her coat, but as she turned to pass the coat to Sandra, she noticed the young woman leaning over the threshold, looking back and forth along the half-moon curve of the street.

"Are you expecting someone, Sandra?"

"No, no, m'um." Sandra closed the door behind her, with one last look along the street. She was frowning. "I was just checking. There was a man out there this morning, then again this afternoon. Looking up at the house, he was. I had a mind to go out and ask him his business, or at least send Eric."

"A man?" Maisie shivered. "What did he look like?"

Sandra folded Maisie's mackintosh over her crossed arms and leaned toward her in a conspiratorial manner. "Well, that's the funny thing. Teresa said it wasn't a man at all. She came up the kitchen steps and had a look from around the side wall, and she said it was a woman all bundled up to look like a man."

Maisie was just about to ask another question, when Sandra interjected.

"Oh, and there was a telephone call from the operator this afternoon, saying that a connection has been booked from Canada for Miss Maisie Dobbs." She looked around at the clock. "Oh, look at the time, it's booked for half past seven, so you've only got a few minutes."

"Thank you, Sandra. That will be Master James."

Sandra shook her head. "It's amazing, when you think of it, the way you can talk to someone all the way across the world nowadays."

Maisie smiled. "It certainly is, Sandra. I'll go immediately to the library and answer the call myself."

"Right you are, m'um."

"THIS IS THE operator for Miss Maisie Dobbs. Connection to Toronto, Canada."

"Yes, thank you." Maisie heard two operators speaking, one with a Canadian accent; then the resonant voice of James Compton could be heard clearly.

"Maisie, can you hear me?"

"Yes, James, I'm here. It's so good of you to telephone."

"Couldn't ignore a telegram from the intrepid Maisie Dobbs, could I?" James laughed. "To tell you the truth, it's hot and humid here; I've been stuck in my office on Yonge Street since dawn and thought I'd liven things up a bit. And I must confess, I was intrigued by your questions."

"You were the first person I thought of." Maisie pressed on. "James, when you were in the Flying Corps, were you ever required to do—and I know *do* probably isn't the right word—but were you ever required to do a stop-start landing?"

"God, I hoped I'd never have to think about all that again."

"I'm sorry."

"Oh, no, it just seems so long ago, but there again, just like yesterday. I was so young—we were all so young."

"I know, James." Maisie looked around at the grandfather clock, then turned back. *He's lonely. And still so vulnerable.*

"Now then, you know, I may have tried it once, but frankly, training didn't really last as long as you might think. I was an observer first, which trains you to—well, observe. Then I began flying; then, as you know, I copped a Blighty while standing on the ground, if you please. Lovely way for an aviator to go out!"

"So, stop-start landings? Why would you need to execute such a maneuver?"

"Now you're sounding like my old CO." James paused for so long, Maisie wondered whether the line had failed.

"James?"

"Yes, I'm here. The only reason for doing a stop-start is if you need to go up again immediately. For example, if you have landed and suddenly you come under fire, you have to go up again. We'd have to get the aeroplanes up in the air to protect them and us. Or if you are delivering something that can be thrown out: a communication pouch, for example. Mind you, you can do that from the air. Then there are the really brave and secret missions."

"Brave and secret? That sounds like a *Boy's Own* adventure."

James laughed. "Just a bit tongue-in-cheek. Of course, some of us thought the whole war was going to be a *Boy's Own* adventure. Then we got over there, and things were not quite as we imagined."

"So what would have been brave and secret?"

"Maisie, some of us weren't out there long enough to know much more than what was required of us when we received daily orders, and we were glad if we made it to the end of the day. However, it was *understood*, let's say, that there were a few who crossed into enemy territory to do more than just report back on where the Hun was in relation to where we all thought they were. They went in with someone but came back alone."

"You mean that the *someone* was left behind?"

"Yes, that's about the measure of it."

Maisie frowned, ignoring the minutes ticking by. As much as was allowed by the telephone cord, she began to pace. "James, forgive me, but I want to ensure I understand what you are saying. An aviator would take on a passenger, cross over into enemy territory, land the craft just long enough for another person to leap out, and then the aviator would be off and away again before anyone had even known they were there—assuming the whole thing was not observed."

"Yes."

"Gosh."

"Quite."

"Were you ever asked to do such a thing?"

A laugh cracked in the receiver, which Maisie moved slightly. "Oh, Maisie, I was never that good!" The laughing stopped. "And now that time has passed, I wonder where I ever acquired the nerve to do what I did. Certainly couldn't do it now! But that level of courage, keeping one's nerve for that kind of thing—no, not me."

"James, you've been most helpful. One last thing: Did you ever know Ralph Lawton, perhaps as children?"

"Oh, Ralph, Cecil Lawton's son. You know, we sort of knew each other as young boys, but we weren't pally or anything like that. He was a bit soft, you know, the type who always tried to please mummy, that sort of thing. Not exactly one who would be reading *Boy's Own!*"

"I see. Then you didn't know him in the Flying Corps then?"

"I knew he was in but never actually came across him. Probably wouldn't have recognized him, you know."

"Thank you, James. Well, it's doubtless time for lunch in your neck of the woods. I'd better go now." Maisie began to close the call, but felt that James wanted to speak longer. "Is everything all right, James? I've heard through the grapevine that you're courting a very nice young woman."

"News travels. And I hear you are seeing a doctor—and not because you're ill!"

"Touché!"

"But it isn't the same, is it?"

Maisie frowned. She now pictured James in her mind's eye, James going home to an empty apartment, sitting alone with a drink in his hand. More than anyone, she knew how deeply he had loved Enid, who had worked at Ebury Place and had shared a bedroom in the servants' quarters with Maisie. Before the war, Lord and Lady Compton had sought to end the liaison by sending their son to Canada to become familiar with the family business there, but he returned to England—and to Enid—when war was declared. Enid had soon left the Comptons' employ to work in a munitions factory, though she and James continued to see each other. It was her death in an explosion, in 1915, that had spurred Maisie to enlist for nursing service. *The past still haunts us.* She worried about James, who had suffered so, crushed by his loss and tormented with memories of the war and of what might have been. A near-breakdown had led to his return to Canada, a country where he had reclaimed a sense of peace, of the old joy that had been his in earlier years.

"Now then, you're not getting maudlin, James? I know Lady Rowan is aching for grandchildren, so she's waiting to hear of an engagement soon."

The melancholy seemed to lift. "Oh, I'll try not to disappoint her. After all, we aren't getting any younger, are we?"

"No, James. Now then, this telephone call will cost a fortune—" And indeed, as Maisie spoke, the operator interrupted and the call was ended with only time to bid a quick farewell.

Maisie left the library and went to her rooms. A bath had been drawn for her, and the vapor of lavender oil lingered in the air. She stood by the window for a few moments, the telephone conversation with James whirling around in her mind. *Could Ralph Lawton have been engaged in work that was brave and secret?* If so, might that have led to his death? After all, his aeroplane went down behind enemy lines. And what if he was, did it have any bearing on the discord between the Lawtons regarding Agnes's belief that her son was dead? No. They probably didn't even know what work he was involved in. *Or did they?* Might Ralph have been so pleased with his accomplishments that he told his parents, eager for some recognition of worth from his father? Or might he have told Jeremy Hazleton? *And what if he had?* Maisie shook her head. Ralph's papers were fairly straightforward, whereas Peter Evernden's . . . that was another matter.

As she turned from the window, a slight movement on the street caught her eye. Was someone watching her? It was quite dark now, but there, out on the street? She leaned closer. No, there was no one there.

Later, as she sat in her rooms having eaten only half a supper of fish and vegetables, Maisie leaned back into the armchair and reflected upon her day. She knew sleep would come as soon as she closed her eyes, along with the nightmares once more. So she would sit in silence and stillness before going to bed, to quiet her mind and soothe her soul. Yet as tiredness claimed her, James Compton's words spun in her mind. *But it isn't the same, is it?*

"MAISIE, I AM so glad to have caught you before you whiz off to your office in that little red car of yours!"

"Hello, Andrew, how are you? And how are your patients after the emergency? It sounded terrible."

"It was. There's a new hotel being built along the seafront. The scaffolding failed and some twenty men and boys were injured—some quite seriously. Two men were killed."

"Oh!"

"Yes, there will be a big inquiry. So, I was busy all weekend and missed you. Will you come on Saturday?"

"I'm sorry, Andrew, I can't."

"Can't?"

Maisie felt the tension in his voice. "I'm leaving for France on Friday, Andrew. Maurice is coming with me. I think we'll be gone a week or ten days, something of that order."

"I knew it. My competition is an older man!"

Maisie laughed. The tension had gone. "Yes, didn't you know that already? I promise I will come to Hastings as soon as this part of my case is complete."

"Promise?"

"Yes, that's what I said. Now, I have to leave. Busy day ahead."

"Look, I know we have telephones, but would you write?"

"I promise I'll put pen to paper—and I'll telephone as soon as I can."

Replacing the receiver, Maisie left the library where she had taken the telephone call, collected her document case and mackintosh, and made her way toward the kitchen. Deep purplish rings under her eyes betrayed her troubled night, when memories and nightmares conspired to tear into her heart and mind. One minute she was on her way to France, the boat pitching amid white-capped waves; the next she was in Kent, trying to reach her father across the orchard, ripe red apples dripping blood as she ran through avenues of branches, which turned to human limbs as they brushed against her face, the spots of red on her woolen dress and white apron expanding so that the garments became heavy and sodden, and all the time her father moving farther away and her legs weaker and weaker, until she woke with a start, hot and feverish.

Leaving via the kitchen door, Maisie made her way to the mews, where she would collect the MG.

"Nice mornin', m'um." Eric was making a final sweep across the MG's bonnet with a yellow duster. "Just a cat's lick and a promise before you leave."

"Thank you, Eric. She looks lovely."

"My favorite motor, that one." He tapped the bonnet to indicate a job finished. "Mind you, I'll want 'er for a good few hours before you go over there to France. Don't want anything going wrong, now, do we? And I'll make up a kit for you, some spares, so that if anything *does* go wrong, you won't have any of them Frenchies trying to put a Peugeot part where a Peugeot part has no place to be."

"Oh, good point, Eric. Mind you, she hasn't let me down this far, so I doubt if she'll let me down in France."

"Well, the miles you drive, you never know. Better safe than sorry, that's what I say."

Maisie took her seat in the MG, and Eric closed the door. "Yes, better safe than sorry." She waved and drove carefully from the cobbled mews.

It was as she pulled out onto the main road that Maisie noticed a man on the corner. A man who at first seemed quite nondescript, with a plain mackintosh buttoned to the top so that neither shirt nor tie could be discerned. He wore brown trousers and a brown felt hat; as she drove past, he pulled out a newspaper and opened it wide. Curious, Maisie doubled back in time to see the man leave Ebury Place. She could see why Teresa might have thought the man was, in fact, a woman, for his steps were shorter than the stride normally taken by a man. . . .

THE ACCIDENT HAPPENED in a flash, so quickly that afterward she realized that, only twenty minutes before, she was driving along, her mind full of the things she had to accomplish before leaving for France, and now this had happened: the MG nose first into a lamppost and she with a rather nasty cut on her forehead. Her head was throbbing as she answered questions, sitting in the motor car with a handkerchief to her forehead while a police constable stood before her, notebook in hand, assuring her that a doctor was on his way and no, he couldn't let her just go on without at least being looked at, and he had to make a report in any case.

"So, you say that a person ran toward the curb, as if they weren't going to stop, so you took avoiding action—and the person just vanished?"

"Yes."

"And, just so I have it here in your words, what was your avoiding action?"

"Well, I swerved to miss him. . . ." Maisie frowned. "Yes, *him*."

"So the person who walked out in front of you was a man?"

Maisie faltered.

"I think she's concussed, poor girl. Been knocked silly." A woman among the group of onlookers voiced an opinion.

"Please, madam, if you don't mind." The police constable moved toward the group, whereupon a police vehicle arrived followed by another motor car with a DOCTOR sign placed on the dashboard. The constable looked around, nodded at his comrades as they alighted from the motor car, and proceeded to speak again to the crowd. "Now then, now then, move back, go on with your shopping, ladies, there's nothing to see here."

"Well, it's not a life-or-death case, just giving you a nasty headache, I expect." The doctor examined the cut on Maisie's head as she remained in the driver's seat of the MG, then reached into his bag and began pulling out a tincture and dressings. "I've got some brand-new bandage here—it's only been issued to certain hospitals and in small quantities, but I managed to get my hands on some—it's got sticky stuff on one side so there's no need for pins and a swathe of gauze around your head. I'll be able to give you a nice neat dressing. Don't get it wet and mind how you take it off, though." The doctor spoke while attending to the wound, pulling out the brand-new bandage, measuring a short length, then placing it over a square of lint.

"I'll be able to take care of it. I was a nurse."

"If that's the case, I'll have to double-underline the rest prescription! We'll get the police here to take you home now. You're to go to bed for a good twenty-four hours and see your usual doctor tomorrow."

"I can't. I've got to get to my office."

The doctor looked at the MG, his forlorn countenance leaving a sick feeling in Maisie's stomach. "Not in this, you won't. No doubt the police will have it towed to wherever you want it taken." He looked at Maisie intently. "You know, you're very lucky to be alive. If you had hit another motor car or bus, or even the side of that building, it would have been curtains for you. Thank God there was nothing coming in the other direction—and at this time in the morning! No wonder the chappie who ran out in front of you made off. The blithering idiot!"

"You know, I really am all right, though my motor is . . . not." Maisie felt a prickling at the corners of her eyes, and her head was still pounding. The MG was more than simply a motor car to her, it was her first big purchase as a business owner. And it represented so much.

The doctor stood up and peered over the crumpled bonnet. "You know, I'm not a mechanical man, but I think someone with a bit of know-how will be able to sort this out for you in no time. So you do as I say, be sure to see your doctor tomorrow, and all will be well. Now then, I'll just talk to the constable here and ensure that they'll be taking you back to your home."

Maisie nodded and pressed her hands against her eyes. As if going back to the starting line at a race, she went through events leading up to the collision again, picturing almost every yard of the journey until the last image when she had gasped, quickly turned the wheel to avoid a disaster, and. . . . She knew the police would have questions about the person who caused her to swerve, the person who started this awful chain of events. Maisie pressed her fingers against the bandage again, willing her mind to work harder, to recover.

"Ready, miss? Let's get you home then."

Maisie stood up, allowing the police constable to support her.

"No, take me to Fitzroy Square. Please. My office is there; my assistant will help me."

"But, miss, the doctor said—"

"It's all right. I know what I'm doing, constable. I was a nurse." Maisie's eyes filled with tears. *Yes, I was a nurse.*

"I REALLY THINK you should do what the doctor said, Miss, and take a bit of a rest. You never know with a bang on the 'ead." Billy placed a mug of strong sweet tea in front of Maisie, who was sitting alongside his own chair at the table where they had pinned out the Ralph Lawton case map.

"I'll be all right, Billy. Come this afternoon, I'll be a lot better than the bruise around that gash might suggest. Thank heavens I had my hair cut and now have a fringe to cover it up."

Billy doodled on the edge of the paper with a red pencil. "So, you say that this fella—if it was a fella—came from the station and sort of rushed at the curb as if to run out and then stopped, by which time you'd swerved."

"Yes, that's about it."

"And then the man—or woman, for that matter—just vanished? Into thin air. Like a ghost."

"Yes."

Billy pressed his lips together and glanced sideways at Maisie, but she looked up and caught his eye.

"I promise you, Billy, I know what I saw. If you doubt me, then put your cards on the table now!" Maisie scraped her chair back, stood up abruptly, and began to pace, looking at him all the time.

Billy turned, his elbow resting on the back of the chair. "Miss, you've been right busy this past few weeks and, speaking direc'ly, it don't take the brains of a gnat to work out that you've a lot on your plate. It wouldn't surprise me if—"

Maisie interjected. "If I hadn't imagined it? Then what about the person seen at Ebury Place?"

"Could've 'ad nothin' to do with you or anyone else at number fifteen. Could've been one of them people what works for an estate agent, eyeing up the properties."

"No. It wasn't."

Billy sighed. "Awright, then, let's look at who else it could've been. We ain't got any really dodgy cases on at the moment, 'ave we? I mean, who would want to do that to you? It's terrible."

Maisie stopped, then paced back to the table, whereupon she took her seat again. "No, let's ask another question: What is the message?"

"What d'yer mean, Miss?"

"The accident could have killed me, but it didn't. It was a strange accident, made to seem as if it were entirely my fault, with no one able to back me up, no witnesses to the pedestrian's odd behavior. I couldn't even tell whether the person was a man or a woman, though at first glance I would have said it was a man. Billy, I don't think it was an accident that was supposed to be fatal. I think it was a warning. That was the message."

Billy held up three fingers and counted them off: "Avril Jarvis, Ralph Lawton, Peter Evernden. Which one?"

Maisie leaned back in her chair.

"Miss, what you would ask me, if I were in your shoes, is *What do you feel?*" Billy placed his hand on his middle. "What do you feel *inside* about the accident and who caused it?"

Maisie placed her hand on her waist, mirroring Billy. "My immediate thought is that it is to do with the Lawton case; however, I now have a sense that all is not as it at first seemed with Peter Evernden. His records are missing from the repository."

"Is that unusual? Seems like what with all them files and all them relatives, somebody's papers are bound to go missin'."

"On the contrary, they keep excellent records and access is restricted to family members with prior permission to visit. I was able to make my appointment to view only after Priscilla had given her written permission."

"But ain't the brass allowed in there?" Billy was rubbing his chin now. "P'raps one of the higher-ups needed the records."

"Or perhaps they have *never been there*. Perhaps they are somewhere else. Or destroyed. *Perhaps*, Billy, they are to be kept away from prying eyes."

THE REMAINDER OF the day was spent attending to details pertaining to the accident on Tottenham Court Road. After hearing about Maisie's close shave with disaster, Maurice took over finalizing the arrangements for their passage to France.

On a normal day, the telephone might ring one, two, or three times; however, it seemed that today, once Maisie had placed the receiver in the cradle, the telephone bell would immediately sound again. Even though she had telephoned ahead to warn that the MG was being towed to Ebury Mews, as soon as the damaged motor car was delivered into Eric's care, word spread quickly. Frankie Dobbs was the first to telephone as soon as he heard the news. A telephone had been installed in the Groom's Cottage at Maisie's expense following his own accident, a serious fall earlier in the year, though Frankie would have preferred not to have such a thing in his home. When it rang he would look at the black machine for some time before answering the call—invariably from Maisie—as if the receiver might explode upon placing it next to his ear. But he lost no time in calling when he learned of her accident.

"I should come up there right now, my girl, and bring you back to Kent. Runnin' around in that motor all on your own. I've a good mind to go straight to the station now."

"Dad, I promise I'm all right." She placed her fingers on her forehead, which was thumping yet again. "Now you know how it feels, eh, now the boot is on the other foot?"

Frankie Dobbs was quick to respond. "I've *always* known how it feels, young Maisie!" Frankie had a habit of sounding rather cross when he was most worried about his daughter. "And this 'going to

France' for a fortnight; can't do you any good, can it, what with the foreign food they give you over there?"

Maisie began to laugh, then winced as the pain increased. "Dad, the food is the least of my worries. I promise you, it's just a bump and a scratch, nothing more than when I fell out of the tree in Granddad's garden when I was five."

Frankie sighed. "I'll never forget that either—I thought your mother was about to have a heart attack! Well, you mind, my girl. And you've to get on the blower to me again tomorrow, just so's I know you're all right. When are you coming home?"

"When I'm back from France, promise."

"Right then."

"Dad—" Maisie hesitated. Telephone conversations with her father usually ended with the words "Look after yourself," or perhaps "See you soon." She swallowed. This time there was more she wanted to say. "Dad—"

"What is it, Maisie?"

"Dad—I   I love you."

Frankie seemed to falter. "Just you take care, my girl. Just you take care."

After Frankie, Maurice telephoned several times, Lady Rowan twice, and then Andrew Dene, who insisted Maisie see a friend at St. Thomas's. "He's a skull man, Maisie. I insist!"

Eventually, Maisie agreed to telephone the surgeon for an appointment before she left for France, though it occurred to her that at this moment, with her motor car requiring repairs, new travel expenses, and her ambition to put a down payment on a property of her own, to say nothing of a second excursion to Taunton by Billy, she could ill afford the expense of a medical consultation. Her head throbbed. It was definitely time she went back to Ebury Place.

Later, after a hot bath and a supper of hearty chicken broth with dumplings brought to her room by Sandra, Maisie finally laid her head back on her pillow and closed her eyes. She had rested for only a few moments when she opened her eyes and gazed for a while at the single red rose that Sandra had placed on the tray along with her supper. Frowning, she quickly reached over to her bedside table for the clutch of papers given to her by Priscilla. Maisie reread the letters written before Peter returned to England for what she and Priscilla had assumed was training and promotion, and then she read again the letters sent at a later date, letters so short by comparison. And there it was, the line that intrigued her: *You would love the gardens here, Pris, the roses are gorgeous at this time of year.*

If there was one thing Maisie knew about Priscilla, it was that her friend was no gardener and hated roses in particular. Maisie closed her eyes and recalled Priscilla at Cambridge, pulling a face when a bouquet of scarlet roses from a smitten suitor was brought to her room by the porter.

"I never saw a rose I could trust, Maisie. All very beautiful but with thorns that can rip one's skin if one isn't careful. The boys chased me into the rose garden when I was a girl, and I have never forgotten it. My father gave them each the stick for their trouble! Watch a man who sends you roses, Maisie!"

And there was something else. The letter was dated November 1916. Winter. Roses are at their best in June.

THIRTEEN

Maisie woke suddenly, morning light teasing its way through the curtains at an angle that suggested she had overslept.

"Oh, no!" She leaped out of bed, then held on to the back of a chair for support, her head beginning to ache again. "I'll take a powder, that'll do it." There was much to accomplish today, and Maisie did not want to be hampered. With resolve, she told herself that it was time to pull herself together, get affairs in order for her fortnight's absence, and ensure that her fee from Sir Cecil Lawton was well earned. Today she had to see Sir Cecil, and she had also arranged to meet Detective Inspector Stratton for tea; she wanted to know how the case against Avril Jarvis was progressing. At her instruction, Billy would travel to Taunton again on Saturday in an effort to see the girl's mother, which might be difficult as Avril's name was now in the newspapers, along with the news that she had been remanded in custody at Holloway Prison, charged with the crime of murder. Maisie vowed to do all she could to ensure that Avril would not spend the rest of her life behind bars.

Dressing quickly, Maisie added errands to her mental list of tasks that must be completed before the journey to France on Friday and tried to consider only positive aspects of the trip. France in mid-September would be lovely, with city dwellers back in Paris following the summer *vacances* and those making the pilgrimage from overseas to visit military cemeteries now fewer in number. Yes, she would get through her work here, and each day she would see only the new, only the rebirth of a land once decimated. Thus resolved, she tilted her navy cloche in a way that disguised any hint of a cut or bruise, took her black document case, and made her way toward the Victoria underground station. She did not tarry to visit Eric in the mews: she wasn't up to receiving his prognosis on the health of her MG just yet.

It was as she walked along that Maisie felt a prickly sensation at her neck, akin to the feeling that one gets when one is being observed, perhaps across a room, between the shelves of books in a library, or when one is shopping. It was a trigger that made Maisie instinctively turn around to identify the observer, stopping quickly before looking down the street upon which she had just walked. The street was empty, so she continued on her way, struggling to maintain the determination embraced only ten minutes ago as she left Ebury Place.

Descending into the underground, she was dismayed to find the platform busy, an indication that trains were slow and limited this morning. Though the day had greeted London with an early morning chill, the air around Maisie was already too warm, too humid, and she began to perspire. Taking a white linen handkerchief from her bag, she lifted her hat slightly and pressed it to her brow. She swallowed, the bitter salty taste in her mouth adding to her discomfort. People jostled her as she walked along the platform to a place she thought might be less crowded, but she was pushed and shoved closer to the edge, where warm air rushed from the tunnel. *I wish I had stayed at home. I wish, this once, I had called a taxi-cab. I wish—* suddenly, Maisie was aware of that other sensation again, that someone was watching her, following her every move. She glanced around, first right, then left. The sweat at the nape of her neck dared her to turn, dared her to look behind her.

She was at the very front of the platform when she saw him and gasped, dropping her case and holding her hands to her mouth. And as the train came from the tunnel, Simon—*Simon*—shouted to her: "Move, Maisie! Move!" And as she moved, pushing her body sideways at the very moment the train came alongside, she saw a hand reach out. A hand that was meant to connect with her body, meant to push her forward onto the rails.

Arriving passengers forced Maisie backward as they surged onto the platform and then to the exits. Maisie faltered, feeling both hot and cold at the same time. Panic was rising within her. She could not get on the train, could not let her body be sucked into the hot mass of humanity as it shuttled onward to the next stop. Instead, as the train pulled out of the station and disappeared into the dark tunnel, Maisie remained on the empty platform, clutching the retrieved black case to her chest. There was no Simon now. She knew Simon would at this moment be sitting in his wheelchair, which would have just been taken to the conservatory, where he would be left to spend the morning alone until he was pushed away to be spoon-fed a meal that his mind had no ability to identify as breakfast, lunch, or supper. With her hands and legs still trembling, Maisie left the underground as quickly as possible. In her heart she knew Simon had saved her. His spirit had reached out to her as surely as the hand had reached forward to push her to her death.

"I RECKON YOU should tell Detective Inspector Stratton about this, if you don't mind me sayin' so."

"What can he do, Billy? It's not as if I'm dead!"

"No, but you could've been, couldn't you? Eh? And then where would we be?"

"There's *nothing* he could do—or *can* do, for that matter. I stand a better chance of getting to the bottom of all this myself."

Billy was thoughtful. "I'm beginning to get a bit worried about you, Miss." He sat across the desk from Maisie, who was leaning forward in her oak chair, going through the events of the past hour in her mind while flicking through the morning's mail. "First there's someone—man or woman—in a mackintosh at Goodge Street station, and now another someone trying to do away with you on the underground. What's it all about?"

Maisie looked up. "I do not believe it has anything to do with Avril Jarvis, so the connection is with either Lawton or Peter Evernden—and I have to say that the informal investigation on the part of my old friend is looking more complex every day, especially as we have no military records."

"And you say the brother's letters to Mrs. Partridge were a bit strange?"

"Yes, though one has to be careful not to leap to conclusions. As you know, probably more than most, everything is different in a time of war. People do and say things they might never otherwise say. We have to avoid passing judgment on what someone wrote when they were about to go back to the Western Front, probably with more responsibility than they had when they enlisted. *And* with the knowledge that they might very well be taking their last look at home."

The skin around Billy's eyes crinkled as he spoke, his face betraying a high level of concern regarding the events of the morning. "But you reckon there's something in this business of the roses? And as far as you know, 'e wasn't the gardenin' type?"

"He knew Priscilla hated roses."

"If I was playing devil's advocate, as you would say, Miss, I might point out that 'e could've been doin' that deliberately, pullin' 'er leg a bit. Or per'aps it was the name of the local pub, you know, and it was another way of sayin' that 'e'd nipped out for a swift one at the Rose when 'e wasn't s'posed to. Sounds like a pub to me."

Maisie smiled. "Nice idea, but I don't think so." She looked at her watch. "I have to get on to Lord Julian now." She reached for the telephone receiver. "I need his help."

Billy moved to his own desk as the call was placed to Lord Julian's office in the City.

"Good morning, Lord Julian."

"And good morning to you, Maisie Dobbs! To what do I owe this telephone call? I hope my friend Lawton is paying you!"

"Yes, of course, Lord Julian. I need some information, and I think you might be able to help."

"Fire away. Pen at the ready."

Maisie thought there were times when he sounded remarkably like his wife and reminded herself that it was hardly surprising, given that they had now been married for over forty years.

"It's about the MP Jeremy Hazleton."

"Oh, yes, I've spoken to him occasionally at Westminster. Quite a firebrand. Could well be prime minister in a few years, wheelchair or no wheelchair—and a man decorated for bravery in a time of war is always apt to be a vote-catcher. But I'm not sure I know more about him than the next man."

"Probably not, but you do have access to more information than most."

"My War Office connections?"

"Yes. I am not family, so I have no means of obtaining his service record. I'd like to know more about his military career."

"I'll see what I can do. Will you still be in town tomorrow evening?"

"Yes."

"Right you are. I will be returning to Chelstone tomorrow, but if you come to my office we can speak in confidence. About four o'clock?"

"Thank you. I'll see you at four tomorrow, Lord Julian."

"Good. Until then."

"Yes, until then."

Maisie replaced the receiver.

"That man's really got connections, eh? The old school tie and all that. Fancy bein' able to just pick up the blower and 'ave everything at your fingertips!"

"At least he's a good man, Billy. Essentially a good man. He'll get me what I need."

"Do you think there's something off about this Hazleton?"

Maisie pushed some papers into a desk drawer and locked it, placing the key in her document case. "Other than his connection to Ralph Lawton? I don't know yet. Put it this way; I *wonder* about him. . . . Now then, I have an appointment. I'll be back this afternoon; then I have to see both Sir Cecil and Stratton. Could you visit the woman who called this morning regarding her husband? It looks like a case for you while I'm gone."

"I'll get to it right away, Miss. Nice to see the work coming in at a steady clip, innit?"

"Very nice, Billy. Very nice indeed!"

MAISIE LEFT FITZROY Square and was about to walk up toward Warren Street station, when she thought again. Looking over her shoulder, then both right and left, she turned back into the square and crossed into Charlotte Street. Breathing a sigh of relief, she felt a weariness that seemed to begin in her head and then seep down even into the bones of her feet. She had told Billy about events on the underground platform, keeping calm, speaking in a controlled manner. She had telephoned Lord Julian, making an appointment that would keep the momentum of her investigation moving forward at a time when she had a great desire to curl into a ball on her bed and never move again.

She remembered feeling this same way as a child. She had gone with her mother to visit the doctor. Not the doctor who ran the clinic on Tuesdays over on the corner, where her mother would take a florin from her purse, put it on the table, and go though a doorway that led to the doctor's office while Maisie waited outside, banging her feet together as she sat on the too-high chair, reading her book, waiting and waiting. No, on this occasion they were going to another doctor, a doctor for whom quite a few pound notes had to be taken from the earthenware jar that stood on the mantelpiece over the stove. It was afterward, as they were leaving, that they saw the young dog, and he must have been young because his paws seemed far too big for his legs. His tongue was hanging out with glee as he ran out in front of one of those new motor cars that came around the corner far too fast, popping and banging on its way to kill a poor little dog. Maisie had squealed in terror and her mother, her mother who had herself winced in pain as she lifted up her beloved daughter, brushed Maisie's hair back with her hand, speaking gently to her. Then later, as she curled onto her bed in the small house in Lambeth, she had been gentled again by the soft hands at her brow and the voice that told her that there should be no tears because the little dog had gone to heaven, which was the best place to be. Maisie had wept until sleep claimed her, knowing in her very soul that her mother's words were meant to encompass far more than the sudden death of a poor little dog.

And here she was again, that urge to be soothed clawing at her insides each day, the knowledge that those who would readily calm her—Andrew, her father, Maurice, even Khan—could not.

Traveling to her destination by bus and on foot, Maisie was vigilant, keeping a watchful eye around her. As she reached the tall Georgian house, now converted into an office below with flats above, she thought of Madeleine Hartnell again. *There are two who walk with you.* Should she go to see her again? The thought was quickly countered with another as she recalled her grandmother, the one who could see every bit as well as Madeleine Hartnell and whom they said Maisie took after. *Don't you ever dabble, young Maisie. The minute you start with the spirits, they'll never leave you alone.* She shivered as she entered the oak-floored office with furniture that had been polished to a brilliant shine.

"Good morning. Maisie Dobbs to see Mr. Isaacs."

A short man in late middle age pushed back his chair at the back of the office upon hearing his name given to the secretary.

"Ah, yes. Miss Dobbs." His hand was extended in greeting as he came toward her. "Charmed, I'm sure. Now, per our telephone conversation, I have several properties that would be perfect for an up-and-coming, if I may say so, young woman such as yourself." He flicked through some papers. "All by the river, as you indicated in your telephone call, and all in your price range. It's a very good time to be investing in bricks and mortar. There's a new block of flats in Pimlico that are particularly interesting . . ."

Maisie nodded and smiled, as she took the sheet of paper. *Move forward. Do not stop. Keep moving, and the past will be kept at bay.* The trouble was, as Maisie knew only too well, her job demanded that she reside in the past for most of her working life. And the past was a dark abyss into which she was quickly descending.

FOURTEEN

Maisie arrived next at Sir Cecil Lawton's chambers and was ushered into his office by a pupil, who pulled out a chair for her on the opposite side of the grand desk.

"Good afternoon, Miss Dobbs. How is your task progressing?" Allowing her no time to answer, Lawton collected some sheets of paper and placed them on one side before pulling back the copious sleeves of his gown, resting his jacketed forearms on the desk, and clasping his hands together. "I fear I have given you an almost impossible task. You are no doubt more used to searching for people who are known to be alive, rather than known to be dead." He pursed his lips.

Maisie nodded, looking across at her client, who could not now meet her eye-to-eye. "As I said before, Sir Cecil, it's an unusual assignment, but the sort of thing that is not unknown. Of course, the demands of such an inquiry are more difficult for you to bear."

"What do you mean?"

"I mean you have assumed I will not find any evidence to suggest that Ralph lived on after his De Havilland went down, and I agree; it seems most unlikely. But"—Maisie paused before continuing—"*but*, Sir Cecil, have you thought of what might happen if he *had* survived the crash? How it might be if he is, as your wife suspected, still alive?"

"As we both know, that is highly unlikely."

"Sir Cecil, the more I inquire with regard to your son, the more questions I have. I must ask for complete honesty from you."

"You have had my word already."

Maisie stood up and walked to the window, where she stood for just a moment before turning back to face Lawton.

"I know we have talked about this before, but I must ask again: If Ralph was alive as Mrs. Lawton maintained, what events, what discord, what fears might have prevented him from being in touch with you, particularly when the war was over?" Maisie looked at Lawton directly as she pressed him.

The man who one moment before had seemed controlled, and in complete command, leaned forward and placed his head in his hands. Maisie made no move. If anything, she assumed a more relaxed position, resting her hand lightly on the windowsill. When Lawton did not change his posture, she took her seat once more, silently, and placed her hands together in her lap. Breathing deeply, Maisie narrowed her eyes. Soon an image formed in her mind's eye, of a boyish youth standing next to an older man. The young man's earnest look revealed a wish to please, a wish to be accepted by the older man, whose very demeanor made him appear intractable, resolute. Unmovable.

"I could not accept him as my son."

Maisie opened her eyes as Lawton leaned back in his chair and swept his hand backward across his forehead and into his hair.

"Go on."

"His choice of friends and close associates was untenable."

"But a young man who grows to become a highly regarded Member of Parliament would appear to have been a good choice as a friend for the son of a prominent KC." Maisie knew she was continuing to push Lawton. She wanted to hear the words that would corroborate the scenario her instincts had led her to imagine.

"He is a respectable MP *now*, Miss Dobbs."

"And married."

Lawton's eyes met Maisie's for the first time. "Yes. And married. If you have already deduced that my son had no interest in women, Miss Dobbs, why on earth do you ask these questions?"

"I am interested in you and Ralph together, father and son."

"I know he tried to prove himself to me, that despite"—Lawton turned from Maisie for a moment—"despite his choices and behaviors, he wanted my—well, I don't know what he wanted."

"Love?"

"He was my son. I wanted my son to be a man to be looked up to."

"And that precludes the love of a son by his father?"

Lawton shook his head. "A man in my position cannot have a son running around in the circles Ralph chose, even when he was in the service. Was it too much to ask that he be married and have children?"

"And live a lie?"

"And live within the law."

Maisie nodded. "Then back to my first question. What if Ralph had survived the crash—and I know his remains were found—but what if?"

"I believe his love of his mother would have risen above his hatred of me."

"You believe he hated you?"

"Yes. There was no love lost between us. If you must know, notification of his death was . . . was . . ."

Maisie was silent. She would not help Lawton find his words, knowing instead that such emotions could be relieved of their chains only in the personal struggle of confession. Some moments passed before the man lauded as a great legal orator could give voice to his thoughts.

"I did not grieve for my son as he was when he joined the army and then the Flying Corps. I grieved for the boy. I grieved for what was not. We were not the only ones to suffer great loss, as you know. One just gets on with it. If anything, it was a relief, for the discord inspired by his choices caused great pain for his mother, as great as losing him."

"So really, Sir Cecil, you wouldn't want him found even if he had survived."

Lawton shook his head. "My son is dead. You have been retained as a mark of respect to my wife. Of course you have a further interest, now that I am defending Miss Jarvis. Thus I fail to see what this interrogation is expected to achieve."

Now Maisie leaned forward with a gaze so direct that Lawton could not fail to look back into her midnight-blue eyes.

"It was necessary to hear directly from you the nature of Ralph's personal associations. I cannot and will not toil in a fog of evasion on the part of the very people for whom I am working."

Maisie left Lawton's chambers, pondering the cases in hand. Two things in particular occurred to her as odd: It seemed ironic that the only person worthy of her trust thus far was a young girl who stood accused of murder. And then there was the intriguing reference to roses in Peter Evernden's letter. Yes, that nagged at her constantly now. The rose. Maisie imagined a rose, imagined the bud tight until it was ready to open, the delicate red petals gradually peeling back in the sun, then falling to reveal the rosehip, another locked door. Yes, the rose: delicate, strong, and guarded by thorns that could draw blood in a second if one reached out without due care. The rose. Traditional emblem of secrecy and silence.

STRATTON WAS PACING outside the "caffy" where they had agreed to meet on Tottenham Court Road. Maisie noticed that he repeatedly checked his watch, and she made a mental note to pick up her own precious timepiece from the mender's on Charlotte Street before returning to the office.

"I'm sorry to keep you waiting, Inspector. Am I very late?"

"Good afternoon, Miss Dobbs. No, you're not late at all. But I do have another appointment this afternoon, so I must leave promptly."

"Right you are." Maisie stepped forward into the café and walked toward a small table near the window that had just been cleared. Communication with Stratton had been rather stilted since the summer, when his invitations to supper or the theater had been met with refusal. Maisie had considered any meetings that went beyond the bounds of their professional relationship a poor decision, though she had entertained the idea for a while. And though she was now walking out with Andrew Dene, there was still something about Stratton that Maisie found rather likable.

They ordered tea, toast, and jam and moved the conversation quickly to the case in hand.

"The Jarvis case will go to trial in January."

"I see." Maisie shook her head, declining the sugar pot, which Stratton had pushed toward her. She watched as he scooped two large teaspoonfuls into his cup of tea and stirred briskly.

"She stands accused of murder. There are no other suspects."

"But what about a lesser charge? The girl was abused, was pushed onto the streets."

"So are a lot of young girls. Go down to Soho, Miss Dobbs. Whether we like it or not, the streetwalkers are as young as ten or eleven. And they don't murder the pimps."

Maisie pressed her lips together. "What if—just what if—she's innocent?"

Stratton placed his cup down on the saucer with a crack that attracted the attention of onlookers. Maisie did not flinch but, instead, ensured that she looked at him directly. She sipped her tea.

"She is guilty." Stratton leaned back. "Look, I know you don't care for Caldwell, and I admit he can be an abrasive tyke. *And* I know you had words with him during my absence—he had every right to insist that any new information was brought to our attention—but he's a terrier on a case. He has proof beyond doubt that the girl is the killer."

Maisie nodded. *Yes, I'm sure he has.*

"In any case, I understand that you have engineered it so Sir Cecil Lawton will be defending her in court. She'll stand a better chance than most."

"If she survives Holloway."

"Don't underestimate the girl. The months spent on the streets will have hardened her. She'll survive Holloway very well."

The thought of incarceration in Holloway Prison made Maisie realize that she had had enough of the conversation. She had hoped to find out more about the police case against Avril Jarvis, but the attempt was proving to be fruitless. She pushed her teacup away to indicate that it was time to leave. Stratton seemed surprised.

"Of course, you will be called as witness by the prosecution."

"As well as for the defense, in cross-examination, Detective Inspector Stratton."

Stratton smiled. "Of course."

As they stood, conversation became general in nature. Then, as Maisie brushed her hand against her forehead, she exposed the dressing concealed by her fringe.

"Heavens, what have you done to yourself?"

"Oh, it's nothing. Just a bit of a whack, I'm afraid. Someone coming through a door as I was leaving, you know the sort of thing."

"You should be careful. Have you had it looked at?"

"Oh, yes. It's all right. Just pinches a bit at times."

"Everything awright, Miss?"

"Yes, thank you, Billy." Maisie had taken off her hat and coat and was settled in a chair by the window, looking at the case map spread out in front of her.

"Stratton any 'elp to us today?"

"Not really, not in terms of Avril Jarvis."

"Well, we can't expect much from 'im really, can we?"

Maisie changed the subject. "You've got your tickets for Taunton?"

"Yes, I'll go down on the early train Saturday, then come back on the last train. I want to get 'ome by the end of the day. You're off to France on Friday then?" Billy was frowning.

"Yes, I'll be leaving early too." Maisie bit into her bottom lip.

Billy frowned even more deeply, then slapped his forehead. "Glad you reminded me. Mrs. Partridge telephoned. Never answered the telephone to *abroad* before, so it was nice to talk to 'er."

"Mrs. Partridge telephoned? What did she say?"

"Oh, it's all right. She said she'd place a call later, so the ol' dog 'n' bone should be ringing any time now." Billy was interrupted by the loud double ring from the black telephone on Maisie's desk. "Talk of the devil. Bet that's 'er now!"

Maisie walked swiftly to the desk and picked up the telephone receiver. "This is Maisie Dobbs."

"Don't you give the number anymore? Has that gone out of fashion?"

"Priscilla!"

"I'm glad you recognized me, old girl."

"Not so much of the old, Pris."

"Sorry. Look, I just wanted to confirm your dates. When will you come to Biarritz? I know that if I don't nag, you won't come."

"It's an expensive nag, isn't it. This telephone call must be costing a fortune."

"When are you coming?"

"I leave for France on Friday, so I would imagine in a week."

"Book your seat, then. I want to make sure you are coming, so I will expect a telegram from Paris with your arrival time next Wednesday or Thursday."

Maisie sighed. "All right."

"Don't sound so dull, Maisie. You'll love it here. You need the break. Now then, how is the flat-hunting going?"

Billy had left the room, so Maisie felt free to speak. "I've actually found a very nice property. In Pimlico, a new block. Rather modern, and only a few streets from the water."

"Ugh."

"What's wrong?"

"Well, Pimlico's not bad, I suppose, but that awful swill they have the cheek to call a river—I bet you were a little mudlark as a child, searching for treasure when the tide went out! But each to her own. When are you moving in?"

"Not so fast, Priscilla. There are some problems."

"Such as?"

"I'm a woman, a spinster. They don't like to give property loans to women."

Priscilla sighed. "Yes, I thought you might run into that old chestnut. But never fear, your friend is here. Leave it to me."

"What do you mean?"

"Just leave it to me. There are people, Maisie, who would drive stakes through their toes rather than offend me, so I will appear to be offended if they do not help."

"Who?"

"My bankers, of course. No, don't consider arguing. The old boys' club isn't just for boys, you know."

"You're not to do anything of the sort. In fact, I forbid it, Pris—I can do this alone."

There was a sigh from Priscilla, who did not counter Maisie's objection but moved instead to the subject of her brother. "Maisie, what about Peter? Do you think there's a chance you'll be able to find out anything?"

"I'll do my best, as you know, but his records have been hard to trace." Maisie continued quickly, to avoid an interruption by Priscilla. "You know, there's something in one of Peter's letters that I am curious about."

"Go on."

"What's all this about roses? Was he interested in flowers?"

Priscilla laughed. "What do you mean?" There was a brief pause, then before Maisie could speak again, the voice on the line continued. "Oh, yes, I know what you're talking about now." Maisie heard her draw upon her cigarette, then cough. "To tell you the truth, I didn't exactly know what he meant, so I just passed over it. I remember thinking it was a reference to Patrick and I was too dense—and tired—to get the joke."

"Yes?"

"Well, when the boys were younger—and remember, I was the youngest and a girl, so I was left out of just about everything—Pat thought they should form a sort of Evernden secret society. They used to run off into the woods, their jackets fastened around their necks like capes, pretending to be highwaymen—you know what boys are like! They would leave letters under one another's pillows, that sort of thing, and they had this special wax seal. I think they'd found it in the attic, where they held their inner-circle meetings, raising old pewter cups filled with ginger beer." Maisie heard Priscilla's voice catch as she spoke of her beloved brothers. "Anyway, the seal was a rose. They'd leave a trail of red wax all over the place and drive my mother mad. As I said, I was definitely left out of the game, but I thought Peter mentioned it in his letter as a reference to Pat and Phil, that they were both well, or something like that."

Maisie frowned, running the telephone cord through her fingers, deep in thought.

"Hello?"

"Sorry, just thinking. Look, there's something you can do for me, Pris. I want you to think—and I do mean *think*; please don't just say you've done it—really think about anything and everything Peter may have said about being in France, even if it's nothing to do with his service."

"All right, I'll think about it. Whatever is going on, Maisie?"

"I'm not sure yet." The conversation was interrupted by an

operator and the call ended. Billy entered the room at that point, so she was slow to replace the receiver. In the one or two seconds before the receiver met with the bar that cut off the line, Maisie heard another click. She lifted the receiver to her ear again. "Hello. Hello? Is anyone there?"

The line was silent.

"So what actually 'appened, Miss?"

"I told you. The operator disconnected the line and then there was another click."

"Well, p'raps you missed the first one, where she pulled out the jack."

"Billy, I heard that. This was different. It was seconds after, as if there was someone else on the line. Listening." Maisie knew she was becoming tense, could feel the muscles in her neck begin to pull.

Billy frowned. "Miss, you'd 'ave to be pretty 'igh up to eavesdrop on a personal line. Mind you, I will tell you this: My mate who works on the exchanges reckons them operator girls sometimes listen to the calls, you know; they wave to each other if they've got a good one on the line so that everyone can get an earful."

"Charming!"

"But I don't reckon the calls that come 'ere are very interestin', not compared to some of 'em, you know, women cryin' over their 'usbands to each other, the more personal goings-on." Billy paused. "Who'd want to listen to what you're sayin' to Mrs. Partridge?"

Maisie was silent for a moment, then replied, "The search for her brother's last known whereabouts has just become even more difficult." She turned and looked at Billy. "It seems that not only are his records missing but, unless I am mistaken in my supposition, he was engaged in very dangerous work during the war."

"Weren't we all, Miss? If you don't mind me sayin' so."

"Granted. Of course you're right. But I believe his work might have been a bit more covert, and I think he tried to tell his sister as much."

"Bit more what?"

"Secret, Billy. I suspect he may have been assigned to an intelligence position—which could be anything from code-breaking to intercepting messages. Who knows? A lot of that kind of work was pretty mundane on a day-to-day basis."

"And a lot of it weren't anything a sane person would do, Miss, and that's a fact."

"Which is why I'm suspicious about the line."

Billy nodded. "Look, I'm going to walk around outside and 'ave a dekko to see if I can see anything unusual. Of course, if someone were listenin' it could be done at the exchange or closer, right 'ere in the buildin' even."

"All right, go on, Billy, though I suspect you won't find any evidence of a listener. In the meantime, we must take care with conversations on the telephone. No details of any cases must be divulged in a telephone call—or in a letter, for that matter. Only in person with the client or anyone with whom we may need to discuss particulars."

"Right you are, Miss."

As soon as Billy left the office, Maisie slumped into a chair by the window and placed her hand on her forehead where the wound from the motor car accident was pounding. *Who is following me? Who tried to kill me? Who is out there, listening?* She began to consider those she had made inquiries with over the past two weeks: Avril Jarvis, Priscilla, Madeleine Hartnell. Then there was Jeremy Hazleton and his wife. Sir Cecil Lawton, along with the manservant, Brayley. And of course Stratton. *Think. Think. Who would wish me dead—and why?*

APART FROM PACKING, Maisie had only one more commitment before she set off on Friday morning via train for Dover: the meeting with Lord Julian. The travel plans were now finally set. To avoid coming into London, Maurice would join Maisie's train at Ashford, and they would travel together to the ferry connect with the Golden Arrow's ferry service. During her absence, work would begin on the MG. She had received the estimate for repairs, and Eric had taken his favorite motor along to the garage where it would remain for several weeks. He had promised to visit the repair shop several times to check on progress, to ensure that the MG came back, in Eric's words, "spick-and-span."

Maisie arrived at the red-brick offices belonging to the Compton Company on Arbuthnot Street fifteen minutes early, according to the clock on the outside of the building. She decided to walk for a while to ensure that all the necessary questions were in her mind, ready to put to Lord Julian, should the opportunity arise. Maisie loved the City, the legacy encapsulated in that one square mile of London. There was something about this area and its proximity to the river that was a lifeblood—a poisoned lifeblood—of such a powerful place. *Perhaps there is something here for me*, thought Maisie, as she waited for the moments to tick by until her appointment.

"Maisie, jolly good to see you!" Lord Julian stepped forward from his desk and came around to shake her hand. His secretary left the room with her head slightly bowed.

Maisie took the seat indicated by her former employer. "It's kind of you to see me, Lord Julian."

"Not at all, but I'm a bit overextended on time, I'm afraid." He handed an envelope containing several sheets of paper to Maisie. "Here are some of my notes on Hazleton. Only had access to the files for a very brief period, you understand."

"Thank you, I'll read them this evening. Did anything stand out?"

Lord Julian shook his head. "Not really. It all seemed rather a shame, actually. He appears to have been a fine young man—not that he isn't now; that's not it. But you'll see that originally a far better prognosis regarding the outcome of his wounds was put forward. Must have been terrible for the poor fellow to relapse and end up in a wheelchair when at first they thought a couple of canes might do."

"I see." Maisie frowned and flipped open the envelope. Remembering Lord Julian's limited time, she apologized, replaced the notes, and put the envelope into her document case.

"I am most grateful. Thank you, Lord Julian," said Maisie, standing.

"A pleasure. Anything else while I am still here?" It was a perfunctory offer, with no reply anticipated. She was quick to respond.

"Actually, I do have one question," said Maisie. "And no answer is required at this moment, but please let me know if anything comes to mind."

"Go on."

"Lord Julian, do you have any contacts in military intelligence? Anyone you served with at the War Office who would be able to trace records belonging to someone who may have been with the intelligence corps? I need confirmation of an affiliation."

Lord Julian shook his head. "Not me. I can't think of anyone I could call upon; there were, after all, different intelligence organizations. And wasn't the corps—such as it's been since the war—disbanded last year?" He paused. "Of course, there are those I know, but with that sort of work, we're going into a different type of terrain." He paused, then smiled. "But Maisie, *you* know the very person who could probably answer all of your questions."

"I know someone? Who?"

Lord Julian laughed. "And I thought you knew everything!"

"Who is it?"

"Why, Blanche, of course. Talk to Maurice."

"Maurice?"

"Yes. What do you think he was doing in the war, Maisie?"

Maisie shook her head, now spinning with convergent thoughts once more. "I—I knew he worked all over Europe, and even in Mesopotamia. And I knew it was highly confidential. I just always thought it was political, to do with his contacts, those people he'd known forever. But intelligence?"

"Our Maurice has a finger in a lot of pies, Maisie. He is the sharpest, most acute man I have ever known. I expect he will take the true extent of his wartime exploits to his grave, but I do know one thing: He was involved with the secret service and with several branches of military intelligence."

Maisie nodded, thanked Lord Julian again, and left the building quickly. Rushing along the narrow streets with tall buildings on either side, she made her way toward the water. Dusk was falling, the smog a yellow vapor around her, the light casting shadows that appeared alongside her as if they were ghostly street urchins from another time. Maurice. *Maurice?* Was his request to join her on this excursion a coincidence? Or was it motivated by something else. *I knew that something was wrong.* But what did she know? Maurice's voice echoed down the years. *It's guesswork, hard work, guesswork again and supposition, taking what we have learned and applying it to what we know now, even when the cases are different. All cases challenge us: to reconsider who we are, how we see ourselves in this world, and how we view the past, the present, and the future from the unique observation point of our individual humanity. The needling out of information, of knowledge, is like trying to remove the tiniest splinter from a finger. The trick is to tease out truth without causing blood to flow—literally and figuratively—our own or that of another human being.*

Could it all be coincidence? No. *No.* One of her first lessons from Maurice, the one that was repeated time and time again in case after case until it was imprinted on her very soul, was: *Coincidence is a messenger sent by truth.*

And what was the truth of Maurice's insistence on traveling with her? *I will have to remember every single lesson, every single move and conversation.* The words came to Maisie instinctively as she watched the water flow murkily on its way downriver, toward the gushing torrent where the Thames met the sea. And she hoped against hope, especially now, especially when she needed her mentor more than ever before, that she and Maurice would be working not against each other, but together.

PART TWO

France, September 1930

FIFTEEN

Maisie left London before seven in the morning, her clothes, books, and papers packed in a small case of dark brown leather with straps across to ensure her belongings were secure. She carried her black document case and wore a gray-and-blue tweed jacket with a pale gray silk blouse, light gray woolen trousers, black shoes, and, to top off her ensemble, a dark gray hat with a broader brim than usual, a black band and a dark blue feather on the side, which was attached to the band with a deep blue stone in a sapphire cut. She had collected her watch from the mender's yesterday, and it was now pinned in its customary place on the left-hand lapel of her jacket. The clothes were not new, though she had retrimmed the hat herself recently. But the case was very new, a gift from Dene delivered the day before. Two hours after that first delivery, a large box of chocolates arrived for Maisie, and included a simple message: *With love.* The second gift caused Maisie to shake her head, for she knew Dene to be impulsive at times and had recently taken to sending her chocolates. She had not the heart to tell him she did not care for such sweets and, as usual, left the box in the kitchen with a note: *Help yourselves!*

Carrying her mackintosh over her arm, she boarded the train

clutching her luggage tightly. She had telephoned her father the night before, wishing deeply that she were traveling to his cottage and the embracing familiarity of the place that was now firmly his home, though he was London born and bred.

"Who's that?" Her father's words upon picking up the telephone receiver always caused Maisie to smile.

"It's me, Dad, unless you were expecting someone else."

Her father laughed. "It's this bloomin' piece of nonsense. Can't get used to the thing."

"At least I know I can reach you if I need to." Maisie paused. She could feel her father's tension, though he did not speak. "Well, I'm off tomorrow, so I thought I would telephone. I'll see you on the way back. I'll come straight to Chelstone from Dover when we arrive back in England."

"Will you be awright, love?"

"Yes, of course, you know me. I'm always all right."

There was a pause before her father continued. "I do know you, Maisie, and I know this little shindig over there is botherin' you."

"I said I'll be all right."

"Well, I know what your mother would say."

Maisie shivered and once again felt a sudden urge to turn around.

"What did you say, love?"

"I said, what would Mum have said?"

Frankie Dobbs was slow in responding, and Maisie knew that even after all these years, he ached for the company of his wife. "I reckon she would have told you to get on over there to France. She would have told you to slay your dragons, Maisie. Do your work and slay your dragons. Then come home."

Maisie reflected upon his words as the train pulled out of Charing Cross Station and knew he was right. Her father, whom she had never taken to be a philosopher, was absolutely right. She must do her work, slay her dragons, and then come home.

. . .

THE TRAIN PUFFED and chugged its way though Kent. Sitting by the window, Maisie delighted in seeing a fresh ground-mist lingering above the fields. She loved this time of year in Kent, when autumn was in the air, the leaves just beginning to turn, their pale yellows and deeper greens a promise of the rich reds, browns, and golds to come. And this was hop-picking time, the train almost full of Londoners on their way to Paddock Wood, to Goudhurst, Charing, Yalding, Cranbrook, and Hawkhurst, and to every other Kentish town and village with farms where the hops were hanging heavy on the bines, waiting to be picked. Of course, many had already traveled by charabanc, others in lorries laden to the gills with boxes, but many would take the train to Tonbridge, then change for the branch lines that would deliver them to their final destination. Pots and pans, folded bed linens pushed into old pillowcases and tied with string, shabby suitcases, boxes, and tilly lamps were stowed in the luggage racks, and throughout her journey, Maisie sat silently and smiled, listening to the banter she knew so very well. The talk was of how the hops might be in this field or that field, for this grand exodus of Londoners went to the same farms each year and knew the land as well as any country farmworker. They talked about the hopper huts, whom they might see, and the singsongs they would have at night when the picking was done. Maisie almost wished she were going with them instead of to France.

The next stop was Ashford, and as the train began to slow, Maisie pulled down the window, looking out for Maurice. Finally she saw him, standing on the platform, two suitcases held by the Comptons' chauffeur.

"Maurice!"

"There she is, sir, over there." George pointed to Maisie, and Maurice looked up.

Expecting Maurice to step up into the carriage, Maisie frowned when a porter joined them and then boarded the train while they waited on the platform.

"This way, miss." He took Maisie's luggage from the rack and indicated for her to follow him.

"Where are we going?"

"Gentleman said you'd be in second class, so we're moving you to first. He's got the tickets."

Maisie shook her head and followed the porter, who took her to join Maurice, now settled in the first-class carriage. After the porter had stowed Maisie's new leather case, Maurice pressed a coin into his hand and waved through the window to George, who touched his cap and turned to leave the station.

"This is rather extravagant." Maisie settled into the seat, placing her document case next to her. She automatically let her hand remain on the case, then saw that Maurice had noticed and removed her hand quickly.

Blanche smiled. "Yes, perhaps. Though when one reaches my age, one is inclined to indulge in comforts where one can. I thought it would give us an opportunity to speak in confidence, Maisie—to reconnect with each other in person. It has been some months."

"Since early summer, Maurice."

"Ah, yes, and you have been seeing more of Andrew."

Maisie blushed. Andrew Dene was another protégé of Maurice Blanche, though not as close as herself. "Yes, we've spent time together. He's good company."

"Oh, I think there's more to it than that." Maurice looked out of the window for a moment. "Well, on Andrew's part anyway. I would have thought you were very well matched, the two of you."

"As I said, he's good company. I enjoy our time together."

"May an old gentleman make an observation?"

Maisie inclined her head. She wanted very much to say no but instead replied, "Of course."

"Well, just one comment; then let's discuss the true purpose of your journey and your case."

"Go on."

"You know, particularly where Andrew is concerned, I think it may well be possible for you to have your cake and eat it."

"I don't know what—"

Maurice held up his hand. "That's all, Maisie. Now then, the case of the aviator."

Maisie paused for a moment, then opened her document case and took out a map. She moved to sit next to Maurice, the map on her knees. Maurice took out his spectacles, placed them on his nose, and looked at the point Maisie indicated.

"This is where Ralph Lawton's De Havilland went down. It was just outside Reims, in the village of Sainte-Marie, which was occupied by the Germans. The German authorities went through the correct channels of notification, and his remains—well, such as they were; I understand the remains in this case comprised only metal identification tags that were all but melted—his remains were repatriated after the war and now lie in the cemetery at Auchon-Villiers."

Maurice took off his spectacles and frowned. "Maisie, it is awfully difficult to completely incinerate a human body, as you know. Your studies in Edinburgh would have encompassed the effects of fire on flesh and bone."

"Granted. However, this particular aeroplane, the Airco D.H.4, was not referred to as the Flaming Coffin for nothing. The fuel tank was situated precariously in a position that resulted in the most horrible outcome if shot down. It was a long-range craft equipped with a powerful twelve-cylinder engine that would give over six hours of flying time and therefore had a huge fuel capacity. Now—"

"You have become an expert on aviation."

Maisie shook her head. "Not really. James Compton was an enormous help, and I have access to Ralph's flight records, as well as his personal journal."

She looked at Maurice, watching his response. He gave away nothing but simply nodded and replaced his spectacles, peering toward the map. Maisie continued.

"Now, this craft was generally used for bombing runs into enemy territory and would usually have an observer, but it was also quite nimble, able to make fast and accurate changes in direction. Interestingly enough, Ralph was flying alone that day and was not carrying bombs; the journey would have been quite swift, with the plane easy to maneuver."

"I see."

"So what was he doing with no bombs and no observer over enemy territory? Why didn't he try to fly back across Allied lines before crashing? He was an experienced aviator, one who would never let his aeroplane get into enemy hands—even if he knew it would burn to a cinder."

Maurice removed his spectacles again. "Remind me of your remit, Maisie."

"To prove that he is dead."

"Then I see no need to investigate Ralph Lawton's assignment at the time of his death. You need only to corroborate accounts of his death, visit the grave and you have completed your task."

Maisie frowned. "But Maurice, we've always worked diligently, answering each and every question that arises in order to come to a completion of our case. It is how you have taught me; it is ingrained in the way I work."

"That was not always possible when I worked alone, as you are doing now."

"I'm not alone. I have Billy."

"Your having Billy is not the same as my having you for an assistant."

"What do you mean? Billy has been an excellent choice." Maisie sensed the annoyance rising. She had never before felt this way with Maurice.

"Billy is a good choice, yes. He is a workhorse, without a doubt. But with you, I had no need for constant vigilance." He paused. "One constructs one's business according to one's resources. I was most fortunate in being able to entrust so much to you. I sense that you do not have the same advantage, so you must, on occasion, take the case at face value, do only what you must to conclude, and move on."

Maisie shook her head in disbelief. "Maurice, I must continue with this case as I have planned, and I must follow where the clues, guesses, and suppositions take me. Clearly there must be an end to such a case, and we both know there is a time limit. But I will go forward according to my training from you and according to that which I feel is right."

Maurice regarded Maisie intently. "Indeed. But at what cost?"

Maisie felt her eyes prickle at the corners. *He knows. He knows I am distressed.* At that moment the train began to decrease speed to an idle chugging as it approached Dover. She turned to look out of the window again, knowing Maurice's eyes were still on her. *But what if he wants me to draw back for another reason. Is he here to hamper my inquiries? Is that why he came?*

"Ah, we have arrived." Maurice looked at his pocket watch. "I think we have time for a good lunch before the Golden Arrow arrives and we board the ferry with the other passengers. You know what they say about travel by sea, Maisie. A good lining to the stomach!"

A porter came aboard to collect the luggage and Maisie stepped down from the carriage, turning to ensure that Maurice was on secure footing as he alighted onto the platform. And as she took his hand, she felt a shiver move along her arm into her neck. Her stomach lurched. The dragon was awake.

FOLLOWING LUNCH IN the dining room of the Railway Inn, Maisie excused herself. Making her way to the hotel reception desk, she asked to use the telephone and was directed along the corridor to a wooden booth with concertina doors. Maisie looked around her, wishing she could shake off the constant sense that someone was watching her. Reaching the telephone, she closed the doors behind her and pulled the bolt across to ensure privacy. She dialed All Saints Convalescent Hospital in the Old Town, Hastings, and when the call was answered she pressed the button to connect.

"May I speak to Dr. Dene, please?"

"Yes, of course, I'll put you through."

Maisie imagined the receptionist turning to the others in the administration office and raising her eyebrows as she said, "Miss Dobbs, isn't it?" Could there be another who called? wondered Maisie.

"Maisie, darling!" Dene's enthusiastic greeting dispelled any doubts in her mind, though she had worried since Priscilla commented on his bachelorhood at a time when there was a surfeit of women her age in search of a sweetheart. "Shouldn't you be on the high seas by now?"

"Another hour or so, Andrew."

There was a strained silence for a moment.

"I take it that you managed to fit everything into the case?"

"Oh, yes, Andrew, it's perfect. Just perfect. Thank you again—and thank you for the chocolates."

"Chocolates?"

Maisie frowned. "Yes. The box arrived this morning, special delivery."

There was a delay of several seconds before Dene replied. "Well, I'm clearly not your sole admirer. And here I was thinking I was the only one who sent you chocolates."

"But, Andrew—"

"Perhaps they were sent by a grateful client."

"Yes, of course. I wonder. . . ." Maisie could barely concentrate.

"Is there anything you need, Maisie?" Dene had already sensed that the telephone call might not have been made for sentimental reasons, though they had not seen each other for several weeks.

Maisie brought her thoughts back to the present. "Actually, Andrew, there is. I need your expertise."

"*My* expertise? Gosh, do I look as if I have criminal tendencies?" Dene laughed.

Maisie checked her watch, then with one hand reached into her document case, which she had placed on the small triangular wooden seat in the corner of the telephone box. She pulled out the notes given to her by Lord Julian concerning Jeremy Hazleton. "No, it's your medical knowledge that I'm after, Andrew, you're the only orthopedic surgeon I know."

"And you certainly don't know any cranial experts, do you; you didn't keep your appointment to have that head of yours looked at!"

"It was kind of you to arrange it, Andrew, but there was no time. Anyway, my head feels much better. Now then, it's about a man who sustained injuries that have led to paralysis, though at first it was thought he would have a better outcome. Look, if I just read out these notes from the attending physicians, could you tell me what it all means?"

"Fire away, my intrepid one, fire away!"

Some fifteen minutes later, Maisie replaced the receiver, promising to telephone Dene as soon as she was on home soil upon her return from France. Her curiosity regarding Hazleton had deepened, for Dene's comments and assessment had served to broaden the gray areas evident in the MP's medical history. But there was something bothering her even more as she reached for her purse, which was tucked into a corner of the document case. She took out a coin and lifted the receiver once again, hoping that all was as it should be at Ebury Place. She hoped her call would reach Sandra in time. The double ring repeated several times. Maisie's frown deepened.

"The Compton residence."

"Sandra? Sandra, listen, there's—"

"Oh, m'um, it's you!" Sandra exclaimed, as if she had been running.

"Sandra, is everything all right?"

"Well, I don't know if it is." She began to weep, then checked herself. "I'm sorry, m'um."

"What's wrong?" Maisie clutched the receiver to her ear.

"It's Teresa. Been taken very poorly, she has. The doctor's here now and they're taking her to the infirmary. His Lordship has said—"

"What's the matter with her?" The apprehension was clear in Maisie's voice.

"She was working away, m'um, then suddenly—it was only a few hours after you left—well, she just sort of keeled over, clutching her belly and crying. She was screaming with the pain."

"Oh, God!" Maisie could feel the pain increasing inside her, a sympathetic discomfort as the story unfolded.

"It was the middle of the morning, and Teresa said, 'Well, if no one else is going to dig in, I'm going to have one of those chocolates that Miss gave us, set me up for a good day's work it will, a bit of chocolate.' So, she digs in, has a bite out of one of the chocolates, and says, 'Oooh, that's too bitter for me. It's that dark chocolate; I prefer it sweeter.' So she pushes the box away and off she goes with the polishes, but then she starts screaming—"

"Is she all right?" Maisie could hear the cry in her voice.

"We called the doctor straightaway. I got a glass of salty water, m'um, and made her drink it, held her head up and poured it down her. Then I stuck my fingers down her throat, so she'd bring whatever it was up again and—"

"What does the doctor say?"

"He's pumped her out and he reckons she'll be all right, though she'll be poorly for a while."

"And what about the chocolates, are they safe?"

"Oh, safe as houses, m'um. I said straightaway, I know where those are going."

Maisie held her breath, anticipating the reply from the always-efficient Sandra.

"I opened the door to the kitchen fire—I'd just stoked it up to start making a batch of bread—and I threw them in, I did. Can't have chocolates that have gone bad lying around."

"Oh, no!"

"Did I do something wrong, m'um? I do think Dr. Dene ought to know, so as he can go back to the confectioners and—"

"The box of chocolates wasn't from Dr. Dene."

"Oh." Sandra began to understand. "Oh, dear me. Oh, m'um, I *am* sorry, I didn't think. I should have kept them, shouldn't I?"

Maisie knew that poor Sandra had been through enough already. "Look, Sandra, tell the doctor that you will require a complete report. Ask him what substances would have such an effect on a person. If you have any problems, please inform Lord Julian that you have spoken to me and I will need to see the doctor's assessment regarding the cause of Teresa's sickness."

"Oh, m'um . . ."

"Lord Julian will understand—and he won't bite you, Sandra, you know that. Just give him my message."

"Yes, m'um."

"And you are sure Teresa will be all right?"

"Yes, m'um, that's what the doctor said. But I'd better go. She's being moved to the infirmary soon and we've got to keep at her with the water. Doctor says she's got to keep drinking. I tell you, m'um, we're all at sixes and sevens."

"I will call you tomorrow, from France."

"From France, m'um?"

"Yes. Tell Teresa that I am thinking of her. I am so sorry."

"Oh, it's not your fault, m'um. Who was to know that the chocolate was off?"

Maisie ended the call and leaned against the door. *Another attempt.* She closed her eyes. *I must be doubly vigilant.* She thought of Teresa. *And not only for myself.* Finally, pulling back the concertina doors, Maisie stepped into the dimly lit corridor. Maurice Blanche was standing just a few yards away.

"Maurice! I thought you were going to enjoy a pipe before we left the hotel."

Blanche took out his pocket watch, checked the time, and snapped the silver cover. "We had better be off, Maisie. Our ferry will be leaving soon. Come along."

Maisie tensed again. From the moment they stepped into the taxi-cab, visions of the past haunted her once more. She had not crossed the English Channel since her days as a nurse, clustered together with her fellow members of the Voluntary Aid Detachment. She remembered hearing the *ba-boom* of cannonade in the distance, the pitching and tossing of the vessel, and the terrible sickness that gripped her from the moment she boarded. And she remembered the rain that soaked through her cape and the damp, the seeping, smelling damp that remained with her every day of her service in France, a damp she could still feel, even on the warmest summer's day. As the taxi-cab made its way to the port, Maisie turned to Maurice and recounted the conversation with Sandra, watching him frown, nodding as she spoke. She felt warmed by the exchange, for it seemed like old times. His concern revealed his regard for her and for her work. Was her doubt a sign of her own distress? She thought of the accident on Tottenham Court Road, of the hand that had reached out to push her in front of the train, and, now, of a gift of chocolate laced with poison. No. Someone was out to kill her.

They were shown to the first-class lounge and chose to sit in a far corner, alone. Maisie simply hoped for a millpond sea, a calm crossing into the past, for the present was becoming as dangerous as anything she had ever known.

THE FERRY DEPARTED promptly, for the Flèche d'Or train service to Paris would leave Calais at ten past two on the dot. Maisie remained in the lounge for just a few moments, then decided that her already unsettled stomach would benefit from a walk on deck. Perhaps it was best to spend the entire passage looking out at the horizon, a level point to concentrate her thoughts. Though there was much to occupy her—Teresa, Ralph Lawton, Peter Evernden, the fact that she really didn't want to go to Biarritz—she found it was the voices from the past that accompanied her across the Channel. The noisy chatter of Iris, the nurse with whom she had served at the casualty clearing station; the calming deckhand who had pressed hot cocoa and cake into her red raw hands and told her to drink and eat to stop the queasiness. In 1916 her ship was no ferry, but a requisitioned freighter taking supplies and horses over to France, the animals lined on the deck and tacked up ready to be mounted as soon as they docked in Le Havre. But the destination wasn't Le Havre this time, wasn't a port teeming with battalions of troops from across the globe, young men to replace those who had died in their tens of thousands in France and Belgium. Yet there *was* a reminder of the war, as Maisie bought a cup of tea and proceeded along the deck to a quiet place where she could lean and look out across the whitecaps toward France. Many of those on the ferry were making their pilgrimage to the last resting place of a loved one. Maisie watched as two women walked along in front of her, each wearing a linen poppy on a lapel, a poppy they would leave behind to say, *I have come. I have not forgotten.* Were they mother and daughter-in-law, perhaps? If Simon had died, would Maisie have made such a journey with Margaret Lynch, his mother? And would Margaret have one day touched her on the arm and said, "Life must go on, Maisie dear. He's passed now, and you are of the living."

Maisie sipped her tea and turned again to the gray-green sea, to the prow of the ship rising and falling and the bow wave crashing across the foredeck. Could she ever properly explain how time had passed, how she had buried her love for Simon for years and pressed on with her work, her mind settled if not soothed by the demands of being assistant to Maurice Blanche? And now, what would Margaret Lynch say to her, if she allowed their paths to cross? Would she say, "Ah, you came, after all this time, you came. But he is lost, so go now. You have made your peace, move on." Maisie knew Simon's mother was happy to know that she visited him, that even though she went only once a month, he would not be forgotten when she herself was gone.

Maisie finished her tea and walked along the deck, pulling her mackintosh collar up around her neck and her hat more firmly down on her head. The dark clouds overhead were a portent of the weather that would accompany them on their journey, and Maisie smiled. It was a smile of irony, for the weather exactly mirrored her recollections of the war. Though there had been fine days, days that were hot, days when the flies tormented the dying and living alike, there always seemed to be a darkness when Maisie recalled that time in her life. And now she was facing it all over again, looking back at the past to understand the present. How she felt for Agnes Lawton, for the ache that had grown out of all control, for the grief that consumed her mind, leading her to the doors of those who would exploit her. What was it about Hartnell that caused Maisie to reflect upon her time and time again? She had played games with the mind of a sick woman. *How dare she!* Maisie hit her hand against the guardrail, causing several people to look her way and then back at one another. Amid the excitement of late holidaymakers there was always a contingent of mourners, the sad and bereaved, so her impulsive action was quickly ignored.

Then there was Avril Jarvis. What new information had Billy acquired? Would he have anything that might help in her quest to lessen the sentence against the child? And what of the girl herself? Maisie knew immediately that Jarvis was no ordinary streetwalker but one whose gifts sustained her in unimaginable circumstances. Such gifts must not be squandered.

"Ah, there you are!"

Maisie turned. "Maurice. Are you refreshed?"

Blanche rested his forearms on the guardrail. "Indeed. The value of taking a short nap is underestimated, Maisie. You would do well to acquire the skill, though I believe that such an inclination is the preserve of those of us in our more mature years."

Maisie smiled and reached inside her mackintosh to check the time. "Not long now." She turned toward the prow. "Yes, look, there's the port. About twenty minutes, do you think?"

Maurice squinted as he looked forward. "Yes. About twenty minutes." He turned to Maisie. "Now then, what have you been thinking about, my friend?"

Maisie leaned on the guardrail again and exhaled. "Oh, you know, the crossings I made when I was a nurse."

"You were only a child at the time."

"I was old enough, Maurice. Many of the boys were younger than I, and we were all old enough to die." She was aware that her tone was short.

Maurice nodded. "Yes, of course." He paused. "And you have no doubt been replaying those journeys in your mind. The scenes you encountered then are before you now even as we speak, are they not?"

"Yes." Maisie did not look at Maurice but at the horizon again.

"And that will continue to happen as this journey progresses. However, Maisie, I have this to say."

"Go on." She turned again to Blanche.

"You should allow yourself to indulge in this remembrance. When you face the past, all you will see is that which has gone before. So I have some advice: Let this be your turning point. Have done with it, and turn to face the future. Only then will the future rise up to meet you. Only then will the distress pass."

Maisie swallowed and made ready to reply, and as she did so it was as if her mother were at her side, for her voice was so clear. *Your father's right, Maisie. Slay those dragons.*

Maurice inclined his head, but this time he did not smile. Maisie touched his arm and returned to the lounge. Collecting her leather luggage and document case, she recognized the feeling that enveloped her. She had been just eighteen then, ready to disembark, to join the throng en route for Rouen, where they would receive orders. Seasickness had gripped her throughout that first crossing, but in the moment just before she stepped onto French soil, she had reminded herself that she was here to serve with strength and compassion, calling upon everything she had learned at the London Hospital and under the tutelage of Maurice Blanche. Now, on this journey, she was in her salad days no longer and she had much, much more to draw upon. She left the lounge quickly to join Maurice and the Flèche d'Or, which would have them in Paris by thirty-five minutes past five.

SIXTEEN

There was little conversation during the journey into Paris. For Maisie, there was only a window to the past as towns, fields, and villages swept by. Was this how France had looked before the war, before the landscape was changed beyond all recognition, before she herself was changed forever? What fears and resentments remained beneath the surface, as communities were rebuilt to mirror the homes, churches, and shops razed to the ground amid constant shelling? Many of the old foundations had survived bombardment and were now used as templates for the massive reconstruction still in progress. How strange it was that the country was like a human being, a different self on the outside but with the old memories, deeply held, buried under the new.

Down through France they traveled, lulled by the *clickety-clack, clickety-clack* of wheel against track. The place-names of battles past echoed in Maisie's mind. First Bethune and Lens; then, to the east, Vimy and Arras; now through the Somme Valley, the once-terrible Somme Valley; then on to Amiens. *Clickety-clack, clickety-clack.* How many are still here, buried, in this place, ten thousand? Twenty thousand? Perhaps one hundred thousand lay at rest beneath fields ready for harvest, healthy crops now growing where millions died. *And what about Peter Evernden, where does he lie?*

They arrived in Paris, where Maurice had reserved rooms at a small exclusive hotel close to the Seine, the Hotel Richmonde. Maisie had no real need to linger in Paris, though in his journal Ralph Lawton spoke of leave spent there with his "dear friend." Was that person Jeremy Hazleton? Could there have been another he would not name? A café was mentioned, and a hotel. She would visit both tomorrow.

Following a light supper during which she and Maurice went over plans for the following day, Maisie returned to her room. She would leave for Reims on Sunday. Until then, in addition to her work, she would also indulge Maurice, who wished to spend time in the company of old friends and invited Maisie to join him with the comment, "You have been starved of such intellectual encounter for some time, Maisie. It will do you good, and you will be able to test your retention of the French language."

The plans settled, there was little to say. Maisie wondered whether she should apologize for her shortness on the channel crossing. She had been aware of resentment building and knew that soon it would surely come to the surface.

ONCE IN HER room, Maisie bathed and then sat on the floor in her dressing gown with her legs crossed. As she sat in silence, unaware of noises from the street outside, still bustling with night owls intent upon remaining awake until dawn, the image in her mind was of those early days of the war, days when she was full of her move to Girton and to a life she had hardly dared imagine. Then that first journey back to Chelstone for Christmas, 1914. Maisie saw again the mass of khaki on the station platforms, standing aside as troop trains went through, and the endless farewells, the stubborn smiles of those who dearly hoped to see a son, brother, or sweetheart again. Hadn't they said it would all be over by now, those politicians, those men who knew? And then her excitement at seeing her father. And Maurice. Maurice had been in London and, it was said, overseas, perhaps France, perhaps Holland. No one really knew, and he said nothing when she went to visit him, simply smiled as she recounted stories of Girton.

"Tell me about your friends, Maisie," he said, "for I hope you have made a friend or two." Maurice had worried that Maisie's standing might have prevented her from seeking close associations.

"Priscilla Evernden is my best friend. Oh, she's very funny at times, really doesn't care for her studies, and spends most of her time planning her next outing. She's a little older than I."

"I see." Maurice relit his pipe and smiled. He was pleased.

"When I scold her about her studies, she simply says the boys, her brothers, keep their parents happy with their accomplishments, especially Peter. He's the eldest, about twenty-five or -six, I think."

"Are they overseas?"

"Yes, they've all enlisted. Priscilla says Peter will do best of all over there, because he's such a whiz with languages."

Maurice smiled. He was fluent in six languages in addition to his native French. "That's rare for an Englishman."

Maisie had been unaware that her excitement was building as she spoke of her friend and her rough-and-tumble yet very wealthy household. "Well, Priscilla says it's a gift and no one knows where he gets it from. He doesn't even know himself. Apparently it was while they were on a holiday in Switzerland when he was about twelve; suddenly Peter began speaking in French and then German to other people in the hotel, and the whole family looked at him aghast."

Maurice paid close attention as Maisie continued.

"He wondered what it was all about and told Priscilla he thought everyone could understand other languages just like that." Maisie snapped her fingers. "I wish I could."

As the scene replayed in her head, Maisie watched again, this time from a distance of sixteen years, as Maurice picked up his pen and wrote something on a sheet of paper. She had glanced only briefly before launching into the next part of her story and barely wondered at the time why Maurice had written PETER EVERNDEN in capital letters. Then he had looked at her and smiled.

"You're doing very well, my dear. I am proud of you."

MAISIE WOKE EARLY on Saturday, dressed quickly, and left the hotel. It was a fine morning with only a few clouds, but a chilly breeze reminded her that the cold nip of autumn was not that far away. Wandering along the busy street, she watched as awnings came down and shops opened for business, many owners completing the morning ritual of washing the pavement. She slowed as the shopkeeper in front of her made a final swab back and forth, twisted the mop to squeeze out excess water, picked up the bucket, and threw the water across the pavement.

"*Ah, pardon, mademoiselle. Excusez-moi, s'il vous plaît.*"

She had forgotten quite how to say "Not to worry. It's all right," so instead she lifted her hand and smiled. The shopkeeper touched his temple with a forefinger, smiled in return, and went back into the shop.

Street cafés were bustling already, with conversation in English and French crackling back and forth and a medley of accents revealing visitors as well as an expatriate community from America, Britain, Spain, Italy, and Africa. Maisie looked at her watch. She would join Maurice for breakfast at nine, so there was time for a cup of coffee before she made her way back to the hotel.

"*Café au lait, s'il vous plaît.*"

The waiter gave a sharp bow and disappeared into the café, stopping en route to pick up a tip, which he inspected first, shaking his head before placing the money in the front pocket of his long white apron.

Maisie sat back in her seat, observing the café's patrons around her. Many were clearly regulars of some tenure, such as the man wearing tweed trousers and jacket that did not match, a monocle pressed against his eye as he unfolded a newspaper, which he read while waiting for coffee and a croissant he had no need to order, for his choice of breakfast never changed. Then there were the two well-dressed women, fashionably attired in late-summer wear of linen and silk. Coco Chanel had made sun-kissed skin a desirable accessory only a year earlier, and these women had clearly taken heed, their faces, hands, and slender ankles suggesting a summer spent on the Riviera. Maisie inspected her own pale hands as she took a mirror from her handbag, snapped back the pewter lid, and looked at her reflection. She pinched her cheeks, then looked up to see the women watching her. They turned quickly, each lifting a cup to her lips. Maisie's attention was drawn away from the women by a group of Americans nearby. Voices were raised, members of the set shifting in their seats, men and women eager to both hear and voice opinions.

"Listen, pal, I think the man will be good for Germany."

"What? Have you read his book, *Mein Kampf*? The man is nuts. Nuts!"

Another man spoke while lighting a cigarette for one of the women, who leaned forward. "Thanks, Frank." She turned from the one who flipped the lighter top with a "You're welcome" and offered her own opinion. "Look, don't you think it'd be a good idea if we all just shut up and let the guy do his job for a while? I agree his ways are strange—all those guys in brown shirts are a bit creepy—but he's brought a lot of hope to the German people. His party was at the bottom of the heap, and now it's second in the polls. Just give him a chance!" She inhaled deeply and was about to continue, when another man leaned into the conversation.

"Give him a chance? Who knows what might happen. If you ask me—"

"Which we weren't, Brad."

Brad held up his hand for emphasis, as everyone laughed at the interruption. "I said, if you ask me, it's trouble down the line. Real trouble."

And so the conversation went on, until the one named Frank stood up. "Am I the only one going to work today?"

The group laughed, beating on the table with their palms, creating such noise that other patrons shook their heads and turned back to their breakfast, perhaps opening a newspaper in front of them with a snap that might have been audible if the Americans had not been so noisy.

"So, what is it today, Frank, an hour's shut-eye and then a thousand words by lunchtime to keep the *Trib* happy, followed by a Pernod for a job well done?"

Standing, Frank addressed the group, his hands resting on the back of his chair. "No rich old man to keep me in clover in sunny Paree. See y'all back here tonight." He scanned the faces. "Martha? Stu? Brad?"

Voices agreed in unison and then, as Frank left, the conversation turned to other matters, and it dawned on Maisie that this was not an early breakfast for the group but the tail end of a night out. Was this the sort of life Priscilla imagined for her? And if this was the life she had missed—well, would she really miss it if it did pass her by?

"*Café au lait.*" The waiter stood in front of Maisie.

"*Ah, merci beaucoup.*" Maisie smiled, picking up the large cup, the blend of freshly ground coffee and hot milk already teasing her to taste the scalding beverage. She blew across the surface, causing a film of foam to push back against the cup, and sipped slowly. More memories surged forth, of a leave in Rouen, of dinner with Simon. Maisie smiled. There were good memories along with the bad; indeed, she knew some people who thought the war brought out the best in them and almost hankered for those days of camaraderie, of purpose. Maisie bore no such desire and, as she scanned the faces around her, reflected on her fortune and the man who had nurtured her educational and professional success. *Oh, Maurice, what is going on?* She finished her coffee, her thoughts on plans for today and tomorrow and then the continuation of her journey.

. . .

MAISIE AND MAURICE took breakfast in the hotel dining room. It was a light, airy room, a former courtyard that now had a high ceiling of glass panes that gave the impression of being in a grand Regency orangery, the morning light casting shadows down upon the flagstone floor and dancing upon fountains embedded in the rough stone wall. Ivy grew up and across the walls, while green rubbery trees planted in large rough terra-cotta pots stood in the four corners. The tables were each clad in a white damask cloth topped with a delicate posy of flowers arranged in a small glass jar. The cast-iron chairs were more comfortable than they seemed at first. Maisie ensured that Maurice was seated before taking her place opposite him. A waiter brought a basket of small fresh warm baguettes, croissants, and brioches, then left, and returned with a silver pot of fresh strong coffee and a matching jug of hot frothy milk.

"*Merci beaucoup.*" Maurice spoke French with the accent of a Parisian.

Maisie smiled as Maurice indicated that she should help herself first. She took a croissant, which she spread with butter and jam. Maurice tore off a piece of baguette, spread it with jam, and dipped it in the large cup of black coffee he had poured for himself. Maisie helped herself to milk, which she added to the coffee Maurice had poured for her.

"So: your agenda for today, Maisie?"

"I think I should ask you, Maurice. After all, you are the one with a social circle here."

Maurice smiled, dipped more baguette into his coffee, and outlined his plans. "Let us walk for a while. Paris is perfect in September, my favorite time. Then we have lunch at noon, which I believe will continue for several hours. My old friends Docteur Stéphane Gabin and Docteur Jean Balmain will join us; both are still teaching at the Sorbonne—did you know that?"

"I would have thought they were retired by now." Maisie had met the two men many years earlier, when they had visited Maurice during her apprenticeship.

"And they are anxious to see you too."

"Me?"

Maurice looked up, wiping a flake of bread crust from his chin. "The first meeting was brief, but you are held in high esteem by both gentlemen. They naturally want to know how you are."

"I see." Maisie paused. "Well, I will join you for lunch, Maurice, but perhaps not for the *après-midi* conversation. I have to visit two places this afternoon: one is the hotel where Ralph Lawton stayed while in Paris, and the other is a club he visited. I found a box of matches among his belongings and want to see what it's like."

"If it is still there."

Maisie sipped her coffee. "Of course, if it's still there."

THE WALK MAURICE had proposed was comfortable if quiet, though Maisie remained vigilant. It was Maurice who had taught her to observe the truth revealed in the movement and position of the body, and he taught her to be attentive and curious about words chosen, instructing her in the ways in which just one seemingly insignificant comment could provide the key to a secret tightly held. She had learned in her apprenticeship that even people with lips firmly sealed would speak volumes in complete ignorance of the clues they allowed to escape. *It is as if we are playing chess*, thought Maisie, as she strolled beside Maurice, careful that her step gave away nothing, as far as she knew. And she kept the conversation light, knowing that Maurice would detect her avoidance. But she could take no chances. She had already decided not to ask questions regarding her recollection of their conversation about the Everdens in the library almost sixteen years ago. There could well be a simple explanation, but Maisie knew it was best to keep her cards very close—indeed, so close she would be the last person to show her hand. Or so she hoped.

LUNCH PASSED IN easy conversation, conducted in a mix of French and English with everyone using words from their own language when there was no easy translation. Maisie quickly regained confidence in French, which she had studied with Maurice in those early days and then again at Girton. Talk went back and forth in such a way that an observer might have been reminded of a tennis game on a summer's day, played not for a wager, or particularly to win, but for the pleasure of connection. Certain subjects caused voices to become tense; for Stéphane to emphasize a point with his jutting lower lip and hands held open; for Maurice to draw back, which was always a sign that he was about to strike with an incisive and well-timed point. Maisie smiled, for the scene might have been one an artist would choose, the men looking as Frenchmen of a certain age were expected to look, enjoying the company of a young woman who was clearly not French but part of the group.

A green salad was served, followed by lamb cutlets cooked to perfection. Red wine flowed, and the talk continued back and forth. The success of Adolf Hitler's party in the September elections took up a good portion of the exchange, with opinions that were deeper but mirrored those of the American group. Then there was speculation about the airship, the R-101, that would arrive in France in just a week or so, en route for India. India, of all places; one could fly to India on a dirigible!

As they sat in the restaurant, a particular venue long favored by the three men, Maisie shivered and looked away from the group as conversation moved to who was doing what now and, inevitably for men of their years, who had passed away. Two waiters ran between tables draped in checked tablecloths. The walls were painted in an old cream-colored paint, now smoke-stained and covered with posters advertising events long past. Music was playing in the background and double doors opened onto the street for fresh air to enter, though there were no tables on the pavement. As she surveyed the room, she felt she was being watched and turned to the corner of the restaurant, closer to the door. Insufficient light prevented her from gaining a view of the solitary diner there, so, not wanting to peer, she turned back to the men and quickly rejoined the conversation, which this time was about the economy. She looked at her watch, squinting to see the time.

"I'm terribly sorry, gentlemen, but I really must leave you now. I have work to do this afternoon."

Jean and Stéphane dabbed at their mouths with table napkins as Maisie reached for her document case, which was on the floor at her feet.

"Ah, Mademoiselle Dobbs, must you go? It has been such a pleasure."

"I'm sorry, Dr. Gabin. My work calls."

Jean smiled. "It is a *fait accompli*, as I think you might say."

They all laughed together. Maurice remained seated as Maisie turned to him. "I trust you won't be out late, Maurice?" More laughter as Maurice inclined his head and smiled. Maisie leaned toward Stéphane and Jean, and exchanged kisses into the air on each side of the men's faces. She squeezed Maurice's shoulder and he pressed her hand with his own. "Later."

"Yes, later. Take care, Maisie."

"Of course." She left the restaurant, walked quickly along a side street until she reached the main thoroughfare, and turned left.

It was as she rounded the corner that Maisie had the distinct feeling that she was being followed and turned to look. The sensation was so strong, so apparent, that she quickly darted into an alley leading to a courtyard, pressing herself against the shadowed wall to avoid detection, and glanced sideways toward the street, waiting.

A tall man hurried past, placing a hat on his head as he walked and looking back and forth along the street. *He was in the restaurant, watching me.* Maisie continued to wait, then looked toward the back of the courtyard, where there was another alleyway. Moving into the light, Maisie pulled a Baedecker guide from her case and flicked through the pages to get her bearings. She moved silently across the cobblestones and out into the alley, looking both ways before stepping out. Once out on the street again, she walked briskly in the direction of the métro. She looked at her watch, thinking quickly. Without doubt, she was being followed. But by whom? And what of Maurice? He was always so aware, so in tune with his environment; would he not have sensed the man in the shadows of the restaurant? Maisie frowned as beads of perspiration peppered her brow, and the wound she thought was healing began to nip at her again. She had pressed the attempts on her life to the back of her mind, feeling safe so far away, across the Channel.

The man following her had moved quickly, his body sharp and almost feline as he looked back and forth and ran across the street, out of her view. Maisie closed her eyes briefly, remembering the man at Goodge Street station who had rushed toward the curb. . . . *No, it's not him. It's someone else.* She turned to face the traffic and, seeing a taxi-cab approaching, lifted her arm. A motor car suddenly seemed a safer choice than walking. The taxi-cab screeched to a halt, and Maisie clambered inside.

"*Montmartre, s'il vous plaît. L'hôtel Adrienne.*"

The driver nodded sharply and Maisie leaned back into the seat, closed her eyes, and tried to empty her mind. She thought again of Madeleine Hartnell: "There are two who walk with you." *I hope so. I do hope so.* Maisie opened her eyes and looked out of the window as the taxi-cab made its way through narrow streets and then bumped across ancient cobblestones and stopped outside the Hotel Adrienne. Feeling alone and vulnerable, she pulled up her collar against a faint breeze that another person might not have noticed.

· · ·

"*ATTENTION. ATTENTION, S'IL vous plaît.*" Maisie stood alongside the deserted polished dark wooden counter and called out for assistance. An old man shuffled through the door that led to the back of the hotel. He was dressed in dark trousers and a white shirt, with a small bow tie and armbands that prevented the long sleeves from bunching up around his cuffs.

"*Bonjour, mademoiselle.*" He smiled broadly, placed his hands on the counter side by side, and spoke in English. "How may I be of service to you?"

Maisie was surprised but did not question how he had ascertained that she was not French. Probably her countenance and dress revealed more about her than she would have liked.

"Monsieur, a dear friend of mine was a guest here during the war, and I hoped you might still have a record of his visit. I am going to his grave next week and want very much to visit the places where he knew some joy before he was killed. Can you help me?"

"It is a pilgrimage, no?"

Maisie dipped her head. "Yes. It is a pilgrimage."

The man came to the front of the counter and took both of her hands in his, smiling kindly. "Yes, there are some who come, like you, and others who were here and survived the crisis. Do you know when your friend visited?"

Maisie pulled her hand from the man's grasp and reached inside her document case. She held out a small receipt, now brown around the edges, that she had found tucked inside Ralph Lawton's journal.

The man pulled a pair of half-moon spectacles from his waistcoat, placed them on his nose, and studied the paper. "*Ah, bon.*" He turned to Maisie. "It is I myself who issued the receipt." As tears welled up in the corners of his eyes, he removed his spectacles and pressed the thumb and finger of his right hand to the bridge of his nose. "*Excusez-moi, mademoiselle.* I saw so many: our own boys, the English and Scottish, the Canadians, the Americans, the Australians. They all came to Paris for a day or two of this or that." He smiled. "You know, the girls. . . ." Maisie nodded and smiled. "And then they were gone." He snapped his fingers. "Gone."

"Can you tell me if my friend came alone to the hotel?"

The man frowned, turning. "*Un moment.* I will have to find the book."

He shuffled into the office, where Maisie could hear doors being opened and closed, papers falling to the ground, and the odd expletive from the hotel owner. Eventually he returned, holding a large faded leather-bound ledger in both hands while blowing dust from the top and sides.

"*Voilà!* I have found the book. Now, let me see." He placed the ledger on the counter and flipped through the pages, commenting occasionally. "Ah, a regular there, an Irish boy. He visited two years ago with his children and wife." He shook his head. "If she knew!" The pages turned, all the time with added commentary, about those who died, those who came back, those who had caused trouble. "So many, but I remember, I remember."

Maisie rested her elbow on the counter and waited, occasionally waving her hand in the air as a small cloud of dust wafted toward her.

"Ah! Good. It is found." He pushed the ledger in front of Maisie, and they leaned over the entry together. "Yes, he is here. He came with his friend." The man put the spectacles on his nose once again, squinted, and leaned closer to the page. "But the man cannot write!"

"No, he can't." Maisie's shoulders dropped as she read Ralph Lawton's signature clearly, followed by another that was barely a scrawl. It could have been a man or a woman's hand, a thought that caused Maisie to turn to the hotel owner. "How do you know it is a man's handwriting?"

His bottom lip jutted out in the manner that Stéphane had shown only an hour earlier, and he held out his upturned palms for emphasis. "It is the burden of my job, mademoiselle, to know handwriting as I am seeing it all the time." He tapped the ledger. "This is the signature of a man."

Maisie opened her mouth to ask another question but stopped when the man touched her arm. "In a time of war, we do not see, we do not ask. They may be dead in a week. We see only the smile, we give the smile in return, and we collect the francs. That is war."

She smiled and reached for the receipt, which had been left on the counter, and returned it to her document case. "You have been most kind, Monsieur . . ."

"Vernier. My name is André Vernier." He executed a short bow in front of her. "It is a pleasure, mademoiselle. Would you care to see the room?"

"Thank you, Monsieur Vernier. It is enough to have seen your hotel." Maisie hesitated, then reached into her case again. "Can you tell me if this club is still in Montmartre?" She held out the match-box.

Monsieur Vernier took the box, bringing it closer to his nose to see the inscription.

"Café Druk. Yes, yes. And it is still owned by the *Indochinoise*." He smiled and handed back the matches.

"What is it?"

"Now I am sure your friend was here with a man." Vernier was still grinning.

"Why?"

"Because, mademoiselle, the Café Druk is for *garçons*, for men."

Maisie nodded. "I see."

"Now let me direct you." Vernier guided Maisie to the street outside. Looking along the street, he held out his arm and proceeded to show her how to find Café Druk. "It will take ten minutes only if you are walking very slowly."

They bid au revoir, the man claiming a kiss on each cheek before he allowed Maisie to leave. She was certain that the man with Ralph during his leave in Paris was Jeremy Hazleton but knew that jumping to such conclusions was unwise, for it closed the mind to other possibilities. One must consider facts as if one has discovered jewels, each gem laid out on a plain surface, a clear mind, and then considered carefully before being arranged in a set.

THE CAFÉ DRUK seemed to have seen better days. The black double doors were chipped and worn, with the head of a giant dragon painted across so that the mouth gaped when a customer opened the door. The dragon's teeth were raised, carved and joined to the door rather than painted; however, the years had taken their toll on the wooden beast, for several of the teeth were missing. The door was ajar, so Maisie pushed it open and walked in, frowning as she became accustomed to the room, inefficiently lit by red lights on the walls, which appeared to be covered in silk.

"*Excusez-moi?* Madame? Is anyone here?" Maisie walked into the shadows slowly, colliding with a chair that scraped back against the tiled floor.

"Be careful, will you?"

"Excuse me." Maisie was aware of a person in the shadows behind the bar, which she could now see was laden with soiled glasses and ashtrays full of cigarette ends. "*Excusez-moi, s'il vous plaît.*"

A laugh that was more of a cackle almost rattled the glasses. "I can speak your language, Englishwoman."

"Oh, there you are." Maisie walked toward the bar, stood very straight, and held out her hand to the woman who was emerging from the shadows.

"And you are?" The woman took Maisie's hand in her own long elegant fingers.

"My name is Maisie Dobbs. I'm here to—"

The woman cackled again.

"What's wrong?"

"So very English, Maisie Dobbs." She pushed her face toward

Maisie, then turned and flicked a switch. Lights came on in the center of the room, making it easier for Maisie to see around her. It looked as if a party had begun a week ago and only just ended.

"I am Eva. What can I do for Maisie Dobbs?"

"I wanted to come here because my friend from childhood came here during the war, when he was on leave and before he died." She took out the matchbox and held it out toward the Indochinese woman.

As Eva reached for the matchbox, turning it to catch the light, Maisie was able to look at her more closely. She was about fifty years old. Her black hair was pulled back tightly, wound into a twist at the back of her head, and secured with two ornate clasps. She wore an evening gown with a hemline that dusted the floor and an embroidered coat draped across her shoulders. Her makeup was smudged, but she was, without a doubt, a beautiful Eurasian woman.

"Yes, your friend was here. How can I help you? Thousands passed through my doors, all of them drowning sorrows before sorrow drowned them. But those were the days, Maisie Dobbs, oh, those were the days!"

"What do you mean?"

"People who are doomed live life with abandon, don't you know that?"

"I was in France too, in the war."

The woman looked her up and down; then she picked up an ashtray and poked at it until she found an inch of cigarette that was worth lighting again. She reached into the box that Maisie had passed to her, pulled out a match, and struck it on the wall behind her. It ignited immediately. She lit the cigarette and shook the match until the flame extinguished, turning to Maisie only after a long draw on the cigarette.

"So, you were in France." She paused, gazing intently at Maisie, who did not look away. "What can I do for you? The war was years ago."

"I just wanted to see where my friend had been."

"Obviously not a boyfriend, a—what did they call them?" She

shook her head. "A sweetheart! No, you weren't a sweetheart; that would have been impossible."

Maisie was silent but maintained eye contact.

"Oh, you Englishwomen. So petite in the mind!" She paused. "My club does not appeal to those who come with their wives, their ladyfriends."

Maisie nodded. "Yes, that I understand, Madame Eva. However, I was just curious, you know, to see." She reached for her bag.

"No, stop." Eva placed her hand on her arm. "Come, come with me." She led Maisie to the back of the club and through an archway leading to a staircase. Once upstairs, Eva unlocked a door with a key on a chain that she pulled from around her neck. She opened the door to reveal a light and airy room with floor-to-ceiling windows that looked out onto the street below. As her eyes moved from one exquisite painting to another, then to the china and furniture from Asia, Maisie felt as if she had entered another world. Eva opened a glass-fronted case and pulled out several photograph albums, which she placed in front of Maisie. The light outside was fading now, and Eva ensured that the lamps were tilted so that she could view the photographs. Unlike André's dusty collection of ledgers, Eva's albums were cherished, each page of photographs covered with a sheet of onion-skin paper for protection.

"These are from the war. My boys, all my boys. Most were lost, but I kept the photographs. They are all of parties here, all of laughter and singing." She walked toward a door to the right. "So do not judge, Miss Maisie Dobbs, for you are alive and able to laugh again, as difficult as that may be." Eva clasped her hands together in front of her. "Nice English lady like tea?" She cackled and walked away, leaving Maisie alone.

Maisie shook her head and reached for the albums, which were all dated, selected one, and began flipping through. It was the faces she was looking at, the boyish grins, sometimes embarrassed as the flashlight caught them unawares, sometimes defiant or waving to Eva, for surely it was Eva who was behind the camera.

"Tea for English missy." Eva returned, set the tray on the table, and added, "I do not keep the juice of cows, so you will have to drink it without milk."

"Lovely, thank you." Maisie smiled and looked up. Eva seemed more serious now.

"You have found nothing?"

Maisie took a sip of the tea that Eva had placed on a table beside her and sighed. "No, nothing." She paused, then looked again. "Oh, my goodness, there he is!"

Eva came around to lean over Maisie's shoulder, so that they were both peering at the photograph in the album that Maisie had pulled onto her lap. The two young men were laughing, their arms intertwined as they each held a glass to the other's lips. Placed on the bar in front of Hazleton was a glass ornament, an orb, perhaps a paperweight, that caught the light in such a way that it reflected into the camera, creating a moment that appeared laced with magic. It reminded Maisie of that other photograph among Ralph's belongings at Cecil Lawton's Cambridgeshire home. There they were, the same two young men. And the same adoring gaze was on Ralph Lawton's face, as he looked away from the camera to the man he held to him in this moment of joy.

SEVENTEEN

 "So it looks like she's pulled through and she'll be back on her feet in a day or two."

Maisie placed her hand on her chest, feeling relief rush through her body. "Oh, Sandra, that is the best news I could've had today." She paused to wave to Maurice, who had just entered the reception lounge, and pointed to the receiver to indicate the call in progress. Maurice nodded and seated himself in an ornate carved chair. Maisie resumed the conversation. "Did the doctor say anything about what caused the malady?"

"He said it was very difficult to say, seeing as I'd made her lose most of what she'd eaten, if you know what I mean, and then made her drink pints and pints of water. Mind you, he said it's a rare bad chocolate that has the same effect as rat poison—"

Maisie took a breath, ready to ask another question, but Sandra anticipated her.

"And he couldn't prove it now without her being a corpse. Even then it would be hard."

"I have to run now. Look, Sandra, I want you to be very, very careful. If anyone tries to deliver *anything* for me, you must send them away." She had considered the evidence value of a suspect package but did not want to bear the risk of a contaminated parcel in the house when she was not there to monitor the situation.

"Not even put them in the courtyard shed?"

"No. Do not accept anything. And if you see any strangers loitering around Ebury Place, you must report them to the police immediately; make sure you inform the staff. I shall place a call to Lord Julian later today when I arrive in Reims. He should be kept apprised of the situation."

"Right you are, m'um."

"I'll say goodbye then, Sandra."

"Goodbye, m'um—oh, and m'um, please be careful."

"Thank you, I will." Maisie replaced the receiver, turned to the bespectacled hotel manager, and paid her telephone account. Maurice, who would be remaining in Paris, had already settled her room fee.

She walked across to Maurice, indicating to a porter that she was ready to leave. Then she reached toward her mentor, placed a hand on his shoulder, and kissed him on each cheek. "I'll see you soon, Maurice."

"Indeed. Take care, Maisie." He looked at her intently. As she left the hotel and climbed into a taxi-cab, Maisie could still feel him watching her.

SHE SPENT THE train journey to Reims in quiet reflection. From her decision to take on the case of Ralph Lawton to yesterday's meetings with André and Eva, she picked over the events and connections of the past two weeks. Each time she considered a person or situation, she approached from another direction, challenging in her mind the way in which she observed the clues left behind. To be sure, there was no actual physical connection between Avril Jarvis and Madeleine Hartnell. But there was another link, as if the presence of one in her life was an indication of the importance of the other.

Maisie remembered asking Maurice, in the early years of her apprenticeship, why it was that he would treat two cases—cases that seemingly had nothing to do with each other—as if they were related. He had tapped his pipe against the fireplace in their old office close to Oxford Circus, inspected the empty bowl, and responded to her question as he filled the pipe again, pressing down the fresh tobacco as he spoke.

"It is a question of serendipity, Maisie. Yes, of course the cases have nothing to do with each other *on the surface.*" He reached for a match, which he held ready to strike against the chimney breast. "But here's the link: In considering the one case, we have to stand in another place, look at our evidence from a fresh angle. Without a doubt, that is a challenge for us; after all, we come to our work with a history, a language, a way of doing things in this world that is uniquely ours—and we can be stuck with it." He paused to light the pipe and draw upon the oaky-sweet tobacco. "But in that moment, another case comes along that demands our mental athleticism, our ability to leap to that other place and look again, for it is so different from the first. Then it comes, that one similarity, that small grain of intelligence that breaks the block in one or both cases. Or, Maisie"—he had looked at her intently—"the task of asking questions, of peeling back layers of the past, reveals something that has nothing to do with the cases and everything to do with ourselves. Do you understand?"

She had nodded, in her youth not quite grasping the weight of his words, but now, as the land swept by accompanied by the dull rhythm of wheels on tracks, she understood it was a lesson she was to learn anew time and time again. And now was no exception.

Arriving in Reims, Maisie secured a taxi-cab driver who was willing to take her to the small town of Sainte-Marie just a few miles to the east of the city. It was a rural area occupied by the Kaiser's army during the war, and it was on the edge of Sainte-Marie that Ralph Lawton's De Havilland fell to earth in a cascade of flames, according to those who witnessed the event.

Maisie's driver took her to a small pension run by a woman who introduced herself as Madame Thierry. She was a petite woman, thin rather than slender, and wore a blue cotton dress with a white apron that still bore the sharp folds of freshly ironed linen. Her long blond-gray hair had been braided and then wound around her head, reminding Maisie of an ornate loaf of bread.

"It is a comfortable room and you will enjoy the view." Madame pulled back the lace curtain. There was a garden with chickens pecking at the grass, vegetables growing in well-ordered rows, and an old hound asleep under an apple tree. Beyond were two fields, separated by woodland, and then, in the distance, a château.

Maisie looked out the window. "What a beautiful château. Who lives there?"

"It is the home of Madame Chantal Clement. She lives there with her thirteen-year-old granddaughter, Mademoiselle Pascale Clement."

Maisie drew back. "Does the child have no parents? A mother?"

"She is gone." Madame Thierry shook her head and added, "The war. . . ."

Maisie knew the comment was meant to prevent any further inquiry. "Of course."

"Now, Mademoiselle Dobbs, let me show you where we serve our *petit déjeuner*; it is a delightful room."

MAISIE WALKED TO the police station first, a two-room building with a counter as one entered, behind which were two desks and a door, which led through to what Maisie assumed were two or three cells. As she rang the bell on the counter, she suspected that the cells were seldom used and then only to facilitate the sleeping off of a liquid repast by a tottering villager. When the gendarme returned to his post, it was with a cup of strong coffee in his hand, so Maisie assumed that the kitchen was probably situated in one of the cells.

"*Bonjour*"—there was a pause as he stole a glance at Maisie's hands—"*mademoiselle*. What can I do for you?" He smiled broadly, revealing two missing front teeth, then placed his cup on the counter as he leaned forward.

"I am Captain Desvignes, at your service."

Maisie took one small step back. "Thank you, Captain Desvignes. I am here on behalf of the father of a man, an aviator, who was shot down close to Sainte-Marie during the war, and I wondered—"

"It was a terrible time, mademoiselle. In Sainte-Marie we prefer to forget."

"Of course." Maisie rested her hands on the counter. "But, sir— Captain Desvignes—I wondered if you could assist me in helping the young man's father. I want to know where the craft went down so I might pay my respects on the father's behalf. He is an elderly man and now, in the twilight of his years, he wants to know that someone has come."

Desvignes sipped the black coffee and ran his tongue across his remaining front teeth. Droplets of coffee clung to his mustache, which he wiped with the back of his hand before taking a handkerchief from his pocket, wiping his mouth again, and then his hands. Maisie waited patiently. *He's thinking, playing for time.* Clearing his throat, Desvignes shrugged. "It was a long time ago. We prefer to forget, but we all remember, do we not, mademoiselle?"

"I was in France myself, in the war." Maisie clutched her hands together, still on top of the counter where he could see them. "I was a nurse."

The gendarme raised his eyebrows and smiled. "You were brave—and so young!" He turned and took his kepi from the nail on the wall where it had been hanging. "Come. Let me show you." He opened the counter flap, came to Maisie's side, and looked at her feet. "Good, you have strong shoes. We will walk." He opened the door for Maisie and flipped a sign outside the door that now announced FERMÉ to anyone who came. Then he led Maisie along a cobbled street to a gate, which opened onto a path leading to the fields beyond the town.

They walked for a mile or so on paths alongside land that had recently been harvested. Captain Desvignes pointed out aspects of the town's history to Maisie, at first saying little about the war. Then, lulled by her easy companionship and ready smile, he revealed more and more. Many residents had tried to leave as the German armies approached, but to move forward spelled even more risk, placing them en route for the British front lines. And because it was a small community, where the old were related to almost everyone else and the young were the promise of the town's future, most of the townsfolk remained, determined not to be ousted by the German advance.

At first they had felt pity for the occupying army, who, as far as anyone could ascertain, were young men plucked from schools and universities to fight after only a few weeks in a training camp. Then the Kaiser's generals decreed that the only method of ensuring security in the occupied population was to rule with an iron fist, demanding obedience, and responding to dissent with punishment.

"It was a foolish move," said Desvignes.

Maisie said nothing, knowing that the captain now needed no encouragement to continue.

"As soon as the fist came down"— Desvignes pounded his right hand into the palm of his left—"we began to wage our own war, and we were determined to win."

Maisie was about to ask a question, when Desvignes pointed to the far corner of a field. "There it is, the place where your flying man went down. We all remember that day, you see, those of us who were here. We do not forget." He removed his kepi and pressed it to his chest, then held out his hand as if the field were his own property. "See how the grass grows? You would never know. No, you would never know."

They walked across the land, Desvignes helping Maisie as she clambered over a fence. Finally they were standing at the point where the aeroplane crashed.

"It was right here, on this very spot?"

"Yes, mademoiselle. On this spot."

"And was the wood there? The trees around the riverbank?"

"Yes, mademoiselle. The woods, they were thicker, so dense you could not see beyond the first line of trees. We thought they would also burn, but the wind turned and our people came with buckets to form a chain from the river."

"I see." Maisie was thoughtful. "Who was here first?"

"It was the gardener, from the château over there beyond the trees."

"Madame Clement's gardener?"

"Yes."

"And then what happened?"

"Others came, from the town."

"And the Germans? Surely they saw the flames. Were they not here quickly?"

Desvignes shrugged. "I think there were some difficulties on the road from town; a cart with vegetables had overturned." He pointed to a small dusty road at the end of the field. "And of course they had a war to fight."

Maisie nodded. She suspected that Desvignes was adept at spicing the truth with a liberal helping of fabrication, and that "difficulties on the road" were likely to have been obstructions caused by villagers.

"And the fire?"

"Ah, well, it was impossible to stop the fire, it was everywhere, so we saved our woodland, our crops. The Germans came after the fire was extinguished, burned out. The plane was nothing, a charred shell. The body—nothing except name tags that were half melted."

"Was there a problem with identification?"

Desvignes shrugged again. "The aeroplane was identified when it crashed, before being completely lost, and I believe there was sufficient information to send word to the British authorities."

Maisie regarded the man carefully. "Did you serve in the war, Captain?"

Desvignes stood to attention and saluted. "Of course. I was wounded at the first Marne battle, in 1914. I was like Madame Clement's gardener, a cripple of war."

They turned to leave. As they did so, Maisie was compelled to look back at the land where Ralph Lawton's De Havilland had burned and at the pointed turrets of the château beyond the trees in the distance. And she wondered how a "cripple of war" could have been the first man to rush to the aid of a British aviator who was burning to death.

CAPTAIN HENRI DESVIGNES escorted Maisie back to the pension, tipped his kepi, and bid her *bonsoir.* Upon reaching her room, she slipped off her walking shoes and lay back on the bed. The room was far too frivolous for her taste: a lace counterpane, lace curtains, lace around the edge of the marble-topped table, upon which sat a china bowl and ewer filled with cold water, and lace around the framed paintings on the walls. As she rested she recalled the counsel of her early years working with Maurice Blanche. *Never rush to a conclusion. Even though the clues point in a certain direction, do not allow yourself to be blinded by assumption. It is too easy to be trapped by the mind closing when a task is considered done.* She was reaching conclusions here, and quickly. Yet there again, new information along with a good measure of doubt emerged with each conversation, each new encounter. She touched her head, stood up, walked over to the ewer, lifted it with both hands, and poured water into the bowl. Taking the lace-edged cotton cloth from the rail alongside the table, Maisie dipped one end in the water, looked into the mirror above, and pressed the wet cloth against the dressing on her forehead. After soaking the bandage, she carefully peeled it back, removing the lint to reveal a livid scar and surrounding abrasion. Maisie cleansed the wound, patted it dry, and pinned back her hair to let the air get to it. As she did so, she smiled, remembering the early days of her nursing at the London Hospital and the sisters in charge, who would march up and down the wards extolling the virtues of fresh air and instructing the nurses to open the windows. "Don't she know we've 'ad enough of the fresh bleedin' cold air over there?" one soldier would quip to another as the nurses hurriedly obeyed orders.

Maisie sat on the bed again and reached for her document case. She pulled out a series of index cards upon which she proceeded to write down even the smallest details of her day, from the moment of waking until now. She noted her desire to confront Maurice, for she had deduced his association with Peter—or *thought* she had. A small element of doubt convinced her that the time was not quite right; possibly there was more to learn. She wrote of her telephone calls to Ebury Place, to Lord Compton, and then to Stratton and then noted her sense of the secrecy among the townsfolk of Sainte-Marie and of her curiosity surrounding the gardener at the château. Threads, threads, threads, some leading to each other, some leading in new directions.

Once again she lay back. The dragon was resting, lulled by her attention to her work.

"Mademoiselle Dobbs!" The shrill voice of Madame Thierry was accompanied by a sharp double knock. "Mademoiselle!"

Maisie leaped from her bed and opened the door. Madame held out an envelope.

"It arrived this past hour. It was on the table when I came from collecting vegetables. Would you like some soup with *saucisson*? It is good, to my mother's recipe."

Maisie took the envelope and smiled. "Ah, I can smell your fresh herbs from here. Yes, I would love some soup."

Madame nodded. "I will call when it is ready. You are my only guest now. The holidays are over; there will be few visitors."

"Thank you. I'll wait to hear your call."

Madame turned and went downstairs. Maisie closed the door and locked it before slipping her finger into the unsealed gap at the side of the envelope and tearing an opening. She removed the fine ivory paper and read:

> *Welcome, Mademoiselle Dobbs:*
>
> *I would be delighted if you would join my granddaughter Pascale and me for lunch tomorrow at noon. Ours is a small town and news of visitors travels quickly, especially at a time when we expect most to have left. Pascale is learning English and would love to have a real Englishwoman to experiment on.*
>
> *We look forward to enjoying your company.*
>
> *Until tomorrow, Madame Chantal Clement*

There seemed little time to respond, though Maisie suspected that any invitation from Chantal Clement was as good as an order. She was clearly the town's matriarch.

Maisie tapped her left hand with the folded letter and walked over to the window. She looked out to the barely discernible lights of the château as they punctured the absolute darkness between the edge of the garden and the fields beyond. A flicker of movement caught her eye, and she turned to look to the left of the garden. Was that a man silhouetted against the apple tree? Maisie stood back to avoid being seen, but in a way to enable a broad view of the garden. Someone was watching her. *Who is that?* She stole another look, then shook her head and admonished herself. A light extended across the garden as the back door opened and Madame called out, "*Philippe! Philippe! Attention!*" Maisie heard the grumble of the old hound as he pulled himself onto all fours and walked toward his mistress in his own good time. *Did I perhaps see a dog and not a man?* Maisie squinted once more and then leaned back, pulled down the blind behind the lace curtain, and turned to the mirror. She splashed water on her face again and dried her skin with the towel.

"Mademoiselle Dobbs! Mademoiselle Dobbs! It is time."

Maisie opened the door. "I'm coming, madame! *Un moment, s'il vous plaît.*"

EIGHTEEN

Maisie awoke to the mouth-watering aroma of freshly baked bread mingled with strong coffee. Instead of leaping from her bed, as she would at home, she lay back and allowed her thoughts free rein. She had not sent a letter to Andrew as she had promised; she must do that today. In truth, she was unsettled in the relationship, unsettled because despite his sunny disposition and readiness to encourage her in her work, along with that very special understanding he seemed to have of her, she could feel herself drawing back. She watched the clouds drift by, large puffy cumulus clouds with deep blue sky in between. Is that how she would be, driven in her work yet drifting in her most personal liaisons? She had drifted into living at Ebury Place, drifted into everything except each new case, or so it seemed. The flat was a good idea, a break, a chance to . . . to *experiment*. Yes, experiment with what she liked and did not like. She would choose the things around her, the furniture, the curtains—and definitely no lace. Maisie got up and walked to the window. Wasn't it easier just to plunge ahead into work? Not to have to worry about living accommodation, about the everyday minutiae of life? Perhaps Andrew would be better off alone or with someone else—someone less confused about the past, someone who had not loved before.

Leaning her head against the window frame, Maisie heard the back door open and watched as Madame stood outside, looking back into the kitchen while pointing into the garden. *"Philippe! Attention! Vite, vite!"* The old hound ambled from the kitchen, across the garden, and took up his place by the apple tree. Maisie looked closer. What had she seen last night? Had she seen the dog move, long shadows caused by the light from windows fooling her into thinking it was a man? She turned back into the room and dressed quickly in brown trousers and a knitted brown cardigan, a scarf for her neck, and her sturdy walking shoes. Grabbing her jacket, she placed a beret on her head before running downstairs and into the garden.

"Bonjour, Philippe." Maisie approached the dog, holding out her hand palm up for him to take her scent. He did not move. She came closer, and it was not until she reached down that she realized that the dog was deaf. At her touch, he turned his head and allowed her to kneel beside him and stroke his gray muzzle and one floppy ear. "Ah, that is why you didn't bark. Or was it you all the time, you old rogue?" The dog moved toward her and licked her face, his tail moving back and forth in what passes for a wag in an old dog. Maisie gave Philippe one last pat and moved to the place where she thought she had seen a man, close to the apple tree. She bent down and touched the ground with her fingers.

Someone was here. The footprints suggested a man's shoe. She called Philippe. Nothing, not even a tremor in the tail. The dog was asleep again.

"Mademoiselle Dobbs! Mademoiselle Dobbs!" Madame Thierry stood at the back door again, this time shouting for Maisie and not her dog.

"Pardon, madame, I was saying good morning to your dog."

Madame laughed. "Then you will have to say it very loud, for Philippe is as deaf as a post. It is his fault that I have become used to shouting."

· · ·

THE MORNING WAS spent in a leisurely fashion. Maisie walked around the town, relaxing as she strolled along narrow cobbled streets. Reaching the town square, she stopped by the war memorial and closed her eyes for a moment of respectful silence. A plaque alongside the adjacent church door piqued her curiosity, so she walked over for a closer look.

FROM THE TOWNSPEOPLE OF SAINTE-MARIE
IN MEMORY OF FRÉDÉRIC DUPONT, MAYOR OF SAINTE-MARIE,
GEORGES BAURIN, AND SUZANNE CLEMENT, WHO WERE EXECUTED
BY THE OCCUPYING GERMAN ARMY IN 1918.
THEY DIED FOR THE FREEDOM OF SAINTE-MARIE AND FOR FRANCE.

They died for the freedom of Sainte-Marie? Suzanne Clement? What connection existed between Suzanne Clement and the woman who had issued an invitation to lunch? Maisie looked at her watch. It was time to make her way to the château for lunch with Chantal Clement and her granddaughter, Pascale.

MAISIE CHANGED INTO a black woolen skirt and cream silk blouse, pulled the woolen cardigan around her shoulders, and placed the beret on her head again, securing it with a hat pin tipped with amber. Once again she took the path that led to the place where Ralph Lawton had burned to death. She stood in silence, the breeze rustling through leaves on the trees nearby as she tried to imagine the crash. Certainly, if one were over enemy territory on a reconnaissance mission, this field was a good choice for an attempted landing with a burning aircraft, a flying coffin—that's if it really was burning at the point of impact.

Had the villagers foiled attempts by their occupiers to secure the field? Had the brave gardener struggled in vain to reach Lawton? Of course he must have tried; was he overcome by the terrible inferno? Captain Desvignes was right, all evidence of the disaster was gone now: no burnt ground, no seared trees. The grass had grown, the round of planting, nurturing, and harvest reestablished, and the war was now a time that most wanted to forget. Yet at the side of the road a collection of shells and ammunition, turned over in the last plowing, awaited collection by the authorities. And so it went on, the earth yielding up her dead along with the terrible tools of war.

A skylark singing high above the fields interrupted Maisie, who looked at her watch. There was just time to walk to the river. Inspecting the ground and the surrounding countryside one last time, Maisie continued on a path that led through the trees and down to the water. It seemed more of a stream than a river, but it bubbled and splashed over rocks and into deep pools, across dams built of fallen branches, she suspected by local children; then the river swirled around the roots of ancient trees and wove its way across the land. Maisie thought it remarkable that the trees were still standing during the war, for so many forests had been lost to shelling. Could Lawton have been saved? Maisie wondered what might have happened had Lawton been rescued. *This is where I would have brought him.* But then what? Where might one hide a wounded aviator in occupied territory?

Not ten minutes later, Maisie walked through a gate from the fields that led onto the carriage sweep to the château. A man running would have cut that time down to three or four minutes. *But a cripple of war?* Maisie was interrupted by the sound of galloping hooves approaching and swung around in time to see a young girl atop a large black horse direct her mount to the fence on the opposite side of the carriage sweep. Maisie gasped but soon breathed a sigh of relief, as the horse cleared the fence with a foot to spare, the rider landing expertly, then bringing the horse to a canter and circling to a trot before approaching her. The girl was almost out of breath but smiling broadly, her dark chestnut hair falling in waves across her shoulders. She wore pale woolen riding breeches, long black leather boots, a white shirt, a scarf at her neck and a brown jacket.

"Hello, you must be Mademoiselle Maisie Dobbs." The girl's English was perfect. She dismounted and patted her horse on the neck before holding out her hand to Maisie. "I am Pascale Clement, and I am happy to meet you."

"I am happy to meet you too, Mademoiselle Clement, though I must say you rather took my breath away with that jump."

She laughed dismissively. "Oh, my Louis is a king; he can do anything." As a groom emerged from the gate that led to the stables, Pascale hugged the horse's neck, pulled a cube of sugar from her pocket and fed it to him before handing the reins to the groom. "*Merci*, Monsieur Charles." She turned to Maisie again. "We have been galloping and jumping across the fields for two hours. It is nothing." She paused and smiled broadly again, a devilish smile that startled Maisie.

"Come, Mademoiselle Dobbs, let me take you to meet Grandmère. She will be watching and I will be taken to task for the jump and for keeping you to myself." As she led the way, Pascale turned to Maisie. "May I call you Maisie, please?"

Maisie tried not to grin. "Oh, I do believe your grandmother might not approve, Mademoiselle Clement."

Pascale laughed, leaning back as she did so. "Of course, you are correct!"

Walking alongside the French girl, Maisie found it hard to believe that she was only thirteen. She was almost as tall as Maisie, moved with an easy, confident gait and had an almost flippant sense of humor, though it was a humor that revealed her age.

"You have met Captain Desvignes, we have heard." She looked at Maisie as she asked the question, placing her tongue over her front teeth, and giggled again.

Maisie could not help herself and laughed too. "Yes, we have met. He is a nice man."

Pascale shrugged. Maisie stole another glance at this girl who seemed so self-assured. Yet hadn't she lost her mother, both her parents, in the war? She thought of herself, of her own loss when she was the same age as Pascale, a loss that lately had pierced her heart anew as if it were only yesterday. She thought of Avril Jarvis, who had lost her mother to a man who sent her away to London and a life on the streets. And here was this vivacious French girl laughing. Perhaps it was her way of rendering her losses powerless in everyday life, as Andrew was wont to do.

"Grandmère, Grandmère, I have found her!" Pascale had led Maisie past the butler, with a wave and an audacious wink, into a spacious drawing room. It was filled with antiques, along with several large Chinese vases overflowing with blooms, yet it was a bright room, with pale lavender drapes and a view across landscaped grounds from the grand glass doors on the far side of the room. Madame Chantal Clement was seated in an armchair, a lavender blanket across her knees. An elegant woman, she wore her silver-gray hair drawn up into a loose knot at the back of her head; the wide collar of her pale-gray silk blouse was open to reveal a pearl-and-amethyst choker at her neck. A pair of deep purple satin shoes were just visible under her long purple wool skirt She took off her spectacles and placed her book on a side table as Pascale entered with her "find."

"Pascale, chérie, please, please calm down. I am sure our guest was not lost and you will wear her out before the day is done." Chantal Clement turned to Maisie and smiled broadly, her deep gray eyes sparkling, and took Maisie's hands in both her own. "*Enchantée*, Mademoiselle Dobbs. We are delighted to have you in our home. You give us an opportunity to practice the English language."

"It's lovely of you to invite me, Madame Clement."

Chantal Clement nodded and turned to Pascale. "My dear, you will not sit at table dressed in that manner; it is most unladylike. Please go to your room and do not join us until you resemble the elegant young woman I am trying so hard to bring you up to be."

Pascale kissed Chantal on the cheek, waved to Maisie, and ran from the room. The matriarch shook her head in mock despair. In that one gesture, Maisie could see that Chantal adored her granddaughter, that she delighted in her energetic disposition, and that it was her love that sustained the girl.

"You are so kind to come, but I fear the afternoon may be wearing for you. This is a small town, except when visitors arrive—and there are only a few of those, despite what Captain Desvignes or Madame Thierry may tell you—so everyone knows everyone else. Pascale especially was thrilled to hear that an Englishwoman was in our midst."

Madame Clement smiled and Maisie intuited a change in her demeanor as she raised her chin and seemed to sit up a little straighter in her chair. She moved the blanket, took a cane from alongside her chair, and stood up.

"Walk with me to the window, Mademoiselle Dobbs. Lunch will be served shortly, so we have only a few moments before the whirlwind returns." They made their way to the windows and stood for a moment in silence. Though she was tempted to comment upon the gardens, the ornamental lake, the statuary, a maze in the distance to the right, and the topiary figures that formed an avenue leading to a rose garden, Maisie waited for her hostess to speak.

"What brings you to Sainte-Marie, Mademoiselle Dobbs? You are not *en vacances*, are you?"

Maisie turned, a half smile on her lips as she replied. "Oh, Madame Clement, I do believe you know why I am here, do you not? If news travels quickly in your village, you know I have come to find out more about the British aviator who crashed during the war in your field."

"Ah, a woman who speaks directly. Are you sure you are English?" She raised her eyebrows and laughed. "And you have had your curiosity piqued, I would imagine, regarding my gardener, Patrice."

"Patrice?"

"Yes. The waging of war became my good fortune, for Patrice was injured at the Battle of the Marne—"

"As was Captain Desvignes."

"The men and boys of the town joined the army together, so

they saw battle together, until they were either dead or wounded. If they were lucky, they came home."

Maisie nodded.

"My usual gardeners were gone to war, so I was grateful when Patrice came back and wanted work. The Germans liked to have a garden to wander in, to take them away from the horrors of battle."

"The Germans?"

"You know we were occupied."

"Of course."

"My house was requisitioned for the officers, though I was allowed to live here too. I was not expected to leave; in fact, I was the gracious hostess."

"That must have been terrible for you."

"There were advantages." Madame Clement turned to Maisie. "A lot can be learned from a homesick soldier with a glass of my very good wine inside him."

Maisie looked into Chantal Clement's gray eyes, eyes that she knew had seen much sadness. "You are very brave."

"And so were you, Mademoiselle Dobbs."

"I beg your pardon?"

"I have learned from Captain Desvignes that you were a nurse. That was courageous of you, and you so young. Did you lie in order to serve your country?"

"Yes," replied Maisie, somewhat surprised at the woman's quick grasp of the situation, that she had been too young for service overseas.

"It is part of war, is it not? We lie for truth to prevail and for goodness to return for all of us."

Maisie allowed a half moment's silence, then spoke again. "Can you tell me what happened to your granddaughter's parents? To her mother?"

"My daughter, Suzanne? Ah, yes. Not like Pascale, quieter, a *dark horse*, I think you English would say."

"Yes."

Chantal Clement shook her head. "It is a long story, Mademoiselle, and it is one that cannot be told in haste. She worked alongside other members of our small community here to thwart the enemy, essentially in passing messages to the Allies and committing acts of sabotage. It will be sufficient to say that our captors were in disarray toward the end of the war, the end of their occupation. They were panicking, and the risks my daughter took were crucial, for she wanted to carry on the work of Pascale's father. But along with our mayor and another, she was executed as an example, a final act of power before the Germans left and we were liberated. The end of the war came too late for Suzanne." She took a handkerchief from a pocket in her skirt and dabbed her eyes.

Maisie was about to speak when a *thump-thump-thump-thump* announced Pascale, running downstairs toward the drawing room. Then the door burst open.

"Grandmère, I am starving! Our lunch is in the dining room and I am ravenous." She turned to Maisie. "That is a good English word, is it not? Ravenous!"

Lunch was filled with light conversation, with Pascale interrupting frequently with "Is this a word that . . . ?" and "How would you describe . . . ?" Madame Clement spoke of a finishing school in Switzerland, and Pascale pouted, saying she would much prefer to live on a farm, or on the Riviera, or even in America. "I want to go to Hollywood to meet film stars."

The older woman rolled her eyes many times and the two sparred playfully, both ensuring that Maisie was part of the conversation and never left out. They were sparkling hostesses. All too soon, lunch was over.

"You will come again, Mademoiselle Dobbs? Can you come tomorrow?"

"Well, I'm not sure, not really. You see, I go to Biarritz on Thursday."

"Oh, Grandmère, Biarritz! May I go, may I?"

"Certainly not! Mademoiselle Dobbs does not want a tall jumping bean of a girl with her when she is on business." Madame Clement frowned and held up one finger to press her point.

"Actually, Biarritz will be my first real holiday ever, to tell you the truth."

"Then you must come tomorrow." Pascale fidgeted as she awaited Maisie's answer. "Please come! I will show you the château and tell you all my secrets."

"Ah, the joys of thirteen: always there is a secret, is there not, Pascale?" Madame Clement stepped toward the door, eager to release Maisie from Pascale's energetic insistence.

Maisie smiled as she replaced her beret. "You have twisted my arm, Mademoiselle Clement. I will come tomorrow morning, but I must leave at noon."

Madame Clement inclined her head. "You are most indulgent, Mademoiselle Dobbs. Thank you."

"What does this mean?" Pascale frowned. "Twisting the arm?"

MAISIE WAS SMILING as she walked across the fields toward the town. Though the story half told by Chantal Clement was one of bravery and sacrifice, leaving much to the imagination, one could not spend time with Pascale and not feel one's spirits lifted. But then again, to what extent did Pascale work to elevate her grandmother's mood? Did she feel, perhaps, that she needed to compensate for her mother's death, to bring constant joy to an aging woman who had lost her only daughter? Maisie nodded to herself as she stopped once again at the place where the earth had been scorched by a burning British aeroplane. Yes, there was too much intensity to Pascale's laughter, her determination to bring light into Chantal Clement's life. And there was another thing that nagged at Maisie, as she allowed her mind to reach back into the past with only the swish of a breeze through the trees and a skylark's song on the air

above. She found herself reminded of those early days at Girton
and the ebullient playfulness of her friend Priscilla.

As Maisie rounded the corner in front of the pension, she
stepped quickly into the shadows, her heart pounding. On the opposite corner, just outside the invisible line that would provide an easy
view of him from the upper windows, was a man. Yes, it was the
same man, the one first seen in Paris. It must have been him in the
garden, and now he was here, watching the pension. Waiting for her.
Well, he's not that good or he would have followed me across the field. Maisie
continued to watch as the man stepped back against a brick wall at
the approach of a motor car. *Perhaps he did follow. But then, perhaps he
had no need, for he knew where I was going.* Maisie took one last look,
turned, and doubled back quickly. She hurried around the houses to
the back of the pension and entered by the kitchen door. Running
into the house, first to her room to collect a small pair of binoculars
and then onto the landing again, she stood by the window. Kneeling
so that her head was just above the windowsill, she lifted the binoculars and carefully pushed the lace curtain aside just sufficiently to
study the man. He watched the house, sometimes looking back and
forth along the street. Then he checked his watch, took one last long
look, and began walking away. Maisie frowned, tapping the binoculars against the windowsill in thought before standing up. Sometimes, there wasn't any particular reason for knowing a thing, one
just knew; there was no other explanation. This man might seem like
any other walking along a street, but it is generally known that people reveal their roots by the manner in which they walk, use their
hands, and generally comport themselves. This man was no exception. Maisie knew that he was not French but English.

"Ah, Mademoiselle Dobbs, Mademoiselle Dobbs!" Madame
Thierry turned on the gaslight from the base of the stairwell and
walked up to greet Maisie, who had been oblivious to the fading

light. "We may not yet have the electricity, but we certainly have illumination. You will fall if you do not turn on the lights."

"Of course, madame. You are right."

Madame Thierry smiled. "It is for you. My very popular guest! A telegram from Angleterre." She held out an envelope to Maisie.

"Thank you."

"I have a fresh soup and pâté this evening, a peasant concoction with chicken. Is that to your liking, or have you been fed too much by Madame Clement?"

"I think just a small bowl, perhaps in an hour, madame."

"*Bon.* I will call in one hour."

"*Merci beaucoup, madame.*"

Maisie went to her room and tore open the telegram. It was from Stratton, as she expected.

RECEIVED YOUR MESSAGE VIA COMPTON STOP HAVE

CONDUCTED DISCREET INITIAL INVESTIGATION PER

INSTRUCTION STOP WILL ADVISE UPON RETURN STOP

WATCH YOUR BACK STOP STRATTON

Much to her surprise, Maisie fell asleep quickly, relaxed, perhaps, by the laughter that accompanied Pascale Clement. But she took two conscious thoughts with her into slumber. First, she wondered why Pascale's surname was that of her mother and grandmother, not her father. The second thought was of Stratton's telegram and his warning: *Watch your back.*

NINETEEN

Pascale was sitting on the fence that ran along one side of the carriage sweep, at the very place where she had flown through the air atop her ebony gelding, Louis, the day before. She was wearing a pretty cotton dress with tiny flowers embroidered into the fabric, yesterday's brown jacket with the sleeves pushed up above the elbow, and brown leather sandals that revealed legs tanned by the summer sun. Her chestnut hair was drawn back into a braid, which made her look her age.

"Mademoiselle Dobbs! Hello!" She waved, jumped from the fence, and ran toward her guest. "Grandmère is asleep, but she will rise just before lunch."

"Is she ill?" Maisie greeted Pascale with the customary kiss on each cheek.

"No, but it is her way. She sleeps poorly and rises very early, so she will often take a nap for a couple of hours in the morning. And she's old."

Maisie laughed. "Ah, what it is to be thirteen, when all others seem old!"

Pascale wrinkled her nose, grinned, and took Maisie's hand as she skipped along beside her. "I will show you the château. It is very large, you know."

"I can see that. But I have been wondering, aren't you supposed to be at school?"

"I have taken all my classes at the lycée for girls in Reims, and now I have a tutor who comes three times each week. This will be for one year; then I will go to Switzerland."

"That sounds very exciting. Are you looking forward to it?"

Pascale shrugged. "Not really. I want to stay with Grandmère, but she says I must spread my wings and a house with an old lady is not the place for a young girl. Yet I like my home here, and I know I will worry about Grandmère if I am away."

Maisie nodded. Chantal Clement was a wise one, but as Pascale told of the plans for her future, a sharp pain like the prick of a pin touched her heart. *I know just how you feel.* She smiled. "I am sure you will love it. Your grandmother is right; you must learn more of the world."

Pascale ran up the steps leading to a side entrance and turned to Maisie as she opened the door. "But it's a complete waste of time—I am only going to come back here to run the château and look after our land, so what's the point? I was not serious about all those other places yesterday. I want to look after Grandmère. And I will have very big parties here too!"

Maisie laughed and shook her head, once again thinking of the one who was so very much like Pascale.

The tour of the château seemed to take ages. They went upstairs, downstairs, into galleries and rooms—some with furniture covered in white dust sheets—along corridors, and even into a ballroom.

"Can you keep a secret?" Pascale wrinkled her nose, the freckles joining together in a way that made her seem even more mischievous than usual.

"Well, I would hope so, Mademoiselle Clement."

"If I show you something that I think even Grandmère knows nothing about, will you promise, absolutely promise, not to tell?" She pressed both hands to her heart and gave her visitor a look that Maisie thought was rather theatrical.

"I promise." Maisie placed her hand on her heart, which had begun to beat faster.

Pascale nodded and crooked her finger to indicate that Maisie should follow her. Leading the way along a narrow wood-paneled corridor, she suddenly knelt and pressed a panel, which snapped open. Maisie raised her eyebrows. She had heard of such devices but never actually seen one; it struck her as something she might read about in a book rather than something to be encountered in the course of her work.

"The Revolution," Pascale explained, as she reached into the space behind the panel.

Maisie pictured a lever or a handle. "Oh, I see."

A small door opened, wide enough for them to crouch and enter a dark space. As Pascale closed the door, Maisie found that she was able to stand up.

"Wait here. I will return."

Pascale's footsteps could be heard treading lightly on wooden floorboards. There was some shuffling, and the girl returned with an illuminated oil lamp. "Come, follow me again."

The passageway led into a wood-lined room about twelve feet square. Heavy frayed curtains hung from a small window that looked out onto the slate roof. There was a limited view of the fields beyond—even, Maisie noted, of the place where Ralph Lawton had perished. Maisie said nothing, at first, but looked around the room. An old chaise longue on one side by a bookcase with works in French and English, a table and a cupboard on the other. Pascale opened the cupboard to reveal a set of cups, saucers, and plates and a tray of cutlery, accompanied by the smell of musty blankets and pillows. Maisie sneezed and Pascale closed the door quickly.

"Shhh! We mustn't make any noise."

"What is this room? Who knows about it?"

"Well, I think Grandmère must know about it, but she doesn't know that I know."

"And you say it was used in the Revolution?"

"That's what I think, but if I ask, she'll know I know."

"How did you find it?"

Pascale shrugged her shoulders and sat on the chaise, patting the place next to her. "By accident, playing with my toys when I was a little child."

"I see." Maisie sat next to Pascale.

"I think my mother came here, because I have found some of her books." She leaped up and took several books of poetry from the bookcase.

"These are all in English."

Pascale nodded. "Of course, she was fluent. I myself speak five languages."

"Five?" It was all Maisie could say as she regarded the young girl, who moved to lean over her shoulder while she leafed through the books.

"Yes. It is not difficult for me, you see; I just know. It is not easy to explain, but I know about their words and sentences when I hear foreign people speak." She shrugged. "But I do like to have exercise in using the language, especially those phrases I cannot find in a book. 'Twisting the arm' is like that."

Maisie felt her mouth become dry as she whispered, "Can you tell me about your father too?"

Pascale blushed and twisted her lips together. She looked straight into Maisie's eyes as if trying to read her. Maisie did not flinch but looked directly back. Pascale was the first to look away. "I am not supposed to know. I am only to know he was a hero and gave his life for France before even knowing I was to be born. My mother worked with our townspeople to foil the Germans, so they killed her. That is what I am supposed to know."

Maisie swallowed hard. "And what is it that you are not supposed to know?"

Pascale twisted her mouth again. "Can I really trust you, Mademoiselle Maisie Dobbs?"

"Yes, you can, Mademoiselle Pascale Clement."

The girl smiled and then became serious again. "My father was the gardener. He was a cripple."

Maisie nodded. *Yes, I know.*

"They came here together. That is why I am not to know about it. I don't know why Grandmère would never tell me, for they all worked together for France in the war. Then my father was killed trying to help the man who crashed on our land, and Mama was taken a year later, when I was just a few months old."

"You know your father was killed trying to save the aviator?"

"This is what I know: that the gardener tried to save him and then the aeroplane exploded."

Maisie shook her head and said no more. Standing as if to leave, she walked across to the cupboard and then to the bookcase, before stopping for a final look out of the window.

"I have another secret, you know." Pascale's breathing was short. Maisie could see she was burdened, not only by a girlish need to share her secret but by the knowledge that what she knew was of importance.

"Ah, you are a woman of secrets." Maisie smiled at the girl and reached out to touch her arm. It was a calming gesture.

"This is a secret that even Grandmère does not know."

Maisie said nothing, just smiled to encourage her young guide.

The girl leaped to her feet and moved the bookcase to one side. At first there seemed to be nothing there; then she tapped a panel and a very small door opened, this one barely large enough for a person to slither through. She lay down on her stomach, reached back into a pocket for a box of matches, lit one, and then beckoned to Maisie, who followed Pascale's lead by lying down beside her. They both peered into the tiny cavern. Pascale pulled out a leather-bound journal and a collection of photographs bound in ribbon.

Pascale handed the photographs to Maisie. Some were formal, taken in a studio, whereas others were obviously taken outside. At first Maisie thought the woman might be Chantal in her younger years and then realized it was Suzanne Clement, Pascale's mother.

"You have looked through these, of course?"

Pascale nodded. "There are some of my mother, some with people in the village. And there are some of the man who may be my father."

Maisie shuffled the photographs. "Ah, yes, I can see why you would believe that."

"Do you think I look like that man?"

Maisie smiled at Pascale. "Perhaps a little." She turned away. *You look more like your aunt.*

"Grandmère has some photographs of me when I was a baby, with my mother. Of course, I was not born in the town. No, I was born in Reims."

"I see." Maisie understood. She turned her attention to the leather-bound book. "And what about this? Have you read it?"

Pascale blushed. "I started, but it didn't make any sense to me."

Maisie flipped through the pages, stopping here and there to read a sentence or run her finger under a word. "No, it wouldn't." She closed the book and turned to Pascale again. "Would you mind very much if I took this book with me? To read? I think I can understand it. I will explain more when I see you again."

Pascale frowned. "But you are going to Biarritz!"

Maisie placed her hand on the shoulder of her new confidante. "And I will be back in a few days."

"Do you really, really promise?"

Maisie reached for the girl and held her close. "I promise you I will return the book. And I never break my promises."

Pascale returned Maisie's hold with thin girlish arms around her waist. "I trust you, Mademoiselle Dobbs."

MAISIE PUSHED THE book into the shoulder bag that she was carrying and left the room. After following Pascale again along corridors and then down to the entrance hall via yet another staircase, Maisie was about to leave when Chantal Clement opened the door that led to the drawing room and came forward to greet them. She wore a pale pink blouse with a high neck and long cuffs, which topped a skirt of pink-and-gray-flecked wool. An ivory shawl was wrapped around her shoulders, and once again she used the cane, though her spine was straight and she did not stoop.

"Ah, there you are. Have you exhausted our guest?" She smiled, then regarded Maisie with a half smile. "It is quite lovely to see you again. I trust my granddaughter has looked after you."

"She has been a delightful hostess. You have a wonderful home, Madame Clement."

"The château has been in our family for centuries, but it is too large for just the two of us and of course our servants. I understand that even in your country a large household is a thing of the past."

"That's true. So many men did not come back from the war, and then there's the economic situation. . . ."

Chantal shook her head. "Yes, it is the same everywhere. And when I am gone, this white elephant will become the property of Pascale."

The girl ran to her grandmother's side. "No, no, you can't go anywhere, Grandmère. I won't let you!"

Chantal laughed. "Ah, *chérie*, I do not plan to escape your clutches just yet." She turned to Maisie. "So, she told you all her secrets, did she?"

"Oh, a few." Maisie winked at Pascale. "But I promised not to tell."

The back-and-forth teasing directed at Pascale continued for another moment or two; then Maisie insisted she must leave to ready herself for the journey to Biarritz the following day. She kissed Pascale on both cheeks and turned to Chantal, who drew Maisie to her with her free hand. She kissed Maisie on one cheek and then, after kissing her quickly on the second cheek, she whispered, "The secrets of the château stay in the château, Mademoiselle Dobbs."

Maisie drew back, smiled again at Chantal, and nodded. *I would love to know your secrets, Chantal Clement.*

. . .

MAISIE ARRIVED BACK at the pension, stopping several times to ensure that she was not being watched before reaching the back garden and letting herself into the house through the kitchen door. She was startled to see the captain and Madame Thierry drinking coffee at the scrubbed pine table.

"*Bonjour*, madame, Captain Desvignes."

"*Bonjour*, Mademoiselle Dobbs. How are you today? I understand that you will be leaving Sainte-Marie tomorrow." Desvignes ran his tongue across the place where his teeth were missing, then smiled with his lips firmly closed.

"Yes, I am *en vacances* to Biarritz, then I will come back to Sainte-Marie again." She turned to Madame Thierry. "I will need a room, perhaps two rooms, for my return. In about five days?"

Madame cast a glance toward Desvignes, then turned to Maisie. "But of course. You will always be welcome at my pension, Mademoiselle Dobbs. A friend will be joining you?"

"Yes, an old friend. I believe she will like Sainte-Marie very much." Maisie addressed Desvignes. "I did not know it was Madame Clement's gardener who was killed while trying to save the British aviator."

"Yes, that is so. Did I not tell you?" Desvignes held out his upturned hands. "Was the detail important to you?"

Maisie shook her head. "Not really. The aviator's father will be pleased to learn that someone tried to save his son, but very sad to know he died in the attempt."

"We all made the attempt but were too late."

"Yes, you were all so brave." Maisie smiled at both Madame Thierry and Captain Desvignes. "Now I must go. Time to pack for tomorrow."

Maisie left the kitchen and hurried upstairs. Locking the door behind her, she pulled several sheets of paper from her document case, took the book from her shoulder bag, and placed it on the table. She pushed back her chair, walked over to the ewer and filled the bowl with cold water—which she once again splashed on her face—and dried her skin with another lace-edged towel A glass carafe filled with fresh drinking water was on the side table, and Maisie poured herself a full measure, which she sipped while walking back and forth across the room.

Everything pointed to Peter Evernden being the gardener, Patrice. Of that she had no doubt. The fact that the gardener had perished along with Ralph was new information. *Was it the truth?* Maisie continued to pace back and forth. What if . . . what if Peter did not die, but his presence at the crash made his position vulnerable? *No, no, go back to the beginning.* Why was he in Sainte-Marie? *Back farther. Peter Evernden was an intelligence agent.* She paced, stopped, paced, and stopped, drawing together the suppositions that had nagged at her for days, along with recent clues. With her heart beating faster, Maisie began to dwell upon a suspicion arrived at, much to her dismay, even before she arrived in Paris. *What if Maurice recruited Peter Evernden based upon my description of his linguistic gifts?* She held her hand to her mouth and put down the glass. Then she paced again, her arms clutched around her, each hand rubbing the top of the opposite upper arm. *Let's say he was transferred to intelligence work and tried to tell Priscilla in the language of boyhood secrecy shared with his brothers.* The assumed name, Patrice, was taken in honor of Patrick, the brother who had founded their boyhood secret society. The guise *a cripple of war* was to anchor him in the community as a man who had fought alongside his fellow men and boys of the village and returned wounded. He had met Suzanne Clement and fallen in love; their affair had produced Pascale. Had Peter known his lover was with child before he died? *Perhaps.* She remembered Priscilla, explaining family names, her brothers Peter, Patrick, and Philip. "It's all Ps, you see, a family tradition, plus it makes it easier when ordering name tags for the school uniforms. I think the teachers must have thought, *Oh, no, here comes another P. Evernden!*"

Quickly she allowed the events to come together, giving voice to the way in which Fate had synchronized the paths of two men, each an expert in his wartime field of endeavor. And Fate had brought their bereaved to Maisie in the same way, engineering her discoveries to this point in time, when Truth would have her way. She had avoided drawing conclusions too quickly but now acknowledged the obvious. *Ralph was an expert in stop-start landings. He delivered Peter to his assignment behind enemy lines. They wouldn't even have known each other. No names would have been exchanged, and they probably didn't even see each other's faces.* Now she stood at the window. *So, later, when Ralph's De Havilland was hit by enemy fire, he knew a landing must be attempted.* And where better than a field already tested, a place where he might, just might, find help if he survived?

Maisie heard a noise downstairs, the muffled sound of Captain Desvignes and Madame Thierry talking and then the front door opening and closing. She left her room and went out onto the landing, moving the lace curtain to one side as she had before. Maisie watched as Desvignes walked across the cobbled street, which appeared gray in the dusky light of late afternoon. Then a man stepped from the side alley, from the same place where she had seen him yesterday. He joined the captain and they walked away, toward the police station.

Returning to her room and locking the door behind her again, Maisie wiped the sweat from her brow and inadvertently scraped her hand across the almost-healed cut. It began to bleed profusely.

"Blast!" She grabbed the damp towel and held it to her forehead.

She would have to be doubly watchful, even more on guard to protect her findings and ensure that the integrity of her work was beyond question. Above all, she had to be very, very careful. *Am I being watched by the secret service? The war was over twelve years ago; surely there is nothing to protect.*

She opened Peter's leather-bound book, sat down, and took up her pen. When she first worked with Maurice he would give her an assignment each Friday, to be completed by Monday, as a teacher might present a homework problem. The assignments were written in code, and Maisie's first task was to break that code, be it based on numbers, language, or a combination of the two. "The mind must be trained as an athlete trains the body, the muscles stretched until they are tired and then strained again. If we are to leave no stone unturned in our work, the mind must be lithe, must be agile. These assignments will ensure your mental acuity."

She began working on Peter's coded entries.

TWENTY

Maisie lifted her head from the table. Six o'clock in the morning. When had she fallen asleep? She had stopped only to take a late supper of yet another bowl of Madame Thierry's delicious soup, packed her suitcase for her departure the following day, and continued her task.

The code used in the leather-bound journal had lacked the complexity she expected and was based on assigning a number to each letter of the alphabet. The problem was that the number was different for each page and even each word, depending on the nature of what was being recorded. Sometimes a page was inscribed on the basis of a five-four-three-two-one code, so that the word DOBBS might be spelled *ISEDT*, with *I* being five letters away from *D* and so on. If the first letter in a word was *z*, then the code began at the beginning of the alphabet. But then the code would change again, and another combination would be used. Though each code might essentially be simple to break, complete interpretation of the pages was a time-consuming task. *And the book was not supposed to be found in the first place.* In discovering the hiding place, Pascale had proved that the curiosity of a child will often prevail over the training of an adult. In fact, Maisie wondered if the journal should have been written at all; it had revealed to her the place where she would find the definitive proof of Peter's identity and affiliation.

She rubbed the sleep from her eyes and stretched. The dreams had come again. Were they dreams or nightmares? She remembered one in which her mother was walking ahead, turning back to admonish her: "Come along, Maisie, hurry up; you don't want to be left behind, now, do you?" But try as she might, she could not keep up; her legs were like lead. She was running but not moving, and when she looked down it was into a river of blood-soaked mud that sucked at her feet and legs. "Come along, Maisie, come along." She struggled to wrench herself free of the mud and reached out to her mother, who instead held out her hands to two young girls, two Maisies, but they weren't her, and her own mother was walking away, holding *their* hands. Then all three turned to her and beckoned, the girls smiling as they revealed themselves. One was Avril Jarvis and the other Pascale Clement. *Come along, Maisie. Come along or you'll be left behind.*

She shivered and looked at her watch. It was over. It was a dream and it was over. In her exhaustion she had allowed the dragon free rein, and she knew the dreams would come again the moment she succumbed to sleep. She must keep a clear head. The driver would not arrive to transport her back to Reims until half-past eight. There was just enough time to run to the woods and find the place indicated in Peter's journal. She had to keep her promise to Pascale, that the book would remain their secret, but now she knew where to find solid proof that Peter Evernden had been here during the war.

She dressed in her woolen trousers, a blouse, cardigan, stout shoes, jacket, scarf and beret and once again left the house by the back door. Philippe snuffled and moved as she walked past him but continued his old-dog snoring without waking or looking up at her. She slipped through the gate, making her way toward the trees beyond the place where the De Havilland had crashed. A ground-mist was lifting as the grainy light became slowly brighter, sending muted shadows across the fields. The dawn chorus had already commenced, and though she could hear farmworkers in the distance she felt alone.

The trees seemed to cluster together even more, as if to shield the inner sanctum of forest animals from the cold air. Maisie walked to the right, looked carefully at the surrounding fence, and began counting. Here and there it seemed as if a post had been replaced, but essentially, the fence appeared to be much as it was when first constructed at the turn of the century. *Number twenty. Turn right into the wood.* Maisie knelt down and slipped through the fence. She was looking for a particular oak tree, a very old one, possibly the grand-father of the wood. Dry leaves crackled underfoot, and each time she heard a twig snap or leaves rustle, she stopped and listened, her heart beating, her breath steamy in the morning air.

This must be the one. It was the broadest oak. Maisie walked around the perimeter of the tree, then knelt between two roots in particular, looking for the place close to the ground, where the bark had grown away from the trunk in a shape that resembled a small doorway. When Maisie was at Chelstone, she had heard children in the vil-lage call them fairy doors, for they resembled an opening into a sto-rybook world. *This is the place.*

Maisie pulled the Victorinox knife from her jacket pocket, se-lected the largest blade, and brushed back the peaty decomposing fallen leaves; then she struck the ground and began to dig. She would only need to go down about a foot or so. Using both hands to scoop back the earth, she finally felt her fingers touch metal. *It's here.* Leaning back, Maisie looked around once more and then brushed debris from the tin. *Yes, this is it.* It was almost seven o'clock. She must not tarry, and certainly she should not risk being seen coming from the wood. She was obviously still under surveillance. Placing the tin in her pocket together with the Victorinox knife, she filled the small hole and covered it again with leaves. Another quick look, an-other missed heartbeat as a rabbit left its warren, and she was gone. Over the fence, one more glance to right and left, along the fence line and across the field, keeping close to a rough stone wall, then up to the houses. Maisie looked back once toward the wood as she came close to Madame Thierry's garden. She squinted into the now-bright morning sunshine just as a man made his way swiftly across the field and into the woods. It was the Englishman. She looked at her watch and willed the driver to arrive early.

Locking the door of her room behind her, Maisie was breathing deeply as she leaned against the closed door. Her bags were packed. She would wash her face and hands and then wait until Madame Thierry called her to say that her driver had arrived. *No need to go outside again.* She placed the tin on the table, then thought again and put it back in her pocket. She splashed water from the bowl onto her face and dabbed her cheeks with the lacy towel. Then she began washing her hands a second time, scrubbing under her nails with the bristle brush that had been placed with the soap in a china dish. She removed the tin from her pocket and doused it with water to remove the dirt. Maisie considered emptying the bowl of water into the lavatory next to the landing, but thought better of it.

Using a lace towel to dry the tin before opening it, she turned it over to examine the lid. It was a Princess Mary tin, a gift from the nation sent to each and every man serving overseas on Christmas Day 1914. The brass box, bearing an embossed image of Princess Mary surrounded on either side by a laurel wreath, along with the names of the Allied countries at war with Germany, contained a combination of treats, dependent upon whether the man was an officer or soldier. Had Peter Evernden enjoyed a pipe along with his half-ounce of tobacco and card with the picture of the princess? Or was he one of the men who'd received a pencil and a packet of sweets instead? Maisie turned the box over. It was approximately five inches long by three and one-quarter inches wide, with a depth of one and one-quarter inches. A green corrosion had already fused the two parts, but she prevailed and eventually the lid came off to reveal a small cotton pouch with a drawstring. Rust spots dotted the cream fabric but the opening spread apart with ease. And when Maisie tipped up the bag, a chain with two small round coins attached fell into her hand. She smiled. It was just what she wanted, just what she knew would be there: Peter Evernden's identity tags. Intelligence agents did not wear any identification, though the metal tag was issued. The agent would bury the tag somewhere close within the field of operation, to be found later should he be taken prisoner or killed, though in this case the family had already been notified that he was missing, presumed dead. And as Maisie knew from his coded journals, when Peter Evernden left hurriedly on his next assignment, he had no time to retrieve the discs, though he hoped they would be found. *How strange*, thought Maisie, as she returned the tags to the small bag and then to the tin, which she wrapped inside a blouse at the bottom of her case. *How strange that it was the daughter he had never known who discovered the key he'd left behind.*

In the moments remaining before she left Sainte-Marie, Maisie began to consider her strategy for the conversation with Priscilla. Her hotheaded friend would no doubt want to rush to Sainte-Marie to see Pascale, which would not please Chantal Clement at all. In fact, Maisie thought that Chantal Clement's gray eyes revealed the steely determination of a woman who was not scared by much, even the German army in her home. No, she must take care to control Priscilla, to ensure that Chantal was consulted and the situation discussed before Priscilla came within miles of the carriage sweep. But without a doubt, her friend should not be kept from her brother's child any longer.

Maisie paced the room again, listening for the sound of a motor car door slamming, her name spoken at the front door, and Madame Thierry's insistent call from the foot of the stair. *What about Ralph Lawton?* Peter's journal had revealed interesting information about Lawton and the crashed De Havilland. It was the most intriguing part of her assignment thus far. It seemed that, in more ways than one, she was going in the right direction, her intuition at play with the hand of Fate, though at times she felt as if she were being moved through the past like a pawn in a game of chess.

· · ·

THE DRIVER CAME at the allotted hour and, after bidding farewell to Madame Thierry and a drooling heavy-lidded Philippe, Maisie departed as quickly as possible for Reims. Her ticket purchased, she spent only a few minutes on the waiting platform before a piercing whistle heralded the commencement of the long journey to Biarritz: the arrival of the train that would take her to Paris and her connecting train. She found her compartment and took a seat by the window, the better to keep a keen eye on the platform. As the station guard blew his whistle and waved the flag, Maisie closed her eyes and leaned back. But it was a short-lived relief, for as the train began to move she heard the guard shout, the whistle blow again and a carriage door open and close. A late passenger had taken a chance and jumped aboard the moving train. It was without doubt a man traveling alone; a woman, Maisie thought, would not have taken so unseemly a risk. Two people would not have had the time to clamber aboard, but a solitary traveler determined to board would not have allowed a guard with a whistle to prevent him from taking a chance. Could it have been the Englishman? Or was it simply a young man who had not yet learned a sense of life's fragility, a boy determined to visit his sweetheart or rushing to another city to find work. Maisie leaned back in her seat again, her hand clasped around the handle of the black leather document case that now held Peter Evernden's journal. She closed her eyes. *I must not let my fear diminish me.*

MAISIE COULD SMELL the Atlantic Ocean in the distance even before her first vision of waves strung out in lines, wind-driven whitecaps reflecting both sun and cloud as they forged toward the shoreline of Biarritz. And as the locomotive finally reached the buffers, travel-weary men, women, and children surged forth onto the platform. Doors slammed back against the carriages as porters ran to and fro, back and forth, with trunks, suitcases, hatboxes, and, in one case, a rather large hairy black dog sitting on top of a suitcase awkwardly balanced on a hand cart. Despite the flurry of activity and the fact that Priscilla anxiously awaited her arrival on the other side of the barrier, Maisie remained in her seat. She waited until there were fewer passengers on the platform and then took her brown leather suitcase down from the rack, gathered up her document case and handbag, and moved out into the corridor and to the door that opened out onto the platform. She looked both ways before alighting and then walked briskly to the place where Priscilla had stipulated that they should meet.

She continued to walk purposefully until she saw Priscilla in the distance. Relieved, she hoped her friend would not overdo her welcome, but Priscilla was her usual ebullient self, rushing toward Maisie, stopping only to drop her cigarette, which she stepped on and twisted into the ground before continuing. Maisie could not help but notice that her friend was as glamorous as ever.

Priscilla's shoulder-length hair was brushed across her shoulders and topped with a cream beret. Wide ivory woolen trousers were complemented by a navy and cream hip-length cardigan with a just-below-the-waist belt. She wore a navy silk scarf around her neck and navy shoes on her narrow feet. Her slender wrists jangled with bracelets that Maisie could hear as Priscilla approached, taking off her dark glasses as she neared the weary traveler.

"Darling, whatever kept you? I've been waiting for ages, simply ages! And I have left Douglas with the toads—the nanny is still in love and has taken a day off to get up to heaven knows what with her latest *garçon*. Mind you, we did owe her a day off, I must say." Priscilla barely stopped talking to take a breath, though she did turn to the porter who ran in her wake, to point to Maisie's luggage. "Now then, how are you, Maisie?" She linked arms with her friend and strode out toward her motor car, which appeared to have been parked indiscriminately outside the station, with one wheel on the pavement and little room for other motors to pass.

"Oh, my goodness!"

"What's the matter?" Priscilla turned to Maisie, and then to her motor car, a black Bugatti Royale with an eye-catching royal-blue swath of color on the bonnet. "Oh, don't! It's an impossibly large motor car and rather fanciful of me. Frankly, I might sell the thing and buy the new smaller version; it's faster." Priscilla pointed to the car, and the porter scurried away to stow Maisie's luggage. "At least the thing starts in the morning!" Priscilla turned to Maisie again. "You know, I promised myself one thing in the war, when I was forcing my old ambulance across the mud, always wondering how many boys I would lose on the way—I promised myself that I would never crank a motor car again in my life. Then later, after the boys were born, I promised us all that, if ever they were injured or hurt, I would always have a decent motor car to get them to a doctor." The porter opened the passenger and driver's doors; Priscilla pressed a generous tip into his hand before starting the engine and nosing the Bugatti toward the road. "And *is it* a complete extravagance? Of course it is. And if I felt like it, I would buy another to keep the thing company."

"You've made your point, Priscilla."

Priscilla looked sideways at Maisie, then back at the road. "Well, I know you too well, Maisie. Any bit of perceived extravagance can send you into sackcloth and ashes again."

They were silent for a moment, Maisie allowing the ocean air to fill her senses.

"You're exhausted from your trip. I'm sorry, I shouldn't have jumped on you like that." Keeping her left hand on the steering wheel, Priscilla flipped open a silver cigarette case with her right, took out a fresh cigarette, snapped the case shut, reached for a matching silver lighter, and lit the cigarette, which she drew on deeply. "I expect it's because I'm so anxious to know whether you have news of Peter."

Maisie smiled. From the moment she saw Priscilla running toward her at the station, her friend's demeanor had revealed her fears, hopes, and expectations. She should keep her waiting no longer.

"It's a bit more complex than we might have thought, Pris—"

"That's strange." Priscilla frowned, distracted for a moment.

"What?"

Priscilla turned her head to look behind, then swung back to face the road. "That's the first time I have ever encountered another motor car while driving along this road. There are only a couple of houses up here: us, the Crowthers—expats; he was in Mesopotamia—and a Spanish family who've already left for the winter."

Maisie looked behind to see a black motor car some way behind.

"Probably some lost tourist," added Priscilla, shrugging. "Oh, well, he'll find out as soon as he comes to the end of the road."

"Pris, can you stop somewhere—you know, pull in behind some trees or something—around the next bend where he can't see us?"

"What's going on?"

"Priscilla. . . ."

Priscilla didn't notice the color drain from Maisie's face, but she could not miss the sharp intensity of her voice and the use of her full name. She accelerated the motor car, turned into a driveway, and pulled to a halt behind a tree. They sat in silence while the black motor car went past. They were close enough to see the driver and passenger, an older couple, the man with his hat pushed back as if in exasperation, the woman holding a map and frowning.

"Just as I thought, tourists."

Maisie closed her eyes and leaned back in the seat.

Priscilla reached out and took her hand, and Maisie squeezed her hand in return.

She was silent for a moment, then turned to Priscilla. "Let's go home, Pris. Let me have a nice long bath, a cup of tea, and a moment to relax. We have much to talk about."

Priscilla started the Bugatti's engine, which roared into life, and pulled out onto the road. "To hell with the tea, Maisie. I believe I need a gin and tonic!"

TWENTY-ONE

Though the journey had been long and grueling, Priscilla's family gave Maisie no quarter. As soon as the Bugatti drew up outside the white hillside villa, the doors opened and three boys gamboled from the house toward the car. They had heard a great deal about their mother's friend, and, despite the deep voice of their father in the distance cautioning them not to run, were clearly excited by the new arrival.

"Boys!" Priscilla's voice was loud and clear and immediately caused her children to cease their rough-and-tumble welcome, which included pressing questions about what it was like to be an investigator. "Your Aunt Maisie has had a long journey and I am claiming her first! Now then, you can go into the house, wash hands and faces—and behind the ears, if you please, Tarquin Patrick Partridge—and then you can make yourselves useful. Tell cook that you'll be setting the table this evening. *Now!*" Priscilla shook her head and smiled. Maisie noticed immediately that she addressed her sons by both their Christian and middle names, as if to keep alive the memory of the brother for whom each boy was named: Timothy Peter, Thomas Philip and Tarquin Patrick.

The boys began to walk slowly back into the villa. Then Timothy pinched Tarquin on the ear, a scuffle began, and they ran to the rear of the property, toward the kitchen, Maisie supposed. A tall man came down the steps toward the Bugatti, which was being unloaded by a manservant named Giles. Maisie immediately warmed to Douglas Partridge, whose smile was kindly and whose green eyes sparkled. He wore pale beige linen trousers, a white shirt with a burgundy cravat, and a Panama hat to shield his eyes from the sun. The left arm of his shirt had been tailored below the shoulder to accommodate his amputation, without obviously drawing attention to an empty sleeve. He used a cane with his right hand and walked with a slight limp. When he spoke, Maisie detected the wheeze of gasdamaged lungs.

"Maisie, at last. I have heard so much about you. Welcome to our home—though I do hope Priscilla warned you that with our three toads it's more like a lunatic asylum at times!"

Douglas rested the cane against his thigh for a moment as he shook hands with Maisie, then took up the cane again and bent toward his wife, whom he kissed not on the cheek but on the lips. It was not a long kiss, but Maisie looked away. And as Priscilla laughed and gently held her hand to her husband's face, Maisie felt, not for the first time, that events of the past two weeks were plunging her deeper into an ever-widening and lonely abyss.

Douglas excused himself, explaining that he had several telephone calls to make to Paris, while Priscilla turned to Maisie and put an arm around her friend's shoulder. "Come along, let me show you the gardens. We have a lovely view out toward the sea. Douglas will be in his study until supper; his latest book is due out in London in a month and he's rather anxious about it. He's also written a not-too-complimentary piece about the German elections for *The Spectator*."

Priscilla led Maisie along a stone pathway flanked by olive trees and lavender bushes, the walls of the villa on her right ablaze with bougainvillea and passionflower. Steps led up to the broad whitewashed terrace, and a more rustic stairway led down to landscaped gardens and a small, not very successful vineyard.

Maisie found it hard to believe that only yesterday she was stealing across a field in Sainte-Marie, her every move probably monitored by someone who might want her dead. And in this idyll, she must now speak of death with her dear friend. The way Priscilla opened and closed her hands with each step, the fact that her fingers shook as she pointed out landmarks below and—as she described the boys taking part in the olive harvest—pushed her wedding ring back and forth over the joint in her finger, all revealed the depth of her anxiety.

"Shall we sit down?" Maisie pushed her fringe back across her forehead, then shielded her eyes from the late-afternoon sun, now low in the sky. The brightness was causing her temples to ache.

"We should get you some of these." Priscilla pointed to the dark glasses protecting her eyes. "I have some spare pairs, you know." Priscilla started toward the double-glass doors that led into the villa, but Maisie's words called her back.

"Sit down, Pris. It's time we talked about Peter. You cannot wait any longer, and I cannot hold what I have discovered. There are things you must know."

"I . . . I. . . ." Priscilla appeared paralyzed by the idea of impending news.

"Come along, my dear friend. Sit with me here." Maisie smiled and patted the place alongside her on the wooden slatted bench, which was festooned with blue and gold cushions. "Then, when we have spoken, I really must have you show me to my room and I will take a good long bath while you speak with Douglas."

Priscilla swallowed, her throat dry. "Can I just get a drink?"

Maisie sighed. "All right. But be quick."

Priscilla rushed inside the villa, and Maisie closed her eyes. From her place on the veranda overlooking the town of Biarritz, the *clink-clink* of ice on glass was clearly audible through the open doors.

"Here you are. And it's a strong one!" Priscilla handed a glass to Maisie and took a seat next to her.

Maisie held the glass in her left hand and slipped the fingers of her right through Priscilla's.

"I will tell you what I know; then I will tell you what we will do. And before I begin, Pris, this is one time when I will not have you storming ahead without my say-so. Is that clear?"

"I have no idea what you are talking about, but I promise I will heed your word." Priscilla took a large sip from her glass as Maisie set her untouched cocktail on a table alongside the bench and turned to face her friend.

"I have made some discoveries that may come as rather a shock. Peter did not die on the day or at the place where he was listed as missing. That was a deliberate subterfuge to protect him. My original investigation, the one that brought me to France, has surprisingly revealed that Peter was a British intelligence agent. He was operating in occupied territory in a small town outside Reims under an assumed name." Maisie paused, allowing Priscilla time to assimilate the information.

"Oh, my darling, darling Peter." Priscilla placed her glass on the table to the right of the bench and pressed her hand to her forehead, still holding Maisie's hand tightly.

"I believe his job was to liaise with an important civilian who had been recruited to muster local support as well as to protect Peter. I believe his field of operation was extremely dangerous, though my knowledge of the service and his actual brief is limited."

Priscilla pulled a linen handkerchief edged in blue silk from the pocket of her trousers and dabbed her eyes.

Maisie breathed deeply again, her shoulders aching as the weight of her discovered knowledge was moved but not lessened. "There's more. He had to leave Sainte-Marie after a British aviator crash-landed his aircraft while en route to drop more messenger pigeons for Peter's group to use. Peter attempted to save the man's life but had to flee the town for fear his unmasking would reveal the web of activity locally."

Priscilla shook her head. "Oh, my brave Peter—those brave people!"

"Yes, they were very brave. A year later, three of them were executed." Maisie paused again, gauging her friend's demeanor and her capacity to assimilate the information revealed. She went on. "Those killed included Peter's lover, a young woman named Suzanne Clement."

"His lover?"

"Yes. Peter was in love."

"Oh, God." Priscilla began to cry, removing her dark glasses and pressing the handkerchief to her eyes, her tears now in full flow.

"Priscilla, there's still more."

"I don't know if I can stand it."

"Yes, you can. You can stand this."

"What is it?" She turned to Maisie, the tears still running down her cheeks.

"Peter's lover had a child, a daughter whom she named Pascale. She's thirteen years old now and lives with her grandmother."

Priscilla's eyes opened wide, her tears abated. She released Maisie's hand and stood up. "Oh, my God! Where is she?" She began to pace, almost hysterical. "I must go to her. I must see her. She is my family; she is all I have of him—"

"No, you must not. Not yet." Maisie's voice was soft but firm.

Priscilla sat down, reaching for her glass of gin and tonic, from which she took a hefty swig. Maisie continued, her voice quiet and modulated, so that Priscilla had to lean toward her to hear.

"This is what will happen. I must return to Sainte-Marie in a few days. I am tired, Priscilla, and my work is far from over; as you may remember, you are a secondary client. I will speak to the grandmother, Chantal Clement. I will press her to see you, and I believe I will meet with success. Then I will send for you—expect to come to

Sainte-Marie a day or so after my arrival there. You cannot whisk the girl away, for she and her grandmother adore each other. But Pascale knows quite a lot about her father and, I believe, deserves to know even more. And there's something else."

"Yes?"

"I do not yet know where Peter perished, though I'll find out. But I believe you will find Sainte-Marie a fine place for a memorial."

Priscilla took a final sip from the almost-empty glass and nodded. "Yes, I think you're right. It's where he left his heart, isn't it?" She swirled ice cubes around, the *clink-clinking* almost tuneful, and asked one final question. "What does she look like, Maisie?"

Maisie reached for Priscilla. "She's just like you, Priscilla. Down to the bone."

FOLLOWING A LONG hot bath, Maisie pulled on a heavy white cotton robe and wandered onto the balcony overlooking the gardens at the side of the house. Though it was now dark, from her vantage point she could see not only the lights of the town but also, to her right, intermittent house lights on adjacent estates. Motor car headlights occasionally swept up a neighboring hillside or went down again. She checked the sweep of gravel driveway that led from the Partridges' villa out onto the road and down the hill and could see no evidence of another vehicle.

Maisie turned her thoughts to her investigation, which was proceeding like liquid in a funnel, pouring toward an ever-narrowing point until captured in the cup below: In her mind the lives of Peter Evernden and Ralph Lawton were coming together as if orchestrated by the gods of life and death, peace and war. And if she was correct in her decoding of Peter's journals, Biarritz was the receptacle to which Priscilla unwittingly held the key. She watched the lights for just a moment longer. Then she turned into the room and dressed for dinner.

Priscilla's welcoming gift to Maisie had been laid out on the bed to await her arrival. Knowing that her friend was nothing if not sensible and would not have thought of packing evening wear even for a place such as Biarritz, she had ordered an ensemble from a Paris couturier that would fit Maisie to perfection. Long heavy silk trousers in a deep midnight blue were complemented by a sleeveless blouse in pale blue and an Asian-inspired thigh-length jacket in matching midnight-blue silk with a sash of the same fabric as the blouse. Should the evening become cool, there were two additional items: a broad pale-blue cashmere wrap and a knee-length knitted coat, also in cashmere, to wear instead of the silk jacket if necessary. Maisie shook her head. Though she might admire such clothing on others, she would never have considered purchasing such items—nor could she have ever afforded such luxury.

The gift caused Maisie to think of her mother and father, and when she touched the fine cloth, her skin prickled as she remembered her mother's translucent beauty, which needed no augmentation of the kind that riches can buy. Maisie fingered the fabrics, wondering how much the gift she would so graciously accept actually cost. And as she felt the nearness of that lovely spirit once again, she wondered what her father would think about her friend's expenditure, of a sum of money that might have delivered his wife from indescribable pain being spent on mere clothes. But Maisie understood that the gift was part of Priscilla's attempt to assuage her own indescribable pain, pain Maisie knew would be made even worse this evening by her attempt to extract information: information Maisie hoped might lead her to the truth about Ralph Lawton.

TWENTY-TWO

The boys did not dine with their parents and Maisie that night, though Priscilla was quick to explain that usually they had meals together, a ritual rare among many of their friends and acquaintances, who adhered to the maxim that children should be seen and not heard.

"Of course, there are times when Douglas and I would rather have a meal without looking at a runny nose or having to extol the virtues of greens, but fortunately not only is the food much better here but, on those occasions when we need time away from being Mummy and Daddy, we have a high tea in the playroom around six and then a late supper in peace when they've finally fallen asleep."

Maisie ran a forefinger up and down the long narrow stem of the crystal wineglass in front of her as Priscilla's nervousness continued to give way to small talk. She was distracted by her determination to forge ahead with her investigations, a need at odds with a desire to return to England, to have the cases closed so she could move on. But to what? She had telephoned Billy again from Paris, and was both pleased and frustrated by his news that there had been little movement on the Avril Jarvis case. Though his current knowledge of the police investigation had been extracted from newspaper reports, he did inform Maisie that he was working on an interesting tip, but their call had been disconnected at the most inopportune moment, as Maisie had to hurry to catch her train.

"Well." Douglas placed his table napkin alongside his cheese plate and stood up. Taking the cane that had been hooked over the back of his chair, he leaned down to Priscilla, who raised her lips to his. "I'll leave you two to your after-dinner conversation. Don't stay up too long; it's been a wretched day for you both." He smiled at Maisie. "And you must be thoroughly exhausted by now." Douglas smiled once more and left the room.

"Douglas seems to be such a good man, Priscilla. You chose well."

Priscilla leaned forward and picked up her cigarette case, which she then set on the table again. "I'm like a chimney. It's got to stop." She sipped the smooth Barolo instead and topped up her glass. She reached to pour more wine for her guest, but Maisie was ready and placed her hand over her glass. Without sitting back in her chair, she turned to Maisie. "As I have said before, he's my rock, my strength, my anchor in what was—and still is—a very unsettled world."

Maisie nodded. "And he knows I'm going to unsettle that world even more now, doesn't he?"

"Yes." Priscilla tapped the cigarette case. "But I am ready. You have discovered more than I could ever imagine, Maisie. I will help in any way I can; it's an entirely selfish position: The more you uncover, the more I will find out about Peter and where he died."

"First of all, you had your own suspicions about his work, didn't you?"

Priscilla sighed. "How did you know?"

Maisie shook her head. "You aren't a fool, Priscilla. You knew there was a secret; you said as much in London."

"I had my suspicions . . . oh, sod it!" She reached for her cigarette case, flipped it open, and took out a cigarette, which she placed directly in her mouth and lit with the triangular silver table lighter. "It's no good; I can't do without them."

"Pris, I want you to tell me about Biarritz."

"What do you want to know? You would probably do better speaking to the people at Thomas Cook."

"That's not what I meant. I want to know why you chose Biarritz, what caused you to come here."

"Well, you know what caused me to come here, Maisie, I mean—"

"You could have gone to Madrid, to Cannes, Antibes, to the Bahamas, to anywhere that anyone of a certain sort who had seen too much in the war ran away to. Why Biarritz?"

"Gosh, when you put it like that—I did consider other places, but Biarritz meant something to me."

Maisie leaned forward, her hands clasped together on the table. She said nothing, waiting for Priscilla to continue.

"We used to come here for the summers as a family. I was about six or so when we first traveled down; it was just after the boys had broken up from school. We couldn't wait. My father had rented a villa—only about a mile from here, actually, but closer to the beach. And we stayed for six weeks, the whole summer. Of course, it's changed now; it's much more of a resort. Then it was more like a sleepy little fishing village. We came every summer after that, right up until 1913, when we were all a bit too old for buckets and spades and were making idiots of ourselves in the local bars with the friends who would descend on us. It was all great fun, wonderful memories. . . ." Priscilla pressed her cigarette into the ashtray and picked up her glass, taking another sip of the deep red wine.

Maisie nodded. "If you could say—in just a few words, perhaps—what Biarritz meant to you, what you were searching for, what would it be?"

"What kind of question is that, one of those airy-fairy ideas of yours?"

"Priscilla. . . ."

Pulling her long legs up so that her bare heels balanced on the edge of the chair, Priscilla rested her chin on her knees. "All right. I think, if anything, it was the sense of freedom. You know, when we were young, the four of us together, we would burst out of school at the end of term—lucky you, never to have suffered through boarding school—and then we were whisked away to this . . . this oasis of lightness. We were allowed to be wild here, run with no shoes, be young and carefree. And I wanted that back, Maisie. I wanted to get away from the nightmares, from that aching sorrow. I lost them all and I wanted some of it back, if only in the scent on the air, the light as it falls across the floor. I wanted freedom from the grief."

Maisie swallowed hard, reached for her glass, and took a sip.

"But as you know, I did not find my freedom in the sand but rather at the bottom of a bottle—until Douglas."

"Did Peter share your feelings about Biarritz?"

"Oh, my goodness, he most certainly did. Peter loved it here more than any of us, if that were possible. He made friends easily— of course it helped that he was absolutely fluent in the language and the dialect, which is so important. In fact, Daddy always said that, by the end of the summer, Peter was more Basque than British!"

"What do you know about what happened in the town during the war?"

"Ah, now it's on to history!" Priscilla shrugged, then went on. "Of course, we did not come in 1914. Daddy thought that what with one thing and another, it was best to stay at home, so we ended up at Cowes, which was all very well except for the weather. And we all loved the boats. You know, when I first came back to Biarritz—in 1920, I think it was—there were still lots of soldiers here. The Hotel Palais, which was originally built to be the royal palace, had been requisitioned for use as a hospital for the wounded throughout the war. They were shipped here by train—apparently they came in droves—and then afterward even more came to convalesce. Quite a few remained—and some they never could identify, you know. Lost their memories, their minds. I remember meeting a couple in a hotel when I first came here who thought they would find their missing son among the injured. They left disappointed. And they weren't the only ones."

"I see."

Priscilla turned to Maisie. "Why are you interested, Maisie? What has all this got to do with Peter? Rest assured that if he were here I would have found him."

"No, that's not it, not at all." Maisie paused, wondering to what extent she should share her thoughts with her friend. "I was wondering whether Peter might have——"

"I don't know how you do your job." Priscilla's tone was sharp.

"What do you mean?"

"Prodding here and poking there, all the time searching for a reason for this and an explanation for that. It's a wonder you solve anything."

Maisie looked at Priscilla intently. "No, it's not exactly like that. Sometimes it's as if truth were like a festering wound, ready to break open and be cleansed. It seems as if the information I am seeking is just there, lying in front of me on the path, asking to be discovered, asking for a kind of solution—or absolution. Then again, it can evade me, like a small splinter that escapes under the skin. Then I have to wait, be patient. I have to wait for it to fester."

"And what do you think of Peter and the other case?"

Maisie leaned back in her chair and closed her eyes, aware that her chosen metaphor had revealed something of her personal turmoil. She changed the subject. "Tell me more about your friends here, about your life. We haven't had this much time together since Girton."

"Well, seeing as you've asked. . . ." Priscilla stood and pushed back the chair, which scraped on the terra-cotta tiles. "Come to my lair. It is time for you to see my rogues' gallery, and then we must away to our beds. We will be woken by my boys soon enough."

Maisie followed Priscilla along a tiled hallway to a small staircase at the back of the house.

"These rooms are as far away from the playroom as possible," said Priscilla, leading Maisie to the foot of the narrow staircase, where she switched on a light. "I'm not sure that you can see very well here, but you will be able to in the morning."

The stairwell was covered in photographs on both sides, and as Maisie took each step in turn it seemed as if she were caught in a sea of joy, of happy times and, as Priscilla said, of freedom. There were photographs taken before the war, of three boys and a girl, all with the same grin that caused their eyes to appear closed in a mischievous manner. Then the four were older, often joined by friends from school, and there were the parents, on bicycles, leading their brood on a ride close to the sea. Then the Everndens in 1913, the boys now men, Priscilla a stunning young woman, wearing her brother's trousers even then. *Freedom*. Maisie said nothing as she ascended the staircase. Now Priscilla on her own, in a club, glass in one hand, cigarette in the other, those half-closed eyes sad even in the dim light. Then another group, and another. Groups of men and women with smiles not matched by their eyes. As Maisie touched each photograph, Priscilla told the story of the day, the night, the holiday. Soon, Maisie was aware that she was searching for a face in the crowd, a young man who might not resemble any photograph she had already seen. Was this a shot in the dark, this feeling in her gut that Biarritz was not just the place where Priscilla had tried to touch her family again but was a place of refuge for another?

Groups in clubs, parties on white verandas, and gatherings in bars. Then Douglas, at first on the edge of a group, then alongside Priscilla; a year later, walking in the Pyrenees, both shielding their eyes from the sun. There they are with an infant; then with a small boy and a babe in arms. A family. Maisie looked at the photographs on the wall close to the top of the staircase, and as she squinted at the faces she could see life in Priscilla's eyes again. *And joy*.

"What a tribe, eh?"

"It's your history, Pris."

"Come along, time for us to go to bed. You can look again tomorrow—and we've albums to bore you with too!"

Maisie began to descend the staircase, and as she took each step slowly, a sensation, one she knew so well, seemed to grow in her stomach. At first a tingle, then her heart began beating faster. *Stop here. It is here.* Priscilla was waiting to turn off the light.

"What is it, Maisie? Are you all right?"

Maisie nodded, scanning each photograph, touching each image, each face caught in the lens. *I am close. I am so close.*

"Come along, you're tired, Maisie. You'll ruin your eyes."

Maisie was holding her chest to still her now-throbbing heart; with the other hand she fingered the images, some in frames, some pinned haphazardly in place. She turned to Priscilla, her smile warm, revealing nothing.

"This looks like a jolly day out—who are all these people?" Maisie pointed to one photograph in particular, a group of men and women leaning against a motor car with the bonnet up, glasses of champagne in their hands.

Priscilla came to Maisie's side and peered at the photograph. "Oh, that was a day! A group of us decided to take off for a hidden cove, picnic and all, then halfway along the road, *bang!* Something went in the engine, so we all had to clamber out while it was repaired. Needless to say, out came the champers, the foie gras, cheese, bread, and even more champers!"

"Tell me everyone's names." Maisie was aware of some acting on her part, as if she were really interested in each and every person raising a glass to the camera.

"All right." Priscilla was smiling, happy to speak of the day. "That's Polly Woods, what a girl! To look at her, you'd have thought butter wouldn't melt in her mouth. There's Richard—Ricky to his friends—Longman." Her finger moved along the photograph, pointing to each face in turn. "Thadeus More and his wife Candace . . . and there's Douglas, looking serious. Um, this is Julia Thorpe and her fiancé—the first of many—Edmund. And this chappie here, the one you just about see looking up from the engine, is Daniel Roberts." Priscilla paused and pulled a face. "Heaven knows how we squeezed so many into that motor car, but we did! Mind you, Ricky and Daniel were following us, and thank heavens Danny knew what he was doing, once the bonnet was up."

Maisie smiled again, and the women turned to continue walking downstairs. "So, do those people all still live here? Do you see them?"

Priscilla flicked the light switch as they reached the bottom of the staircase. "Polly's heart was broken by a swarthy Spaniard; then she met an American who was here for the summer in '26—I remember him talking about oil a lot. They're married now and she seems to spend most of her time dripping in furs, being petted and pampered. The Mores went back to England, now nicely settled with two children in Pangbourne. Julia lives in Paris with husband number three. Daniel Roberts deals in motor cars, not that anyone ever sees him. He started years ago, literally with his own garage where he did all the mechanics himself. No one really knows him—as I said, he's always kept to himself, rather a recluse. We gave up inviting him to parties years ago. He owns a lovely house about a mile away, the Villa Bleu. Lives there with a manservant, I believe. Paul, I think is his name. Mind you, we all thought that Paul was—"

"And what about the other man?"

"Ricky Longman? It was so sad, Maisie. He died about five years ago."

"Oh."

"Yes, poor man couldn't keep away from the bottle. Died of liver failure. Daniel did everything to help him, nursed him at the end, even." Priscilla's smile had evaporated. "Ricky just couldn't forget the war, couldn't put it behind him. Probably something to do with his hands; they were terribly scarred from burns." Priscilla folded her arms as she spoke "Mind you, scars aren't that unusual among the boys, are they? Look at Douglas. Daniel has some nasty scars too, right here." She lifted her chin and indicated a swath of skin from her ear to her neck, then shook her head. "Ricky's death made me shudder, I can tell you. It made me realize, more than ever, that Douglas had come along at just the right time for me."

Maisie nodded. "I'm glad you found each other."

Priscilla leaned toward Maisie and kissed her on each cheek. "Well, I don't know about you, but I'm all in."

"I think I'll just go out onto the terrace for a little bit of calm before I go to bed."

"You never change, Maisie—and I love you for it! See you in the morning." She squeezed Maisie's hand and turned to make her way along the tiled hallway.

"Good night, Pris."

Maisie opened the French doors and walked onto a terrace at the side of the house. A cool breeze skimmed across her skin, and she pulled the cashmere wrap around her shoulders. A few minutes passed before she turned, came back into the house, and, instead of making her way to the main wing and the guest rooms, switched on the stair light. She mounted the stairs quickly, searching for that one photograph once again, that sunny day amid the many sunny days in Priscilla's rogues' gallery. Leaning closer, she found the image and squinted to inspect the brown-spotted photograph, the now-fading face; then she stepped away, turned off the light, and made her way downstairs and through the night-quiet house.

TWENTY-THREE

It was not until the afternoon of Maisie's first full day in Biarritz that she finally had some time to herself. The house seemed to become silent quite suddenly. The boys attended a local school in the morning, followed by lunch at home and two hours with their private tutor; then, when their pent-up energy seemed ready to raise the rafters, Elinor, the Welsh nanny who had finally returned from the clutches of her Basque boyfriend, took them to the beach. Douglas worked in his study while Priscilla claimed a nap before dinner. Maisie had procured Daniel Roberts's address from Giles, along with directions to his house, and set off, walking briskly down the hill before turning left and continuing on her way.

Eventually, she came to the narrow walled hillside road that led to Villa Bleu. Maisie made her way along the street where the rough walls were overhung with ivy, then stood for a while outside the cast-iron gate that led into the property's walled gardens. She peered through to a cobbled patio interspersed with raised flower beds, still colorful with end-of-summer blooms. The modest villa immediately beyond was painted in a wash of pale blue that seemed to reflect the sky and the sea in the distance. An arched entrance led to a heavy wooden door. Maisie unlatched the gate and made her way along the path.

A wicker shopping basket and a pair of brown leather sandals had been cast aside by the door, along with a wet towel. A leather dog leash hung over the back of a wooden chair. Maisie reached forward and pulled on a knotted fisherman's rope, which rang the large brass bell above. She winced as the clanging broke the afternoon silence. A dog in the distance barked just once; then there was silence again. She reached up and clanged again before hearing the single bark and a man shouting, "All right, all right, I'm coming," in a mixture of French and English. Maisie saw a silhouette pass the window, and the door opened to reveal a tall man with jet-black hair that was wet and slicked back. He was wearing a fine cotton shirt and linen trousers rolled up to mid-calf.

"Bonjour." His greeting was curt.

"Please, do you speak English?" Maisie felt a need for the greater confidence offered by conversation in her native language.

The man raised his hand, his finger and thumb just half an inch apart to indicate his ability. "*Un peu.* A little."

Maisie smiled, and the man smiled broadly in return.

"I was hoping to see Mr. Roberts. Is he at home?"

"Ah, you have a problem with the automobile? Yes? Then you must go to the town, to Mr. Roberts's business."

Maisie shook her head. "No. *Non.* I have no automobile here. I would like to see Mr. Roberts on a personal matter."

The man shrugged and made a point of looking at his watch. "Come in. I will see if he can meet with you. Your name?"

"Maisie Dobbs."

He opened the door wider to allow Maisie to enter the room, which seemed almost chilly in the shadows of late afternoon. "Wait here. I will check." Before closing the door, the man reached for the leather sandals and then padded through the entrance hall, along a hallway, and was gone. In the distance, Maisie could see a veranda similar to those at Priscilla's house, though this one was decorated with shrubs planted in white and blue pots of varying sizes. She heard voices and then shoe-clad footsteps coming closer, along with the *click-click-click* of dog claws on tile.

Daniel Roberts came toward her, accompanied by a black Great Dane walking at heel. At first, she did not recognize the man, for his hair was completely white. It was not the gray of age, or an inherited color, but rather the shock of white that is known to follow terror.

"Miss Dobbs?"

"Yes. It's good of you to see me, Mr. Roberts." Maisie stood firm before Roberts, even though the dog had positioned itself not alongside his owner, but next to Maisie. She reached down with her hand and stroked the broad head. "What a magnificent creature."

"He's rather regal, isn't he? The breed was Attila the Hun's preferred dog of war, you know. They are ever-watchful but seldom feel the need to become a nuisance with incessant barking. His name is Ritz. Short and sweet." He paused, making no move to invite Maisie to be seated in comfort. "What can I do for you, Miss Dobbs? People usually only want to see me about motor cars, and yet Paul tells me that you have no motor here."

"I wonder, can we sit down? I have come to see you on a matter of some delicacy."

Roberts smiled, almost as if he understood the purpose of her visit, and in that moment Maisie knew that, despite the scar that became visible as he turned into the light, this was the man she had seen before in photographs. Leading the way through to the veranda, Roberts pointed to two cushioned wicker chairs with a table in between. Maisie sat down first, followed by her host.

"Now then, I think I should come straight to the point, Mr. Roberts, so that no time is wasted."

"Yes, do." His voice was teasing, almost sarcastic.

Maisie rested her hand on one arm of the chair and turned to face Roberts in a manner that was neither urgent nor too relaxed. He sat up and leaned slightly toward her.

"Mr. Roberts, I conduct inquiries of a highly confidential nature for my clients. A couple of weeks ago I was retained by Sir Cecil Lawton, to prove that his son, an aviator, was indeed killed in the war." Maisie paused for just a second to gauge Roberts's emotions. He had not moved and was completely attentive, though Maisie detected the tweak of a half smile at the corner of his mouth. She continued. "My investigation naturally led me to France and now to Biarritz." Maisie inclined her head and looked straight into Roberts's eyes. "So, Ralph, that is why I am here."

The man before her was silent, the muscles in his neck taut in a way that emphasized the scar where intense heat had seared his flesh. He held her gaze for half a moment and then looked away.

"Ralph?"

"You are mistaken, Miss—"

"Dobbs." Maisie smiled. "I have come a long way, Ralph."

"Look, I'm telling you I am not any Tom, Dick, Harry or Ralph. My name is Daniel Roberts." Visibly shaking, the man stood up and moved toward the door as if to swiftly expedite departure of the unwanted guest.

"Wait!" Maisie remained seated, reaching into her shoulder bag before turning once again. There were two photographs in her hand. "I'm sorry, Ralph, even with time, with scars and with a new identity, I could recognize you anywhere." She held out the first photograph, of two young men laughing after a game of tennis a carefree lifetime ago.

The man was silent again, taking the photograph and looking at it before reaching for the second photograph, which bore the image of the same two young men at the Café Druk. The black dog at his side began to whimper.

"Mr. Lawton? Ralph?"

"Yes?"

"It is you, isn't it?"

Ralph Lawton nodded and then spoke, the words catching in his throat. "It's been quite a long time since anyone called me by that name." He placed the photographs on an adjacent table.

"How long?"

Lawton's eyes flashed and Maisie felt the energy of his delayed anger almost as if it were a sudden cold breeze. Then he laughed. "I don't believe it. The old man finally found someone to track me down!"

Maisie frowned but did not counter the outburst.

Thrusting his hands into the pockets of his beige trousers, Lawton paced back and forth. "Of course, you do realize, don't you, Miss Dobbs, that you can never tell him where I am, can never tell anyone that I am here."

"My client—"

Lawton stopped in front of Maisie and leaned toward her from the waist, his hands still in his pockets. She thought he looked like a recalcitrant schoolboy. "He doesn't want to know. Not really. No, he retained you knowing—believing—that you would only go through the motions, confirm my death, collect your fee, and then he could go on as if nothing had happened, his conscience clear."

Maisie responded quickly, before Lawton could reflect on his words. "Ralph, how do you know the truth of your father's feelings toward you now?"

Lawton paced again, and then he came back to Maisie, taking his chair in a manner that revealed his frustration. "My name is Mr. Roberts, to you, Miss Dobbs." He took a deep breath and leaned forward again, addressing Maisie as one might speak to a person who is hard of hearing. "He-does-not-love-me. He does not even *like* me, Miss Dobbs. He would be appalled to know I am alive. His world—and mine, come to that—would fall asunder if he were forced to acknowledge me again."

"How do you know? After all, time—"

He waved his hand dismissively. "*Come on!* Don't give me any 'time heals' nonsense. You have no idea, *no idea* what you are talking about." Lawton's voice had almost reached screaming pitch, and now he issued a deep sigh. "Look at me. Look at who I am, what I have here." He waved his hand around the veranda, at the house. "Look at my friend, Paul. Then when you see my father, look at him, his world. There is no place for me. There is no place for us as father and son, as family."

Maisie nodded. Yes, she understood.

"You know about your mother?"

He nodded, pressing his lips together and looking away so that Maisie could not see his face.

"I read it in *The Times*." He shrugged, giving a nervous half laugh. "Hardly ever read a newspaper, but a customer left a copy at my garage. I suppose someone up there wanted me to know. . . ." His words drifted. Then he turned to Maisie. "I don't know anything about you, Miss Dobbs, but please don't bring your preconceived notions of family to my house and think you can fit the word *Lawton* into it. We were born of the same blood, but we are not . . . not *joined*. There is nothing *here*." He thumped his chest with his fist, then pressed his closed hand to his mouth. He turned to Maisie with tears in his eyes and went on. "Can you possibly grasp how difficult it was to build a life here? To make something of myself, something I could never have done if I had gone back after the war? I am someone *to myself* here. There I am nothing. Nothing. I am nothing because I am the son of Cecil Lawton, KC, and I am not *sir* material."

There was silence between them. Maisie noticed that as his voice became more urgent, the giant dog had rested his head on his master's knee as if to quell his temper, to calm him. Lawton leaned forward, held his face to the animal's soft cheek, and looked up at Maisie.

"You have done a good job, Miss Dobbs. I am in awe of your tenacity and skill. I suspect, however, that you are a woman of some depth, so listen: I am Daniel Roberts. Ralph Lawton died in a ball of flames when he was shot down in the war. His grave is at Arras; you should visit it to make sure. I am sorry. I cannot help you."

Maisie nodded. "One last thing, Mr.—Roberts. I am curious to know how you came to Biarritz."

Lawton was silent for a moment, considering Maisie's question. Then he turned to her, his eyes narrowed against the sun. "To tell you the truth, I can barely remember it. I did not come out of the crash unscathed, even though the fire didn't start until after I had fought to land in one piece—I had only seconds before . . ." He sighed, then continued. "I was hidden—heaven knows where, in a cottage, a barn, a very lonely place—for a day or two. My wounds were tended by a young woman. I saw the man who dragged me from the aeroplane just once. I remember knowing I had seen him before, that even though he had worn a balaclava and was disguised, this was the man that I'd brought in. He was the reason I was on my way back to that field, to drop a hamper of pigeons— which I managed to throw out." Lawton gave another half laugh. "He came to tell me that I would be taken from the village, that people would pass me from one to the other. I think he was leaving too; it was probably too dangerous for him to stay after my aerobatics display. He told me they would try to get me on a train for wounded that went to the coast, that hospitals for the French soldiers were there, that I should remain mute and I would be considered shell-shocked. I thought my best bet might be to try to get into Switzerland, but they had a plan—and it seemed there were already quite a few German deserters making for the Swiss border." Lawton plunged his hands into his pockets and looked out to sea. "I remember being moved under cover of darkness, as he'd described, from one village to the next. Then I awoke on a train full of wounded soldiers, so I did what I was told and kept my mouth shut." He paused again, shaking his head. "You wouldn't believe how many there were who had no name and no recollection of what had happened to them. I was just another anonymous soldier in a French uniform, another injured soul to bring back to health by the sea and then discharge." Now he looked directly at Maisie. "It was too fortuitous an opportunity to allow it to slip through my fingers. I decided there and then that I could start again. I didn't even need to invent a past for myself. People don't ask a lot of questions here, you see—the answers can be too terrible to comprehend."

Maisie nodded. Once again silence descended until Maisie asked one more question. "Do you know who Priscilla Partridge is?"

"Of course, everyone who was here after the war knew partying Prissie. But there again, people knew she'd had a terrible time; you could see it on her face."

"But do you know who she *is*, Mr. Roberts?"

"What do you mean? Who is she?"

Maisie stood to leave, picked up her bag, and stroked the dog as she stepped alongside the man who called himself Roberts. "Her brother is the man who tried to save Ralph Lawton from the inferno after he crashed."

Roberts held his hand to his forehead and ran his long scarred fingers back through the shock of white hair. "I—I—don't understand. How could she have known?"

"She doesn't. And it's probably best left that way. But I thought *you* would like to know. Goodbye, Mr. Roberts. You have been most kind in allowing me so much of your time." Maisie reached for the photographs as she turned to enter the house, then drew back her hand. She had no further need of them.

"Wait, wait! Wait a minute. Look, what will you say? To my father?"

Maisie inclined her head. "I am not sure yet. My clients place enormous trust in me, Mr. Roberts. I must respect that trust with the truth of my findings. So I do not yet know what I will say. But I also follow the maxim of a dear friend of mine, a doctor, who says, 'First, do no harm.' Hence, I will respect your wishes and your life here."

After shaking Roberts by the hand, Maisie departed the house and walked away quickly into the dusky late afternoon. The sky was clear, the air chilly, so she pulled her new cashmere wrap around her shoulders as she made her way back to the Partridge villa. And as she walked, she knew her work was far from over, for now she bore the weight of truth regarding the true identity of Daniel Roberts.

DINNER THAT EVENING was a sparkling event, with friends invited from around the town, most of them expatriates, many artists or writers, one a photographer of landscapes. Maisie enjoyed a healthy appetite, realizing that lately she had eaten little, barely picking at each meal. There was first a course of terrines and pâtés served with crusty baguettes, followed by salad, then roast duck with a medley of vegetables that were so fresh and crisp that Maisie had seconds. Then a sweet chocolate mousse with candied cherries delighted the guests, and finally the cheese course. In Britain, at such a dinner, the ladies would have retired to the hostess's salon as the cigars and port were brought out, leaving the men to speak of politics and sport. But here in Biarritz, the women remained at table, with one particularly tall woman, an actress, helping herself to a Havana cigar, which she clipped expertly, like a true aficionado.

Back and forth, the conversation crackled with opinions, a raised voice here, a laugh there, perhaps one voice holding court, then another in reply. Maisie found that, although burdened, she laughed with her companions and took part in the debate regarding the future of Europe, for the guests had all served in the war and were fearful of another. It was in the early hours that the company finally departed and Maisie made her way to her room, where she realized that Dene had been at the back of her mind for much of the evening. She had not written, as promised, nor had she sent a telegram. She must do so before leaving Biarritz tomorrow.

For the second night Maisie slept soundly, without visitation from the demons and dragons of her past. The following morning, after a noisy breakfast in the company of the Partridge boys and their father, Priscilla claimed Maisie for herself once more before driving her to the station. They walked down the rustic steps into the grounds below and then among the olive trees.

"I cannot believe you are leaving already, Maisie. You are only just beginning to seem at all rested."

Maisie smiled. "I am feeling much better. But now I have to continue with my work, which is almost over in France. I will be in Sainte-Marie for only a short time—I anticipate only long enough to ensure that all goes well with Chantal Clement—then back to Paris."

Priscilla looked at Maisie, halting for a moment. "And you've other plans before you leave France." It was a statement, not a question.

Maisie patted the grass below, which had dried in the morning sun, then sat down. Priscilla joined her, and at the same moment each woman pulled her legs toward her chest, clasping her hands together in front of her knees.

"Yes, probably before Paris. I was going to go to Arras, but not now. Though I will go back to Bailleul."

"Slaying your dragons?"

"Yes, Pris. If they can be slain, that's what I'm trying to do."

Priscilla stretched out her legs, one ankle crossed over the other, and reached into her cardigan pocket for her cigarettes and lighter. Maisie shook her head as Priscilla went through her ritual of tapping one end of the cigarette on the silver case, pressing it into the holder, placing the holder between her lips and then leaning her head to one side as she lit up. She inhaled deeply and blew a smoke ring into the air. It reminded Maisie of the younger Priscilla, the girl who broke all the rules at Girton.

"You are very acute, Maisie, I knew that when I first laid eyes on you. But I'm not beyond making the odd deep observation myself, you know."

"And?"

Another smoke ring. "Sometimes you can't slay those dragons;

they can't be done away with, just like that." She snapped the fingers of her free hand. "You have to know how not to disturb them, how to mollify them if they become roused, and, above all, you have to come to respect them."

"Go on. I'm listening."

Priscilla turned to Maisie. "I'm not used to this sort of talk, but here's what I think: I think that the dragon is part of us. What happened, happened. We saw into the jaws of a terrible creature as he feasted upon us all. That is war. You have to find a way to acknowledge and live with it."

"I thought I'd done that."

"We all think that, don't we? Until the dragon breathes down our necks again. Look at my husband, the controversial poet and writer; the dragon lives deep inside him, Maisie, and inside me. If you acknowledge it, you can tame it. That's why yours has come alive again, Maisie. You thought that if you just worked hard enough, the past would be kept at bay."

Maisie stood up and brushed her hands against her woolen trousers. Priscilla had touched a nerve. But then Priscilla always touched a nerve. "Well, I'm going back, Pris. It's what I have to do."

Priscilla extinguished the cigarette and placed the stub in her cigarette case. "Yes, I know. Just be careful, Maisie. Be careful." She looked at her watch. "Now then, we'd better get you to the station. Your train leaves Biarritz–La Negresse at twelve."

TWENTY-FOUR

Maisie slept for much of the journey, letting down her guard as the locomotive's rhythm lulled her. Again, there would be only a short time in Paris while she changed trains for Reims, a route necessitated by the inadequacy of the subsidiary lines that might have taken her to Biarritz from Reims without first going north. When booking her original ticket she had queried the reason for going via Paris, and the clerk had simply looked at her over half-moon glasses and informed her that any other route was "only for the train enthusiast."

Maurice was still in Paris, though Maisie had no plans to see him until they met for their return journey to England. She had sent a telegram to inform him that her business would require more time spent in Reims and she would see him at the weekend. She knew that, at home in Biarritz, Priscilla was already packed and waiting for her summons to meet Chantal Clement—and Pascale.

With her head full of plans, of thoughts that vied for her sole attention, though Maisie slept, it was a fitful slumber, for in each dream it seemed as if a simple action became a conduit for blood to flow. As she reached out for luscious blackberries in the kitchen garden at Chelstone, her wrist suddenly caught on the briar, tearing her skin to reveal a vein that opened too easily, the vermilion trickle becoming a stream and then a river. She forced herself to shake off the terrible image, only to find herself back in France in 1917, back in a casualty clearing station where doctors wielded not the tools of the surgeon's trade but those of the butcher, amputating one limb after another. And as she passed instruments back and forth, her heavy woolen uniform skirt began to soak up blood from the floor, a flood that seemed never-ending. Then she awoke, immediately conscious, as the train slowed for arrival in Paris. Looking out of the windows at the rainy day, Maisie shuddered, for the last dream was not fantasy, not an image of the past gone mad. Instead it was a memory, the butcher's apron being the very uniform that doctors had worn while locked in combat with death, the ghoul who had marched alongside every man brought from the battlefield into the casualty clearing station.

She stood up, shook her head, pressed back her hair, and checked her appearance in the mirror above her seat. Maisie was pleased to see that she looked quite well, her face having caught the last of summer's sun in Biarritz. Though she did not care for the new fashionably tanned complexion, she was glad that the skin beneath her eyes was somewhat camouflaged. She collected her bags, ran her hands down the front and back of her wide corduroy trousers and the arms of her brown tweed jacket, and collected her luggage.

As she left the carriage, declining the help of a porter, she heard a door clang behind her. Anxious to be on her way, she had seen no reason to turn, for passengers were disembarking, gathering portmanteaux and cases before being caught in a sea of people moving toward the exit. Now, however, as she walked, Maisie was filled with an urge to look around, to see who had stepped from the train. She was quite certain that she had been the last passenger to leave her particular carriage, so the person who closed the door must have been waiting in an adjacent one. Her hands felt cold and clammy;

her fingers slipped on the handle of her suitcase. She increased her pace, her eyes on the exit and the point at which she would hail a taxi-cab.

She was close to the exit now, walking as fast as she could without running. She repositioned the luggage handle as she went, knowing the act of doing so rendered her body unbalanced as she struggled to keep ahead of whomever it was she could feel at her heel.

A hand caught Maisie's elbow, and she gasped.

"Miss Dobbs?"

She turned, her mouth open ready to scream. The man she faced was the man she had last seen—was it only three days ago?—stealing across the field and into the wood where she had just re-moved the tin containing Peter Evernden's identification tags. The Englishman.

"What do you want?" Maisie covered fear with indignation.

The man retained his firm hold on her elbow. "Remain calm, Miss Dobbs. Please act as if delighted to unexpectedly see an old friend." The man smiled broadly, his lips closed, his gray eyes cold. He kissed her cheek. "Do not scream or otherwise draw attention to us. Give me your luggage and come with me now."

Maisie pulled back her arm sharply and turned toward the gen-darme she had seen pacing back and forth by the ticket counter.

"That won't do you any good at all. Come with me, Miss Dobbs. It would be in your interests."

She stood her ground. "Where do you intend to take me?"

The Englishman was firm and confident. "To someone who can give you the answers you seek."

In that moment, Maisie suspected she knew to whom she was be-ing taken and the reason for such subterfuge. She held out her suit-case for the man, retaining a tighter hold on her document case. She would trust him, but only so far. "Let's get on with it, then."

He did not smile again but simply reached for her case with his left hand, still retaining his grip on her elbow with his right, and steered her through the crowded station until they reached a motor car waiting outside. The driver opened the door, saluting the Englishman as he climbed aboard behind Maisie and reached above each window, pulling down a series of small blinds that obscured any vision of their route. She knew better than to ask where they were going.

THE MOTOR CAR came finally to a halt with an unexpected slowness, as if royalty were being delivered to a palace rather than a captor's prey to his lair. The Englishman alighted first and reached for Maisie's hand, a gesture she accepted to steady her step as she emerged from the back seat. The building before her was on a narrow street of grand homes. It could have been one of thousands in Paris. The stone was gray, the windows long and narrow, with ornate scrollwork in the rendering around the frames. She looked up and saw a face, slightly obscured, watching from the first floor. She nodded and received an acknowledgment with a mere lifting of the hand.

A sweeping curved staircase spilled down into the marble entrance hall. A woman came from an adjoining room to take Maisie's hat and gloves. She was dressed in a black costume of expensive woolen fabric, her hair pulled back fiercely. She moved to take Maisie's document case, but Maisie held on to it with two hands and shook her head. Instead, the woman reached for the Englishman's hat and black coat, but there was no greeting between the two. The man swept back his oiled hair with a hand on either side of his head and indicated to Maisie that they must go upstairs. Once on the upper landing, the man again cupped Maisie's elbow and steered her along a corridor until they reached a pair of tall double doors rich with ornate gold-leaf carving. He inclined his head as he knocked and then walked Maisie into the room. A man sat with his back to them in a leather wing chair alongside the fireplace. A second chair had been placed opposite, with a small table set for tea between the two. A third chair had been positioned by the window. A wisp of smoke from sweet tobacco peppered with nutmeg wafted toward her, but on this occasion she did not smile at the recognition.

"Thank you for coming, Maisie." Maurice Blanche stood to greet her, placing his pipe in an ashtray on the side table.

Maisie moved toward him. "I had no choice, Maurice." She glanced at the Englishman. "Your henchman over there was rather persuasive."

Maurice smiled. It was a smile that was both wise and sad and, Maisie thought, revealed a certain regret. "I am sorry it has come to this." He moved as if to introduce the Englishman, but Maisie interrupted quickly.

"So am I, Maurice. And I want to know the truth!"

Maurice paused for a second and then continued. "Maisie, I would like you to meet my colleague, Mr. Brian Huntley." He held out his hand to the Englishman, who approached Maisie, this time with his hand outstretched.

Maisie grudgingly accepted his greeting. "I suppose you're with the secret service as well."

The man said nothing but took his place by the window. Maurice indicated the second wing chair in front of the fire and did not sit down again until Maisie was seated. She said nothing at first, instead ensuring that she established absolute balance in her posture and kept her eyes fixed on Maurice.

"Was the cloak-and-dagger approach necessary, Maurice? Surely you could have arranged to meet me in a less formal and authoritarian manner."

"Not this time. My official capacity here is not one that you are familiar with. There are certain formalities, ways of doing things we must all follow, thus you had to be escorted here upon your return to Paris."

"I had to be escorted so I would know my place!"

Maurice ignored Maisie's comment and moved on. "In case you are concerned about your train, I should tell you that there will be no need for you to return to Sainte-Marie."

"I see."

"No, not yet. You do not *see* yet, Maisie."

"Then please enlighten me, Maurice."

Maurice stared into the fire for a moment, reaching for his pipe. He seemed burdened, though Maisie was determined that she would do nothing to make the conversation easier for him. She was aware that her own thoughts were becoming less than gracious. *I am so upset with him. So disappointed.*

"Let me first speak to you about my work, though I request that you respect the fact that there are details that cannot be shared." Maurice looked at Maisie and half smiled. "My work began even before the war, when it was clear that certain alliances could lead to an unstable political situation in Europe. Despite what we thought was a world impervious to such conflict—such was the extent of trade between countries, along with economies dependent upon one another for survival and growth—already the fabric woven of goodwill and mutual financial interest was showing wear." He paused as if to consider his choice of words carefully. Maisie could see the extent to which her mentor had been troubled by the need for this conversation, a conversation her actions had made more urgent and more difficult. She leaned forward and poured tea, passing a cup to Maurice. He accepted the refreshment, smiled gratefully, and continued.

"I was asked to assist in certain matters of national importance, especially concerning the manner in which we obtained information. Suffice it to say that, when war was declared, my role took on a quite different complexion. Maisie, as you know, and to speak frankly, my work has always been about people, essentially about the truth of human beings, of their experience, their life, and, indeed, their death. I work with body, mind, and soul, and I have made it my life's work to understand the relationship of each to the others. I was asked to bring that knowledge, if you will, to the development of our intelligence service. On a basic level, though my work had many facets, I studied possible recruits and assessed their suitability for the most dangerous, most important work. Following a string of intelligence disasters, where vital information regarding the movement of German troops and armaments was woefully inadequate and spread between different departments, we had to regroup and look again at our strategy."

Maisie felt anger rise again, only this time it was directed at herself, as much as to Maurice. "And you recruited Peter! I made an innocent comment at an innocent age, and you took advantage—" She reached into her pocket for a handkerchief. "Priscilla was my friend. She was my friend!"

"And she is *still* your friend, Maisie. Let me continue." Maurice moved as if to reach toward Maisie, but, sensing her withdrawal, he simply set his cup and saucer on the table and rested his hands on the arms of his chair. "Maisie, we will never know how long Peter might have lived had he not been recruited to work in intelligence. Indeed, it is worth knowing that his entire original battalion was all but wiped out. Yet you are right: When we spoke upon your return from the first term at Girton, I noted your comment about Peter Evernden's gift for languages. Such a skill is rare and was acutely needed in our work."

"You could have told me!"

"You were just seventeen, Maisie!"

"I was old enough to go to war."

"I should remind you that you were *not* old enough. You lied."

Maisie became silent, aware that she was losing her self-control. She was also aware that she was hurt, that Maurice's secrecy had pained her. *We were so close.*

Maurice was anxious to complete his account of Peter's work. "Initially he took on the most dangerous of battlefield tasks, that of moving across no-man's-land under cover of darkness in order to listen to the enemy in their trenches. The work meant advancing beyond the point where help could be given if he were in trouble, so speed, stealth, and quick thinking were essential to avoid death, injury, or capture." He paused only briefly. "One of our aims was to glean as much information as possible regarding the enemy's Order of Battle. We needed to know what plans were in progress, details of troop movements, deployment of artillery—and it was of paramount importance that we gauge the stamina of the enemy."

Maurice rubbed his chin, as if considering how best to frame the rest of his story. Maisie watched him, wondering when she had ever known him so melancholy.

"You know, Maisie, before the war our notion of intelligence was antiquated at best. The generals had little knowledge of the implications of modern warfare, so we looked back to the South African war, when instead we would have done well to examine the lessons of trench warfare in the American Civil War." He shook his head. "Mind you, one thing we did was to take a leaf from Napoleon's book by sending agents deep into the enemy's field of operation—so we are back to Peter Evernden. Having proved his mettle and ability, he was promoted to the work of a field agent, though not before a return to England for more training in Southampton and London."

"Then he was sent into enemy territory."

"Yes. Once there, his role became even more crucial, even more dangerous. Order of Battle remained at the heart of his assignment; however, he also worked with our local contact to recruit civilians to support intelligence efforts. The selfless contribution of the local people made the difference between a war won and a war lost. His job involved assessing sympathy and enlisting support. He did not know who was above him in the chain of communication, nor would he have known the true identity of the man who transported him. Peter was known only by his French name and personage to most of those in Sainte-Marie."

"I see."

"No, not quite; let me continue." Maurice reached for his cup again and took a final sip of his now-lukewarm tea. "Peter's safety was already in question even before the debacle of the aviator who crashed, but that disaster made it even more urgent that he be moved into a new field of operation, from IC—the intelligence corps—to a secret service assignment that was both deep and broad."

"So he didn't die in Sainte-Marie?"

"No, Peter died in Germany."

"In Germany?" Maisie's eyes revealed her surprise.

"Yes. Even before the end of the war, the enemy's morale was faltering. Desertion, mutiny, soldiers shocked, wounded, and hungry. And affairs in Germany were desperate, with people—women and children—starving to death. Along with the burden of grief there was mass unemployment. Peter's job was to report on the situation and, more especially, to keep us informed regarding the plans and actions of antigovernment and other dissenting groups that were coming together even then. The knowledge was essential for victory—and to know what might befall us all following an armistice."

"What do you mean?"

Maurice stood up and moved toward the fire, holding his hands out to the warmth, splaying his fingers as if blessing the flames. "The tentacles of war reach into the future, Maisie. We may think conflict is over, that we can mourn our dead, build our houses again, take up our tools, fashion our tomorrows, and watch the grass grow over the trenches, but the truth is somewhat more complex. There are always the disenfranchised, those who feel they have lost too much and that the only way to regain their due is through control and ultimately another fight. War debt on all sides, the economic and moral bankruptcy that comes from conflict—any stability in our world since the war is only a myth."

"How did Peter die, then—and when did he die?"

"Peter died in Germany in 1918, in a food riot. Along with other civilians, he was crushed under the weight of people running from the army, which had been brought in to quell the demonstrators. It was most sad, especially as he was to be brought back to England in a matter of days. He was to be demobilized, and eventually his 'missing' status changed to reflect repatriation from a prisoner-of-war camp. I have no doubt that Peter would have become the teacher of languages he had always aspired to be and would have put his wartime work behind him, having never spoken a word of it to a soul. That is the role of an intelligence agent. And Peter was one of our finest."

"Do you know where he died?"

"Yes."

"But I cannot know."

"No, Maisie. You know too much already, though I have persuaded my colleagues of your integrity."

Maisie and Maurice sat in silence for some moments, until Maisie spoke again. "And who was the local recruit in Sainte-Marie? Speaking of the town, I should tell you that Priscilla—"

"Ah, yes, now we come to the question of Sainte-Marie, of Pascale Clement." Maurice looked at his watch, then turned to Huntley. "I think we are ready for our guest now, Brian."

Huntley rose and bowed slightly to Maurice before leaving the room. Maisie turned to Maurice, who was now standing with his back to the fire, awaiting the entrance of his other guest. Darkness had fallen outside. Maisie stood up and walked to the window, where she remained for a moment to watch the street, the rooms illuminated in the mansion opposite, the motor cars below, and the warm glow of streetlamps. There was still much to speak about, and Maurice was bound to ask what Maisie had discovered while in Sainte-Marie and Biarritz. It was as she remembered her promise to Pascale that Maurice interrupted her thoughts.

"I should also tell you, Maisie, that Mrs. Partridge will arrive tomorrow morning here in Paris."

"How—"

Maurice raised his hand as the doors opened following a gentle knock. Huntley entered, holding the door open for the elegant Chantal Clement.

"Maisie, I understand you know our agent in Sainte-Marie, Madame Chantal Clement?"

Chantal Clement was dressed in suit of pale gray knitted fabric, and though Maisie was not familiar with the couture houses, she was sure Chantal was a patron of the famous Coco Chanel. The dignified woman came to Maisie and, instead of taking her hand, held her by the shoulders and leaned forward to kiss her on each cheek. Maisie felt her complexion redden.

"You have walked far in the dark, my dear. I am glad that we can speak openly now."

Maisie pulled back as Madame Clement released her grasp on her shoulders. Turning first to Maurice, then back to Madame Clement, Maisie trembled as she spoke. "Walked far in the dark? You have deceived me, both of you." She swallowed, attempting to modulate her voice. "I want only to bring my friend Priscilla together with Pascale, her niece. She has lost so much, has suffered so deeply from loss, I appeal to you—"

Madame Clement smiled again and set one finger against Maisie's lips. "Shhhh. Do not worry anymore, Maisie Dobbs. You are a good friend to have. Indeed, I wish I had such a friend." She turned to Maurice, smiled, and turned back to Maisie. "Pascale is with me here in Paris. I have already spoken with her regarding her father, and she knows now that her family extends beyond myself alone. She was young to bear such news, but the time had come. I had to reflect that at her age I had already met the man I was to marry, though neither of us knew it at the time." Madame Clement shook her head and addressed her next comment to Maurice. "I believe it is to our detriment that age gives us a certain mistrust of those younger than ourselves, and we fail to see the strength within them to assume the burden of truth."

Maurice nodded as Madame Clement spoke.

"When will they meet?" asked Maisie.

"Tomorrow, in this room." The woman held her hands together in front of her waist in a manner, Maisie suspected, taught by a strict governess. "I will be here with Pascale, who is most excited."

"And what about Priscilla; who will be here for her? Wasn't her beloved brother a 'good friend' to France? Isn't she to be respected and cared for?"

Maurice came forward, placing his hand on her shoulder. "Maisie, it is time that we left France. Mrs. Partridge will be secure here with Madame Clement. Your work is done."

Pulling away, Maisie looked back and forth between Madame Clement and Maurice. It was clear the decision had been made; it was settled. But there was more for her to accomplish before leaving France.

"May we speak privately, Maurice?"

Chantal Clement smiled, touched Maisie on the arm, nodded toward Maurice, and left the room, accompanied by Huntley.

Maurice watched them leave. "You know, Madame Clement is most trustworthy."

"I do not question her, Maurice. I wanted to speak to you alone, now that all decisions about tomorrow have been made."

"It was her place to decide what was best for Pascale."

"Of course. I understand. But it is not your place to dictate when I should leave France."

Maurice frowned as Maisie walked to the fireplace to warm herself.

"I must go to Bailleul, the place where I served in the war. I must go back."

"I see. Shall I come?"

"No. I must go alone."

"As you wish."

"And there's more, Maurice." Maisie turned to face her teacher, mentor, and friend. "I want to know if that man has tried to kill me."

"Huntley? Of course not."

"Then your intelligence friends have not sent out an agent to ensure my silence?"

"I have vouched for you."

"And you are that important here?"

Maurice smiled. "Yes. I am."

Maisie sighed.

Maurice spoke quietly. "Maisie, you have taken on so much lately. A personal dimension to a case can take a toll. Are you *sure* that your life is in danger? Could not the pressure of your undertaking have altered your thinking?"

Maisie sighed again in frustration, turning once more to the fire.

Maurice touched her shoulder. "I will have Marie-Claude show you to the room that has been prepared for you. You may join me in the dining room in half an hour, or you may wish to have supper served in your room."

"I think I prefer to be alone."

"I understand."

"And I will leave for Bailleul tomorrow."

"I will await your return to Paris so that we may travel back to England together."

"You don't need—"

"But I *do*, Maisie. Now then, let me summon Marie-Claude." Maurice reached for the bellpull alongside the fireplace, turning to Maisie as he did so. "Maisie, before you retire, I wish to underline the import of what has been revealed to you. When you leave here tomorrow, you must act as if you have never been in this place. Chantal Clement's role remains active. Should a tragedy befall this country in future, her expertise, her knowledge will be invaluable— as will the dedicated people who worked alongside her. In addition, am I correct in thinking that you have met with a Mr. Daniel Roberts?"

Maisie nodded, saying nothing.

"It is sufficient to say that our department has no interest in him." Maurice paused. "But one more thought occurs to me."

"Yes?"

"In reflecting upon who might wish you dead, it would perhaps behoove you to consider this: If you were to die, what would your demise give to another? What currency is attached to your life?"

"I'm not sure I know what you mean."

"If you are right and someone has been trying to bring your life to an end, how might your death serve that person? The insights resulting from such a question may well provide you with some protection."

Maisie shook her head. "Good night, Maurice." She stepped away as if to leave, then stopped and turned back. Reaching out she took both his hands in her own and leaned to kiss him on both cheeks. "I remain unsettled by our conversation, Maurice, and I think there is still much to be said between us. But I must thank you for your part in bringing Pascale and Priscilla together."

Marie-Claude entered the room and held the door to escort Maisie to her guest suite. As he heard the women's footsteps become distant, Maurice reached for the bellpull and summoned Huntley. His work concerning Maisie Dobbs was not over yet.

TWENTY-FIVE

Maisie left early the following morning, again chauffeured in the black motor car, again with blinds pulled to obscure her view of the street. She did not see Priscilla, which, upon reflection, might be just as well. Chantal Clement was, without doubt, the one to make decisions about matters concerning Pascale's well-being. Maisie knew it was not her place anymore. She had kept her promise to Priscilla and must now move on to her next task and, when that was done, her return to England and the search for answers to more questions, along with a report to Sir Cecil Lawton.

It was late afternoon when Maisie arrived in Bailleul, the driver of her taxi-cab taking her to a small pension run by a Frenchwoman named Josette and her husband, an Australian. As she signed her name in the guest register for one night only, the man, Ted Tavistock, told Maisie he had met his wife during a visit to France and Belgium soon after the war.

"I was supposed to go back to Sydney, but stayed in Blighty for a while. Thought I might have a bit of a look-see before going home, though I was supposed to go back with the regiment—what was left of it, that is." He had led Maisie to a small sitting room, where he reached down to light the fire. "Bit nippy this afternoon, eh?" Ted poked at the flames as they licked up toward the chimney, then stood leaning against the mantelpiece. "Then I came back over here to pay my respects and—to tell you the truth—to see where it had all happened. I wondered what I was up to at first; what was it all about? I mean, I lost my boyhood, my mates, I lost my heart here." He shook his head as if to shake off the past. "Then I found it again when I met Josette. Now of course we do a fair business with all the families who come over to visit the cemeteries."

"Yes, of course." Maisie smiled at Josette, who brought her a cup of milky cocoa.

"So, Miss Dobbs. I bet you were in London during the Armistice, weren't you?"

Maisie stared into the flames, squinting into the past, to a day she would never forget. "You know, I was. I had recovered from a long convalescence and had just started work at a hospital in Camberwell. I remember I was off-duty at the time. One of the nurses rushed into our hostel and told us that the war was over. So we all decided there and then to go straight to Trafalgar Square."

"Well, wouldn't you know it! I was there too!"

Maisie smiled, then laughed, her memories drawn along on the coattails of Ted Tavistock's story. "I remember there were lots of Australian soldiers, and they all linked hands and danced in circles, and then everyone started dancing and shouting. It was so wonderful. The war was over!"

Ted laughed with Maisie. "I tell you, I was one of those blokes! Big old ring-o'-ring-o'-roses, it was. And we were all waving flags and seeing who could find a girl to dance with. Small world, really. It's a small world."

The laughing abated and they both stared into the crackling fire again. Maisie knew they had shared the same thought, that the Armistice did not herald days of joy but was instead short-lived in the face of a collective realization that those lost really would not be coming home again.

"I suppose that's why I had to come back, really, to pay my respects to my mates and say goodbye one last time. Now, of course, I do what I can for the families who come."

Maisie nodded. "Then perhaps you can help me, Ted."

"I'll try, Miss Dobbs."

"I was a nurse close to Bailleul, at a casualty clearing station. But nothing looks the same now. I have no idea where to start and I have only one day before I must return to Paris and then to England. Do you know where the casualty clearing station was? There should be a cemetery—"

"You were there, miss?"

"Yes. As I said, I was a nurse."

Ted shook his head. "One of the saddest stories I heard, that one. Lost some of the doctors—and weren't there a couple of German doctors killed too, prisoners of war who were working with the RAMC docs? Five nurses killed, orderlies, and the boys, of course."

Maisie nodded.

"You were there?"

She pressed her lips together and nodded again.

"You poor love. You poor, poor love. Come on, let's get you settled in your room. It'll be getting dark soon, but I can take you there. Or it might be best to wait until tomorrow morning."

Maisie shook her head and set her cup on a side table. "No, Ted. I have come all this way. I want to go now."

TED TAVISTOCK HELPED Maisie into his old Renault motor car and drove along narrow streets until they were on the outskirts of the town. They passed a smattering of houses, then some fields. Rain had continued a slanting assault across the land, and as they drove Maisie continually wiped condensation from the window. The detritus of war was still there, rotting and rusting into the ground until someone saw fit to remove it. Hulks of tanks and rusting barbed wire were constant reminders, and as rain filled the potholes along their route, Maisie felt her feet and hands grow icy cold, the chill of death reaching out from the past to finger her skin and touch her soul. *This is my underworld; this is the place where my girlhood was lost. This was my hell on earth.*

She wiped the windows again.

"Nearly there, Miss Dobbs. I know this place like the back of my hand, love. Made it my business so I could help the families when they come over, tell them where their boy was lost. I'm what you'd call a bit of a battlefield detective, you know." Tavistock smiled and winked at his passenger.

Maisie nodded, clutching her elbows to keep warm. *I should have waited. The weather might have cleared; it might have been sunny, not like this, not like it was.*

"Here we are then." The car pulled up alongside a row of small houses, each with a vegetable garden. The houses looked old, yet Maisie could not recall houses nearby. She frowned.

"Is this really the place, Ted?"

Tavistock closed Maisie's door behind her as she stood on the grass verge, pulling her old cloche farther down to protect her face from the stinging rain.

"Don't be fooled by the houses. They rebuilt them just a few years ago. See where they used the old foundations? You can always tell by the old bricks at the bottom."

Maisie nodded. From the windows of trains and taxi-cabs she had observed the flurry of house-building all over northern France, villages growing up again where there had been a barren shell-shocked landscape in 1918. The giants had raged across this land, and now it was fertile again. Yet the scars were still visible.

"So, where was the casualty clearing station?"

"Over here, Miss Dobbs."

Tavistock opened a gate into a no-man's-land dividing two houses, and then to the back where, between the two gardens, a Cross of Sacrifice rose toward the dark clouds, ever watchful over a small walled cemetery. She pressed both hands to her mouth and gasped as tears filled her eyes. Wind funneling between the houses whistled past her ears, and she barely heard Tavistock when he told her that he'd wait for her in the motor car. And she didn't hear the crunch on gravel as another, larger, motor car came to a halt behind the Renault.

Walking slowly, Maisie approached the cemetery. This was the place where she had stood, day after day, night after night, in the operating tent, where she had watched blood flow from the terrible wounds of war, where she had seen young lives ebb away, and on each boy's lips a cry for mother, wife, or sweetheart. Rain mingled with her tears as she pulled her coat even closer in a bid to drive back the cold. She unlatched the gate and entered the cemetery, already reading the plain stone markers with so many names she knew. It seemed as if the clouds were enveloping her, the biting wind now a wail between the houses, the rain still slicing into the earth. Reaching out, she touched one stone after another, each time feeling as if she were touching the very flesh of a soldier of the Great War. She fell to her knees and allowed the full weight of her terrible grief to break through the dam of self-will that had taken years to build. *Oh, my God, why now? Why now? Why me, why did I live? Why did they die and I live; why was Simon lost and I spared? Why? Tell me why.*

She could feel the cold rain-soaked soil seeping into her clothing as she remained on the ground, clutching the grass as if to tear into her memories. And as she felt herself sinking lower, felt her shoulder and then her face touch the earth, she knew there were voices above her. She tried to open her eyes against the rain, against her tears, but could not; she could only hear the voices of men. She began to curl her body as if she were a child again, ready to be picked up and held to her mother's heart. A hand touched her fiercely hot cheek, and as she slipped deeper away from the cannonade that now tore into her mind, her last memory was of the warm hand touching her forehead and a soft voice saying her name: *Maisie.*

. . .

DREAMS CAME AND went, and, though her eyes were heavy as she slipped in and out of consciousness, she would hear voices coming and going, feel soft hands and a warm damp cloth on her brow; then the light beyond her eyelids became dark again and she would commence her descent down the long staircase once more. In one dream each step led her closer to a court surrounded by flames and gunfire. The judge was seated before her in long red-and-black robes, his silvery wig obscuring his face as he reached for the square black cloth to place on his head, then he pointed his index finger at her while uttering just one word: *Guilty*. Then his face was revealed: Sir Cecil Lawton. In another dream, as she turned and clambered upward to escape the court of accusation, a woman and a girl were silhouetted at the top of the stair with a bright light behind them. The woman reached out her hand and with the other pulled the girl toward her, to protect her, yet Maisie could not reach the hand, could not drag herself from stair to stair, slipping backward instead toward the inferno.

Then she was in the operating tent, pushing a mop back and forth, back and forth, trying desperately to clean the blood-soaked floor.

"What are you doing, Maisie, love?"

"I'm trying to get this floor clean, Mum, but every time I think it's done I turn around and I've missed a bit. Then another puddle of blood appears, and another." She looked up, distraught. "I just can't get it clean."

The woman took Maisie in her arms. "Hush, love, hush. Leave it now, let it be. You've done your best."

"But it's not clean! The floor's not clean. I've got to—"

"Shhhh." Her mother pressed two fingers against the center of Maisie's forehead. "Your gran was right; she saw that crinkle the day you were born and she told me, 'She'll be a worrier, that one. She'll never rest.'" She placed an arm around Maisie's shoulder and led her from the operating tent and into a long corridor. A speck of light in the distance shone like a single star in the sky. "Come on, love, it's time. Come with me."

Maisie felt the mop slip from her hands as her mother led her along the corridor. She felt small and vulnerable and allowed herself to be led, easing into the protective comfort of her mother's love. The light became brighter, and as they approached she could see the silhouette of a man at the entrance. "You're nearly there, Maisie. Nearly there."

As they reached the end of the corridor, the woman slowed, releasing her grip. "It's time to say goodbye now."

Maisie clung to her mother's pinafore, pushing her head into the comforting place where her neck and collarbone met. "No!"

"It's time to go back, Maisie. Go on, I'll watch you."

As if pulled, Maisie began to walk toward the man, turning only to watch her mother vanish into the unlit corridor. As she slipped back into unconsciousness, a man's deep but gentle voice spoke. *Maisie. Maisie.*

LIGHT CAME, AT first slowly as she opened her eyes, then quickly as she began to focus on the room. A creamy lace counterpane covered a soft eiderdown, warm blankets, and white cotton sheets. She turned her head toward a vase of fragrant lavender on the side table and breathed in deeply. *I am awake. I am not dead. I am back.* She swallowed, her throat dry. A tray bearing a crystal flagon filled with water and a glass topped with a lace cover had been placed on the table with the lavender. Maisie tried to pull herself up, but a sudden throbbing pain at her temples caused her to lie back again. She waited a moment and tried again, eventually sitting up sufficiently to rest on her left elbow while reaching for the flagon. At that moment, the stairs creaked, the door opened, and Josette entered.

"Ah, mademoiselle, you are awake! Come, let me help you; then I must tell your friend."

Maisie shook her head, her vision becoming blurred again. She rubbed her eyes. "What friend?"

Josette poured a glass of water and sat on the bed to support Maisie as she quenched her thirst. "Monsieur Blanche; he has been by your side for many hours. Monsieur Huntley waits also."

"Oh, God." Maisie leaned back on the pillows. "How long have I been here?"

"Just two days."

"Two days!" Maisie leaned forward quickly and pulled back the covers. "I cannot afford two days." As she began to stand, the room appeared to move and she sat on the bed again. "Oh, dear."

"Come now, rest. I will bring you some eggs. You must regain your strength." Josette smiled, tucking in the sheets around Maisie. "And I will tell Monsieur Blanche that you are awake. He has been worried."

Maisie leaned back into the pillows. The dreams of her sleep began to filter back into her conscious mind. She shuddered. *Two days!* Had she been sedated, or had she simply fallen deep into the abyss and only now dragged herself out? She almost dreaded seeing Maurice. The stairs creaked again, followed by a light knock on the door before he entered.

"How are you?" Maurice pulled a chair close to the bed and sat down.

"Ever the doctor, Maurice. In the summer you held vigil for my father, and now it's me."

Maurice inclined his head and smiled. "It is my calling." His face became grave again. "You have been suffering for a long time, Maisie."

Maisie looked away from him, first out of the window, then at the counterpane, where she found a loose thread to worry. "I have no reason to suffer. I am most fortunate; in fact, this year has been one of blessing, if you consider my work, my good fortune."

"Not like those who did not return and those who lost their loved ones? Not like Simon suffered, or Priscilla, or those in the cemetery?"

Maisie nodded. "I don't know why this has come upon me again. Not when everything seems to be going so well."

"That is the very reason, Maisie. How often we are able to pinpoint such a fall in others but not in ourselves. I have seen this coming for a long time." He paused, got up from the chair, and began to pace back and forth, looking at Maisie all the time. "Yes, you rested when you returned from France, you recovered, you were able to work again. In fact, it was your immersion in your work that helped you. But as time passes we find that the clothes of the past do not fit, do not serve us anymore. As you grew, as you matured, the cloak of recovery ceased to cover your pain, your guilt at survival. This year has been one of bounty in many ways: the hard work is serving you, and you have the attention of a man who cares for you deeply. Your relationship with your father has healed. Such a collapse might be expected, Maisie. And these cases you have taken on! My child, you are a human being!"

Maisie pulled the covers to her chin, as if she really were a child. She knew Maurice would notice.

"You had no need to take on more responsibility for the girl, had no need to agree to Priscilla's request—though I concede that your efforts met with a successful conclusion, but not without terrible risk to yourself."

Maisie felt a bitter, salty taste in her mouth. She must defend her decisions. "Maurice, I had to do *something*. I had to help the girl. I have thought and thought about the case. I know Billy has more information and I have been away for more time than I ever should have, but I believe her innocent and I want to prove it. I think I can."

Maurice shook his head. "I am responsible for this sense of purpose that places you in danger."

Maisie reached out to Maurice as he came to her side. "And you were right, Maurice. I can help this girl, can help people with my work. I must return to England now. I must continue."

"But at what cost? You must help yourself first, Maisie. You have a struggle with truth in the Lawton case, and you must protect yourself from someone who would have you dead."

"So you believe me?"

"Of course I believe you! Teresa was poisoned. Your motor car is damaged, and you barely missed being plunged into the path of an underground train."

"I thought—"

"It is my job to ask questions, Maisie."

"Can we leave for England now? I have work to do."

Maurice looked at Maisie, still holding her hand. "We will leave tomorrow morning. I will return to London with you. But you must promise me that you will rest when these cases are brought to a close."

"But I cannot leave Billy again."

"You can draw back a little until your strength is fully returned—in body and soul. And we must spend time in conversation, you and I. I am, after all, a doctor, and at this moment you are my patient. You must heal."

Josette entered the room with a tray for Maisie. Fresh poached eggs with crusty toasted bread lent a welcoming fragrance to the room, even if Josette had prepared far more than Maisie could eat.

"Now then, rest, Maisie. We will leave tomorrow morning, if I consider you well enough."

Maisie nodded and leaned back as Josette set the tray on the counterpane. She was left alone to eat, which she did slowly, chewing each mouthful thoroughly before swallowing, and then sipping the hot herbal tisane. She could only eat one egg and a slice of toast; then she pushed the tray to the end of the bed. Resting against the pillows once more, Maisie knew the truth of Maurice's words. But there was another open wound, which had been open for so long and seemed to weep into her heart even more. She ached for her mother, for the woman who had left her so long ago.

PART THREE

*England, late September
to October 1930*

TWENTY-SIX

Maurice insisted that a return journey via train would be too exhausting for Maisie and arranged instead for them to travel with Imperial Airways from Paris to Croydon Aerodrome. Eric was waiting for them with the Comptons' old Lanchester, to take them back to Ebury Place.

The day was warm and bright, but already leaves that were still green when she had left London were now brown and gold, and the smoggy ocher vapor was beginning to thicken as more nighttime fires were lit to ward off the chill of evening. As soon as they arrived at the Belgravia mansion, Maurice instructed Sandra to escort Maisie to her room and prescribed several days' rest, an order she was too weak to counter, though she did insist upon seeing Teresa for herself.

"I am so sorry, Teresa, I would never have given the chocolates to you if I had known."

"Well, of course you wouldn't, m'um, of course you wouldn't! Mind you, it hasn't all been bad. I'd let myself get a bit thick around the waist, and now I can fit into some clothes that wouldn't touch me a month ago. Almost gave them to the rag-and-bone man, I did."

"It's a drastic way to save a frock, Teresa, but I am very glad to see you well."

"I had to talk to that Detective Inspector Stratton, though."

"Good. I expect I'll see him soon enough."

"Oh, yes, m'um, you will. He said he'd come around as soon as you returned. Now then, shall I bring you a nice cup of tea, m'um?"

Maisie smiled, leaning back in her chair. "Yes, I'd love a cup."

THOUGH MAURICE HAD issued orders that Maisie must not be overwhelmed with callers, he allowed Billy to visit soon after her arrival at Ebury Place. Telephone calls had been received from Priscilla and also Cecil Lawton. Andrew Dene had left a message that he was on his way to London.

"Miss, you look right tired out." Billy had been shown to Maisie's sitting room, entering awkwardly, nervously fingering his cloth cap, which he ran through his fingers. When invited to be seated, he sat on the very edge of the chair opposite Maisie, as if ready to leap up at any moment and leave.

"I'm all right, Billy. Now then, I want you to tell me everything. First, Avril Jarvis. Tell me about your second visit to Taunton. Has Stratton made any headway that you know of? Has Lawton been in touch?"

Billy nodded and, leaning forward, began recounting all the actions taken and events that had happened in her absence. Instead of peppering him with questions, which she knew would fluster him, she waited until he had fully covered his work on each case.

"So, you think the mother is hiding something?"

"Yes, Miss. Like I said, she was right nervous, she was. The police had been around, but only to confirm details of when Avril had left, that sort of thing. And the poor woman had been followed by one of them 'orrible newspapermen."

"I expect it's big news for a small town. But she let you in, that's the main thing."

"I told 'er about you trying to 'elp Avril. But even so, like I said, she was right nervy. Mind you, she's 'ad a terrible time, losing Avril's dad and all. He was only twenty when 'e copped it. Twenty and married with a baby on the way. Terrible. Then she went and married that man who knocked 'er and Avril about."

"And the aunt?"

"Well, she was the first 'usband's sister, as you know. Apparently she never did like the new one, thought Avril's mum was making a terrible mistake—as she was. That's why she more or less took Avril under 'er wing. She said Avril's mum was a weak-willed woman, not capable of stickin' up for 'er own."

Maisie stood up, faltered a little, leaned against the chair, and began to pace.

"Miss, I don't think you should be doin' that. Dr. Blanche said—"

"I'm thinking, Billy."

"But, Miss—"

"Billy, was the mother really intimidated by the aunt?"

"I should say so. Of course, the aunt tried to lend a hand, like you would—they were family, after all. But she weren't backward in coming forward with opinions. And of course, as we know, the locals thought she topped the second 'usband with one of them potions."

Maisie paced, then stopped alongside Billy's chair. "Look, I must see Avril. I need to talk to her. I'll speak to Stratton."

"But Dr. Blanche said—"

"I know what he said, Billy. I can rest when all this is over, but if I am to give Sir Cecil Lawton the ammunition he needs to secure the release of a girl I now believe to be innocent, I cannot rest now!"

Billy fingered his cap again and looked down. "Well, then, speaking of Sir Cecil."

Maisie shook her head. "I am sorry I snapped, Billy. You have worked hard in my absence. Now, tell me about Lawton."

"Well, 'e wants to know when you will visit to present your

report. I told 'im you had caught a bad cold in France and would see him next week."

Maisie nodded. "Good. It's a white lie, but it gives me some time."

Billy looked at Maisie. "Funny old job, that one. I suppose all you can do is tell the man what 'e knows already, eh? That the son is dead."

"Yes, you could say that. I just need a bit of time to consider how I might say it." She paused before continuing, and as she looked back at Billy, she knew he had realized her lie. "Now then, Stratton."

"Well, Miss, we can't forget that we don't know who was be'ind them strange events, can we?"

"I haven't forgotten, Billy."

"I know he'll be over to see you soon enough. In fact, there was talk of protecting you."

Maisie shook her head. "Oh, no, I will not be trailed around London by some wet-behind-the-ears young detective from Scotland Yard. Out of the question."

"I only said."

"I know, Billy. Now then, is there anything else?"

Billy pulled a rolled folder from the inside pocket of his overcoat. "Two more clients, Miss, new cases. I started doin' the basics, like you taught me, and both parties have appointments to see you next week." Billy smiled as he passed the manila folder to Maisie.

Leafing through the notes, Maisie nodded. "Good work, Billy. You have done well in my absence, and I am very pleased. Now then, I will be back in the office for a short time tomorrow morning. Stratton will be here in an hour, and I will ask him for permission to see the Jarvis girl."

As Billy was shown from 15 Ebury Place, he stood on the front step and pulled up his collar against a sudden cool breeze. He shook his head, took a packet of Woodbines from his pocket and lit a cigarette between cupped hands, squinting as a curl of smoke swept up past his eyes. He'd seen it before, during his convalescence after the war. Seen a man swear he was well, that the docs had mended his broken mind. Then before you knew it he was down again, closer to the edge than ever before.

STRATTON MET MAISIE in the library to discuss the case of the poisoned chocolates that would most certainly have caused Teresa's death had Sandra not acted quickly. There had been nothing to indicate the source of the gift, so Stratton's questions to Maisie yielded little, especially as her answers were protective of her work on the Lawton case and her search for Peter Evernden's final resting place.

"Of course, we have to consider that cranky old aunt and that this might have something to do with the Jarvis case."

"Oh, hardly, Inspector."

Stratton frowned. "Hardly?"

"I have done nothing to harm Avril Jarvis, and everything to assist her cause."

"Assist her cause? Oh, yes, Lawton. But you must remember that you first came to Vine Street to question her at the request of Scotland Yard. As far as the aunt is concerned, you're one of us."

"Oh, I think not." Maisie shook her head.

"Surely being one of us is not that bad."

"But what about the other incidents?"

"Yes, what about the other incidents? You should have informed us."

"You knew about the motor car accident."

"But there was the aborted shove on the underground."

"Billy told you?"

"Of course. He felt guilty after hearing about the poisoning. Apparently he had not quite believed you."

"I now wonder whom he's working for."

"Oh, don't doubt that man of yours, he's loyal as a sheepdog. Look, I want to have all the details. And I want to have you protected."

"Yes to the first, no to the second, Inspector."

Stratton walked to the window and then turned to face her. In following his movements, it was obvious to Maisie that he was about to broach a difficult subject, and she knew what it was.

"Miss Dobbs. I believe you have crossed paths with the secret service. Have you considered—and this is in absolute confidence—that you have been in danger due to some knowledge you have acquired?"

"Yes, Inspector, I have. You can rest assured that I am safe in that quarter. I can say no more, but I am safe."

"Good." He paused. "Because there are enemies I can protect you from, but that one is beyond my reach. As long as you are safe."

Maisie smiled, seeing in Stratton's eyes a concern that went beyond that of an occasional colleague but rather one who had just months ago declared his desire for a friendship beyond the confines of their shared work.

There was an awkward pause. Stratton reached for the hat he had set on a side table earlier. "Well, Miss Dobbs, please telephone immediately if you have any additional information for us. In the meantime, our investigations will continue, especially regarding procurement of the substances used in this attempt on your life."

Maisie stood and held out her hand. "And you will let me know when I can visit Avril Jarvis at Holloway? I would like to see her as soon as possible."

"Dr. Blanche has said—"

"Inspector, I plan to commence work again tomorrow. I can visit soon, if you will make the necessary arrangements."

Stratton sighed. "Of course, though it may take several days." He tipped his hat. As he approached the door that led to the hall, it burst open and Andrew Dene rushed in.

"Maisie, darling, I came as quickly as I could."

"Oh!" She stepped back to avoid his taking her in his arms, a move that she knew would embarrass Stratton. "Andrew, let me introduce Detective Inspector Richard Stratton of Scotland Yard. Inspector Stratton, this is my friend Dr. Andrew Dene."

Stratton offered his hand to Dene, who greeted him with his usual sunny smile. "Very good to meet you, Inspector. Off to box up a few more criminals, eh?"

Stratton looked at Maisie, then Dene. "Of course." He smiled at Maisie. "I will be in touch about tomorrow, Miss Dobbs."

As Stratton left, Dene pulled Maisie to him. "I have been so worried, your father even more so. Let me take you to Chelstone or to Hastings, Maisie. I know Maurice said you must rest. Come, let me take you away from London."

"No, Andrew, not yet. I have telephoned Dad, I know he's worried, and I have assured him I am well. I know Lady Rowan is probably 'beside herself' with worry too. I promise I am all right. I was simply overcome during my visit to Bailleul. It has passed and I am recovering." Dene opened his mouth to object, but Maisie affectionately placed her finger on his lips. "I must finish my work, Andrew. Then I will rest. But my work comes first."

Dene looked at the floor, then back at Maisie. "Yes, I know."

MAISIE'S RECOVERY SEEMED to be taking longer than she had expected, though no one else was surprised. But each day she grew stronger, at first taking on one task, then another. She had received a letter from Priscilla with news of a wonderful meeting with Pascale Clement, of her regard for Chantal Clement, and of their joint plans for a memorial for her beloved Peter in the woodland where Maisie had found his identification discs. They knew nothing of her find, only that Peter had loved to walk there because it reminded him of his childhood home. Already the boys could not wait to see their cousin and were making plans for her to spend summers in Biarritz, though her grandmother had yet to be consulted.

She caught up with pressing errands, first carefully wrapping

Peter Evernden's journal in fine tissue paper, then brown paper with string, before placing it in a box to which she attached a label bearing Pascale Clement's name. An accompanying letter instructed Priscilla to allow no one but the girl to receive or open the package. Having polished the Princess Mary tin so it looked almost new, Maisie returned Peter Evernden's identity discs to their hiding place and wrapped the tin in a sheet of tissue paper before setting it alongside Pascale's gift. She closed the box and secured the parcel, ready to send to Biarritz. The letter did not give details as to how she came upon the treasure, but explained that she thought it only right that the tin and its contents should now belong to Priscilla, though her possession of the items must remain a secret.

WORD CAME FROM Stratton that arrangements had been made for her to visit Avril Jarvis at Holloway on Tuesday, September 30, at ten o'clock, and that her request for a private meeting had been honored. The black Invicta motor car arrived at a quarter past nine, an early departure that would allow time for a meeting with the governor of the women's prison. In preparation, Maisie had woken early for her ritual of meditation. She had taken a taxi-cab to Hampstead, to spend time in conversation with Khan, followed by silence and absolute stillness. In those hours she had seen again the pinhole of light that became larger and larger. She was moving away from the edge. She was healing.

"I thought you might like to see a copy of the pathologist's final report—though as far as anyone at the Yard is concerned, you've never seen it." Stratton reached into a leather briefcase and pulled out a sheaf of papers for Maisie to look at as the motor car made its way across London.

She leafed through the papers, then took each page and read carefully. "The killer was right-handed, and at the second lunge the blade entered here." She touched her mackintosh at the place on her chest to the left of her breastbone. "Hmmm. And a thirteen-year-old girl is supposed to have the strength to push a knife through clothing, flesh and bone."

"Anger gives untold strength. You know that."

"Wouldn't you be angry?"

"I'm not saying she deserves to hang, for God's sake. Your friend Lawton will no doubt seek a manslaughter charge rather than life in prison. She's fortunately too young to see the black cloth."

Maisie remembered the judge of her dreams placing the square black cloth of death atop his long silver-haired wig. She sighed, exasperated, then handed the file to Stratton, leaned back in her seat, and closed her eyes, reliving that first meeting with Avril Jarvis. As she did so, she went back again and again, focusing on one particular movement as the girl reached out—what was it for? Water? And then the moment when she touched the girl's back, feeling the tension that warned of a secret held. She opened her eyes.

The smoke-blackened castellated walls of Holloway Prison loomed ahead. Gates opened for the Invicta to enter, and the car drew to a halt to allow Stratton and Maisie to alight and enter the prison. Following a meeting with the governor, they were led to a small room, not unlike the room at Vine Street where Maisie had first met Avril Jarvis, though this time there was no window. A table was positioned in the center of the room, with a hard wooden chair on either side. She chose the seat facing the door by which Avril would enter.

"I'll wait outside," Stratton said, before leaving the room.

Moments passed. Then the heavy door opened and Avril was led in. The woman guard pushed the girl into the wooden chair and stood in a corner.

"There is no need to guard me. You may wait outside."

"If you please, madam, I—"

"Please leave us."

She flashed a glare at Maisie. "I'll be right outside."

"Of course." Maisie smiled and thanked the guard, who she knew would have been duty-bound to remain in the room but had possibly been instructed to allow leeway in this case.

Maisie regarded Avril Jarvis. Despite her incarceration, she seemed to be faring better than when they first met. The hell she was enduring now was clearly not as dark as the one before.

"How are you, Avril?"

"All right, miss."

Maisie stood up and walked around the table, keeping her eyes on Avril, so that eventually the girl had to look up at her.

"What are you doing, miss?"

"Causing the walls to crumble, Avril."

The girl was unnerved and frowned.

"Stand up." Maisie's voice was soft yet strong.

Avril pushed back her chair and stood, her hands at her sides. Maisie noticed the slightly shorter right arm. It was when she reached for the arm to wash it gently at their first meeting that Avril had flinched.

"Did you kill your uncle?"

"I reckon I must've."

"You don't remember?"

"That's what I said, what I've said all along."

"Could you have killed him?"

"Could I, miss?"

"Yes, could you?"

"Well, he wasn't no saint, so I reckon I could."

"Avril, you are lying."

"No, miss, I ain't lying."

"Avril, I will concede that you may have passed out. I will concede that you may have felt like killing such a brutal man, but I know you could not have done it."

Avril looked down. Maisie moved to a place directly in front of her.

"Avril."

"Yes, miss?"

"Look at me."

Avril looked up.

"I want you to lift your right hand and hit me as hard as you can."

The girl's eyes opened so wide that Maisie almost smiled.

"I can't do that, miss."

"No one's here to see. Just you and me. Now then, do as I say. Hit me as hard as you can."

Avril swallowed and lifted her left hand.

"No, Avril. You are not left-handed, you are right-handed. Your right hand."

Avril Jarvis lifted her right hand and then, with her face reddening, she pulled down her fist with all her might and lunged at Maisie, who closed her eyes as the fist connected with her chest. She did not fall back, did not lose her footing. Instead, as she opened her eyes; she saw the girl standing there with tears flowing.

"You couldn't have killed that man, Avril. You could barely move me." Maisie stepped around to the girl's back and pressed at the very point where she held her secret. "This is the muscle that does the work in your back, isn't it, Avril? The one that compensates for your arm. Roll up your sleeve—all the way to your shoulder."

Avril Jarvis rolled up the sleeve of her rough uniform dress to reveal an arm that was bent above the elbow.

"What happened to you, Avril?" Maisie reached into her black bag and pulled out a handkerchief, which she passed to the girl.

"I was ten when me stepdad first talked about me going away to London. I was scared, miss, right scared. I tried to run away, but he found me and dragged me back again. He beat me, said I was good for nothing and it wasn't worth spending good money on food for me. I was working out in the fields then, even though the school board man came round, but he didn't do nothing when he saw me stepdad, he was that scared of him. I ran away again, and he came after me—drunk, you know." She sniffed and rubbed her eyes and nose with the handkerchief. "So I thought that if I killed myself, it would be all right. He wouldn't be able to touch me then, would he? And I would be out of it, out of the way, if I was dead."

Maisie nodded. "Go on."

"So one day he said he was sending me away to work in London and Mum was crying and saying 'No, no, no,' so I ran off and hid in a tree and when he came up to drag me down I just let meself go. Right far up in the branches, I was. I broke me arm. Hurt me back as well. That's why I've no strength. 'Course, we didn't have the money for a doctor, so my stepdad just put a bit of wood along my arm and put a bandage around it and said that by the time I went to London, I wouldn't even notice. I was twelve when I came up here. And my arm still hurts." She began to weep, and as the tears flowed, Maisie held Avril Jarvis to her. "I want to go back to my mum, miss."

"You will, Avril. Don't worry, you will."

IT WAS ALMOST dusk by the time Maisie returned to Ebury Place, Stratton's driver having brought her back alone while the Inspector remained at Holloway. She went directly to her rooms, stopping only to accept Sandra's offer to bring her supper on a tray later, perhaps a nice piece of steamed cod for strength.

A fire was already alight in the grate. Maisie slipped off her coat, draped it across the back of the chair, and slumped down, rubbing her temples as she did so. Images of the day flashed into her mind as she allowed the tension of the past few hours to seep away. She had summoned both Stratton and the guard, and as they entered the barren room where Maisie stood alongside the girl, Maisie placed a hand between the girl's shoulder blades to encourage her to stand tall. She could not afford to bend. Avril Jarvis needed to be upright and firm, and Maisie ensured that she was nothing less than strong at this time, even if she crumbled when taken back to her cell.

"Inspector Stratton, I would like to draw your attention to a physical disability suffered by Miss Jarvis."

Stratton frowned but knew that Maisie was not one to waste time. "What is it, Miss Dobbs?"

Maisie turned to Avril. "Please roll up your sleeve again." The girl obeyed, her thin damaged limb revealed to Stratton. "As you can see, Miss Jarvis sustained an injury some time ago that has rendered her weak and deformed, though the disadvantage is not immediately noticeable. She has compensated well."

Stratton leaned closer to look at the girl's arm. She began to tremble quite visibly but regained composure when Maisie smiled and touched her shoulder.

"The fact is that Miss Jarvis has little strength in that arm. Of course, you must have a doctor test her ability and physical dexterity, though I feel it should have been noticed at her preliminary medical."

"What are you saying, Miss Dobbs?" Stratton looked directly at Maisie. He knew very well what she was saying.

"Miss Jarvis could hardly push me away with that arm, and she certainly does not have the might to drive a knife into the heart of a man."

Stratton turned to the guard. "Please return Miss Jarvis to her cell."

The guard took Avril Jarvis by her left arm. "Come along, Jarvis. Now then, don't dawdle, get along."

The door closed behind them.

"We have already discussed this, Miss Dobbs. What about rage, anger?"

Maisie shook her head. "As you know, I have medical training, so I can make a preliminary assessment—and again, I am surprised that her disability was not noted earlier." Maisie glanced at Stratton as she began to pace. "Another assessment, possibly by an orthopedic surgeon, along with further consultation with the pathologist, will confirm that Avril Jarvis did not—could not—have killed the man referred to as her uncle."

"If she didn't, then who did?" Stratton shook his head.

"Ah, that I cannot tell you. Clearly the girl was first on the scene. She removed the knife from the body, an act that caused her to collapse and have no memory of subsequent events." She paused, then played her next card. "You might entertain the possibility, Inspector, that the girl has absolutely no knowledge whatsoever regarding the identity of the killer. Her 'uncle' was a Soho ne'er-do-well with dubious associations. If a thirteen-year-old girl did not kill him, I am sure you could compile a list of undesirable characters and known felons who would have been only too glad to bring an end to his life."

Stratton sighed, shook his head, and turned to the door, gesturing for Maisie to go before him. "I have work to do here, Miss Dobbs. I will have to call upon you again. However, I think we can assume that, if your suspicions are corroborated, Avril Jarvis will be released to her family in due course."

As she gazed into the fire, Maisie smiled. *Home with her mother.*

Maisie left her room only once before supper was brought on a tray. In the library she placed a telephone call to Sir Cecil Lawton's chambers and, though she did not speak to him directly, she instructed a pupil to inform him that she would visit him at his estate in Cambridgeshire on Friday, with a request to let her know if the arrangement was not convenient. Maisie planned to make the journey by train, though she had received word from Eric that the MG was "Ready when you are, miss!" But she was not quite ready.

Of course, she could have seen Sir Cecil in his offices; however, her client, the father who had asked her to prove his son dead so his conscience could rest, was not the only man she wished to visit at the Lawton estate.

TWENTY-SEVEN

In the two days between the meeting at Holloway and her journey to Cambridgeshire on Friday, Maisie spent time at her office in Fitzroy Square, though she did not arrive until mid-morning each day and left before four o'clock in the afternoon, a good thrce hours before her customary time of departure. There was another interview with Stratton regarding the Jarvis case, along with commencement of work for the new clients who required the services of Maisie Dobbs, Psychologist and Investigator, and who had seen Billy while she was in France. France: It seemed many weeks ago now, yet she must bring her pilgrimage back into the present for Lawton. She had still to compose both her verbal and written reports.

Maurice had remained in town for several days to monitor Maisie's progress; although he was not in agreement with her insistence upon working, he could see that with her return to routine she had begun to step away from the chaos of her memories. Dene had returned to Hastings, but not before extracting a promise from Maisie that she would spend the weekend at Chelstone with her father, possibly remaining there until Monday.

On the morning of October 3, she set off for Cambridge, to be collected at the station by Sir Cecil's chauffeur and driven over to

Saplings. Lawton's manservant, Brayley, was there to greet her when the motor car pulled up alongside the house. He did not allow his eyes to meet hers but instead executed a shallow bow before offering to take her coat.

"Sir Cecil will see you in the drawing room, Miss Dobbs." He spoke as if their conversation on the street in Cambridge had never happened, as if he had never warned her to cease her investigation on behalf of his employer.

"Thank you." Maisie walked past him, not waiting for him to escort her to the drawing room. She knocked and entered.

"Ah, Miss Dobbs. Good morning. I understand you have been unwell, a chill caught while in France." Lawton betrayed his nervousness with cordial chatter. "I must say, that was probably all my fault for sending you there on a wild goose chase in the first place, but jolly good show for going and for being so thorough with your investigations per my brief to you. Of course, it's not as if I didn't know, you know——"

"Sir Cecil, may I sit down?" Maisie thought it interesting that this man who was so assured in court was actually quite clumsy outside his preferred milieu. But then, this was no ordinary interview.

"Yes, do take a seat. Brayley will be here with morning coffee shortly. I must say, I am gasping for a cup."

"Sir Cecil, I have arrived at the following conclusions regarding your son."

Sir Cecil Lawton was sitting on the edge of his buttoned leather chair. Now, realizing that it made him look less than the important man he was, he sat back and tried to assume a more relaxed position. "Go on."

"I began by comparing Ralph's records with what we have been given to understand occurred in France. I can tell you that your son was a brave aviator who served his country to the highest standards. He accepted the most dangerous of assignments."

Lawton nodded. Maisie paused to consider his posture, his demeanor. *Is there sadness? Does he demonstrate regret?*

"In fact, I do believe you may be unaware that on several occasions he delivered intelligence agents to their fields of operation behind enemy lines, work that demanded skill and courage." Maisie saw Lawton raise his eyebrows, but he said nothing. *He wants only for me to tell him that his son is dead.* "Naturally, this information is in complete confidence. We are both bound by our loyalty to our country, Sir Cecil, and this information was procured at considerable risk."

"Your report will remain within the walls of this room."

"Thank you. The assignment that led to the crash was a particularly dangerous one executed at dusk. He was required to fly into enemy territory to drop a hamper of carrier pigeons for use by an agent he had previously transported to the area. His De Havilland came under enemy fire and he crashed. His craft exploded into flames upon impact."

"And my son was killed."

Maisie paused until Sir Cecil met her eyes with his own. She had considered her words with care. "I can confirm that Ralph Lawton died in the inferno."

Sir Cecil exhaled deeply, though Maisie could see that it was a sigh of relief and not of regret.

"As you know, his remains are buried at Arras and commemorated there, along with others from the Flying Corps who gave their lives in the war."

"Did he suffer? Do you think he suffered?"

Maisie reflected on the scarring on the neck and hands of the man who called himself Daniel Roberts, or the young boy in a photograph with his best friend, and on the man who had now found a semblance of peace.

"I cannot make this easier for you, Sir Cecil. I believe he suffered, though he is in a better place now."

They were silent for a while, during which time Lawton's manservant came to the drawing room bearing a mahogany tray with a silver coffee service and white china cups and saucers. The strong smell of fresh coffee brought Maurice to mind, and Maisie felt his presence, remembering his teachings upon the nature of truth. They had spent many hours of her apprenticeship speaking of the distinctions between fact and truth and the nature of the lie. Indeed, it was the powerful yet cloudy haze between those distinctions that had been at the heart of their recent discord.

"You have done well, Miss Dobbs. I wish my wife were still with me so that she could also hear your report. It would have served her better than the lies she heard from those crackpot mischief-makers."

"Your wife did what she thought best, Sir Cecil. And their words brought comfort along with turmoil." Maisie paused and reached into her document case. "My written report will follow. In the meantime, I have brought my final invoice, together with an accounting in respect of expenses for your perusal."

Lawton reached for the envelope, taking out the page that bore Maisie's account. "Let me deal with this now. I will return in a moment with a check for you."

"Thank you."

Maisie stood and looked around the room, noticing a collection of silver-framed photographs on a sideboard. She walked across the thick carpet and examined each photograph in turn. Most were taken in studios, formal sittings of Sir Cecil and Lady Agnes Lawton individually, as a couple, and then with their son, a frail-looking boy, with a countenance that seemed sad. Then she turned to another photograph of father and son. Though it was not taken in a studio, it had the hallmarks of formality, of the rules of behavior that each was bound to maintain. Maisie smiled, remembering the wall of photographs at the Partridge villa in Biarritz, of the three boys caught laughing, perhaps scrambling over their father in good-natured high jinks, then another showing Douglas with his arm around his eldest son as they both peered into a tide pool, trousers rolled up, heads close. There was truth in the images in front of her, a truth that helped her bear the weight of the story she had recounted to Sir Cecil: Ralph Lawton had suffered but was now free.

"There you are." Lawton entered the room and handed Maisie a check. She glanced at the figure and noticed that the amount was a sum greater than that indicated in her final bill.

"Sir Cecil, I—"

He held up a hand. "Not only did you execute your investigation to a degree of thoroughness beyond that which I expected, but I have received word that charges against Miss Avril Jarvis have been dropped. She will be released on Monday. Of course, there are some administrative details, but the result is minimal work for my chambers."

"Thank you, Sir Cecil."

"Thank *you*, Miss Dobbs. My wife can rest in peace now, as does my son."

Maisie walked toward the door, turning to her client on the threshold. She held out her hand. "You can rest too, Sir Cecil. You have kept your promise. Good day."

AS SHE LEFT the room, Maisie was met by Brayley, who was to escort her to the motor car for her return to the railway station. She stopped, touched him on the arm, and pointed to the corridor that she supposed led to the kitchens.

"May I have a word?"

The man faltered, his face reddening. Their last conversation had proved adversarial on his part, but in this house he was subordinate. "Of course, m'um."

They walked along the corridor until they reached an alcove with a bay window looking out onto the grounds.

"This will do." Maisie looked around to ensure that they were alone. "You threatened me, Mr. Brayley?"

"Please, m'um, in my loyalty to my employer, I suffered a lapse in judgment. I beg of you, please do not speak to Sir Cecil of my visit to see you."

"If I was going to speak of it, I would have done so by now. And after you came to see me, you came to watch me, to discover what I might have found out by following me."

The man shook his head. "I just wanted to protect him. His son had a . . . a past. It would be a terrible thing if people knew, if your investigations revealed the truth."

Maisie paused, again checking the pulse of the conversation. "And was it you who caused me to crash my motor car? Was it you who ran from Goodge Street station into my path?"

The man frowned and shook his head. "I don't know what you are talking about. Yes, I admit, I followed you on two occasions and was even watching you come and go from your accommodations. I thought I might be able to talk to you again, but I did not try to cause you injury."

Maisie frowned and nodded. She believed him but was not mollified. "You acted foolishly, Mr. Brayley. I could have you locked up for your behavior."

"I beg of you—"

Maisie raised her hand. "Be calm. I might have sought to protect my employer in the same way." She looked out at the view over the gardens, and then back at the manservant. "You must never speak of this again, of the promise Sir Cecil made."

"I never have, m'um."

Maisie pulled on her gloves. "I'm ready to leave now."

They walked toward the waiting motor, and as the haggard manservant held the door for her she whispered to him, "Your secrets are safe. Goodbye, Mr. Brayley."

As the motor car made its way slowly down the gravel driveway, Maisie leaned forward to watch as the flat fenlands swept past. So Brayley had tried to scare her, had tried to hamper her investigation into the life and death of Ralph Lawton, but he had not tried to kill her. Now she must move on, to explore the next possibility. Though tired, she knew she was regaining strength. And she would need strength to meet the person who would have her dead.

· · ·

IT HAD BEEN another long day. Tomorrow she would go to Chelstone, though she had not decided whether to drive or travel by
train. When she arrived back at Ebury Place, Sandra informed her
that Eric was anxious to see her: He had collected the repaired MG
just that morning and could not wait for her to see it. Despite the
fact that she was gasping for a cup of tea, Maisie went directly to the
mews that ran parallel along the rear of Ebury Place, to the garage
where the Compton motor cars were kept. The old Lanchester was
kept shining. Despite the fact that Lord Compton was now generally
transported in the newer Rolls-Royce, he preferred to retain the
Lanchester for sentimental reasons. "It's a damn good motor," he
had been heard to say to George, his personal chauffeur. Though
dwarfed by the Lanchester, the MG took pride of place and was
gleaming as Maisie entered the garage.

"Oh, my goodness! What a wonderful job!"

Eric moved around the vehicle bearing a chamois, which he used
to buff a hardly visible mark here or a speck of dust there. "I tell
you, that Reg Martin is a right genius with a motor, specializes in
coach work, and is a true craftsman." He paused to stand back and
admire the MG. "You wouldn't even know what she's been
through."

Maisie nodded. "She's a treat, Eric." She raised her eyebrows.
"But now I had better see the bill, hadn't I?"

Eric shook his head. "All taken care of, m'um."

"What on earth do you mean? The man doesn't work for nothing. In fact, in these times I'm amazed he's still in business. Why am
I not to have a bill?"

"Better talk to His Lordship. Came out here himself, he did,
while you were over there in France. Unlike him, really. You know,
he don't say much, His Lordship, but he instructed me to have the
bill sent to him, said he got you into this, and if you hadn't been
working for his friend this wouldn't have happened."

"Oh, dear. I do so hate to be beholden." Maisie touched her forehead, fingering the now-healed scar.

"Nah, you ain't beholden, m'um. It's him that's beholden; that's why he's paid for the repairs. Now then, when're you taking her out? You could take her down to Kent tomorrow. Nice run down early in the morning—"

Maisie shook her head. "No, Eric. Perhaps early next week. Perhaps I'll take her for a spin then."

Eric frowned. "Right you are, m'um. Soon as you're ready, she'll be here, spick-and-span."

Maisie thanked the young man and turned to leave, but just as she reached the door, he called to her.

"M'um?"

"Yes?" Maisie turned to the young man.

"Just in case you change your mind, I'll have her out in the mews nice and early. And if you like, what with it being your first time out after your accident, I'll go with you. I can come back on the train. I remember talking to old Reg, and he said that after a driver has come a bit of a cropper, it's nice to have company."

Maisie smiled. "That's a very generous offer, Eric. I'll let you know if I change my mind."

Reaching her rooms, Maisie sat at her desk, reaching into her document case for the manila folder in which she had kept her notes on the Lawton case. A clutch of index cards were tucked inside the flap, ready to place into the card file when the case was closed, so that all references would be maintained for future use, should they be required.

She tapped her green fountain pen on the edge of the wooden desk. On Monday she would travel to visit Jeremy Hazleton and his wife. She needed to see Ralph Lawton's old friend one more time. Maisie made a church and steeple with her fingers, resting her head on clasped hands with her elbows on the desk. She thought for a while, then took out the notes she had made during the conversation with Andrew three weeks ago, when she had sought not a personal conversation but, instead, his medical knowledge and his specific training in orthopedics.

A fire crackled in the grate, drawing Maisie away from her desk to the armchair. She gazed into the flames licking up toward the chimney, allowing her mind to wander the caverns created by the hot coals before her. *Perhaps I should get behind the wheel again. Perhaps I should accept Eric's offer. I'll see how I feel in the morning.* But as she fought to keep her heavy eyes open, a sensation crossed her heart that she immediately put down to one of trepidation regarding the act of driving a motor car again. She was so tired she did not consider that her intuition had spoken.

Maisie rose later than usual to a day that seemed bright enough, but with a few threatening clouds in the sky. She bathed, collected her weekend bag, and took the liberty of knocking on the kitchen door and entering the servants' domain.

"If you don't mind, I thought I'd have a quick cup of tea here. It's so quiet in the house, I feel like the only person in the world!"

Sandra and Teresa were counting linens and Eric, the footman cum chauffeur, was leaning against the sink, a cup of tea and a biscuit in hand. He turned quickly as Maisie entered.

"Don't stop drinking your tea, Eric. I've just come in for a bit of company. In any case, I wanted to speak to you about the MG."

"She's been outside in the mews since seven this morning, m'um, waiting for you just in case you decided to drive."

"Well, I think I should." She smiled at Sandra, who had just placed a fresh pot of tea and a china cup in front of her. "It's a fine day, so I'll take the bull by the horns. I am delighted to have her back, so I will drive!"

"Good for you, m'um!" Eric put his cup into the sink and went toward the back door. "But if you think you need someone—"

Maisie raised a hand. "No, that's not necessary, Eric, but your offer is a kind one, as I said yesterday."

"Right then, I'll just run the duster over her one last time and get her started for you."

"I'll be there in about fifteen minutes."

Eric touched his cap and left the kitchen. Sandra and Teresa looked at each other and shook their heads.

Maisie joined Eric in the mews exactly fifteen minutes later, the MG's engine idling as he continued to sweep the duster back and forth across the bonnet. "There won't be anything left of Mr. Martin's paintwork if you go on like that!" said Maisie.

"Got to have her perfect for you." He pushed the duster into a back pocket and reached for Maisie's bag, which he placed in the boot before opening the door. "Take it nice and easy, m'um, and you'll forget that little bump on the Tottenham Court Road ever happened!" He tapped the bonnet twice as Maisie put the car in gear and drove slowly out of the mews.

Through London, out along the Old Kent Road, and on toward Sevenoaks, the traffic was light and the weather good, though not quite good enough to brave the elements with the roof drawn back. At first driving no faster than ten miles per hour, Maisie quickly gained confidence and by the time the city streets had given way to the new suburbia and then the Weald of Kent, it seemed that Eric was right: The accident might never have happened. She would put it all to the back of her mind. River Hill lay just ahead; then she would be on toward Tonbridge, followed by Chelstone. She turned her thoughts to lighter matters as she drove, changing gears to pass a horse and cart and then accelerating to fifty miles an hour along the almost-empty road.

The girls in the kitchen had been full of talk about the airship that was to leave England for Paris at the weekend. The R-101 was a feat of engineering and a symbol of spirited adventure. Maisie found that their conversation was often about such things, of the places they would go "if they had the money," of the houses they would live in if they were blessed with riches, and the clothes they would wear if they married a wealthy man. The kitchen was their cocoon against the reality of the economic crisis that gripped the country.

Counting her good fortune, Maisie changed gear as she approached the hill and applied the brake pedal at the top. She heard the whine of the gears, a force she expected to be accompanied by the pull of the brakes. She pressed her foot to the brake pedal again: nothing. She changed to an even lower gear, sitting forward as the long winding hill curved downward, but despite her dexterity with the controls of the MG, she felt the car begin to careen out of control. *Oh, God, please, help me.* She pressed the brake pedal to the floor hard again, yet still there was nothing. She pulled back on the gear and played the hand brake back and forth, all measures that proved inadequate to this dangerous mix of gradient and velocity. Now, both hands on the wheel, she felt her body twist and turn with each curl of the road, the hill pulling her down, down.

A car coming up the hill swerved to avoid a collision as she spun across the road, the man shaking a fist as his motor car climbed the verge. Time was standing still again, just as it did on Tottenham Court Road, just as it did when the hand reached out to push her under the wheels of a train, just as it had in France. She was barely halfway down, the MG gaining speed with each second, screeching in the lowest gear as the motor car shuddered against Maisie's fight to steer. Her knuckles were white against the wheel, her bottom lip beginning to ooze blood where her teeth had broken the skin. The canopy of trees above the road allowed the sun to glint through, her terror now peppered with shards of light flashing before her. She spun around a corner. "Oh, no!" A slow-moving lorry was lumbering along just a few yards in front. Maisie pulled the wheel to the right, thundered past the lorry and barely avoided another motor car on the opposite side. She spat the salty blood from her mouth as the bottom of the hill finally came into view. The hill began to level out, though the MG was still moving fast. Ahead, the side of the road merged into a graded verge and ditch. With another lorry ahead and a series of vehicles coming in the opposite direction,

Maisie pulled the steering wheel hard left, bumped across the verge and closed her eyes as the MG thumped into the ditch and off the other side, into a hedge.

She swallowed deeply, the sweat pouring from her brow stinging her eyes. Slowly she moved to switch off the engine. Two motor cars had pulled over and a man and woman now ran across the grass toward the MG. The man pulled open her door and the woman knelt alongside her.

"Are you all right?"

Maisie nodded. She could not speak.

The man reached into the MG and helped Maisie to her feet. "What happened, brakes go?"

She nodded again, still unable to find words.

The woman took a handkerchief from the pocket of her tweed jacket and pressed it to Maisie's forehead and then, seeing the rivulet of blood from her lip to her chin, held it against her mouth.

"The driver behind me pulled over and ran back to the police box. They'll be here in a minute," said the man, as he looked around toward the road. "Come on, miss. Sit down here on the grass." He took off his mackintosh and placed it on the damp ground. "Terrible place to have your brakes go, terrible. Mind you, looks like a new motor to me." He shook his head and smiled wryly. "Someone got it in for you, love?"

TWENTY-EIGHT

Maisie sat with her father at the kitchen table of the Groom's Cottage, Frankie silently watching his daughter as she told another version of the events that led to the MG's final resting place in a hedge beside the road: It was all the fault of a wayward squirrel who had run into her path and, not wanting to kill an innocent animal, she swerved to avoid the creature. Her father nodded as she recounted the story and observed a certain fire in her eyes that he had not seen for a while.

"You know, Maisie, there was a look your mother could give, and the minute I saw it I knew she was not only determined but that nothing would stand in her way. I've seen that look in your eyes twice before, Maisie: when you told me you were going away to the university, and when I told you I had a mind to shop you to the authorities for lying about your age when you enlisted. Now then, I don't rightly know what's goin' on in this 'ere case of yours, my girl, but I do know when I see your mother in you and I can see it now. You just mind you don't get into any more trouble. *Squirrel, my eye!*"

Dene arrived later. Maisie was talking with George, the Comptons' chauffeur, when Dene drove up in his Austin Swallow. Maisie's bad luck in meeting an errant squirrel on the road was not the only topic of conversation that day as news came in that the famed

R-101, largest airship in the world, had met a fiery end, crashing in France.

Dene nodded to George and leaned to kiss Maisie on the cheek. After ensuring that she was unhurt, he addressed both Maisie and the chauffeur. "Talking about the airship, eh? Can hardly believe it, can you? She passed over Hastings last night, though I must say I was not one of the hardy souls out there waiting to watch her go over in the dark. Terrible business, terrible. A horrible way to go. They say there are only about eight survivors, don't they?"

George nodded and the conversation went on until Dene asked what the plans were to retrieve the MG.

"Well, I had a word with the owner of the garage myself this morning, and apparently the bodywork isn't badly damaged, surprisingly enough. Some deep scratches and a dent, but nothing that Reg Martin can't take care of, though I'm sure he'll have something to say about it all, just having finished the job after the last one!" Maisie gave George a sudden glare as he spoke, which he understood and did not mention the brakes. "Of course, there are a few other mechanical matters to attend to, but all in all, the motor should be ready in a few days."

Dene turned to Maisie. "You should be careful. Were you driving too fast?"

"Andrew!" Maisie frowned but took the tease in good heart, eager to change the subject.

George departed to continue with his work and Maisie walked toward the paddocks with Dene.

"So, what will you do without a motor car? You'll have to stay in one place for a few days."

Maisie shook her head. "I have to put a case to rest before I can take more time off. I already lost time after France, so I have work to do."

"Do you feel well enough?"

She nodded. "Much better. I must get to the bottom of a question that has been nagging me, but I promise I will come to Hastings as soon as the work is done."

"And what about a motor car? What will you do about transportation?"

"I will be going back to London on the train tomorrow morning. I have to go to Dramsford on Monday afternoon; then I believe I will not need to leave town to complete my work, so I'll use the underground and buses. I managed before I had the MG and can do so again, I'm sure."

"One of the advantages of being in London, I suppose." Dene looked thoughtful and was quiet for a while, and Maisie suspected that he had been holding on to the possibility that she might choose to live outside London. It was an observation that reminded her that she must contact the solicitors regarding the flat in Pimlico. She was not ready to move to another town, especially one that was far from London.

Maisie turned to Dene, eager to avoid a misunderstanding. "And one of the advantages of being in London is that it is always a pleasure to visit the seaside. I'll come to Hastings, Andrew, when this particular job has been completed, and it will be soon. Then I will rest and we can make up for time apart."

Following dinner at the Groom's Cottage with Frankie Dobbs, Dene left Chelstone, taking Maisie in his arms and kissing her deeply as she walked with him to his motor car.

"I worry about you, Maisie. I know how France must have been for you, and I know you've taken on something very important in this case." He paused, holding her to him. "I will never question your work, Maisie, but I will caution you to take care. I don't know what I would do if—"

Maisie pressed a finger to his lips. "I know what I am doing, Andrew. Remember who my teacher was."

Dene nodded and then squeezed her hand as he climbed into his Austin Swallow. "I'll see you soon, then. Perhaps next weekend?"

She waved to him as she replied. "I'll telephone you in the week, Andrew."

Waving as he drove away, Maisie walked slowly back to the Groom's Cottage, to sit beside the fire with her father before going to bed and rising early the next morning to catch the train to London. Yes, she was still tired, could still feel the weakness lingering in each joint. But her father was right; this accident had galvanized her again, had ignited the fire of her resolve. She *would* confront Jeremy Hazleton and his wife. And she *would* find out who wanted her dead.

She stopped alongside the window that looked into the small sitting room where her father reached toward the bellows alongside the fireplace. As he tended the fire ready for her return, flames leaped up, creating a flickering light across the framed photograph of her mother, set on the mantelpiece above. Maisie was transfixed by the photograph, and in that moment it seemed as if the image moved, though surely it could not have. But that night Maisie fell asleep feeling as she had in childhood, that she was safe at home with both her mother and father.

MAISIE ARRIVED AT the Hazletons' house on Monday afternoon. Eric had offered to drive her, saying that Lord Compton had asked him to ensure that the Lanchester be given a good run every now and again, and now was as good a time as ever. He parked the majestic motor car on the street and, as he opened the passenger door for Maisie to alight, he looked up at the house and the winding path that led to the front door.

"Gaw, m'um, wouldn't like to be the one who has to lug the shopping up them steps."

Maisie stepped onto the pavement, pulling on her gloves and checking the position of her black hat. "I think the back entrance is a little more forgiving. That's where they keep their motor car. In fact, it has to be easier, as the owner cannot walk; he was wounded in the war."

Eric nodded. "I'll be waiting for you here, m'um."

"I shan't be long—that's if they even let me in!"

Maisie smiled and began walking up the steps. She noticed curtains move and knew that Mrs. Hazleton had already seen her from the drawing room window and was in all likelihood rushing to the door to send her on her way. As she reached the entrance, it was indeed Jeremy Hazleton's wife and not the housekeeper who answered the doorbell.

"What are you doing here? I thought I made myself clear. You were told not to come to this house again!" Her usual grayness of complexion and attire was hardly dented by the rise of color to her cheeks, which only served to accentuate hollows above her jaw and under her eyes.

"Good morning, Mrs. Hazleton. I would like to see your husband, though my questions will not concern Ralph Lawton directly nor compromise his memory of that friendship. I need only to ask for his assistance in a personal matter."

"What do you mean?" The woman continued to speak through the narrow margin of space allowed by the partially open door.

Maisie smiled again, concentrating on exuding warmth. "It will take only a few moments, Mrs. Hazleton."

"Let the woman in, for God's sake. Let's get it over and done with," Jeremy Hazleton's voice bellowed from the hallway.

Charmaine Hazleton opened the door ungraciously and stepped aside for Maisie to enter. Jeremy Hazleton wheeled his chair forward, then jerked his head to one side. "Let's go into my study, Miss Dobbs." He turned to his wife. "It'll be all right. I'll take care of her."

Hazleton steered his wheelchair into the room as his wife stood behind Maisie, her eyes revealing an intense dislike of the unexpected and unwelcome guest. Maisie closed the door behind her but knew Charmaine Hazleton would eavesdrop.

"So what do you want?" Hazleton reached the desk and swung the chair around until he was facing Maisie. His eyes reflected not only his anger but, as Maisie recognized, his fear. "Did you find out everything you wanted about Ralph?"

Maisie remained standing, then paced back and forth, her eyes meeting Hazleton's. "Yes, I did." She stopped alongside his desk and picked up a glass paperweight, holding it to the light. It was immediately recognizable as the ornament on the bar in front of Jeremy Hazleton in the photograph taken at the Café Druk in Paris. She now understood that the piece had been a gift from Lawton to his lover. Hazleton seemed uncomfortable but said nothing. Maisie continued to hold the paperweight as she paced and spoke to Hazleton. "I understand the depth of your relationship; however, I am not here this time to talk about Ralph." She turned the paperweight, then passed it from one hand to the other. "My first question is about me, actually. And about your wife. My life has been threatened, Mr. Hazleton, and I am here to know why your wife ran from Goodge Street station in a bid to make me lose control of my motor car. Perhaps you can tell me." She looked at Hazleton and increased the distance between her hands as she passed the paperweight back and forth. Still Hazleton said nothing about the ornament, though he did respond to her question.

"What rubbish! My wife has not been anywhere near an underground station for months."

"And she wasn't in Belgravia this weekend?"

"Absolutely not!"

Maisie increased the distance between her hands again so that now she was throwing the paperweight slowly back and forth, seemingly lost in deliberation of his response.

"I say, be careful!"

She smiled. "Oh, I am careful, Mr. Hazleton, which was why I was injured and not killed on Saturday."

"I have no idea what you are talking about, I've told you!"

Now Maisie held the paperweight in one hand only, but continued to play with it as she paced, throwing it up in the air, first just a couple of inches from her palm, then three, then four. "I think we do need to go back to Goodge Street station, don't we, Mr. Hazleton?"

Hazleton became flushed, pulling his wheelchair to the side of the desk. "That is a very valuable piece, I'll have you know!"

"Oh, don't worry, I was quite good at rounders as a child, though we did play in the streets, so one could always get a good bounce." Maisie threw the ball some two feet in the air and caught it again, then moved her arm to repeat the throw.

Hazleton made a guttural cry and launched himself at Maisie, who stepped back toward the wall as this man who claimed to be a cripple ran at her. "Give that to me!"

As he reached for the paperweight, Maisie tightened her grip. When Charmaine Hazleton burst into the room, she saw her husband standing in front of Maisie Dobbs.

"What have you done? Look at him!"

"I don't think I can take any credit for spontaneous healing, can I?"

Hazleton dropped to his knees and began to weep as his wife hurried to his side. "We're done for. We're finished."

Maisie remained calm. "You will be if you don't start telling the truth." She flashed a glare at Charmaine Hazleton. "I want to know exactly what is going on here." Turning to Hazleton, Maisie held out her hand. "Now then, stand up, Mr. Hazleton, because I know you can."

Hazleton staggered to his feet.

"Sit down, both of you."

The two were seated, Charmaine Hazleton next to her husband, who had staggered to his wheelchair.

"Which one of you was at Goodge Street?"

The couple exchanged glances; then Hazleton's wife spoke. "Oh, for heaven's sake!" She turned to her husband. "She's bound to have told the police by now. That's probably one of them outside in the motor car."

Maisie did not offer information concerning whom she may have told of her visit. "Mrs. Hazleton, you'd better explain, and quickly."

"Yes, it was me. First of all, I wanted to speak to you again. I thought if I explained everything, it would stop you in this ridiculous search for Ralph Lawton. I followed you, began to find out where you went, the route you took to your office. I watched you leave your home on that day and, suddenly"—she looked at her hands and then reached across to her husband—"I wanted to scare you, wanted to see you off. I know it was stupid, utterly stupid. I knew I could make it to Goodge Street before you came into Tottenham Court Road. We had too much to lose." Biting her lip, she held her breath, then began speaking again. "We have built a life here. My husband's past is . . . is of no consequence now. He needs me. He needs *me*."

Maisie looked from Hazleton to his wife, assessing the situation. She stood up and began to pace again, then stopped in front of the man, now in his wheelchair. "And why on earth have you lied about your condition? You were badly injured, yes, but there was no reason for you to remain in a wheelchair. I'm surprised you haven't been found out."

The Hazleton couple seemed dejected, as if all energy had left them, so that they leaned toward each other for strength. Had she not been a victim of their deception, Maisie knew that she might almost have felt sorry for them.

"I . . . it was after the war. . . ."

"Go on."

"It was when I was still in a wheelchair and beginning in politics. I could walk, but I was still unsteady." Hazleton swallowed, his throat dry. "There was a meeting of constituents, just a small group. They'd seen me on and off in the wheelchair in the early days, but I was walking. Then I stumbled, came a cropper in front of everyone. It was awful. I wondered what they must have thought."

"I am sure they had the utmost compassion—after all, anyone can fall."

"But not a politician!" Hazleton's voice cracked as he went on. "I lost my footing and could not face it happening again, and Charmaine"—he looked at his wife, a gaze followed by Maisie, who had now got the measure of the delicate balance in their relationship—"Charmaine said it would be best to use the wheelchair when I was out and to walk only in the house, just in case."

"I see."

"And there was more. It seemed as if the image of the crippled MP meant something to people. It seemed to stand for what everyone had been through, I suppose. In any case, I became convinced that the fact I was wheelchair-bound helped me to become popular, to win my seat. My wife was another reason. A politician cannot survive without the right people behind him. If my friendship with Ralph came out. . . ." He reached for his wife and held her hand.

Maisie pressed on, touching her forehead. "You could have killed me."

"We had so much to lose!" Charmaine Hazleton drew her hand to her mouth.

"What about tampering with my motor car last Saturday morning?"

"I—I don't know what you're talking about." Hazleton seemed genuinely perplexed.

A trickle of perspiration ran from Maisie's forehead as she began to understand that the amateurish attempts by the Hazletons did not run to interfering with motor cars. "And what about on the tube? Was Goodge Street your only visit to the underground in your attempts to kill me?"

The couple exchanged glances again. Hazleton spoke. "I promise you, Miss Dobbs, we wanted to scare you, to stop you in your wild goose chase in search of a man who is dead. Yes, of course we had secrets to protect, but to kill you? No."

Maisie swallowed. "You have placed yourselves in a very difficult and vulnerable position."

"Please, don't do it, don't report us. Please forgive us, we were blinded by—"

"Your ambition?" Maisie snapped.

Hazleton shook his head. "No. Not in the way that you think." He paused, took a handkerchief from his pocket, and drew it across his brow. "I was so afraid of falling, and I—we—wanted to do good. We'd both seen too much that was bad, that was evil. I lost my dearest friend, and Charmaine had seen young men try to make lives for themselves again despite terrible wounds. We thought that by working together, being a team, we could represent those who have no voice, especially after the war and especially now. My disability drew attention, and with it a belief in what I had to say."

"Don't you think that what you had to say counted for itself?" Maisie's anger was rising.

"We were misguided."

"Misguided? You could have killed me! And you lied to your constituents."

"Their voices were heard!"

"Nevertheless—"

"Please, Miss Dobbs, we will be ruined."

Maisie paced again. She stopped twice to look at the Hazletons. Making her way back and forth, she had become attuned to their fears and hopes: to a wife so afraid of losing her place as carer and much-needed partner that she would encourage a man to remain in a wheelchair; to a man strong enough to fight on the battlefield and in the House of Commons but fearful should his past be revealed. In her silence she asked for the strength to forgive them and to do what was right. She wanted to leave the house, wanted time to consider their actions and the implications of their lives. Then she looked at the couple once more and knew that to have them wait for her response would be cruel. Hadn't all three of them seen too much that was cruel already?

Finally, she turned to the couple, her resignation clearly heard in the sigh that came before she spoke. "Sit down and we will discuss the terms of my silence." And as she said the words she threw the glass paperweight toward Hazleton, who reached out for it to make the perfect catch.

TWENTY-NINE

"Well, good mornin', Miss! It's nice to see you bright and early again. And may I say you are looking very well indeed!" Billy was not quite sure that his employer was looking very well indeed, but there was certainly an improvement in her pallor, and he had spent enough time in hospitals himself to know that a bit of encouragement worked wonders.

"Yes, I am feeling better, Billy." Maisie looked up from her work and set the top on her fountain pen. "I'm just completing my written report for Sir Cecil. I'm late with it, but he knows I've been a bit under the weather. Anyway, pull up a chair. There's something I have to tell you before you hear it from someone else."

The color drained from Billy's face as he turned from hanging his coat on the hook behind the door. "What is it, Miss?"

"Don't worry, Billy, I'm not closing up shop."

"Whew, you 'ad me scared there, Miss. Everything else all right?"

Maisie leaned back in her chair, partly to give the impression that there was nothing to worry about and partly to exude a certain command of events. "What I was going to say was that, before you hear it from Dr. Dene or Inspector Stratton, there was an accident on Saturday."

Billy frowned. "Who? I mean, was it you? Are you all right?" He walked across to Maisie's desk, taking a seat only after she held out her hand toward the chair a second time.

"Yes, it was me, and frankly it was not an accident. The brakes on my motor car failed. I was lucky—in fact, I have been very lucky—but someone is quite intent upon finishing me off."

"I must say, you are looking pretty calm about it, Miss. I mean, if that were me, I'd be lookin' over me shoulder all the time. Per'aps you ought to talk to Stratton again—about protection, I mean."

"There *was* protection, Billy. It transpires that the man who ran from his motor car to summon the police *was* the police. Fine lot of good it did too. No, I do believe I'll find the answer somewhere in the Lawton case —all the attempts seem to have started from the time I took it on." Maisie shook her head. "I just feel as if there is something I'm missing, something I could almost reach out and touch, but—"

Billy shook his head. "I've been wrackin' me brains as well, really I 'ave." He paused, then leaned forward. "Look, I don't think you should be out and about on your own."

"You sound like my father."

"No, don't take it like that, Miss. I reckon I should see you to and from work. It should be part of the job until the bloke's be'ind bars. After all, if you go, Miss, then there ain't no work for me, is there?"

Maisie leaned forward. "Right you are. I'll take you up on your offer, Billy. Now then, I'd like you to get on with the new cases while I finish this report." She took out four index cards and passed them to her assistant. "I've underlined four names there. See what you can find out about each person. Start with the card file, check if anything is cross-referred to the client folders, and move on to the newspapers."

"Speaking of which." Billy pushed back the chair, walked over to his overcoat, and pulled two newspapers from an inside pocket. He turned back to Maisie, placing the newspapers on her desk. "*The Times* and the *Express*. There's a story in there that will interest you, Miss. Reminds me of that poor Lawton woman."

Maisie looked up, frowning. "What's that?"

"Well, turns out there was a séance yesterday at that place run by a man called 'Arry Price. I'm sure I've seen that name on one of the old cards, a friend of Dr. Blanche's, wasn't 'e?" Billy did not pause, continuing his story with increasing rapidity of speech. "Anyway, there was this séance—I tell you, even the thought of it gives me the willies—and there was these people who are interested in that sort of thing, and a medium that the Price bloke 'ad tested as bein' on the up-and-up. Well, they were there to try to contact that author bloke, you know, the one passed on a few months ago. What was 'is name?"

"Do you mean Conan Doyle?" Maisie leaned forward, wondering what story Billy was about to tell.

"Yep, that's the one! Anyway, as I was sayin', they're all there, doin' whatever they do at these get-togethers, and you'll never guess what—they only got a message from that captain of the R-101, you know, what went down over the weekend." Billy ran his finger along the lines of newspaper print. "A woman name of Eileen Garrett was the medium and, as it says 'ere, this 'Arry Price of the Psychical Institute knows who's real and who isn't. . . ."

Maisie picked up her document case. "I know very well who he is, Billy. Remember I told you about those cases Maurice and I worked on after the war, when there were so many fraudulent mediums and psychics claiming to have a message from the other side, the same sort of people who took Agnes Lawton for a ride? Well, Maurice consulted with Price." Maisie paused, remembering her first experience of giving evidence in court as each defendant was tried. Closing her eyes, she recollected the scene, her attention drawn to one person in particular, sitting in the gallery unaccompanied, and the way she leaned forward to listen, completely focused on Maisie as she gave her report. She opened her eyes. "Billy, I must see Price immediately."

Billy frowned, automatically helping Maisie into her mackintosh before reaching for his own coat. "I don't understand, Miss, what have we got to do with the R-101?"

"Nothing and everything." She opened the door and stepped from the office, waiting for her assistant to lock the door behind him. "Let's just say a coincidence has reminded me that I should probably have spoken to Mr. Price a good month ago."

"So, where are we going now?"

"The Laboratory of Psychical Research." Maisie turned to Billy as they walked downstairs and out into the square. "You're all right, aren't you, not worried about going there? Because if you—"

Billy shook his head, though he seemed pale to Maisie. "Nah, I'm all right, Miss. As my old dad used to say, it ain't the dead what can 'urt you, no, it's the livin' you've got to watch."

MAISIE AND BILLY arrived at the laboratory and were fortunate to gain a brief audience with Price, a man renowned in a field that had many naysayers and followers whom unbelievers thought fey at best. Courtesies followed, during which time the health of Dr. Maurice Blanche was the topic of conversation before the true purpose of their visit was discussed.

"I remember that case very well indeed." He shook his head. "I shudder when I think of the thousands who were harmed by such people. And to think that in the midst of war, Ouija boards were selling like hotcakes and anyone with an old shawl and a red table-cloth was taking money from the bereaved! But that case was particularly nasty. I seem to remember that the fakes were in league, weren't they?"

Maisie nodded, while Billy fidgeted uncomfortably in his seat. "They formed a fraudulent ring, taking life savings in exchange for words from the other side. Even though they could have been charged under the provisions of the Witchcraft Act, they were sent to Holloway for their underhand business dealings, which had ultimately led to the suicide of a young war widow, though the defense argued that she was of unsound mind to start with. Two were released after serving their respective terms, and one died in prison—from a heart ailment, I believe."

Price nodded, then consulted his watch before taking up Maisie's list. "Miss Dobbs, I will ask one of my colleagues to assist you with these names and give you a report as to their activities. As you know, we keep records on all practicing mediums and psychics, as far as we can. I must go now, what with the press and one thing and another."

"Of course, thank you." Maisie shook hands with Price, while Billy drew back, as if to touch a man who worked with spiritualists, mediums, and psychics might pull him along an inescapable channel to another world. Price, in his hurry to attend to other matters, did not in any case offer his hand.

A tall, thin young man entered the room some moments later. His black hair was parted in the center and combed back, and with his dark blue pinstripe suit he wore a red-and-blue bow tie at the neck of a starched white shirt. "Ah, Miss Dobbs, Mr. Beale. Delighted, I'm sure. Archibald Simpson at your service. Now then, let's look at these three women." He placed three manila folders on the desk in front of him. "This one will be of particular interest to *you*, Miss Dobbs." He leaned toward Maisie, handing her the top sheet from a substantial collection of papers.

As she read, the renewed color that Billy had remarked upon earlier drained from Maisie's face. She handed back the sheet of paper. "Thank you. I think that will be all."

"But—"

"What is it, Miss?" Billy leaned toward Maisie as if ready to protect her.

"Mr. Simpson, may I use your telephone? I will of course reimburse you for costs incurred." Maisie stood up, anxious to take action.

The man stuttered, surprised at the change in Maisie's demeanor. "Of-of course. Come this way." He held out a hand for Maisie to exit the room first, followed by Billy, who hurried as if scared he might be left behind.

Simpson accompanied Maisie to a small office with a telephone, while Billy waited anxiously outside; he had not wanted to let Maisie out of his sight. She came from the room ten minutes later, bade farewell to Simpson again, and left the building quickly, Billy at her heels.

"What's going on, Miss? Who'd you 'ave to get on the blower to?"

"Stratton."

"For protection?"

Maisie shook her head as she looked left and right along the road and hailed a taxi-cab. "No. I need Stratton for the purpose of witnessing." She turned to Billy as they clambered into the black motor car. "My word alone will not count. Neither will yours."

"What's going on, Miss? And where are we going?"

"I'll tell you on the way. I can make mistakes and I did—in not asking the right questions at the right time. Now then, let's get going."

BY THE TIME Maisie and Billy arrived outside the shiplike building, two police motor cars were parked along a side street and the only visible evidence of their presence was Stratton, leaning against the corner of a shop nearby, with Caldwell on the opposite side of the road talking to a woman with a shopping bag, possibly one of the new female recruits to criminal investigation disguised as a passerby. Maisie nodded to Stratton as she and Billy made their way to the main door of the building. She had no need to speak with him. Enough had been said on the telephone.

"All right, Billy?"

"I dunno. I reckon I was better off when I was crawling around clipping wires in no-man's-land. Least you knew who your enemy was in wartime, none of this spirit lark." Billy paused and squinted. "'Ere, what are they talkin' into over there?"

Maisie stole a glance at the police. "It's a new police wireless radio, Billy. It was invented at the request of the chief of police down in Brighton. Scotland Yard have been testing it for about a month now—looks like it might come in handy today."

"Well, I never."

Maisie felt a sensation across her neck, as if an icy breeze had touched her. She closed her eyes briefly and touched her chest to feel her own heartbeat with her fingertips. Even now she must show compassion; she must listen and act with integrity. She pressed the doorbell, then introduced herself again using the speaker. Mrs. Kemp was brisk in her response.

"Well, I'm just about to leave as it's my half day, but Miss Hartnell will see you."

Maisie nodded to Billy, then opened the door as the buzzer sounded. Before the door closed, Stratton, Caldwell and the woman slipped through. They walked across the courtyard to the stairs. Maisie pointed to a shadowed nook underneath the staircase that led to the upper flat, crooked her finger for Billy to follow her, and indicated an archway where he would wait. She walked to Madeleine Hartnell's flat alone.

Mrs. Kemp was pushing in a hatpin to secure her beret as Maisie arrived. "I must be off now. Miss Hartnell is in the same room where you saw her before. She knows you're on your way, and I've just taken in refreshments while she prepares."

Maisie nodded. *While she prepares.* Madeleine Hartnell would want time alone before seeing a client, just as she herself would meditate to still her mind before a meeting. The housekeeper left, hurrying toward the staircase, whereupon Billy stepped from his hiding place and walked toward the door that Maisie had ensured was left on the latch. Maisie saw him glance over the balcony to watch the housekeeper's departure and to check that Stratton was on his way.

No bright sunlight was shining through the windows on this gray London day. Instead, a sickly yellow smog lingered as people went about their business with scarves pulled across mouths and noses to avoid breathing in the toxic air. The house harbored a chill that not even red-hot coals in the grate would ever dent. Maisie shivered as she knocked on the door to Madeleine Hartnell's room.

"Come in."

Maisie opened the door and entered. Hartnell was wearing a long narrow black dress with an eye-catching double-stitched seam at the hips and a silver belt at the waist. A boat neckline accentuated her collarbones, and her milky-white skin seemed to reflect the single strand of creamy pearls and matching earrings. Her platinum-blond hair shone, and her lips were made full with a liberal coating of red lipstick. Maisie knew that her visit had been expected. "It's good of you to see me, Miss Hartnell."

Hartnell pointed to the armchair that matched her own, then leaned forward to pour water into two glasses. She pushed a glass toward Maisie and lifted the other to her lips. Maisie reached for the glass, sat down and leaned back.

"Did you expect me?"

"I had an inkling."

Maisie nodded. She understood.

"You know why I am here." It was a statement, not a question.

Hartnell smiled slowly and turned to her, blinking in a languorous way that reminded Maisie of a cat waking, perhaps when someone has made an unwelcome noise to shatter a sleepy silence. "Yes."

Maisie kept her own movements equally unhurried. Not only must she retain a cool demeanor that mirrored Hartnell's, she had to give her witnesses time to take up position. She deliberately brought images of her mother and Simon to mind; her next thought was of Andrew Dene. It was this last image that rendered her calm. Calm enough to make her play.

"So, how did you find out who I was?" Madeleine Hartnell barely moved.

Maisie stood up, claiming an upper hand. She picked up the glass of water to augment the impression of calm, though she did not take a sip. "At first I didn't. You've changed, after all."

Hartnell gave a half laugh accompanied by a smirk that ill became her.

"Your blond hair, your clothes. . . ."

"Courtesy of a hairdresser and a very good seamstress, who knows how to fit me precisely. I've grown up, Miss Dobbs."

Maisie nodded, remembering the young girl who could not take her eyes off her in court over ten years ago, the young girl who had seen her mother sent down on the basis of evidence given in court, Maisie's evidence. The young girl who was now an embittered and dangerous woman.

"I know why you tried to kill me, *Miss Adele Nelson.*"

Hartnell's eyes narrowed, her smile evaporated. She lost no time in rising to the bait but stood up, close to Maisie. "Oh, no, you do not, Miss Dobbs, you have no idea why. You think you know—just because you've discovered my true name, a name I had to change because it was slurred by my mother's trial—but that fine mind of yours has stalled on the surface of the story, just as it did when that old tyrant and his young ambitious assistant put poor Irene Nelson away. It was the death of her!"

"Your mother died of natural causes. A postmortem indicated an enlarged heart, and her medical examination upon reception at Holloway revealed an irregular heartbeat, so—"

"An enlarged heart! Yes, she did have an enlarged heart. It was filled with grief, then when there was still room in that heart she tried to help people. Of course she had an enlarged heart. The body does as the soul moves it!"

Maisie's throat was dry. Though she would have loved to sip the cool water, she knew her retort must be quick. "She tricked poor widows out of their savings. She worked with two others—Frances Sinden and Margaret Awkright—to commit a crime. A dead soldier's young widow was brought so low by their dealings that she took her own life! Miss Nelson, you must understand, your mother, Sinden, and Awkright acted in a fraudulent manner." Maisie paused, frustrated. "You were just a child, after all."

The woman flared, her hair almost silver against a complexion that mirrored her volatility. "I was fourteen! I was old enough to know what was going on, and I remember *you*." She poked a finger at Maisie. "Yes, you. In court." She barely choked back her fury. "I remember you in court, giving your evidence, turning to the jury with those big eyes to talk about the bereaved. I'll tell you who was bereaved: My mother was bereaved when my father died in France, that's who was bereaved. She tried to help herself and others in the only way she knew."

Maisie placed the glass on the table. "She did not have your gift."

"You killed her!" Nelson stood up and crossed her arms, clutching her elbows as if to soothe herself.

Maisie was silent. In her mind's eye she saw the image in her dream of her mother reaching out to her while holding the hand of a girl in the shadows. *Did I deny this girl a mother's love?* She began to falter but reminded herself that she must not let down her guard. She stood up and looked at Nelson directly. "I did not kill your mother. I was acting in the best interests of the innocent bereaved victims who had been tormented—tormented by the actions of three very misguided individuals. You were too young, and too impressionable to see the truth."

Nelson leaned closer to Maisie. "Truth? You speak to me of *truth*? You self-serving creature, you. I will tell you truth. My mother died in a rat-infested damp prison cell with common criminals, with prostitutes, with murderers. A woman with an *enlarged heart* died with the dregs of London, and I loved her. I *adored* her." Her voice caught. "And I vowed that one day, *one day*, I would call you and that horrible old man to account." She leaned her head back and began to laugh, stopping suddenly to speak again. "Oh, how I was blessed when you came here to me, how I feasted upon my good fortune! I had been biding my time, but Fate brought you to me and I knew my moment had come."

"Miss Nelson—Adele." Maisie realized the woman was barely listening to her, intent only upon what she had to say, words that had been rehearsed every day for almost ten years. She walked to the window, playing for time, wondering how she might pacify a woman so blinded by grief she could barely see. Turning, she spoke. "Miss—"

"You witch!" Adele Nelson was pointing a small ivory-handled pistol directly at Maisie, her eyes blazing, her red lips drawn back across her teeth. In the other hand she held her glass of water, which she raised to her mouth, still focused on her quarry.

Maisie did not move, did not shout, did not cry out in terror, instead drawing upon every lesson from Khan, to ensure that each cell in her body remained calm. Fighting the urge to move too soon, she assumed instead a look of concern, as she would if encountering a child with a grazed knee after a fall.

Nelson laughed, raising the pistol, her finger unsteady around the trigger.

"Adele, don't be silly, love." Maisie heard the words come from her mouth, heard herself speak as her own mother might have spoken, so softly, seeing not a woman blinded by the need for revenge but a young girl alone in court, a girl who stared at her as she gave evidence and who, afterward, was left alone to make her way in the world without a soul to accompany her. Then, as Nelson drew back the trigger, slowly, her eyes now duller, Maisie realized that the time for talking had passed. She could soothe neither the woman's aching heart nor her tormented soul.

As Nelson's index finger moved again, almost imperceptibly,

Maisie launched her whole body at the woman, clutching her wrist as she lunged, raising the pistol into the air. A single shot cracked, and Maisie cried out "Stratton!"

A flurry of activity ensued, the police crashing into the room as Maisie knelt to the ground beside the woman who had called herself Madeleine Hartnell.

"Blimey, she 'ad a gun!" Billy crouched beside Maisie. "You all right, Miss?"

"Yes." She turned, looking up to Stratton. "Why didn't you come in earlier? Surely you'd heard enough?"

Stratton reached toward Maisie's shoulder and pulled her back, kneeling next to Nelson. He pressed two fingers to her carotid pulse, her skin soft against his rough hand. "She's gone."

"I know she's gone, but she didn't have to do this. . . ."

Stratton stood up and, taking Maisie by the elbow, pulled her aside as Caldwell and the woman went to work, securing the room and using the radios to summon assistance and the pathologist. "I was about to come in."

Maisie shook her head. "She could have been saved. It did not have to be like this."

Stratton turned to face Maisie directly. "No, it did not have to be, but it was. And she had every intention of killing herself. It was not your glass that was poisoned, it was hers."

Maisie looked once more at the lifeless body of Adele Nelson, then walked over to the tray.

"Oi! Don't touch that, it's needed for evidence."

She ignored Caldwell and picked up the glass of water that Adele Nelson had poured for her. She dipped her little finger into the liquid and then touched it with the tip of her tongue. She shook her head and turned to Stratton. "You're wrong, Inspector. She meant to kill us both."

EPILOGUE

October and November 1930

The rest of the month allowed Maisie little time on her own, with many hours spent at Scotland Yard before being able to begin the process of putting the cases of the past weeks behind her. The MG had been returned in full working order, and Maisie was once again driving around London and Kent with ever-growing confidence. She wanted desperately to spend time at Chelstone with her father and in Hastings with Dene, but she knew she could not rest until she had completed her final accounting. It was a task made urgent by daily telephone calls from Dene.

She delivered her final report to Sir Cecil Lawton and, though the meeting was brief, saw a man who was now at peace. Maisie found herself hoping for a time when there would be no cause for a man and his son to be divided in such a way, but now, reflecting upon the look on the man's face, which so resembled that of his son when the younger man spoke of his life in Biarritz, she felt less unease in her decision, though she knew there would always be an element of doubt.

On the return journey from Cambridge, Maisie drove past the house where Jeremy Hazleton lived with his wife. The house bore a banner outside promoting Hazleton, the tenacious public servant. At a recent rally, he had spoken of his fight to walk following the wounds sustained at the Battle of Passchendaele. Using a cane for support, he reached for his wife's hand and talked to the crowd of his fears, of the resilience a wounded veteran needed to undertake even the simplest tasks. He was outspoken, demanding greater support for the soldiers who had come home injured—and for those who cared for them, as his dear wife had cared for him. Barely referring to his notes, he repeated his commitment to the disenfranchised and outlined a new course, pressing home the need for more help for the many homeless children in London, the young girls forced into a life on the streets, the boys who became hardened criminals before they had reached manhood. He spoke eloquently of new measures to stop those who traded on the young down-and-outs and promised to devote a considerable amount of parliamentary time in putting an end to such abuse. He vowed that his voice would become louder and louder until this work was done. His speech over, he was helped from the podium, walking into the cheering throng who gathered around. In private he knew that he dare not draw back, for not only was Maisie Dobbs in the crowd listening to his every word that day but she would be following his career closely in the months and years to come.

Maisie visited two graves to pay her respects. At the grave of Agnes Lawton, she placed fresh flowers and whispered, "He is alive. You can rest." Later, in the cemetery at Balham, Maisie stood with Mrs. Kemp as Adele Nelson was buried, then placed a single rose on the grave as she walked away. The funeral over, a plain stone memorial bore not her assumed name but the name her mother had given her on the day she was born.

Avril Jarvis did not return to her home in Taunton immediately but was instead taken to Khan's school in Hampstead, to be healed with compassion and guided by those who would help renew her broken young spirit. Maisie had known instinctively that Avril had certain gifts that must be given room to flourish in the light, unlike Adele Nelson, who had never found peace, living instead in a dark hell. And Maisie knew that *she* would not rest until she found peace with the outcome of her work. In her years of working alongside Maurice, she had learned that such atonement could come slowly, with a recognition of lessons learned along the way.

Maurice remained in London before returning to Chelstone, more from concern for Maisie's well-being than his own needs. They spent time together in quiet conversation, each working to repair the fabric of their friendship, so that the past might be remembered with warmth as they worked with the fresh canvas to create a bond for the future. They both knew that her trust in him remained compromised and understood that what had happened could not be undone, only accommodated. But the rupture had brought with it an unanticipated gift. Maisie now felt more independent of her teacher, better able to trust her instincts rather than harking back to her apprenticeship. Yet she knew, too, that to continue her recovery she would need his guidance. She was not out of the woods.

She collected the keys to her new ground-floor flat at the end of October, her hand shaking as she signed the many papers required for purchase of the property in Pimlico. A letter from Priscilla was handed to her following completion of all necessary documents.

My dear Maisie,

However can I thank you; I shall be forever in your debt. It was most unfair of me to land you with the task of finding Peter's final resting place, but as you probably guessed, I could not do it myself. Not only would I not know where to start, but if anyone were to undertake the search for me, I wanted it to be someone I trusted, and I would trust you with my life, Maisie Dobbs.

I am now a loving aunt to my brother's wonderful daughter, even if I say so myself. I have learned to be a bit more restrained around old Chantal, though I do believe she thinks my boys should have been beaten like carpets long ago! I am sure you will adore your new flat, and I am thrilled that my solicitors could help you. In fact, I wanted you to have this letter today because it's such a wonderful day, and I am so delighted for you! Congratulations, Maisie, on your new home! I cannot wait to see it and am sure it will make me hunger for the single life, though that's just between us.

Douglas, the boys and I will all be in Sainte-Marie for Armistice Day. I've had a memorial placed in the woods close to the Clement estate. It so reminds me of England, I can just see Peter walking there to feel as if he were at home. The stone memorial will be placed at the foot of a huge old oak tree. Peter was a magical person, he cast a spell over everyone who met him, so he deserves to be remembered in such a place.

Well, I must go now, the boys . . .

Maisie closed the letter, replaced it in the envelope and tucked it among the papers she pushed into her document case. She would read it in full later. Shaking hands with the clerks, Maisie thanked them, commenting that she knew they must have worked very hard to secure the mortgage on her behalf, as she was more than aware of her position as a spinster. As she left, the men turned to each other and smiled. Their client, the very wealthy Mrs. Partridge, had given strict instructions that Miss Dobbs must never know that her mortgage was guaranteed by the Evernden family trust.

MAISIE LEFT HER office early on Monday, in the second week of November, for an uncustomary midweek visit to Dene in Hastings and her father at Chelstone on the return journey. But before she closed the door behind her she left a small package on Billy Beale's desk. She knew he would be embarrassed by the gift, would run his cap through his hands as he thanked her later. She would tell him that the gift was really in the interests of the business, another tool in their work together. But he would be touched by the gesture anyway.

The sea air in Hastings whisked over the clifftops as Maisie strolled with Andrew on the East Hill, stopping to look down across the Old Town. Clouds in a myriad of shades of gray scudded across the sky. Though it was not raining, the wind was full of cold moisture as it whipped up, causing Maisie to clutch at her hat.

"You'll lose that thing if you're not careful. I told you it would be better to go without."

Maisie laughed as she finally gave up, pulling the hat from her head and releasing her black hair to blow around her face. She turned to him as he placed an arm around her shoulders. "So, are you going to reveal the surprise? You've kept it to yourself long enough now." She swallowed, wanting the "surprise" to be over and done with so that she could respond and then deal with whatever came next.

"Oh, yes, that." Dene grinned at her, as his fringe flopped into his eyes. "I held back—thought I'd wait until all that France business was over. Well now, I don't know if you will like this, but I'm hoping you will."

"Go on." Maisie smiled weakly.

"Well, I'm delighted, to tell you the truth."

"About what?"

"About the fact that starting in the new year I will be lecturing in orthopedic medicine at St. Thomas's." Dene's grin seemed to fill his cheeks. "But don't you worry, Miss Maisie-Dobbs-about-town, it's not a full-time position. In fact, I will only be seeing my students once every fortnight and for special courses, so I won't be breathing down your neck when I'm in London." He continued, barely taking a breath. "It's a wonderful opportunity, all as a result of that paper I wrote on rehabilitation of spinal injuries. The Board of Governors at All Saints are very enthusiastic, of course—it helps the hospital's reputation—so everything is on the up-and-up, as they say!"

"Oh, Andrew, I am just thrilled for you. It will be lovely to have you in London." Maisie spoke the words honestly, for she knew that Dene lifted her spirits and brought a brightness to her life that she had not felt in years.

Dene smiled at her, then frowned in mock seriousness. "I suppose you could be having your cake and eating it, eh, Maisie?"

"I suppose." She teased him in return.

Dene pulled Maisie to him and kissed her. "Well, that will do for now."

Maisie pulled away, taking his hand. "Come on, let's get some fish and chips. I know it's early, but I'm starving!"

As they walked down the steps to Tackleway, and then through a twitten to Rock-a-Nore, where the fishing boats had been hauled up onto the beach following the morning's catch, Maisie remembered Priscilla's comment about Andrew Dene.

"Andrew, I hope you don't mind me asking this, but—"

"Uh-oh, never at rest, eh, Maisie? Go on, fire away!"

"Well, why haven't you ever married? I'm sure you've had plenty of opportunities."

Dene paused and reddened slightly. "I confess, I have come close to popping the question, but, you know, the life of a doctor is not always conducive to partnership, although the job here is better than working full-time at a London hospital. To tell you the truth, whenever I thought about it, my next thought was that I could be jumping the gun, that the perfect woman for me might be just around the corner, and I realized that the girl I was with was not the one for me if I was thinking in that way. My reticence told me that I was unsure, which just wasn't right. And I know—lucky old me to be in that position. It boils down to something my mother said about a cousin who was getting married following a very short courtship: *Marry in haste, repent at leisure.* And I never was one for repenting, you know." Dene began to laugh and the wind whipped up again as they walked along the seafront. "Is that a good enough answer for you, Maisie?"

"Yes, it's good enough, Andrew."

"Of course, there's another reason, you know."

"What's that?"

He looked out across the sea then, his unruly brown hair flying up into his eyes again. "I'm really a Bermondsey boy, ain't I?" He grinned as he affected the accent of his boyhood, then grew serious. "And not everyone can understand how I came from there to here, if you know what I mean."

Maisie turned from him and began to walk toward the fish and chip shop, then looked back to Dene and smiled, holding out her hand.

·   ·   ·

THE FOLLOWING DAY, November 11, at twenty past ten, Andrew Dene switched on the wireless so they could listen together as the correct time was broadcast from Greenwich at half past the hour for the nation to synchronize watches in readiness for the two-minute silence at eleven o'clock. Maisie looked at her watch and imagined Billy Beale taking out his new wristwatch, then checking to ensure he had the correct time. After pressing bright red fabric poppies into each other's lapels alongside their service medals, Maisie and Andrew, respectfully dressed in black, made their way to the war memorial. Once there, they joined with other townsfolk in the Armistice Day ceremony to remember the local boys and men who had died in the Great War. When the names of the fallen were read aloud, Maisie looked around her. People were pressing handkerchiefs to their eyes, perhaps nodding as a name was read, or squeezing the hand of a woman who had lost her husband, a couple their son, a child her father. Maisie leaned against Andrew as the speeches were made and prayers said, remembering the events of the past two months, of those whose lives she had touched who had already experienced wartime's cruel hand of death. She thought of children orphaned, of Avril Jarvis and Madeleine Hartnell, of Pascale Clement. She thought of those who had risked their lives, of Peter Evernden, of Ralph Lawton, and of the wounded Jeremy Hazleton.

A local boy not yet a man lifted the bugle to his lips, and, as the Last Post sounded, Maisie held her breath, closing her eyes. She felt Dene step forward, a veteran of the Great War, raising his deep resonant voice above the salty wind as he spoke the words:

> "They shall not grow old, as we that are left grow old:
> Age shall not weary them, nor the years condemn.
> At the going down of the sun and in the morning
> We will remember them."

Maisie saw the casualty clearing station in her mind's eye, saw her beloved Simon locked in his cavern of shell shock. *I was a nurse.*

A single tear slipped between the lids of each closed eye as she touched the treasured watch that had been her talisman for so many years. Dene returned to her side and Maisie felt the reassuring weight of his arm around her shoulders, pulling her to him. *I will remember them.*

ACKNOWLEDGMENTS

The act of writing a novel is generally thought to be a solitary journey from that first awe-inspiring blank page to *the end*. However, the fact that most authors offer acknowledgments speaks to the presence of a team in the background, offering advice, support, information, a shoulder to cry on, or someone to share a laugh with. The team is often a blend of new contacts and old friends, and when I think of mine I know I have been more than fortunate.

Holly Rose, my very dear friend and writing buddy (and brilliant writer herself), is entrusted to read the first draft of anything I write. Someone give the woman a medal! My Cheef Resurcher, who knows who he is, is not only a wonderful friend—and conspirator—but one to whom I turn in my quest to bring color and depth to the life and times of Maisie Dobbs.

I have drawn upon the knowledge and expertise of the following while writing *Pardonable Lies*. In the U.K.: James Powers of Somme Battlefield Tours, who along with his wife, Annette, made my visit to the battlefields of the Somme and Ypres an unforgettable pilgrimage; the knowledgeable and extremely efficient staff of the Imperial War Museum and of the National Railway Museum; Ian Langlands of Smith & Nephew, who was kind enough to search the company's archives for information on the history of adhesive bandages. Deepest thanks to Carolyn Bleach, Deputy Secretary of the Intelligence Corps Museum at Chicksands, and also to Major (Retd.) A. J. Edwards, OBE, historian at the Military Intelligence Museum—any errors with fact in the story are all down to the author, but cannot diminish the integrity and bravery of the Intelligence Corps. In France: Thanks to Pascal Berger of the AJECTA Association, and to my friend Stéphane Bidan. In the U.S.: I am honored to be a member of the Great War Society and must thank Secretary Mike Hanlon for being a wonderful support and resource.

I am blessed, too, in my editors: Jennifer Barth at Henry Holt in New York and Anya Serota with John Murray in London. Heartfelt thanks must go to John Sterling, president and publisher of Henry Holt, for his inspiring support of Maisie Dobbs. My agent, Amy Rennert, is both a very dear friend and mentor as well as cheerleader extraordinaire for Maisie Dobbs, and thanks must also go to Dena Fischer of the Amy Rennert Agency.

Finally, saving the best till last, to my husband, John Morell—thanks, love, for your unfailing encouragement.

Read on for an excerpt from Jacqueline Winspear's
next Maisie Dobbs novel,
Messenger of Truth,
available in paperback from Picador.

PROLOGUE

Romney Marsh, Kent, Tuesday, December 30, 1930

The taxicab slowed down alongside the gates of Camden Abbey, a red-brick former mansion that seemed even more like a refuge as a bitter sleet swept across the gray, forbidding landscape.

"Is this the place, Madam?"

"Yes, thank you."

The driver pulled alongside the main entrance and, almost as an afterthought, the woman respectfully covered her head with a silk scarf before leaving the motor car.

"I shan't be long."

"Right you are, Madam."

He watched the woman enter by the main door, which slammed shut behind her.

"Rather you than me, love," he said to himself as he picked up a newspaper to while away the minutes until the woman returned again.

THE SITTING ROOM was warm, with a fire in the grate, red carpet on the stone floor, and heavy curtains at the windows to counter draughts that the ancient wooden frame could not keep at bay. The woman, now seated facing a grille, had been in conversation with the Abbess, Dame Constance Charteris, for some forty-five minutes.

"Grief is not an event, my dear, but a passage, a pilgrimage along a path that allows us to reflect upon the past from points of remembrance held in the soul. At times the way is filled with stones underfoot and we feel pained by our memories, yet on other days the shadows reflect our longing and those happinesses shared."

The woman nodded. "I just wish there were not this doubt."

"Uncertainty is sure to follow in such circumstances."

"But how do I put my mind at rest, Dame Constance?"

"Ah, you have not changed, have you?" observed the Abbess. "Always seeking to *do* rather than to *be*. Do you really seek the counsel of the spirit?"

The woman began to press down her cuticles with the thumbnail of the opposite hand.

"I know I missed just about every one of your tutorials when I was at Girton, but I thought—"

"That I could help you find peace?" Dame Constance paused, took a pencil and small notebook from a pocket within the folds of her habit, and scribbled on a piece of paper. "Sometimes help takes the form of directing. And peace is something we find when we have a companion on the journey. Here's someone who will help you. Indeed, you have common ground, for she was at Girton, too, though she came later, in 1914, if my memory serves me well." She passed the folded note through the grille.

Scotland Yard, London, Wednesday, December 31, 1930

"So you see, Madam, there's very little more I can do in the circumstances, which are pretty cut-and-dried, as far as we're concerned."

"Yes, you've made that abundantly clear, Detective Inspector

Stratton." The woman sat bolt upright on her chair, brushing back her hair with an air of defiance. For a mere second she looked at her hands, rubbing an ink stain on calloused skin where her finger always pressed against the nib of her fountain pen. "However, I cannot stop searching because your investigations have drawn nothing. To that end I have decided to enlist the services of a private inquiry agent."

The policeman, reading his notes, rolled his eyes, then looked up. "That is your prerogative, of course, though I am sure his findings will mirror our own."

"It's not a he, it's a she." The woman smiled.

"May I inquire as to the name of the 'she' in question?" asked Stratton, though he had already guessed the answer.

"A Miss Maisie Dobbs. She's been highly recommended."

Stratton nodded. "Indeed, I'm familiar with her work. She's honest and knows her business. In fact, we have consulted with her here at Scotland Yard."

The woman leaned forward, intrigued. "Really? Not like your boys to admit to needing help, is it?"

Stratton inclined his head, adding, "Miss Dobbs has certain skills, certain . . . methods, that seem to bear fruit."

"Would it be overstepping the mark if I asked what you know of her, her background? I know she was at Girton College a few years after me, and I understand she was a nurse in the war, and was herself wounded in Flanders."

Stratton looked at the woman, gauging the wisdom of sharing his knowledge of the private investigator. At this point it was in his interests to have the woman out of his hair, so he would do and say what was necessary to push her onto someone else's patch. "She was born in Lambeth, went to work in service when she was thirteen."

"In service?"

"Don't let that put you off. Her intelligence was discovered by a friend of her employer, a brilliant man, an expert in legal medicine and himself a psychologist. When she came back from Flanders, as far as I know she convalesced, then worked for a year in a secure institution, nursing profoundly shell-shocked men. She completed her education, spent some time studying at the Department of Legal Medicine in Edinburgh, and went to work as assistant to her mentor. She learned her business from the best, if I am to be honest."

"And she's never married? How old is she, thirty-two, thirty-three?"

"Yes, something like that. And no, she's never married, though I understand her wartime sweetheart was severely wounded." He tapped the side of his head, "Up here."

"I see." The woman paused, then held out her hand. "I wish I could say 'thank you' for all that you've done, Inspector. Perhaps Miss Dobbs will be able to shed light where you have seen nothing."

Stratton stood up, shook hands to bid the woman good-bye, and called for a constable to escort her from the building. As soon as the door was closed, while reflecting that they had not even wished each other a cordial Happy New Year, he picked up the telephone receiver and placed a call.

"Yes!"

Stratton leaned back in his chair. "Well, you'll be pleased to hear that I've got rid of that bloody woman."

"Good. How did you manage that?"

"A fortuitous move on her part—she's going to a private investigator."

"Anyone I should worry about?"

Stratton shook his head. "Nothing I can't handle. I can keep an eye on her."

"Her?"

"Yes, *her*."

Fitzroy Square, London: Wednesday, January 7, 1931

Snow had begun to fall once again in small, harsh flakes that swirled around the woman as she emerged from Conway Street into Fitzroy

Square. She pulled her fur collar up around her neck and thought that, even though she did not care for hats, she should have worn one this morning. There were those who would have suggested that the almost inconsequential lack of judgment was typical of her, and that she probably wanted to draw attention to herself, what with that thick copper-colored hair cascading in damp waves across her shoulders—and no thought for propriety. But the truth was that, despite drawing glances wherever she went, on this occasion, rather like yesterday morning, and the morning before, she really didn't want to be seen. Well, not until she was ready, anyway.

She crossed the square, walking with care lest she slip on slush-covered flagstones, then halted alongside iron railings that surrounded the winter-barren garden. The inquiry agent Dame Constance had instructed her to see—yes, *instructed*, for when the Abbess of Camden Abbey spoke, there was never a mere suggestion—worked from a room in the building she now surveyed. She had been told by the investigator's assistant that she should come to the first floor office at nine on Monday morning. When she had canceled the appointment, he had calmly suggested the same time on the following day. And when, at the last minute, she had canceled the second appointment, he simply moved the time by twenty-four hours. She was intrigued that an accomplished woman with a growing reputation would employ a man with such a common dialect. In fact, such flight in the face of convention served as reassurance in her decision to follow the direction of Dame Constance. She had, after all, never set any stock by convention.

It was as she paced back and forth in front of the building, wondering whether today she would have the courage to see Maisie Dobbs—and lack of pluck wasn't something that had dogged her in the past—she looked up and saw a woman in the first-floor office, standing by the floor-to-ceiling window, looking out across the square. There was something about this woman that intrigued her. There she was, simply contemplating the square, her gaze at first directed up to the leafless trees, then at a place in the distance.

Sweeping a lock of hair from her face, the visitor continued to watch the woman at the window, for it occurred to her that she was staring, not at anything in particular in the square, but at something far away. She wondered if that was her way, if that window was her place to stand and think. She suspected it was. It struck her that the woman in the window was the person she had come to see, Maisie Dobbs. Shivering again, she pushed her hands deep inside the copious sleeves of her coat, and began to turn away. But then, as if commanded to do so by a force she could feel, but not see, she looked up at the window once again. Maisie Dobbs was staring directly at *her* now, and raising her hand in a manner so compelling that the visitor could not leave, could do nothing but meet the other woman's eyes in return, for in some inexplicable way the investigator would not allow her to depart. And in that moment, as Maisie Dobbs captured her with her gaze, she felt a warmth flood her body, and was filled with confidence that she could walk across any terrain, cross any divide, and be held steady; it was as if, in lifting her hand, Maisie Dobbs had promised that from the first step in her direction, she would be safe. She began to move forward, but faltered as she looked down at the flagstones as if into the abyss. Turning to leave, she was surprised to hear a voice behind her, petitioning her to stop simply by speaking her name.

"Miss Bassington-Hope . . ."

It was not a sharp voice, brittle with cold and frozen in the bitter breath of winter, but instead exuded a strength that gave the woman confidence, as if she were indeed secure.

"Yes—" Georgina Bassington-Hope looked again into the eyes of the woman she had just been watching in the window, the woman to whom she had been directed. She had been told that Maisie Dobbs would provide a refuge wherein to share her suspicions, and would prove them to be right, or wrong, as the case may be.

"Come." It was an instruction given in a manner that was neither sharp nor soft, and Georgina found that she was mesmerized as Maisie, holding a pale blue cashmere wrap around her shoulders, stood unflinching in windblown snow that was becoming an icy sleet, all the while continuing to extend her hand, palm up, to gently receive her visitor. Georgina Bassington-Hope said nothing, but reached out toward the woman who would lead her across the threshold, and through the door alongside which a nameplate bore the words, MAISIE DOBBS, PSYCHOLOGIST AND INVESTIGATOR. And she knew in her heart that she had been directed well, that she would be given leave to describe the doubt-ridden wilderness in which she had languished since that terrible moment when she knew in her heart—knew before anyone had told her—that the one who was most dear to her, who knew her as well as she knew herself and with whom she shared all secrets, was dead.

CHAPTER 1

"Good morn', Miss Bassington-'ope. Come on in out of that cold." Billy Beale, Maisie Dobb's assistant, stood by the door to the first-floor office as Maisie allowed the visitor to ascend the stairs before her.

"Thank you." Georgina Bassington-Hope glanced at the man, and thought his smile to be infectious, his eyes kind.

"I've brewed a fresh pot of tea for us."

"Thank you, Billy, that will be just the ticket; it's brassy out there today." Maisie smiled in return at Billy as she directed Georgina into the room.

Three chairs had been set by the gas fire and the tea tray placed on Maisie's desk. As soon as her coat was taken and hung on the hook behind the door, Georgina settled on the middle chair. There was a camaraderie between the investigator and her assistant that intrigued the visitor. The man clearly admired his employer, though it did not appear to be a romantic fondness. But there was a bond, and Georgina Bassington-Hope, her journalist's eye at work, thought that perhaps the nature of their work had forged a mutual dependence and regard—though there was no doubt that the woman was the boss.

She turned her attention to Maisie Dobbs, who was collecting a fresh manila folder, and a series of colored pencils, along with a clutch of index cards and paper. Her black wavy hair had probably been cut in a bob some time ago but was now in need of a trim. Did she not care to keep up with a hairdressing regime? Or was she simply too busy with her work? She wore a cream silk blouse with a long, blue cashmere cardigan, a black skirt with kick pleats, and black shoes with a single strap across to secure. It was a stylish ensemble, but one that marked the investigator as someone who set more stock by comfort than fashion.

Rejoining Georgina, Maisie said nothing until her assistant had seen that the guest had tea and was comfortable. Georgina did not want to confirm her suspicions by staring, but she thought the woman was sitting with her eyes closed, just for a moment, as if in deep thought. She felt that same sensation of warmth enter her body once more, and opened her mouth to ask a question, but instead expressed gratitude.

"I'm much obliged that you agreed to see me, Miss Dobbs. Thank you."

Maisie smiled graciously. It was not a broad smile, not in the way that the assistant had welcomed her, but the woman thought it indicated a person completely in her element.

"I have come to you in the hope that you might be able to help me. . . ." She turned to face Maisie directly, who did not turn away at her gaze—and few people were able to do that with Georgina Bassington-Hope. "You have been recommended by someone we both know from our Girton days, actually."

Maisie knew that Georgina Bassington-Hope had been at Girton several years before she herself had gone up to Cambridge, in 1914. "Might that person have been Dame Constance?"

"However did you know?" Georgina seemed puzzled.

"We rekindled our acquaintance last year. I always looked forward to her lessons, and especially the fact that we had to go to the abbey to see her. It was a fortuitous connection that the order had moved to Kent." She turned to Georgina. "So why did you visit

Dame Constance, and what led her to suggest you should seek me out?"

"I must say, I would have had teeth pulled rather than attend her tutorials; however, I went to see her when . . ." She swallowed, and began to speak again. "It is in connection with my brother's . . . my brother's—" She could barely utter another word. Maisie reached behind her into a black shoulder bag hanging across the back of her chair and pulled out a handkerchief, which she placed on Georgina's knee. As the woman picked up the pressed handkerchief, the fragrant aroma of lavender was released into the air. She sniffed, dabbed her eyes, and continued speaking. "My brother died several weeks ago, in early December. A verdict of accidental death has been recorded." She turned to Maisie, then Billy, as if to ensure they were both listening, then stared into the gas fire. "He is—was—an artist. He was working late on the night before the opening of his first major exhibition in years and, it appears, fell from scaffolding that had been set up at the gallery to allow him to construct his main piece." She paused. "I needed to speak to someone who might help me navigate this . . . this . . . doubt. And Dame Constance suggested I come to you." She paused. "I have discovered that there was little to be gained from badgering the police, and the man who was called when my brother was found seemed only too pleased when I told him I was going to talk to an inquiry agent—I think he was glad to get me out of his sight, to tell you the truth."

"And who was the policeman?" She held her pen ready to note the name.

"Detective Inspector Richard Stratton, of Scotland Yard."

"Stratton was pleased to learn that you were coming to see me?"

Georgina was taken aback by the response, and intrigued by the faint blush revealed when Maisie looked up from her notes, her midnight-blue eyes even darker under forehead creases when she frowned. "Well, y-yes, and as I said, I think he was heartily sick of me peppering him with questions."

Maisie made another note before continuing. "Miss Bassington-

MESSENGER OF TRUTH · 357

Hope, perhaps you could tell me how you wish me to assist you—
how can I help?"

Georgina sat up straight in the chair, and ran her fingers back
through thick, drying hair that was springing into even richer copper curls as the room became warmer. She pulled at the hem of her
nutmeg-brown tweed jacket, then smoothed her soft brown trousers
where the fabric fell across her knees. "I believe Nicholas was mur-
dered. I do not think he fell accidentally at all. I believe someone
pushed him, or caused him to fall deliberately." Now she turned to
Maisie. "My brother had friends and enemies. He was a passionate
artist and those who expose themselves so readily are often as much
reviled as admired. His work drew both accolades and disgust, dependent upon the interpreter. I want you to find out how he died."

Maisie nodded, still frowning. "I take it there is a police report."

"As I said, Detective Inspector Stratton was called—"

"Yes, I was wondering about that, the fact that Stratton was
called to an accident."

"It was early and he was the detective on duty, apparently,"
added Georgina. "By the time he'd arrived, the pathologist had
made a preliminary inspection—" She looked down at the crumpled handkerchief in her hands.

"But I am sure Detective Inspector Stratton conducted a thorough investigation. How do you think I might assist you?"

Georgina tensed, the muscles in her neck becoming visibly taut.
"I thought you might say that. Devil's advocate, aren't you?" She
leaned back, showing some of the nerve for which she was
renowned. Georgina Bassington-Hope, intrepid traveler and journalist became infamous at twenty-two when she disguised herself as
a man to gain a closer view of the lines of battle in Flanders than
any other reporter. She brought back stories that were not of generals and battles, but of the men, their struggles, their bravery, their
fears, and the truth of life as a soldier at war. Her dispatches were
published in journals and newspapers the world over and, like her
brother's masterpieces, her work drew as much criticism as admira-

tion, and her reputation grew as both brave storyteller and naive opportunist.

"I know what I want, Miss Dobbs. I want the truth, and will find it myself if I have to. However, I also know my limitations and I believe in using the very best tools when they are available—price notwithstanding. And I believe you are the best." She paused briefly to reach for her cup of tea, which she held in both hands, cradling the china. "And I believe—because I have done my homework— that you ask questions that others fail to ask, and see things that others are blind to." Georgina Bassington-Hope looked back at Billy briefly, then turned to Maisie once again, her voice firm, her eyes unwavering. "Nick's work was extraordinary, his views well known though his art was his voice. I want you to find out who killed him, Miss Dobbs—and bring them to justice."

Maisie closed her eyes, pausing for a few seconds before speaking again. "You were very close, it seems."

Georgina's eyes sparkled. "Oh, yes, we were close, Miss Dobbs. Nick was my twin. Two peas in a pod. He worked with color, texture, and light; I work with words." She paused. "And it has occurred to me that whoever killed my brother may well want to silence me, too."

Maisie nodded, acknowledging the comment deliberately added to intrigue her, then she stood up, moved away from the fire, and walked across to the window. It was snowing again, settling on the ground to join the brown slush that seeped into shoe leather only too readily. Billy smiled at their guest and pointed to the tea pot, indicating that perhaps she might like another cup. He had been taking notes diligently throughout the conversation, and now knew his job was to keep their guest calm and quiet while Maisie had a moment with her thoughts. Finally, she turned from the window.

"Tell me, Miss Bassington-Hope: Why were you so reticent to keep your appointments? You canceled twice, yet you came to Fitzroy Square in any case. What caused you to renege on your contract with yourself on two—almost three—occasions."

Georgina shook her head before replying. "I have no proof. I have nothing to go on, so to speak—and I am a person used to dealing with facts. There's a paucity of clues; indeed, I would be the first to admit, this looks like a classic accident, a careless move by a tired man using a rather precarious ledge upon which to balance while preparing to hang a work that had taken years to achieve." She paused briefly, then continued. "I have nothing except this," she pressed her hand to her chest. "A feeling here, right in my heart, that all is not as it should be, that this accident was murder. I believe I knew the very second that my brother died, for I experienced such an ache at what transpired, according to the pathologist, to be the time of his death. And I did not know how I might explain such things and be taken seriously."

Maisie walked towards Georgina Bassington-Hope and gently laid a hand on her shoulder. "Ah, you have most definitely come to the right place in that case. In my estimation, that feeling in your heart is the most significant clue and all we need to take on your case." She looked at Billy and nodded, whereupon he flipped over a new card. "Now then, let us begin. First of all, let me tell you about my terms and the conditions of our contract."

Author Interview and

Discussion Questions for

PARDONABLE LIES

JACQUELINE WINSPEAR

Author Interview

1. *Some writers claim that their characters come to them fully formed and complete, others discover their characters over the long process of writing a book. What is it like for you to return to Maisie Dobbs on this third outing, and what new things do you discover in your ongoing relationship with the character?*

In a way, it's like a long-term relationship. With each book I have felt as if it were a two-way process in which the character is revealing herself to me at the same time as I am developing the character, based on imagination and historical research.

2. *Detective novels are fraught with conflict, and yet, in yours, a great deal of empathy is extended to all characters involved. Sometimes it is hard to spot the antagonist. Would you talk about why you take this complex approach to the mystery novel?*

I'm not really interested in the black and white, the "goodies and baddies." I find the complexity of the gray areas more compelling, more intriguing. As I have said before, there are angels and demons in all of us, and I am interested in the relationship between the two within the "ordinary" person.

3. *In* Pardonable Lies, *there is almost as much tension in whether Maisie will tell the truth to Cecil Lawton as there is in her pursuit of the truth itself. Would you agree that, sometimes, just making the right moral decision is like a mystery to be solved?*

In a way, yes, though I think it might be more accurate to say that there are layers of mystery, and moral decisions are part of that complexity. In *Maisie Dobbs,* the question of what happened to Simon was a mystery in itself. And Maisie Dobbs, the character, is a mystery—her thoughts and actions keep the reader turning the page.

4. *An interesting detail toward the beginning of* Pardonable Lies: *As Maisie Dobbs approaches Ms. Browning's house, she notices that the railings of the flat have recently been replaced, the old railings taken and melted down for the war effort. These are the small, forgotten details that make a believably constructed period piece. What do you think is the secret of evoking that period in history on the page?*

I think the secret, if there is one, is in judicious application of the research. I gather copious amounts of research material, but I use it in a ratio that can be compared to an iceberg—only about 7 percent of it is visible above the water. I don't make a huge effort to get everything in—otherwise the reader might as well pick up a nonfiction book. Instead, the story dictates use of research material—every fact must support the story. Then I just trust that my research informs every line—in the way characters address each other, their thoughts and conversations, and so on.

5. *From Maisie Dobbs and Avril Jarvis, to Priscilla Evernden and Madeleine Hartnell, this is a story largely moved forward by the actions of women. Is it a part of your objective, as a writer, to show the active role that women have played in history?*

It's not an "objective" so to speak, but I do have a real interest in the lives of women between the wars, and the barriers that were brought down simply because there were two million more women than men, as revealed by the 1921 census—a direct result of wartime losses. Those barriers went up again later, but I certainly believe an archetype was born in that time—the independent British woman.

6. *One of the ways in which* Pardonable Lies *departs from previous Maisie Dobbs novels is in your use of dreams. Why have you chosen to write Maisie's dreams into the story. Do you feel they reveal another dimension of Maisie's inner life?*

I believe dreams can be enormously powerful, that they can provide a portal to understanding emotions, and to—as you say—the "inner life." Maisie, in *Pardonable Lies*, is going through what might be termed a 'dark night of the soul'—so her dreams are intense and important.

7. *Maisie is unique to her time period, and to the detective genre, in that she practices meditation and creative visualization, as learned from her guru, Khan. Why do you feel this is an important part of Maisie's characterization? Does meditation, or yogic philosophy, perhaps play a part in your own life?*

They didn't call it "creative visualization" then, but there was certainly an interest. You see, that's the interesting thing; we tend to think that such practices are new, or at least the Western interest in them is. However, among certain scholars in particular, there was an intense interest in Eastern philosophies at the turn of the last century—certainly the "Raj" days of the British Empire contributed to that. I have books on yoga, for example, going back to the early 1900s. I think it's an important part of Maisie's characterization because she's had exposure to such scholars—Khan is one—during her apprenticeship to Maurice Blanche.

8. *The awful portent of World War II strikes a quiet, but sustained, note through your novels. Late in* Birds of a Feather, *Billy says that his biggest fear is that there will be another war, and his children will be forced to enlist, and in* Pardonable Lies, *Maisie overhears a conversation in a Parisian café about whether Hitler is good for Germany. Do you see the presence of World War II becoming stronger in the series? Will it arrive?*

World War II is definitely a specter casting a shadow—and history bears this out. You'll see it again in *Messenger of Truth*. And in time it will arrive, though I can't say much about that at the moment!

9. *The relationships of Ralph and Maisie to their respective fathers is juxtaposed in that they are both alienated from their fathers, but for different reasons (Ralph for moral and emotional reasons, while Maisie's estrangement is more intellectual). Would you comment on these parallels, and perhaps talk about how you plot and create them in your writing?*

Some things are not "plotted" as such, but seem to fall into place. I think the "falling into place" happens because I become immersed in the characters, so there are parallels that are there, but that I do not consciously develop—they just happen.

10. *Peter Evernden, it turns out, was killed in a food riot during the war; in* Maisie Dobbs, *Enid is killed by an accident at a munitions factory. Part of your unique perspective on World War I is that you identify the myriad ways that it imperils the citizens of a country, beyond the realm of combat. Would you talk about your perspective on war in general, its necessity and consequence, as played out in your novels? Do you see war as a scourge, or more objectively as an agent of fate? Or both?*

What interests me is the experience of ordinary people. To tell you the truth, although I can repeat certain dates, statistics, and so on, what I am really curious about is what happens to ordinary men, women, and children in extraordinary times. And I think, if anything, what touches me deeply is that some things never change—for example, I was watching a segment on TV yesterday evening about the 16,000-plus wounded coming home from Iraq—it'll doubtless be many more by the time this is read. The point was made that head injuries and multiple amputations form the majority of disabilities to be faced by the returning servicemen and women. Though the time was different and of course battlefield medicine is different, that was pretty much the story in the Great War—some 1,350,000 men returned to Britain with serious wounds, 60,000 to 80,000 of them with profound shell shock. How do we support those people as they grow older? Will we be courteous and helpful to the old man who has to take longer in the grocery store because he cannot *think* quickly due to wounds sustained some fifty years earlier? Or will we forget? Will we become impatient in a way that we might not have if faced with a young man clearly just home from war? That's the sort of thing that makes me sad. I remember, when I was a child, there were two brothers who lived locally. They had both been wounded in the Great War, both blinded—and when I say "blinded" I mean that they did not have eyes in their sockets. They would walk to the small grocery store in the hamlet where we lived, one with his hand on the shoulder of the other, just as the blind wounded were led along during the war. They were always so courteous, so kind, and I remember being terribly upset that they had had to live with such terrible wounds—and I must have only been four or five at the time.

11. *What does your unnamed "Cheef Resurcher" do for you, and could you share an example of one way in which vigorous and resourceful research directly influenced this book?*

Ah, my "Cheef Resurcher" who cannot be named! All I can tell you is that he is a retired international man of mystery who happens to have a real interest in the history of the Metropolitan Police—and he loves research and history in general. I ask him lots of "could this have happened?" type questions. He has illuminated many of the gray areas for me, so if someone says, "The police wouldn't have done that" because, say, it isn't in written procedure, I can safely say I have it from the horse's mouth that such a thing could have happened. Here's a small example: In *Pardonable Lies*, there is mention that the woman police auxilliary lived upstairs at Vine Street Police Station. There were no official "section houses"—accommodation provided for police constables—in those days, so at that time, that's exactly where the women recruits to the police lived. I wouldn't have known that had my Cheef Resurcher not told me.

12. *Maisie Dobbs is soon to make a jump to television. Could you share with us how it might be conceived for the small screen, and what it is like to hand your beloved characters over to a team of people who will collaboratively reimagine her? Do you have a dream cast?*

The TV serialization rights have been optioned, which is of course terribly exciting. I think the thing an author has to bear in mind is that it is a completely different media, that every word, every image on the page cannot be transferred directly onto the small screen, and that there are shortcuts that have to be taken to communicate certain events. Also, each Maisie Dobbs book probably has the material for two or three separate TV "cases." Obviously one has to trust that the characters will be presented in a way that reflects the books, especially as TV viewers will forever after "see" the characters as they are on the screen. I would not have allowed the rights to be optioned if I did not think the company concerned would do their best to honor the books. I don't actually have a dream cast, to tell you the truth. There are so many new, absolutely brilliant actors and actresses on the scene in the U.K. now that I just hope to be pleasantly amazed. I have to say, though, that I always thought Anthony Hopkins would make a terrific Maurice Blanche, and Maggie Smith a great Lady Rowan; however, they don't tend to do TV series—more's the pity!

Discussion Questions

1. Three significant figures in *Pardonable Lies*—Avril Jarvis, Pascale Clement, and the younger Maisie Dobbs of the detective's own tormented recollections—are all about thirteen years old. Why does the novel choose this moment in the three girls' growth and development as a focal point for observation? Do the three girls have anything in common apart from age?

2. Although a number of mothers, including Agnes Lawton, Irene Nelson, Mrs. Jarvis, and Maisie's own mother, are essentially absent as characters, they exert profound influence over events in the novel. What is the significance of the theme of the absent mother in *Pardonable Lies*?

3. In quite a few classic detective novels, including *The Maltese Falcon* and *Farewell, My Lovely*, homosexual characters experience violent or disrespectful treatment. Does the treatment of homosexuality in *Pardonable Lies* fundamentally differ from that in older detective fictions? How and why?

4. Compare Maisie's current relationship with Dr. Andrew Dene and the role that her crippled ex-lover Simon continues to play in her life. Which is more important to Maisie, and why?

5. Maisie lied about her age to go to war and now routinely risks her life as a private investigator. Nevertheless, Priscilla Evernden observes that Maisie has "kept to the safe places." Is she right? Explain.

6. Many of the characters in *Pardonable Lies*, including Maurice Blanche, Ralph Lawton, Jeremy Hazleton, and Maisie herself, engage in elaborate deceptions. Is there a deception in the novel that you consider less "pardonable" than the others? Why?

7. Is there a deception in the novel that you consider more "pardonable" than the others? Why?

8. Like Jacqueline Winspear's previous novels, *Maisie Dobbs* and *Birds of a Feather, Pardonable Lies* is haunted by inescapable memories of World War I. In a sense, the war is the great crime from which the legal offenses and ethical transgressions of Winspear's novels are the offshoots. How are the webs of falsehood and deception in this novel a response to the experiences and traumas of war? Do the lies in the novel make the aftermath of the war easier to bear, or do they compound the war's original immorality?

9. Although Jacqueline Winspear frequently focuses on the physical and psychological scars of warfare, *Pardonable Lies* offers instances of something beautiful or noble that has emerged from the horror. Examples include the birth of Pascale Clement and Ralph Lawton's heroic service in the Flying Corps. How does the novel's introduction of these silver linings enrich or complicate Winspear's depiction of the war and its aftermath?

10. Maisie often uses her training as a psychologist to take decisive control of a situation. Nevertheless, she sometimes experiences social situations in which she feels a lack of control. What are some of these situations, and why does she find them daunting?

11. The daughter of a costermonger, Maisie has risen somewhat above the limitations often encountered by members of her class. However, issues pertaining to class persist in the novel. Compare Jacqueline Winspear's treatment of aristocratic characters like Sir Cecil Lawton and Priscilla Evernden with her rendering of characters like Billy Beale and Lady Rowan's servants.

12. Maisie, who gives such extraordinary courage and support to others, must continually battle an inner sense of her own inadequacy. What are the sources of this feeling, and does she triumph over it?

13. Maisie knows a great deal about comforting others. Consider, however, the persons from whom she derives comfort. Do they have anything in common? To whom does she turn for particular kinds of support, and why?

14. In Chapter 8, Maisie asks herself, "What do I believe in?" Is this question answered in the novel? Does Maisie have beliefs that either strengthen or hinder her in her work or in her life?

15. Jacqueline Winspear offers a number of detailed descriptions of her characters' clothing. Given that Maisie is such a cerebral character, highly focused on the inner workings of the mind and heart, what may be the purpose of such external descriptions in the novel?

16. What role do Maisie's nightmares play in the unfolding of the plot and her character?